THE
SUMMONS

DENNIS McCALLUM

NAVPRESS
BRINGING TRUTH TO LIFE
NavPress Publishing Group
P.O. Box 35001, Colorado Springs, Colorado 80935

The Navigators is an international Christian organization. Jesus Christ gave His followers the Great Commission to go and make disciples (Matthew 28:19). The aim of The Navigators is to help fulfill that commission by multiplying laborers for Christ in every nation.

NavPress is the publishing ministry of The Navigators. NavPress publications are tools to help Christians grow. Although publications alone cannot make disciples or change lives, they can help believers learn biblical discipleship, and apply what they learn to their lives and ministries.

© 1993 by Dennis McCallum

Library of Congress Catalog Card Number: 93-38603
ISBN 08910-97686

Cover illustration: Dean Fleming

The stories and characters in this book are fictitious. Any resemblance to people living or dead is coincidental.

McCallum, Dennis.
    The summons / by Dennis McCallum.
        p. cm.
    ISBN 0-89109-768-6
    1. College students—Michigan—Fiction. I. Title.
PS3563.C33445S86   1993
813'.54—dc20   93-38603
                                               CIP

Printed in the United States of America

FOR A FREE CATALOG OF
NAVPRESS BOOKS & BIBLE STUDIES,
CALL 1-800-366-7788 (USA)
or 1-416-499-4615 (CANADA)

ACKNOWLEDGMENTS

My heartfelt thanks goes to the following readers and editors who helped me with this book: Scott Arnold, Judy Basso, Cindy Botti, John Circle, Lee Campbell, Katie Downs, Phil Frank, Jennie Hale, Larry House, Scott Kaymeyer, Darlene, Scott, and Martha McCallum, Dave and Amy Merker, Dave Norris, Mark Ogilbee, Doug and Chris Patch, Dorothy Thompson, and especially my wife, Holly.

To BoK & Amy
with appreciation for
your help on this & our
common mission for Christ

12/16/93

1

Less than four months before the arrest, Sherry sat looking across the littered dinner table at Jim Clemmons. She tossed her long, curly, light brown hair over her shoulder and sat back further in her padded, semicircular dinner chair. With one ear, she listened to his uninteresting conversation, a polite smile plastered on her face. *He's really not that good looking,* she observed. *That's a short-sleeved shirt, but he rolls up the sleeves anyway to show off his muscles.*

Jim carried on with his story, oblivious to any effect it might be having, ". . . so I just realized this was the lift that could get me on the team and I got total focus, you know?"

Sherry nodded.

"And I just busted through every barrier with sheer power of will. That 380 pounds just sailed up!"

"That sounds like a lot of weight." She raised her eyebrows and tried to sound interested.

"Well, for me it was an incredible weight. I only weigh 195. So anyway, I figure if I just keep. . . ."

Sherry was able to let her mind wander without Jim realizing it. *I bet he's on steroids. I could live with that if he'd just be real sometimes. Four dates now, and he never talks about anything real . . . no interest in using his mind, only his body . . . he has no idea what's going on in my life. How could he, when he only talks about himself?* She looked out the picture window of the Acropolis restaurant at the river, now almost covered in the falling darkness. Two mallards drifted near the woods on the far bank. *I don't think this relationship's going anywhere,* she thought with resignation.

Before long she began to complain about not feeling well, and got Jim to take her home, which he was all too willing to do. No doubt he would be expecting another roll in the hay like two weeks ago. *It's not going to happen!* Sherry determined. She stopped and faced him at the door to the cedar wood apartment building, resolved to end the evening right there. He advanced upon her and kissed her, but she was cold as ice.

"You'll probably catch whatever I'm getting," she warned.

He had felt her stiffness. "I get the feeling there's more wrong here than you being sick," he challenged.

"Well, maybe there is, Jim." She instantly decided she might as well get it over with. "I really don't know how I feel. I'm not sure I want to date anyone in particular at this point in my life."

"I don't understand," he pleaded, backing away with his big hands out. "I thought things were going great!"

"Yeah, well, it's probably just me. I warned you I was a little messed up these days." She fumbled getting her keys out of her purse.

"What do you mean 'messed up'?" He grabbed her arm so she would look up at him. "Are you saying there's someone else?"

"No, there isn't anyone else," she said with an annoyed frown as she jerked her arm away from his grasp.

"Well?" He stood with his hands on his hips, trying to look like Paul Bunyan, demanding an explanation.

She tried to soften the tone of the conversation. "Jim, you're a nice guy, and you deserve somebody who has her head together. I just don't want you to get real involved with me and then find out I'm not there for you."

"Hey, I'm willing to take my chances!" he declared, moving so he was partly blocking her way to the door.

"Well, give me a call sometime if you want, and thanks for dinner," she said, smiling weakly but not quite looking into his eyes. Looking past him to the door handle she said, "Excuse me, I'd like to go in now!"

She tried to elbow him aside and open the door, but before she could, he grabbed her and threw her into a tight and unwanted embrace. "Don't tell me you don't want what I have anymore!" he hissed.

He tried to kiss her as she struggled, turning her head away from him. "No, Jim! Cut it out!"

But he corralled her with his muscular arms and kissed her hard for a moment, pressing his body fully against her.

"Jim, get your hands off me!" She thrashed and twisted, suddenly filled not only with disgust, but with real fear.

His powerful arms were like steel bars around her. "You're just trying to deny what you know is real!" he persisted.

Suddenly, the light in the foyer of the building came on as someone's feet became visible walking down the steps. He relaxed and looked up. Sherry broke free, elbowing him sharply in the gut as she turned away. It didn't seem to have much effect. He only let her go because of the woman coming down the steps. In an instant, Sherry had the security door to the building opened and darted inside. She never looked back, but fled up the steps to her apartment, stumbling briefly on the top flight, now almost hysterical.

She jabbed desperately at the keyhole, looking back at the steps to be certain he wasn't following her. After what was probably a matter of a few seconds, but seemed to be minutes, the door flew open, and she jumped in, slamming it behind her and throwing the bolt. For a moment, she leaned against the door, breathing heavily. But as she realized she was safe, she let down and suddenly burst into tears. Sinking to the floor against the door, she shook with sobs of relief and disgust. *Oh, . . . God . . . How could I ever have thought I might like such a creep?* she shouted to herself in her mind.

She picked herself up, still partly bent over, holding her stomach as though she might vomit. Hurriedly she walked over to the kitchen sink and spat several times as the memory of his forced kiss flashed through her mind. Downing a glass of water, she went to the mirror hanging in the kitchen. Her lipstick was smeared and her eye makeup was running. Periodic sobs still rose as she tried to pull herself together.

He had seemed so vicious during his so-called kiss. Her fingers played over her lips as it dawned on her they were bruised and sore from the attack. With a shudder of revulsion, she realized he had not kissed her—what he did was an act of violence; an act of rage; of anger. *So that's what it's like to be raped!* she marveled, slowly recovering some of her composure as she wiped her face with a Kleenex. *That was the terror I felt. That gorilla might have dragged me off and raped me right then!* She checked the bolt on the door again, satisfied it was secure, and latched the chain and the lock in the handle as well. Standing back from the door, she sized it up. It was steel and seemed sturdy. She decided she trusted it. She went back to the sink and spat into it once again.

This time she washed her hands and face. The cold water felt good, but she still felt dirty. *I'm acting like some Freudian monkey,* she chided herself. But it didn't matter. She felt like taking a shower, and that's what she decided to do. But first she went to her window and carefully peeked out toward the green and pond behind the apartment building. She wanted to make sure he wasn't out there looking up at her window. No one was in sight.

Of course, Sherry hadn't been sick, and she felt fine up until Jim attacked her. The real problem was that her whole life seemed to be going wrong somehow. *And now this! This just fits in beautifully with where I'm headed!* She shook her head and again shivered as waves of nausea swept over her. While undressing, she thought of checking the door bolt again, but realized that would be neurotic.

The apartment had a nice shower-bath, and since it was still early for her, she decided to take a hot bath so she could relax. Settling back in the warm water she found herself once again mentally looking over her life, as she had so often lately.

For several years now she had seen herself as successful in the important areas. She was an exceptionally beautiful woman, and men seemed to line up for a chance to go out with her. She had always been beautiful, but once in college, her tall, slender frame had filled out, becoming shapely enough to turn heads when she walked across campus. With her bronzed complexion, beautiful green eyes, and classic features, she had her pick of the men on campus. For the past four years she had relished that power while exploring the frontiers of possibility in the world of romance.

But far more important to Sherry than her looks was her intelligence. Now in her senior year at Michigan State University, she had a quiet inner confidence in her intellectual gifts, and she wanted someone who could appreciate her mind. Unfortunately, most of the really sharp-thinking guys she met were nerds. As she played with some of the suds floating in front of her, she again wondered where it was all heading. Why wasn't she excited about anything anymore? Why didn't her life seem to have a purpose? How could she have gotten involved with such a gorilla?

She also wondered why she wasn't hitting it off with any of the guys she had dated lately. She had a sense that, like her mother, she should probably settle down with some "nice, academically-inclined guy," but the idea repulsed her. Sherry felt a deep longing in her heart for a certain man. She wanted the challenge of a man who was sharp-thinking, and able to relate to others. But she also wanted him to be good looking and cool. *I guess I'm pretty hard to please,* she admitted as she lifted her left foot and used her toes to let in some more hot water.

Sherry thought about her dad, a research biologist for Great Lakes Pharmaceuticals, quietly going to work each morning and coming home to their house on Lake Michigan to watch the news and read scientific journals. David Martin was a kind man and, like her mom, still good looking after thirty-some years of marriage. But he never had much to say, and his social life was nil. She visualized herself married to a man who had no friends or interests outside the family, and it seemed suffocating.

Sherry felt a certain distant love for her father, and she admired his scientific brilliance, which she heard the other scientists extol at company functions. He had taught her how to think critically and scientifically at a very young age, and he had painstakingly trained her to develop the power of careful observation during their walks at the beach and through the nearby woods. He not only quizzed her on the names of all the plants and birds, he would lecture her on how every bio-system worked.

She smiled as she remembered those warm summer days. She knew her dad was the reason she seemed to have a head start on other students at school. But she didn't admire his social life, which seemed boring, or the fact that he seemed to have no ultimate purpose for his life. *I may like him, but I don't have to be like him*, she reflected as she got out of the bath and dried her hair in front of the partially fogged mirror.

Her mother didn't seem to mind their closed-in, limited life. Their marriage was friendly, if not very passionate, and Mom's occasional angry outbursts were always taken in stride by easy-going old Dad. Sherry's mother was far more strong-willed than her father. She was a quick thinker, too, but intuitive in her thinking, not critical like him. Clara didn't analyze things, she just seemed to *sense* them. She was ruled by passion. Sherry admired the fiber her mother demonstrated when dealing with others, but she deplored the fact that she couldn't approach an issue critically. Clara usually blurted out some verdict or impression, before she even understood the issue.

It wasn't until high school that Sherry even became aware of this shortcoming in her mother. But once she saw it, she knew she didn't want to be like her mom either. Sometimes she felt like she had inherited her dad's mind and her mom's will. At other times, she worried that she had only inherited her mom's will—and her uncritical passion, too. There were so many things she had done during the past few years more out of intuition and desire than anything else. She looked down at the imitation marble molded counter and fingered the small cigarette burn at the edge of the sink. One of her temporary lovers had left it there. *That jerk!* Sherry shook her head. *What are you doing with your life? Any fool should have seen Jim Clemmons was a brute savage!* she rebuked herself again. *I'm going to start carrying that mace again*, she resolved as she finished drying off.

Sherry wanted more than what her parents had. She wanted a man who was active and dynamic, who could offer strong opinions, but who would care about hers—someone with the passion to accomplish something important with his life. Was there such a person? And what would be important to accomplish, anyway?

After pulling on her nightshirt, she sat on the side of her bed, again feeling the depression settling like dust in her mind. For some reason, excelling at academics and romance wasn't as exciting as it used to be. Her grades were down a bit lately, although the history department had already indicated there would be a place and even a fellowship for her in graduate school next year.

Mostly, she didn't have as much desire to excel as she once had. When she first came to college, it was exhilarating to outdo other students in class. But the competition wasn't leading anywhere. *I'm sick of it all!* she thought miserably. She didn't really know what she wanted to do with her life. It seemed like there should be some urgent desire to do something, to accomplish something . . . but Sherry wasn't sure what really mattered anymore.

As she reflected on the emotional turmoil haunting her lately, one thought kept aggravating her. *There must be something wrong with me!* As she wondered how she had become the person she was, she realized she was grateful she wasn't from an abusive or a broken family like so many of her friends. Growing up in their shore-front home on Lake Michigan had been peaceful, if somewhat cut off from the rest of the world. Her brother was almost nine years older than she was, and she had never felt close to him. By the time she was in school, he was always out with his friends, so she grew up virtually as an only child.

She felt tired and decided to go to sleep early. Lying back in her bed, she almost groaned as she sank deeper into the intangible sense of emptiness that had been hounding her lately. *I need a drink!* she thought. But something held her back from the liquor cabinet. She was worried about this new tendency to get high when she was alone. In earlier years, she never felt the need to get stoned to cover her problems. Lately, she had been doing it often. She decided to resist the urge for a change.

As she rolled onto her side, facing the mirror on the sliding door to her closet, she stared at the sleek figure she used to believe was her passport to happiness, and continued to think about her life. Her friendships were increasingly irritating to her, but she wasn't sure why. She knew she was sensing that these friends, especially the men, didn't really care about her. Then again, she had to admit she wasn't sure she really cared much about them either. There were little problems festering in various relationships. She had recently admitted to herself she didn't have any good friends, and men certainly didn't seem to be the answer.

She didn't like to judge others, but she was finding herself sitting at parties and mentally disapproving of the shallow pseudo-relating going on there. How stupid and false they seemed! So much of the talk about ideals seemed false too. Underlying the slogans people threw around, she knew they were all pretending; all just as lost and lonely as she was. She didn't feel they could understand her in a deep way even if she did open up. But she didn't feel safe opening up to them. *This party lifestyle's getting old*, she thought.

I wonder if I'm just a rat in a maze, like the ones in psych lab? It was painful to think of her life passing by like that of an animal: driven by instincts and primitive needs, trying to pretend the things in her life were important, only to sail into oblivion and nothingness at the end. She knew that was how her father viewed it, but for some reason it didn't seem to bother him. She hadn't seriously considered God for years, but as she lay alone on this Saturday night she was wondering about the whole spiritual area again.

Every time Sherry let her powerful mind move freely into the area of ultimate meaning, it took her to the same place. Either she was the product of evolution—a sack of chemicals on a chunk of matter in the middle of nowhere—in which case nothing mattered. Or . . . or what? That was the big question. Looking within herself, she knew the only alternative was the existence of a creator God. She wondered why her dad had ruled this possibility out. He was never clear on that point. He just said religious people were ignorant.

Tonight she again felt a burning inside her she couldn't deny—if God didn't exist, her life was pointless. Sherry was terribly lonely in a universe that was empty and headed nowhere.

I can't believe I'm thinking about religion again! That course must be making me think about this all the time. At the urging of her advisor, she was taking a course in comparative religion.

On this night Sherry wondered whether there was a God out there, and whether she could ever encounter Him. She sensed she needed to find an answer to this question or she was in danger of drifting deeper into her addictions; into her pain-killing techniques; into sex and drugs. With no meaning or direction for her life, there just wasn't any reason to resist her urges in these areas.

But there was a barrier in the direction of God also. Whenever Sherry thought about God, she also thought about all the problems she had with religions she had studied. She was a critical thinker, relying on her mind more than on her feelings. At least this is what she wanted to be. She could never be a part of some religion that included what she considered nonsense. She found the idea of blind faith repulsive.

She thought back to the village priest she had watched in Brazil during her work-study summer on the Amazon after her sophomore year. With loathing, she remembered watching the superstitious rituals the villagers observed during their attempts to heal. The village priest seamlessly combined Macumbo ritual with Catholic ritual during one healing service. As he pronounced the sacred words used by Macumbo shamans to cast out demons, he waved a Bible and a crucifix over the infected abscess on a young boy. She shook her head as she remembered how clearly she had discerned the situation. Instead of leading the people toward learning, healthy living, and productivity, the priest was a ball and chain around their ankles. *Oh, how I hate religion! If I have to be addicted to something, it isn't going to be some stupid, primitive superstition!* she thought defiantly.

Still, she wondered if God might be the answer.

She sat up again on the side of her bed and felt the cheap but new shag carpet with her feet. Jim's attack that night had exposed absolutely the sickness of her way of life. *I have to stop fretting about this. This time I'm going to do something about my life,* she thought. She knew enough about the ethical teachings of Jesus to have a measure of respect. After all, Dr. Forsythe, her comparative religion professor, seemed to speak of Jesus in respectful terms.

Then she remembered that the girl across the hall was some kind of church-goer. Maybe she should ask if she could come along. *Yeah, tomorrow's Sunday!* she realized with a smile. *What better source to find out about Christianity than a Christian?* She wasn't sure what she was expecting to see or find, but as Sherry lay back down and rolled over to go to sleep, she was glad she planned to do something. If there was a God, wouldn't He see her desire to know about Him? *How could it do any harm to go to church?*

It felt good to know she was actually going to do something, but visions of Jim troubled her dreams that night.

2

The next morning it was sunny and warm outside, a perfect early-fall day. Sherry dressed with a hopeful feeling. *I'm not going to wear a dress,* she thought. *Why should God care what I wear? If He's there at all, He could see me last night with nothing on at all!* Still, she did wind up putting on a nicer blouse than usual. She wanted to approach this thing honestly, and she thought this was a little false: like she was coming out of her natural way of life because of outside social pressure. But she justified it: *Well, I don't want to stick out when I get there.*

Sherry had seen Becka leave for church at 9:30, so it was no surprise when she knocked on her door at 9:10 to find her in a trim and proper navy blue dress-suit. Becka was heavy, but she had a pleasant face. Before, Sherry had felt annoyed watching her. She knew that if Becka did something better with her brunette hair than the straight page-boy she wore, and lost some weight, she would be quite pretty. "I wonder if you'd mind if I came along with you to church this morning?" she asked.

"Oh, not at all!" beamed Becka. "I'd be delighted!"

Sherry smiled and quickly went back into her apartment. She grabbed her purse, and for a moment, she stood still. It seemed like she might be entering a new phase of her life. *Is it safe? I don't know, and I don't care,* she told herself as she ran out to meet Becka.

They drove to the church in Becka's car, talking busily all the way.

Something bothered Sherry during the drive, but she couldn't put her finger on exactly what it was. Becka had been pleasant and friendly and had shown interest in Sherry during the conversation. She asked questions about Sherry's background, including church affiliation, which Sherry wasn't at all reluctant to answer. Sherry wasn't shy, and she wasn't generally afraid of people. She liked to think she was as assertive as the next person and certainly had nothing to hide. No, there was something else.

She knew she and Becka didn't move in the same social circles and that Becka was somewhat retiring. On the other hand, the few conversations they'd had were pleasant, and besides, Sherry didn't believe in judging others. Still, she felt that she lived in a very different world than

Becka, and it bothered her a bit. She realized Becka probably had never partied much, maybe not at all. She wondered whether Becka could really understand someone like her. *Get a grip! You're going weird!* she told herself.

As they drove past the manicured grounds and into the parking lot of the church, Sherry felt a tightening in her throat and her mind began to swim. *Why do churches have to look like churches?* She thought about her comparative religion class. In other societies, the temples, pagodas, and shrines were always distinctive. They never looked like the other buildings in a city. It made Sherry suspicious for some reason.

She remembered that the church in her Brazilian village was the only building made of stone; all the others were sticks and thatch. *There must be an explanation,* she thought, *but there's something depressing about it. It's as if religion has to go on in some kind of special building. It just doesn't make sense.*

As Sherry entered the lobby with Becka, she was introduced to several people. She even saw a couple of students from the university. *There's something I don't like about this kind of thing,* she thought. Of course she was careful not to let any uneasiness show. Why did this kind of interaction, greeting others and saying a few pleasant things, bother her so much? She wasn't sure.

When they moved toward the door to the sanctuary, organ music swelled up from within. As she took the program from the usher and went to her seat, a wave of negative feeling surged over her. *I guess I don't like church music*, she reflected. But she also wondered why Christians played organs. *Nobody else listens to this kind of music, do they? Why does religious music have to be so different?*

Sherry realized this thought was somehow similar to the thought she'd had earlier about the church building itself. There was a difference in the area of music—religious music. *That's it! Their buildings are different from all other buildings and their music is different too!*

Sherry was on a roll. As she looked around, one thing after another confirmed her impressions. The seat beneath her was not normal. These long wooden benches: Pews! And where did that word come from? She remembered her dad once told her they cost even more than normal seats. *Why would anyone want to pay more for something so uncomfortable?*

She looked up at the stained-glass windows to her left. They were beautiful mosaics of biblical scenes, and yet, something about them struck Sherry as odd. *Why aren't there any windows overlooking this nice wooded lot?* she wondered. The low lighting, colors, organ music, and group singing created an unusual feeling.

The choir stood to sing. *That's another thing. What's with those robes?* Sherry realized she hadn't been to church for a long time.

Several times during the service, the worship leader signaled for everyone to stand. *What does God care whether I'm standing or sitting?* she wondered. She felt mildly irritated, but went along with it because she didn't want to make a scene.

She watched the man in front of her, whose jowls rippled as he robustly sang, "Be Thou my vision, O Lord of my heart. . . ." *Hmmmm . . . strange. Why would God like this Old English?* Sherry knew the Bible was written in Hebrew and Greek. If God was able to translate His thoughts into these languages, or for that matter, into Old English, why couldn't He translate them into the language of today?

Sherry's attitude was deteriorating. Increasingly she was sitting back as a critic, observing the service from the outside. By the time the preacher stood up in his black robe with a colorful mantle strip, she was quite cynical. *The man of God has to dress differently,* she noted ironically. The message was on Abraham and Isaac and the need for faith. Her interest began to return as she listened to the ideas the preacher was discussing. This was certainly different from her Bible-as-literature course at the university. This guy treated these stories as though they actually happened, even the miracles!

It didn't take Sherry long to realize that if she ever accepted the idea of God, she was going to have to be prepared to accept the possibility of miracles. *Wow, that would lead to a totally new way to read the Bible!* she thought. *You couldn't label everything supernatural as myth and legend like we do in historical study; anybody who believed in this God would have to consider the stories real. Otherwise, the whole thing would be worthless!* Her curiosity was pricked as she wondered what it would be like to read the Bible from this perspective. At the same time, she sensed there was a whole new group of problems lying ahead.

Her attention focused back on the preacher as he came out from behind the pulpit, held up his arms, and gave a benediction. She instantly snapped into her former critical frame of mind, remembering the quasimagical blessing the shaman-priest had bestowed on the villagers when they left the healing service. *I suppose this is different,* she admitted, *but why does he have to raise his hands like that? There sure are some things I'd have to understand a lot better before I could get into this.* She was glad to be leaving as everyone stood and gathered their things at the end. Becka introduced her to Reverend Barclay who was greeting people as they filed out. She politely shook the preacher's large hand.

She didn't conceal her mixed feelings from Becka. On the way home, she asked Becka to explain some of the things she had noticed that day. She asked why so many features of churches were so different from things in the rest of society and explained what she had noticed.

Becka was a little defensive as she tried to think of answers. She pointed out that some of these things were traditional, and some were probably intended to express reverence.

"So they aren't required then? If I don't like traditional things, does God call for this show of reverence even from me?" Sherry asked. Becka hesitated and seemed confused. Sherry helped her, "For instance, does the Bible say we should stand up and sit down?"

"Well, I don't know about that, but I know the priests in the Bible wore robes."

Sherry was stunned by this last statement. She turned her eyes back to the road, her head reeling. *That's right! Robes! So God does require that! How can that be? It just doesn't make sense. What does He get from seeing them dress this way? But wait,* she thought, playing with the end of her hair. *I know there were no organs in biblical times, or Old English either. But there were robes and there were rituals, too! Rituals! What are they? Why would God want people to go through some repetitive process? What's His motive?*

Sherry imagined God like a big overgrown person with a hoop in His hand. He was saying to the little mouse-sized people on His table, "Here, jump through this. Now do it again! Keep doing it for the rest of your lives!"

Sherry turned back to Becka. "Look, I don't know whether I'm ready for this."

Becka paused to think. "Well, something must have made you ask to come in the first place," she said.

"Yeah, I don't know. I guess I've been wondering about God lately. But there's a problem here I don't feel I can face yet."

"Is it anything I can help with?"

"I don't know. . . . I don't want to say too much right now, because you've been very gracious and I don't want to be offensive."

"Don't worry about me," Becka pleaded. "I won't be offended!"

Sherry looked her in the eye. *Maybe,* she thought. *But I don't think I'll take the chance.* "I know you won't," she lied. "But I just want to compose my thoughts more." She knew this would end the conversation, and it did. Becka looked disappointed and acted a little awkward after that.

Well, that's her problem. I can't help what I feel, thought Sherry.

3

Sherry worked as a waitress at The Bratcellar, and was scheduled for a long shift that Sunday afternoon and evening. With her good looks and outgoing personality, tips were consistently higher for her than for most of the other servers. She liked to think it was also her sharp memory and knack for efficiency, but she was pragmatic enough to have modified her German barmaid uniform so it was more revealing than required. *It never hurts to use any asset you have,* she reasoned. *If these rowdies want to give me money for having a look at some extra leg or a little cleavage, that's fine with me.* She tried to avoid going out with guys she met at work; they were all animals anyway, as far as she was concerned.

This night, periodic waves of fear and revulsion continued to wash over her as she remembered the brutality Jim had inflicted on her. She kept a sharp eye out for him in the restaurant because he knew she worked there. Halfway through her shift, she went and got her mace canister from her locker and carried it in her skirt pocket the rest of the night, just for security.

Although she viewed Jim and most of the men there that night as animals, she was troubled with another thought: *I feel like I may be an animal, too.* She was sure now it was the rats in psychology lab making her wonder whether there was a difference between herself and other animals. Today, she noticed several of the men who were leering at her were good-looking guys, and she sensed her own desire to respond. *I'm no different from one of these apes!* she thought with disgust as she stood waiting to use the adding machine to total a bill.

Sherry used to think she had control of her sexuality, but the past couple of years had been rough. She had let herself fall for a guy—harder maybe than she should. Sure enough, the relationship ended bitterly. Duchan's constant efforts to control her were exasperating, and she gradually grew nauseated by his jealousies. When he again pressed for them to live together, not just on the weekends, she had told him she wanted out.

In the resulting relational vacuum she had slept with several guys during short, unimportant romances. She justified it by pointing out she needed comfort because she had been through a lot. Somehow, it never seemed very comforting. Although she was sickened by some of the memories now, especially Jim's attack, she thought, *Who're you trying to kid? You're no different from any of them. We're all the same; creatures of instinct driven to a fate we don't understand and can't control.* A wave of depression and shame rolled over her.

Yet, she questioned whether these thoughts were necessarily true. One thing was clear: Her frustration with men was surely a part of what was driving her to do strange things, such as visiting a church.

While working that evening, she waited on a table where two guys and a girl were sitting. The dark-haired guy looked up at her with beautiful blue eyes deeply set into a handsome, sensitive face. He broke into a smile at the sight of her, but remained polite. Later, she "scoped him out" from the waitress station. It seemed like he had recognized her, or was he just reacting to her looks with some sort of come-on? She had to admit he was good-looking as she viewed his lean, athletic figure while he joked and carried on with his friends. The way they were acting, it looked like the girl with them was not his date.

Later, as she laid his hot-pepper brat sandwich on the table, she got a closer look. It seemed like she might have seen him somewhere before, but she couldn't place him. *It was probably from some party,* she reflected as she walked back to the station. *I just hope I didn't make a fool of myself there.* Suddenly, a strong temptation welled up to go back over and try to get his attention a little more. *You fool!* she scolded herself. *You almost got raped by that goon last night!* She was disgusted that, even though she was reeling from hurt, she was already checking out yet another man. She felt like an addict again.

How deeply she longed to be held closely by a man who cared for her but was his own person!

The tips weren't as good as usual that evening. She tried to close her problems out of her mind and focus on work, with only partial success. Later, at her apartment, she listened to her little gray answering machine. She was suddenly electrified to hear Jim's voice! "Sherry, we need to talk. Please call me back. I'm sorry! . . ." She quickly hit the erase button. *He has a lot of nerve!* she thought. *I should have called the police! I should have had that fool arrested!*

It took over half an hour for her to cool off and start relaxing. *I know what I'll do. He always goes to bed early. I'll let him know where he stands on his answering machine. That way I won't have to talk to the jerk!*

She felt better knowing she had a plan for dealing with Jim, and she was glad to be alone with some time to sort out her increasingly turbulent feelings.

Although her church experience that morning had raised more questions than answers, interestingly, it had not dampened her new interest in spiritual things. She was disappointed with the church, yet she felt she had seen something in this "differentness" that marked everything Christian—no, everything religious. She suspected these "different" things were manmade and had nothing to do with God. She walked into the small kitchenette and began to do the dishes she had left earlier.

The conversation with Becka about priestly robes and her thoughts about rituals had thrown her into even deeper confusion. *If it's in the Bible . . . and that's a big "if," I guess . . . that either means God approves of it, or . . . the Bible doesn't really reflect what God thinks. . . .* A moment later, she shook her head. *No, I know a lot of these things couldn't possibly be in the Bible.*

She dried her hands with a fresh towel, and went over to water her African violets by the window. *Of course! The church is a traditional institution. It's manmade. Look at your own research in medieval history! I have to check this out more directly for myself. I ought to get a Bible.* She looked around. *I already took that one from Bible-as-literature back for money.* Sherry nodded to herself. *Yeah, I'm supposed to be a budding "scholar" in the history department, after all. Why not read the source material?*

This thought excited her to an unexpected degree. Here was a direction to search that matched her abilities perfectly! *Too bad I sold that one,* she thought. *What about going over and asking Becka if I could borrow her Bible? No, I don't want her to know I'm looking into this more.* Something about letting Becka know she was still interested bothered Sherry. She realized she also didn't want any of her friends to know she was fooling around in the area of religious thought. *This is something I'm looking into for myself. It's none of their business.* The thought of some of the snide remarks she might hear from the crowd she used to live with at the dorm made her growl inwardly, *Fools! I can't talk about anything important with them!* Her judgmental spirit was creeping in again.

She went back to the couch to get her shoes. She was going to go to the religious bookstore up on Main Street right then to get a Bible.

Then she realized the store would be closed by now, as would all the others on Sunday evening. *The library! Nah, it's too far to walk on campus.* Besides, she knew for some reason she didn't want to borrow a Bible—she wanted to *own* one. As the realization sank in that she wouldn't be able to get one that night, she flopped down in her chair, smitten with surprising disappointment and frustration. She couldn't believe she was so intent on getting a Bible—*Heck! You never read the one you got at church when you took that class.*

She began to think about her childhood again. Her street, Lake Shore Drive, was a small affluent residential street with houses on one side, and the eastern shore of Lake Michigan on the other. It was a beautiful street lined with trees, but it was also isolated. The neighborhood was bounded by miles of farmland in every direction, except for the little village of Saugatuk at one end.

Saugatuk is a picturesque artists' retreat and tourist village which draws bohemian artists and intellectuals, as well as partying tourists from several states. As a teenager, Sherry had begun hanging around in the village, going to parties and meeting young artists and intellectuals. Her beauty always opened doors for her, and the people she met often lived relatively wild "alternative" lifestyles. One thing that intrigued her was the way the bohemian community seemed to use their minds more than her friends at school. Many were intelligent and sensitive idealists.

It was at one of these parties when she was only sixteen years old that she met Bruce Jager. He was several years older than Sherry, tall, bronzed, and well-built. She fell for him utterly. From him she learned about sex, drugs, and wild living. It seemed she grew by years in just a few weeks. But within a few months, he was advocating an "open" relationship, which seemed to mean he would be free to run around with other women. Sherry broke off their romance and retaliated by running around with several of Bruce's friends. As they sparred with each other over the course of the next year, egged on by the gossip in their little circle, Sherry grew disenchanted with life in Saugatuk.

By the time she was eighteen, she wanted to get out and try something different. She found it burdensome to think of just living for the sake of a routine like her parents, but she couldn't see herself just lying around and getting stoned the rest of her life either. She was different from most of her partying friends in one way; she continued to get excellent grades while they flunked out and dropped out of school. She picked a university in eastern Michigan, several hours' drive from home. There she began to run with a wild crowd—a crowd with which she was again becoming disenchanted.

Sitting in her easy chair with her watering pot in her lap, she vacantly combed her toes through the brown shag carpet. How amazing it was that she could remember virtually nothing about the teaching she received when she went to church with her family. She had quit going at thirteen, and her parents had never gone very much anyway. *That church just seemed like a social thing for old people,* she reflected. *I vaguely remember they dealt with the Bible somehow, but I really don't remember anything! "Be good!" That's about the extent of it.*

Church certainly hadn't been a central part of their family life. Her mom sort of took God for granted, but Sherry was never sure whether she was even serious. God could have been something like the tooth fairy for all she knew. Her dad didn't even believe in God. She was sure of that.

She tried to study, but just getting her books out was enough to convince her she was too depressed to study that night. She took another hot bath instead.

Looking at her watch as she slipped into her robe, she saw it was nearly midnight. She went to the phone and stood staring at it. *What if he answers and I have to talk to him?* No. *There's no way he'd be up at this hour.* His jock thing meant he had to get up at 4:30 in the morning. She picked up the phone and dialed his room at the athletic dorm. His roommates also had to get up early. Sure enough, the machine answered.

She waited for the beep. "Listen here, mister tough guy. I don't ever want to see your face again! Don't call me and don't show up! We have nothing to discuss! Do you hear me? If I see you again, I'll have you standing in front of a judge, and that's a promise! I wonder what your coach would think about you attacking women on campus? Just leave me alone, and that's final!" She slammed the receiver down as a big grin spread across her face. *That ought to hold him,* she nodded, and turned to go to the kitchen for a late snack. *Yesssssss!* She made a fist and drew it in, rejoicing at the chance to get back at him. It was one of the most exhilarating things she had done in a while.

At a quarter to one in the morning Sherry still wasn't at all sleepy. She went to her cabinet and got out her bottle of Jim Beam. Again she worried about her drinking and drug habits, especially when she was alone. But she decided tonight it wouldn't hurt to have a nice strong drink. *Hey, it's medicinal! I'll just have a nip to mellow out here and get some sleep.* With the lights out, Sherry sat in her favorite chair in front of the window and drank deeply from her straight up double whiskey.

She was glad she had a third floor apartment with a view out of the picture window. She could see a faint reflection of herself in the window because of her bluish planter light. At the same time she could look through and see a couple sitting on the bench out by the pond in back.

She knew she was attractive, but she caught herself posturing in the window to study the reflection of her graceful and voluptuous figure. *How long will my shape last? And what does it matter anyway?* she thought. She was glad she wasn't homely, and that she had a good figure, but there was no denying these assets weren't delivering the sense of satisfaction they had in the past. *Nothing seems to be delivering satisfaction these days*, she admitted. As Sherry stared out the window, sorrow welled up within her, and she began to cry. *What's wrong with me? I'm losing my mind! And I hate emotional, neurotic women!* She wiped tears away, but sobbed again. *Who am I? What's the point? Why do I feel so lonely?* Her questions seemed to sail out into nothingness. There were no answers. She wondered whether love was a real thing, or only a manifestation of the breeding instinct.

The tears just kept coming, as she felt the deep misery of loneliness and lostness. It was over an hour before Sherry finally dragged herself off to bed.

4

When Sherry got up, she was a wreck. She had to summon considerable willpower to rise and get ready in time to make her 8:00 a.m. senior seminar on modern Western intellectual history. This was only the second week of the fall quarter, and she didn't want to miss a session. She had to scurry quickly across campus under an overcast sky, her thoughts moody and still a little depressed. At least it was a seminar. Sherry always enjoyed a good debate.

The topic of the seminar was ethical systems in modern Western thought. As she listened to the other students talk approvingly about the reading by Aldous Huxley, she was disturbed. She decided to challenge their thinking. "How do we think we can develop a system of moral right and wrong apart from some moral authority?" she challenged. "I think if we say there are morals, it implies the existence of God."

"There's nothing inherently necessary about a deity concept in moral thinking," responded the skinny guy with long hair and a tie-dyed T-shirt. "We can develop a system of ethics based on the preservation of society and, consequently, the preservation of our species."

"Sure," Sherry answered. "But you're begging the question. The real question is 'Why should anyone care about the preservation of our species?' Why should our species be the only one to survive? And for that matter, wouldn't the world be better off without us? You're making a values judgment before you establish a basis for values."

The guy tossed some of his straight dark hair over his shoulder. "It's in the nature of every species to try to survive."

"Yes, but all you're doing is describing what *is*, not what *ought to be*. You might as well argue that everything that happens is 'in the nature' of the species. War is also 'in the nature' of the human species." She was gesturing with her hand like a tomahawk as she spoke.

"War is destructive to society, so it's not in the interest of the preservation of the species," he rejoined.

"You're arguing in a circle," she came back quickly, with some tension in her voice. "Instead of defending your basis for a moral system, you're just repeating it in other words. Why can't you accept the fact that it's 'in the nature' of species to become extinct?" Her eyes flashed with a little more anger than appropriate in this setting.

He recoiled slightly, but gathered himself within seconds. "Because it's also in their nature to resist extinction."

"Then in that case, 'ethics' is the futile effort of species to preserve themselves. It must apply equally to flies, worms, and dinosaurs, as well as to humans."

"No, because humans have more intelligence."

"A mouse may have more intelligence than a fly. Does this mean mice have ethics but not flies? Where's the dividing line?"

Again it took him a few seconds to reply, but then he said, "I don't know where the dividing line is. But that doesn't mean there isn't one."

Sherry sat back in her chair with frustration written all over her face. "Look, let's get the larger picture here," she tried again. "Okay, suppose a breeze blows this piece of paper off my desk to the ground." She pushed a note paper off the front of her desk. "Is that a morally good event, or a morally bad one?"

Her opponent hesitated. "That's not a moral event at all."

"Why not?" Sherry waited for an answer.

"Well, paper is just matter . . . it's just gravity acting on matter . . . it's not moral."

"So if it's just matter responding to physical laws like gravity, it's not moral."

"Yeah, that's right."

"But from Huxley's point of view, our earth is a material object, and everything on earth is also matter, including us. An atheist has to say everything is just matter responding to physical laws. So how can anything be moral or immoral?"

"I don't see the connection." He shifted in his seat uncomfortably.

Sherry was frustrated. She tried again. "Look, there is no spiritual dimension for Huxley, right?" He nodded. "So, the matter on our earth happens to be arranged a certain way, strictly the result of chance, and that way happens to include organisms like flies and humans. Right? Now, one day, this whole world will flame out along with the rest of the solar system. At that time the matter assumes a new arrangement, again by chance. Since this is our source and our destiny, how can we argue in the meantime that anything matters on a *moral* level?"

There was a long moment of silence as the students digested what she had said. One girl near her let out a quiet "Ooooh, she's right!"

Sherry looked over and saw the girl smiling.

"I see exactly what you're saying," the girl beamed at Sherry.

"Well, I don't see what that has to do with it," said the long-hair. "Just because something isn't eternal doesn't mean it has no meaning or importance."

Sherry shook her head. "Show me why, under this system, any one of us has more importance than the fly we swat," she fired back.

There was another silence, as the long-hair faltered. At this point, the professor broke in, "Well, I would rather focus on understanding Huxley's view than on discussing this area in abstract terms, if that's all right with you, Sherry."

She looked around at the professor. "Yeah, sure, whatever," she said, settling back in her chair in resignation, but it wasn't fine. Sherry felt a sickening feeling as she spent several minutes wondering again whether she was an animal. She remembered what she did when she slept with the guy from art class. With a shudder she tried to focus her mind back on the class.

Afterward, she bolted from Franklin Hall and started walking briskly toward the Christian bookstore she knew was on Main Street one block over. The class had left her more determined than ever to press further in her investigation of religion. As she was walking, someone called her from behind. She turned, and saw it was a quiet guy from the seminar. He came trotting up. "Mind if I join you for a minute?" he asked pleasantly.

"Well, actually I'm in sort of a hurry," she said defensively, still walking and not looking at him.

"Oh, that's fine," he replied. "I just wanted to touch base for a minute."

"Fine." She turned to face him. "I've forgotten your name."

"Jack Collins." He smiled.

"Hi, Jack, I'm Sherry." Suddenly, looking him full in the face, she was rocked by the realization it was the same guy she had waited on in The Bratcellar the night before!

He reacted to the visible shock on her face. "Yes, it was me at the restaurant last night. I almost said something then, but you seemed busy."

"Oh, brother!" she laughed, laying her hand on her chest. "I thought I'd seen you somewhere before! I hope you're not following me."

"Well, not yet anyway." He smiled and tipped his head to one side.

"So what's happening with you, Jack?" She started walking and he fell in beside her.

"Oh, well, I noticed you sound like you're a Christian," Jack suggested.

"No, I never said that," she answered in an objective tone.

"Oh . . . well, I guess I'm just used to hearing that kind of argument, you know, theistic-based ethics, from Christians. You must be coming from some religious point of view," he ventured.

"No, I wouldn't necessarily say I am. I'm just thinking this area through right now."

"Oh . . . so, this is unusual. You're not religious, but you're apparently considering things from that viewpoint," he mused.

"I don't see what's so strange about that," she challenged.

"I'm not saying it's strange. It's just unusual. I guess with things like you were saying today, a lot of people need to have something like that pointed out to them by someone else. I'll tell you, you're thinking very clearly, in my opinion."

"Thanks." *How can this be happening to me?* she agonized. *I decided to stay away from this guy, but now he's chasing me!*

Jack carried on merrily. "Yeah, after listening to you today, I wouldn't be surprised if you end up finding some answers in Christianity."

"Well, I'm not so sure. I just went and checked out Christianity yesterday, and I wasn't too happy with what I saw." She shot him a sideways glance.

"What do you mean you 'checked it out'?"

"I went to a church."

"Oh, and you saw some things that bothered you?"

"You bet I did," she nodded.

"Ah, yes. So often the case. . . ."

She wouldn't let him go on. "Look, I don't want to offend, but I don't even know if I really want to have this conversation. What are you, some kind of preacher?"

"No, but I am a Christian."

"Well, Jack, you seem like a nice guy . . ." she hesitated. "And I might even be interested in talking with you about this stuff at some point, but to be perfectly honest, I don't feel very comfortable getting into it right now, and I have to be somewhere." She stopped walking and faced him.

"That's fine," he said meekly. "Just let me know if you want to bounce some ideas off someone. I hope you're going to give Christianity more of a chance than a visit to a church."

"I don't know," she lied.

"There's some of us who don't even go to church, you know." He shrugged appealingly.

She stopped and let the statement register. "No, I didn't know that." She looked curious. "Are you saying you think it's bad to go to church on Sundays?"

"No! It's just that there are a lot of different ways to approach Christianity. Just be sure you get the whole picture," he suggested.

There was a moment's pause as she thought about talking further, but decided against it. She wanted to be more prepared before getting into any conversation like this. "Yeah . . . well, I guess I'll do that. Listen, I'm sorry for being rude. But maybe we could take this up some other time?" She noticed his deep-set, sharp blue eyes again, and the slight grin on his face. He was very handsome.

"Yeah, I'll see you Monday," he said politely. "I'm sorry for holding you up, but I would like to talk a bit some time."

"Sure, that'd be okay." She gave him a nod and a smile.

He smiled back, and took off across the street, briefly turning back to wave. She nodded. *Don't even think about it!* she warned herself as she sensed attraction to him . . . or was it from him? *In your condition, that guy would have you eating out of his hand in no time!* She turned to go to the bookstore.

5

Sherry was feeling peculiar about this Bible thing. *Wow! I've never felt so strange about buying a book! What is this?* She reproved herself: *I don't know why you're so eager to read this book when you've had plenty of chances to read it a hundred times over. Oh, no! What if something's happening to me?!* With a chill, she remembered her thought two nights before that if God existed, He would see her desire to know Him. She felt her nerves becoming more agitated as she strode hurriedly toward the store. *You're doing this to yourself! You're going to convince yourself God's talking to you, and become a religious nut! Now get a grip and shut up!*

As she entered the Open Door bookstore, Sherry's eyes drank in the displays. There were T-shirts, CDs, and rows of books and greeting cards. The floor salesperson asked if there was anything she could do. She was a pleasant-looking brunette about Sherry's own age but much shorter. In fact, she was quite petite, with a very feminine, delicate, almost girlish voice. She greeted Sherry with a friendly, open look on her face, and smiling blue eyes above a black T-shirt and jeans. A tag on her shirt bore the name Lisa over some kind of fish design.

"So, this is a religious store?" Sherry asked matter-of-factly.

"Well, I guess you'd call this a Christian store."

"Good. What about other religions?"

"We do have material on all world religions if you're interested, but we feature the Christian perspective."

"Uh, okay. For now, I guess I just want to buy a Bible."

"Okay. Our Bibles are right over here." Lisa led her to a large bookcase full of different kinds of Bibles. Every size, shape and color imaginable were lined up on row after row.

"I can't believe this! I thought this was a simple thing; you know, just go and buy a Bible."

"Well, they're all Bibles. What did you have in mind?"

"You know—a Bible. One I can read."

"Okay, so you're not buying it as a gift?"

"No."

"Well, it depends on how much you want to spend, and what version you want."

"I don't want to spend much, and I don't know what version I want. What do you mean by *version*? Are you saying there are different Bibles?"

"No, they aren't different Bibles. The English Bible is a translation of the original Bible." Lisa took Sherry's ignorance in perfect stride and never altered her pleasant and accepting demeanor. "Any time people translate a text they can differ slightly in the way they say things."

"Well, yes, I'm aware of translation problems in historical texts." Sherry felt stupid for asking a question for which she should have already known the answer.

"And then there's the issue of what source texts were available at the time of the translation."

"That must be relatively similar for all of them I would think."

"Actually, it's not. Many of the best texts of the Bible have been discovered only in this century."

"You mean people are still relying on translations older than this century?"

"Oh, yeah! The *King James Version* is still our most popular Bible," and she handed Sherry one.

"Of course! The *King James Bible*." Sherry flipped it open and read a line: *The wind bloweth where it listeth.*

There it is! This is where they get the "thee's" and "thou's." She turned to Lisa. "This has to be hundreds of years old! Why would people want such an old translation?"

"A lot of people were raised reading the KJV and they feel comfortable with it. Some even think it's the best version in terms of accuracy."

"How could they think that? You just said the best texts were discovered recently. I know about the Dead Sea Scrolls."

"I never said it *was* the most accurate. Most don't think it is. In fact, I would recommend one of the newer versions. Such as the *New American Standard Version*. . . ." She groaned as she stretched up to reach a Bible on the top shelf. She handed it to Sherry, who began to flip through it. "With this one, the Lockman Foundation began with the *American Standard Version* and invested over forty thousand hours of scholarly research, a lot of it on texts that weren't available earlier."

"Then that version has to be superior! I don't see why there's any market for the old one."

"I think it's a traditional thing. You know?" Lisa said with a smile.

Sherry wasn't smiling. She didn't like things she couldn't understand. "Traditions are things like eating turkey on Thanksgiving Day. I don't see where that fits in when it comes to finding out what God has supposedly revealed of the truth. Why wouldn't people want the most accurate text they could get?"

"I guess I don't know the whole answer to that." Lisa chuckled. "Why don't you look at one of these New International Versions? This one's inexpensive and it has comments by scholars on each page."

"No, I don't want anyone else's opinion on the page. If I need that, I'll get it elsewhere."

"Okay, here's the same version with nothing but cross references to other passages in the Bible."

"Yeah . . . this looks pretty good. Is this one the best translation you know of?"

"It's one of the best. And it's cheap for a full-sized Bible."

"How much?"

"Twelve ninety-five."

"I'll take it."

As Lisa rang up the sale, Sherry watched her with interest. She liked Lisa. She had seemed to be no-nonsense, and she knew some things. "So you must be one," she challenged.

"One what?" Lisa looked up.

"A Christian."

"Yes, I am." She smiled pleasantly.

"Were you born that way and just never changed?"

"No," her smile grew. "I became a Christian about five years ago. You can't be born a Christian, even though a lot of people think they are." She tore off the receipt and thrust it into the colorful sack.

"How do you know that?"

"Well, it says so in the Bible. Here, let me show you in yours." Lisa pulled Sherry's new Bible back out of the sack and opened it. Holding it up with her finger on the page she said, "Here, check out verses 11 through 13."

Sherry read the section in John 1:

He came to that which was his own, but his own did not receive him. Yet to all who received him, to those who believed in his name, he gave the right to become children of God—children born not of natural descent, nor of human decision or a husband's will, but born of God.

She thought about it for a moment before looking up. "You must be referring to this thing, 'not of natural descent.'"

"That's right. If you could be born a Christian, it'd be natural descent. Receiving Christ by personal faith is the only way to get in touch with God."

"I didn't see anything about faith there."

"Faith is the same word in Greek as 'belief.' Here the verb *believe* is used."

Sherry wasn't used to sounding stupid, and she could see this woman had done some thinking about this stuff. She decided she didn't want to discuss it any further until she had done some reading. "Listen, I might want to talk with you about this at some point. Would that be okay?"

"Sure! I'd love to talk. It's my favorite subject. Why don't you give me your number?"

"I'd rather not, if you don't mind. But I'll take your number at home if that's okay."

"That's no problem. Here, let me write it down." Lisa scratched her number on a pad. "I hope you won't be afraid to call me."

"No. I don't think I'll be afraid." She stuffed the number in her backpack and looked up. "If I don't call, it's because I decided there's nothing to talk about."

"Well, I sure think I could show you some interesting things."

"Yeah . . . well, there's a good chance I'll call you sometime." She folded her backpack shut and looked up, ready to go.

"Then I'll talk to you later," Lisa said as Sherry put the shoulder strap on and turned to leave. Before she could reach the door, Lisa called after her, "You know what book of the Bible would be a good one to read first?"

"What?" Sherry turned back to face Lisa.

"The one we were just reading from, the Gospel of John."

"I was planning to read from the beginning."

Lisa shook her head. "I don't recommend it. The early parts of the Bible are important, but they're harder to understand, and a lot of it relates to conditions in ancient Israel more than today."

Sherry raised one skeptical eyebrow. "I'm not prepared to say any of it relates to today."

"Well, if you read John, you may change your mind."

Sherry hesitated for a moment before breaking into a smile. "Okay, I'll read John. Thanks for the help."

6

As Sherry walked out onto the street, a brisk west wind whipped at her. The overcast sky had darkened. It looked as if a depressing fall drizzle might set in soon. She wished she had worn a jacket. Her long hair danced in the breeze as she walked. Several times during the walk home she looked down at her backpack with her Bible in it. *I don't know, it's probably ridiculous to think a book's going to tell me that much.* She saw Jean across the street—her pretty little Italian friend from the dorm who seemed to get hurt by others so often. She waved but kept on walking, thinking about her Bible. *That part Lisa showed me was kind of interesting. I'm going to read that verse again when I get home.*

Suddenly, she felt a tug at her shirt. Spinning around she saw Bill, another one of her ex-boyfriends. He was staring down at her with an arrogant smirk.

"Hey, what's happening, Sherry?"

"Bill! You scared me to death." Her angry frowning face stared straight ahead as she continued to walk.

"Oh, getting a little jumpy, are we?" he patted her back sarcastically.

"Don't be weird, Bill," she said as she threw her shoulder back, pushing his hand off her.

He walked on for a few steps next to her. She could tell he was working up to something.

"So, I haven't seen you for a while. How would you like to get together and do something sometime this week?" He tried to sound nonchalant.

"I don't think so." She wanted to put him down firmly so he wouldn't keep bugging her. He was always so horny.

"Why not? Are you seeing someone?"

"That's none of your business." She shot him a sidelong glance.

"Come on, I'm just trying to be friendly."

"Well, I'm busy with classes, and I'm tired of going out with guys."

"Hey, we could just go out socially, as buddies."

Fat chance! I can see this guy coming a mile off, she thought. "Well, give me a call sometime. I don't want to think about it right now."

"I know about your answering machine. This is a brush-off."

"Take it anyway you want."

"Fine!" he boomed as he turned and strode off across the street.

She blanched in anger and fear at his coarse language. *Why, you miserable idiot!* she thought. *How could I ever have been interested in these creepy men?* Now another voice seemed to speak: *You're judging again.* She argued with herself. *So what? That guy deserves judgment! Two days after we broke up he was in the sack with Charlene! He thinks he's the savior of all women! He's as false as they come!*

Anger again mixed with depression as Sherry thought about her past relationships. It always seemed that she would detect something false, something selfish and ugly in each relationship, and it would become hard to respond naturally. She realized she used to enjoy men, but lately she was getting pretty cynical. It was depressing to think of these failed romances. She wasn't sure why her relationships always failed—whether it was the men or her. She always seemed to be the one who actually broke off the relationship, either directly or by giving the guy a hard time. But these guys seemed so immature . . . so selfish.

Well, I don't want to think about it anymore, she told herself as she reached the apartment. Standing and fiddling with her keys while unlocking the door, she realized that she was standing in the place where, just two nights earlier, a man had attacked her. Just thinking about it made her turn and look around. Nobody was there.

Boy, am I glad I got this apartment! she thought, as she dumped her stuff on her blue desk. Her parents' support and her academic scholarship gave her enough to live in the dorm and pay tuition. But she had found that by working at The Bratcellar she could afford this decent flat.

She had lived on the eighth floor of the dorms for the first two years of school, but she didn't miss that lifestyle one bit. The constant lack of privacy had begun to grate on her. It was becoming increasingly enjoyable to come home to a quiet, empty apartment. She had leased the apartment so her love life could be private. But lately, she liked it more because it gave her room to think.

Within five minutes she had a sandwich and was seated at her desk in the corner of the living room, next to the window. Her new Bible sat in front of her. She stared at the brown cover as she munched her ham and cheese with lettuce. She was getting two distinct feelings. A miserable skepticism was warning her she was wasting her time and even making a fool of herself. Yet there was a sense of impatience and even dread as she considered the possibility she might see something more real than she wanted to find. She considered putting off any reading in the Bible until later, but instead scolded herself. *Coward!* she thought, as she opened it and found the book of John.

> In the beginning was the Word, and the Word was with God, and the Word was God. He was with God in the beginning.
>
> Through him all things were made; without him nothing was made that has been made. In him was life, and that life was the light of men. The light shines in the darkness, but the darkness has not understood it.

She stopped reading and looked out the window. *That sounds catchy, but I'm not sure it means anything. Who . . . or what . . . is "the Word"?* She looked again. "He was with God in the beginning" and "the Word was God." *This must be Christ. I bet "the Word" is some kind of term for Jesus.* Her speculation was confirmed when she came to verse 14:

> The Word became flesh and made his dwelling among us. We have seen his glory, the glory of the One and Only, who came from the Father, full of grace and truth.

Christians believe Jesus existed before His birth. I don't see any proof of that. It'd take evidence before I could accept something like that! She laid the Bible down. *Still, that one phrase is catchy: "In him was life, and that life was the light of men." Of course He had life in Him. That's a strange saying. There must be more here than I'm getting.* Her eyes settled on the phrase "that life was the light of men." *Probably they're saying that He had the life of God in Him or something like that.* She read part of verse 12 again:

> Yet to all who received him, to those who believed in his name, he gave the right to become children of God.

Well, anyone could say that! There is no proof any of this is true. Even if it is true, I don't know how I could ever know for sure. Sherry hadn't gotten very far in her reading before she stood up and began to walk around her apartment. She suddenly felt strange. She realized she didn't have a class for a couple of hours, and she told herself she was burned out. Deciding to take a quick nap, she stretched out on the couch and drifted off into oblivion.

7

When she got up from her nap, Sherry had to hurry to make it to her German conversation class, which was followed by a lecture in psychology. Through both classes she thought about her encounters with Jack and Lisa, and her Bible sitting at home. She was glad she didn't have to work that night, because she was determined to try again to read as soon as she got back.

When she got home she didn't see anything interesting in the refrigerator for dinner. Cold cuts sounded boring. She decided to run down the street and get a hot chicken sandwich at Burger King. Walking back on the dark, quiet street, she was suddenly stabbed with fear: someone was following her! She stopped walking and listened, too scared to look around.

As she stood listening, her heart pounded in her ears. She concluded looking back couldn't make things any worse, and turned suddenly to look back down the sidewalk. A branch was moving by the corner of an apartment building, but nobody was in sight. *It could be the breeze*, she thought, *although most of the wind has died down . . . if I really want to know, I should go back and see if someone just ducked behind that corner.* But then she thought better. *No way! What if it's Jim?* She turned and ran down the sidewalk to her building and went in quickly.

Still breathing heavily, she slid inside and threw the bolt on the door. *Girl, you're really going crazy! There was probably no one there! You're acting like you just barely escaped, but this is probably nothing but your paranoid fears.* She wiped the beads of sweat from her forehead and sat at her desk. *Okay, you've been through some trauma. You were attacked by a man two days ago and you're scared. That's natural.* She breathed deeply, feeling herself begin to relax.

I should have gotten my mace canister out right away . . . without stopping. If there was a guy there, I gave myself away . . . I froze. She shook her head, disappointed in herself for being too emotional. *If that jerk is following me I'll mace his ugly face 'til it melts off!*

At that moment, her eyes darted to the answering machine. *What if he's on there again?* Her pulse started to rise. She immediately got up and went over to the machine. There were two messages. Her finger hesitated over the replay button, but then she resolutely pushed it.

Neither message was from Jim. She felt foolish. *I'm probably imagining this whole thing. He wouldn't dare face legal problems or jeopardize his place on the wrestling team! Just forget about him!*

Twenty minutes later, Sherry had eaten her sandwich and salad and was reading her Bible again. She was still reading in John, now in chapter 2. It was the story of Jesus turning water into wine.

At first she couldn't get past the notion that the story was about a miracle. *I just don't believe in this kind of stuff,* she protested. But then she critiqued her own view. *That's the whole point! Now you're begging the question.* She chided herself, *I thought we were trying to decide whether to believe in the supernatural, but you've already decided!* She determined she would try reading it like the preacher had—what would the story read like if one assumed supernatural things are possible?

She read the story again and shook her head. *There doesn't seem to be any meaning to the story . . . other than Jesus showing He could do miracles. Maybe that's the point.* Sherry was frustrated. It didn't look like she was going to get any answers from this book. Looking over at her backpack, she thought about calling Lisa. She was reluctant, but then she remembered her own words before she left the store—something about not being afraid to call if there was a reason. She dialed the phone.

A minute later, Lisa answered.

"Lisa? This is Sherry, from the store this afternoon."

"Oh, hi! How are you doing?" Her voice was welcoming.

"Okay, I guess. But I'm having a problem with my Bible."

"What is it?"

"Well, I'm reading in the book of John, you know, and I'm up to the second chapter here, about the water being turned into wine."

"Yes, the wedding at Cana."

"Right, a wedding. You know, even if I believed Jesus could do this kind of thing, I don't see what the point is. I mean, you know, you said this book had meaning for today. What can a story like this have to do with someone like me?"

"Oh, this is a super insightful story! Do you have your Bible there?"

"Yeah, it's right in front of me."

"Here, let me look this up," she said as she apparently fumbled for a Bible and found John 2. "Let me get settled at my desk . . . okay. The key here, Sherry, is verse 6."

Sherry read: "Nearby stood six stone water jars, the kind used by the

Jews for ceremonial washing, each holding from twenty to thirty gallons."

"I don't see anything here."

"Well, Jesus turned this water into wine, right?"

"Yes."

"The important thing to see is that this was not drinking water."

"Oh, because it says it was for ceremonial washing? What's that?"

"Ceremonial washing was a practice developed under Rabbinic Judaism at that time. They had to wash their hands in a ceremonial way before they could eat—it's nothing like our washing our hands before we eat."

"I know they had no knowledge of bacteria or sanitation."

"Right. This was mainly a superstitious practice. They believed people could be contaminated *morally* by contact with evil. So this washing was intended to cleanse their hands of the 'moral filth' of the world, you know, so they wouldn't eat with impure hands and take evil into their system. You can read more about it in the passage cross-referenced in the margin; see where it says for verse 6, 'Mark 7:3 and following'?"

"Oh, yes, I see it. Boy, that's stupid! So they thought they could wash off moral problems with water? Did Jesus believe that?"

"No, He didn't. In fact, this miracle was a direct rejection of the practice. He was saying, in effect, 'I'm going to replace your efforts to wash yourselves from the outside with something really good for the inside.' You know, like the finest wine."

Sherry thought about it for a moment. "Wow! That's pretty cool!" She was becoming more impressed with Lisa by the minute. "So you think there's a symbolic meaning here?"

"Yeah. I don't think John would've mentioned that the stone pots were for ceremony if he wasn't trying to call our attention to that fact, you know? I think Jesus was showing He was going to offer new life in our spirits in place of this external observation of religious rituals."

The thought excited Sherry just a bit. She jotted the comment down on her pad, but she tried to remain restrained. "Now that's a very appealing message. But I don't know whether you really got that from this text or whether you're kind of bringing this in as your own interpretation."

"Well, besides the point I just mentioned, consider that the next 'sign' or miracle John records is similar, in a way, to this one."

"I haven't read that far."

"Well, look at it, starting in verse 13. It only takes a minute to read."

Sherry turned the page to verse 13. "Okay, got it."

"Why don't you read it?"

Sherry read aloud how Jesus went to Jerusalem and rebuked the money changers and sellers of animals and drove them out of the temple.

"Why did He do that?" Sherry stopped and asked with a note of shock.

"Well, these people were profiting from the worshipers who traveled to Jerusalem. They'd make the travelers pay their temple tax with a certain coin, so everyone from other countries had to change their money over. The changers were taking a healthy cut for themselves, some of which they gave to the priests for the privilege of having a stall in the temple."

Sherry quickly saw the point. "So they made a rule, and then got kickbacks from it."

"Exactly. They were doing the same thing with animals brought for sacrifice. They'd say the animals were too blemished to be used for sacrifice, and then make people buy one of the 'unblemished' ones for sale in the temple court. Naturally, there was a kickback on these sales as well."

"Boy, I don't know, Lisa. It seems like religious leaders are always the same. They're all in it for the money. And sacrifices also bug me. I have a lot of questions about rituals and holy places, stuff like that."

"Well, that's often true about religious leaders. But on your other point about temples, there may be an answer here. Let's not lose track of the story. The point is, Jesus drove them out and then He has a conversation with the authorities. Why don't you read it?"

> Then the Jews demanded of him, "What miraculous sign can you show us to prove your authority to do all this?"
>
> Jesus answered them, "Destroy this temple, and I will raise it again in three days."
>
> The Jews replied, "It has taken forty-six years to build this temple, and you are going to raise it in three days?" But the temple he had spoken of was his body. After he was raised from the dead, his disciples recalled what he had said. Then they believed the Scripture and the words that Jesus had spoken.

Sherry's voice trailed off as she thought about what she had read.

Lisa spoke up, "You see, this was another symbolic act. Jesus was saying He'd replace the temple with His body in verse 21."

"It does sound like He's hinting at some sort of symbolism, but I don't get it. How can a person's body replace a temple?"

"Well, the temple was supposed to symbolize the house of God, in fact, it's often called that."

"Yeah . . ."

"Jesus is saying God was dwelling within Him; that He was the true 'house of God' in a way."

"I guess that makes sense."

"It also means there isn't any need for an earthly physical temple anymore. The body of Christ is the true dwelling place of God."

"Whoa! Say that again."

"Okay, you need to know the Bible says Christ's body is the community of all true believers in Him. There are several passages in the New Testament where it calls Christians corporately the 'Body of Christ.'"

"Hmmmm . . . I'm still not sure I'm following your line of thought."

"All right, Christ replaced the outward sanctuary of the temple with His own body."

"Yes, I get that."

"Now Christians, who receive the spirit of God in our hearts, become the body of Christ on earth, so to speak. You can look at passages such as Colossians 1:18 or Romans 12:5 where it says, 'So in Christ, we who are many form one body, and each member belongs to all the others.'"

"Hmmmm." Sherry scratched the side of her head with the back of her pen. "So Christian believers are like a living version of the temple?"

"Yeah, that's right. Well said!"

"So what are you saying about cathedrals and so on today?"

"I'm saying what used to be symbolized outwardly is now fulfilled inwardly. So there should no longer be any temples, as far as the New Testament's concerned. Of course, there's nothing wrong with getting a building to meet in, but it shouldn't be viewed as sacred."

"I've seen Christians on their knees approaching sacred shrines and stuff. What're you saying about them?"

"Well, I guess I'm saying I can't find any warrant for that in my Bible, so those people are misguided and superstitious as far as I'm concerned. You know, I base my views of religion on the Bible, and I guess I'm pretty skeptical about claims from other sources."

Sherry realized Lisa was sweeping away with one motion every problem with Christian history. It was too easy. "It seems like you're saying you stand totally separate from everything everyone else considers Christian."

"That depends. I sure don't believe that someone just calling himself a Christian necessarily means anything. Jesus says, 'Not all who call me Lord will enter the kingdom of heaven.' There are a lot of counterfeits out there, and I don't feel any need to defend them at all."

Sherry winced with resistance to what Lisa was saying. It still seemed too easy. "It's as if you're erasing the blackboard and starting over."

"Yeah, I guess in my mind, I want to start with a blank blackboard. I don't want other human interpretations interfering with my own understanding. I guess then, after I've reached my conclusions, I can look at what others have seen, and there's some good stuff there—but there's some real nonsense there, too."

Sherry was intrigued. *Why not write off the history of the church? Isn't that exactly what I wanted to do myself? Why not reach my own conclusions about the Bible?* Within a few moments, she realized she was very pleased by the way Lisa was able to deal with these concepts. "I think that's a really cool interpretation, Lisa. But I still don't know whether you're reading your own views into the story."

"Well, read the next chapter in John, which explains about the spiritual new birth possible with Christ. That explains what I mean by the Spirit coming into a believer. Also, read in chapter 4 about the woman by the well. There Jesus lays it down about temples and things like that."

"So you're telling me this interpretation is based on the context in John."

"Yes."

"Where do you learn stuff like that?"

"I go to a Bible study on Mondays. In fact that's where I'm going now. We've been studying John, and the guy that teaches the study is really sharp. He has all this great insight and stuff. I guess this passage is pretty fresh in my mind because we just covered it the week before last."

"Really? That sounds interesting. So this is like a church? This guy's a preacher or something?"

"No," Lisa chuckled. "He's just a student at the university, but he's a bright one, and pretty well-read."

"Hmmm. Is this group open for others to visit?"

"Yeah, definitely. You'd be welcome. " Lisa's voice sounded eager.

"Well, I don't want to join anything right now. Could I just visit?"

"Oh, yeah, you don't join anything with this. You just participate as much or as little as you want. Do you really want to check it out?"

"Well, not tonight, but I think I might . . ." Sherry shifted her weight in the chair. "I'm not sure, actually."

"Well, I'll call you next Monday and see if you want to come," Lisa offered.

Sherry paused. "I'll call you if I can make it."

"Okay. Listen, I have to go. Read those passages and we can talk about them if you want."

"All right, I'll do that. And Lisa, thanks, this was kind of fun."

"Sure, I enjoyed talking."

Sherry sat staring at the turquoise phone in her hand for a minute before hanging up. She was really fired up about her conversation with Lisa. This was intriguing stuff! When she returned to reading, it was with new eyes. She was now reading with the sense that these words were possibly full of meaning—not just stories of ancient people.

As she read on, she was captivated by Jesus' claim that one must be "born again." *So, that term comes from the Bible. I thought it was just a way for Bible-bangers to claim they were better than others. This "born of the Spirit" thing sounds wild. What would it be like to have a spirit come into you? I wonder whether that's possible?*

Then she came to the part where it read,

> For God so loved the world that he gave his one and only Son, that whoever believes in him shall not perish but have eternal life. For God did not send his Son into the world to condemn the world, but to save the world through him. Whoever believes in him is not condemned, but whoever does not believe stands condemned already because he has not believed in the name of God's one and only Son.

Sherry put the book down and got up. She walked over to her window and stared out at the rain which was now falling steadily. Wave after wave of jumbled, conflicting feelings swept over her. Something she couldn't explain was happening inside her. She had a sudden desire to speak to God. At the same time, she felt cold fingers of fear. She couldn't believe she was actually contemplating seeking interaction with God's Spirit. Not just thinking about God, but experiencing Him! She argued with herself: *You haven't even looked into this much yet! You hear these claims, but you don't even know if they're true.*

But another voice also spoke: *What's there to worry about? If there's no God, nothing will happen.*

You could convince yourself something happened because you want something to happen. She grabbed the cords to her blinds and held on.

Get real! You're just afraid you're going to lose control. You're afraid something really will happen.

Of course I'm afraid something will happen! What is this thing? I don't even know what I'm talking about here! She walked to the kitchen to get something to nibble on . . . but after staring vacantly at the fruitwood cabinet for a moment, she came back to the window without getting anything.

Sherry looked down at her hands and confirmed they were damp before wiping them on her jeans. It was going to be very hard to go to sleep without at least trying to address God. The minutes ticked by as she struggled with her thoughts and feelings, and her mind kept coming back to the same questions.

When I'm wondering whether I could get into a guy, I go out with him and find out what he's like. That's all I'm thinking of doing here.

Yeah, but that's a real flesh-and-blood guy. What am I talking about here? A spirit! Some God who might not even be there!

She shook her head, disagreeing with herself. *It seems like something's happening in my life lately. God might be there and . . . maybe I should try to talk to Him. How do I know God isn't speaking to me through these feelings? He could be trying to get through to me.*

But another side would answer, *"Feelings! Feelings!" Now we're going to base life on some feeling?*

A moment later she slapped the window sill. *Base my life nothing! I'm just talking about trying to pray here.* She reached over and picked up her new Bible.

Sherry's heart was thumping in her ears. Her breathing quickened. She sensed she was about to do it, but dread and fear held her back. *What are you so afraid of? I'm going to do it and that's final!*

Inwardly, she turned to face God, also turning physically to look out the window for some reason. She had never prayed in her adult life. She felt like introducing herself. *Oh, that's so stupid. If He's God He knows who I am.* She rubbed her eyes, collecting herself.

For several seconds that seemed like minutes, Sherry faced God in her inner person. She couldn't speak. She felt stupid. Tears suddenly began to well up and burst forth. She sat down on the edge of her easy chair and wept, her new Bible clutched in her hands. Still nothing came out. Finally she began to speak in her mind.

Look God, I guess You know I'm still not sure You're there. Well . . . I get the feeling You're there, but I'm not sure. Anyway, I want to know. She sobbed, *I'm sorry I'm such an emotional wreck. I know I probably haven't been living the way You want me to. . . .* She wasn't sure where to go next. *Look, if You hear me, just . . . let me know You're there, okay? Thanks.*

Sherry got up and went to the kitchen to get a tissue. *You have to make yourself relax.* She breathed deeply a couple of times. She felt spent, but a certain relaxed feeling had come over her. She smiled and shook her head. *You're really doing some strange things now, girl,* she thought. She felt like she might have crossed a barrier. There was no ecstasy, no miracle. Just a sense of calm. Sherry felt like she had done the right thing.

That night sleep came easily.

8

The sun was breaking through the puffy clouds as Sherry walked to her first class the next morning. She felt a little sheepish about her experience. *What I did last night was strange, but I don't regret it,* she thought. She wondered whether God was now somehow involved in her life—or if she had imagined the whole thing. *It's not going to be easy to avoid saying something about this to my friends,* she thought.

After going to two classes and spending several hours at the library studying, she felt more relaxed than she had for days. *I probably feel washed out from so much emotional commotion in my life,* she thought. As she watched some birds splashing in the birdbath outside the library, she again thought about God. She didn't say anything to Him, but almost with amazement, she found herself breaking into a big smile! *Oh, boy,* she shook her head to herself, *you're getting weird these days!*

At her late-afternoon lunch at McDonald's, Sherry got a table by the picture window next to Main Street. As usual, the street was packed with students jostling by. She loved to sit and watch people striding by while she ate—the beautiful, the ugly, the happy, the sad. The persona each wanted to project—tough guy, sweet innocent, frat-rats, and gays—they were like a carousel of life turning past her window. For some reason, the window allowed Sherry to stare openly. Although she was in plain view, it felt like she was in a different world from them.

It was a beautiful early fall day in Michigan—the sky had that deep blue that only comes with dry air.

As she munched on her chicken sandwich and watched the faces pass by, she looked down the street and suddenly recognized the guy from the modern Western intellectual history seminar heading toward her. It was Jack all right. She saw him some distance away and had a chance to really look him over without him knowing it. *I guess I'd have to admit this guy's good-looking.* She admired his rather tall, thin-but-athletic build. His dark hair was just a little long over the ears and collar, only slightly wavy, and soft enough to blow a bit in the breeze. He wore a dark blue sweater under a bright light blue and orange windbreaker, and well-worn jeans that fit perfectly. And then there were those eyes. . . .

Sherry gaped at him until, with a shock, she saw him look straight at her, catching her in the act of staring at him! She rolled with the situation, smiling and waving as though she had just recognized him. He stopped, grinned, and turned around to go back to the door. *Uh, oh!* Sherry fretted as she sat up and got ready for him to come back to her table. *Hey, it's no big deal!* She reached up to make sure her hair was in order.

Jack walked up to her table. "So you eat here, too!"

"Yeah," she smiled. "I like to have a little wad of animal lard now and then."

"Mind if I sit down for a minute?"

"No. Not at all. I have to leave soon."

"Yeah, so do I." He peeled off his thin jacket. "So, what'd you think of the Ayn Rand reading?"

"I haven't done it yet," she admitted. As she placed her sandwich to her mouth, she used one hand to partly shield her eyes as she scoped out his chest while he wrestled to get the jacket sleeves off.

"I think you'll find it gets the juices moving," he said as he slid into the seat across the very small table.

She had to swallow. "I just hope I get to it before class."

"So what've you been up to today?" he asked, looking her in the eyes.

"Well . . . I studied after my morning class. I like to read at the library."

"Yeah, I know. The table by the window next to the Simpson courtyard, right?"

She raised one eyebrow. "How did you know that?"

"I've seen you there a number of times. When I saw you in seminar I knew I'd seen you before."

"You mean in earlier quarters or something?" She wiped her mouth after taking the last bite of sandwich.

"Yeah, I always study at a table behind you there. You've been right in my line of sight for the windows a number of times." He smiled playfully.

Sherry realized he was admitting he had been watching her. She looked down in embarrassment and pretended like she was brushing crumbs off her lap. "Oh . . . what do you study?" She wanted to change the subject.

"I'm in the new school of religious studies here."

"Is that in Arts and Sciences?" She held out her French fries to him.

"I don't want to eat your lunch," he objected.

"No, really, I don't feel like eating them," she insisted. He took a couple, and she set them between them.

"No. It's a graduate program. I guess the university felt it was losing too much business to seminaries, so they opened a school of religion. Apparently it's a growing area of interest on campus."

"Well, what kind of religion is it?"

"They don't care. It's a personalized study program sort of based on the history, anthropology, and philosophy departments, mainly." He waved a French fry with ketchup in time with his words. "You just have to give your religious perspective, you know, what we call our 'presuppositions,' at the beginning of your papers, and then keep your reasoning consistent with that. And of course, you have to show that you understand other perspectives in their own right."

"So you're getting a master's degree?"

"Yeah."

"Why are you in my seminar, then? I thought that was for undergrads."

"No, there are a couple of grad students in there. The 700-level seminars often serve for graduate credit." He was steadily feeding on her French fries now, and she ate a couple, too.

"Well, that's not really fair competition, is it?" she grinned.

"I think you'll find grad students are no brighter than anyone else. That long-haired guy you pounded the other day was a grad student." He looked up with a big smile.

"That's ridiculous, and you know it. I didn't pound him at all." She grinned as she felt a blush rising from her collar.

"Right," he acquiesced sarcastically.

"No, I mean it. You're really exaggerating!"

"Uh huh. I guess there's probably some other reason why he left the class about a foot and a half shorter than he entered it."

She laughed heartily. "That's so ridiculous! The prof interrupted before we could even finish."

"Yeah, he saw you were driving him into the ground like a fence-post!" His good-natured smile and chuckle showed he was only kidding.

"I can't believe you're distorting that so much!" After shaking her head for a moment in mock disapproval she went on and changed the subject again. "How long do you have to go on your M.A.?"

"I finish up this year. I'm just taking two classes this quarter, and most of my time's going into my thesis."

"Oh . . . what are you writing on?"

"I'm starting with a passage in the Bible, the seventh chapter of the book of Acts. It's a passage where this guy named Stephen went on trial for his life."

"Yeah. What's the, uh . . . importance of the passage?"

"Well, let's see. In a few words, I'm arguing that this is one of the most important passages in the New Testament; 'The transition point from the ethnic religious framework of Rabbinic Judaism to the notion of a universal faith free from formalistic encumbrance,' as my introduction says. It's probably pretty boring to the average reader."

"That doesn't sound boring to me. I'd like to read it." Sherry liked the idea of an intelligent man who was good-looking.

"You can't do that 'til I get it written. I just have sections of text right now with no cohesion. But this is good. I can get some extra motivation to write if I think you'll be reading it."

His eyes had an extra twinkle that made Sherry look down again. It seemed like his eyes were drinking in her beauty. She was instantly certain Jack was challenging her romantically, and she felt another warm flush come over her. "Well, I guess that's good, I'm glad to help. Is it going to be comprehensible to someone like me?"

"Well, if it isn't, I can explain any difficult parts. I think most of it should be no problem . . . but it'll be good to find out if there are difficult sections. I'm so close to the subject at this point I can't always tell what needs explanation."

"I may not be the best judge of what's complicated. I've been trying to read the Bible lately, but I'm so ignorant, it's a real joke." She reached for the same French fry he did, and looked up directly into his eyes for slightly longer than she should have, but he stared right back. There was a moment of electricity that passed between them; an unspoken communication so quick it could hardly be measured, but so clear it was frightening. Sherry knew she had revealed more than she wanted to. She looked back down and fiddled with her wastepaper during a pregnant moment of silence during which both of them seemed to have forgotten what they were talking about.

Jack got his bearings first. "If you're reading, you'll pick up a lot of the Bible sooner than you think," he went on mercifully. "Tell me about your interest in Christianity. You said you went to a church."

"Yeah, but I couldn't get into it."

"What was the name of the church?"

"Uh, Edgewood something. Edgewood Bible Church."

"Oh, okay, up on Glendale?"

"Yeah, that's it. What do you know about it?"

"Not much, actually. I know it's a Bible-believing church, unlike some. Maybe you need to check out a less traditional Bible study group," he suggested as they finished up her French fries, and started gathering the wastepapers onto Sherry's tray.

"I might be going to one. I met this girl and she told me about one."

"Good!"

"Listen, Jack, I have to go," she lied.

"Okay." They got up, and he indicated she should go first as she went over to dump her wastepaper in the trash. After they wound their way out he held the door. "I guess I'll see you in class."

"Yeah, I'll see you then." She gave him a friendly smile.

"Are you going this way?" he asked, pointing in the direction he had been walking when she saw him.

"No. I'm going the other way," she lied again.

"Okay. I'll see you later, Sherry." He immediately turned and strode off.

Oh, that's just great! she chided herself. *I'm trying to sort out my life, and I just messed up a relationship with someone who seems to know some of the answers. Now I'm not going to be able to ask him questions without him wondering if I'm coming on to him.*

She knew she had basked in the light of his admiring eyes, and had even signaled she was open to something in the way she responded. She felt the power of her uncontrolled desire for a man rise within her like a warm fire in her chest, and a tangible tingle ran up her spine. *The last thing I need now is another man, and especially a Christian! This is going to mess up everything. You just almost got raped by one of these animals!* But she wasn't very convinced Jack was another animal. *He sure doesn't seem like an animal.* She could see what was happening. *You're so weak!* she lamented to herself.

Because she had told Jack she wasn't going his way, she had to walk an extra two blocks out of her way home. She felt twinges of anger and frustration, interspersed with little fantasies of how she could have taken the conversation even further and lured him in closer. She couldn't keep from having these thoughts, even though she knew they were dangerous. Overall, the encounter left her feeling good. *Well, he is awfully attractive,* she thought. *What's so bad about a woman being attracted to a man who likes her?*

No! Not now! You can't afford to get involved with a guy when you're this messed up! She forced herself to think of other things, but the conversation kept creeping into her mind the rest of the afternoon.

9

The answering machine revealed Jean had called, so Sherry called her back around dinner time. Jean wanted to know if she was going to stop over that night and have a beer with the girls at the dorm during their usual Wednesday night gathering. Sherry called and left a message on Jean's machine that she would be there.

Sherry tried to keep up her friendships at the dorm even though she had moved out. At one time she had acted as a sort of *de facto* leader for this group of young women. But she had grown increasingly uncomfortable with the way they looked up to her. She could tell they didn't realize how confused she was much of the time, and so she felt like she had to act more together than she really was. Ever since she had moved out of the dorm, her influence had diminished. These days, she was more like "one of the girls," which was fine with her.

When she walked up to the metal door of suite 8H she could hear the music playing. Leslie let her into the small, smoky living area of the four-bedroom suite. The usual group of women sat drinking with the stereo playing music by the Spin Doctors. She grabbed a beer and flopped down by Jean, a small, dark-haired Italian beauty with a quiet, sensitive disposition.

"What's happening, Blue-Jean?"

"Oh, you know, nothing really ever happens," she said, tugging on her long green sleeves in a self-absorbed way. "I'm definitely finished with men. That's it. Forever. I swear to God I'll never trust one again."

"I think I've heard you say something like this before."

"Oh, give me a break, Sherry. I've been through a lot." Jean's large, beautiful brown eyes flashed with anger.

"I'm sorry," Sherry said with resignation. "What happened?"

Jean seemed to consider giving her a hard time for a moment, but it was obvious she really wanted to share her problem. "Cory told me he couldn't go out the other night because his mother was in town. Then I found out he really went to this party down at his brother's place—some kind of bachelor party for his brother's buddy."

Sherry nodded attentively.

"So anyway, they got strippers to come to the party, and these strippers were really prostitutes, you know?"

Sherry wagged her head and frowned in disapproval.

"So after ogling these naked women, these drunken slobs were taking them back into the bedrooms! Larry was teasing me about Cory being there . . . and he said Cory had a run at one of these girls in the bedroom!"

"That's sickening." She put a sympathetic hand on Jean's shoulder.

"So I confronted him, and what do you think he said?"

"I give up."

"He tried to deny the whole thing!"

"He's such a liar!" Sherry said with disgust.

"No kidding! But see, I'd already played along with Larry and asked who else was at this party. It turned out Mo was there."

"Yeah?"

"Well, I told Cory I'd ask Mo what happened, and you know, Mo wouldn't lie for Cory."

"Good move."

"So then he says to me it's none of my business what he does on his nights out with the boys. And I'm like, 'You said you were out with your mother!' And he just folded up. He starts to plead for forgiveness and he says he was really drunk and all this garbage. . . ." Jean looked at her hands as she wrung them and then wiped the beginnings of a tear.

Sherry felt sorry for Jean and gently rubbed and patted her back, trying to comfort her. It was a little hard to sympathize because everyone in the dorm had known for a long time Cory couldn't be trusted—including Jean.

"Well, Cory's a real jerk all right. You're better off without him."

"Oh, Sherry, you're always so strong." She looked up with her large dark eyes brimming with tears.

"I don't think that's true."

"Yes, it is. You don't let guys make a fool of you." She wiped away the tears that ran down her dark-complected cheeks.

"I feel like a fool a lot of the time," Sherry insisted. "Especially with men."

Jean wasn't listening. She looked down, shaking her head. "I don't know what the future holds. You just can't trust them, or else the ones you can trust are so nerdy. I just don't know. . . ."

Sherry wasn't sure what to say. In her heart she sort of agreed. The evening progressed and Sherry listened to the jabber of the girls with a growing sense of dismay and depression. As she listened to Lydia going on about wanting to be reincarnated as a whale, it made her feel separated from the social flow of the evening. She began to stand off from the others and hear their words in a critical light.

She pretended to be interested in Gina and Leslie's animated discussion about the cute blouses for sale at a shop downtown. Later, as they critiqued some of the clothing worn by various friends, she looked through the deepening smoke haze and watched Mary writhing in a sensuous dance to the music, her lithe body outlined by the fluorescent light over the planter. The old Led Zeppelin number seemed to be blaring louder than before. For some reason, it intensified her feeling of distance from what was happening. *How different these people are from Lisa. Their lives seem to go around in circles, and their conversation never amounts to anything. They're all just as lonely as I am.* She lifted the beer in her hand and swallowed a big mouthful. *I can see myself at forty having these conversations over the phone.* She subtly shook her head to herself in dismay. *How dreadful!*

They began passing around a small, glass water pipe with somebody's donated weed in it. Sherry took a deep hit and passed it on. As the familiar tide of sensual confusion rose in her mind, the conversation became increasingly bizarre. She sensed herself being pressed down into the chair by an unseen weight, and she listlessly watched the other girls giggle and carry on. A fatalistic sense arose in her that the whole human race was doomed. *Everyone's so eager to create an impression. They really put on the act*, she marveled.

"You don't have much to say tonight, Sherry," Leslie challenged, standing in her jeans shorts with one foot on the coffee table and a cigarette sticking out between the fingers of the hand resting on her knee.

"That's because there isn't much happening," Sherry lied.

"How's that hunk jock you've been seeing? Did you ever check him out between the sheets?" Several giggled at that suggestion. Leslie was so bold.

"We're not seeing each other anymore. I . . . he was a stupid jerk."

"Oh, I'm sure! A guy with a bod like that could be as stupid as he wants with me!" The girls laughed, as Leslie looked around to check their reactions.

"Hey, he almost attacked me when I told him to get lost. I mean it, that guy's dangerous! He's a real idiot!" Sherry said.

"What d'ya mean, he almost attacked you?" Leslie pressed.

"Man, he grabbed me and forced a kiss on me . . . like that was going to make me change my mind or something." Sherry made a disgusted face that drew snickers from several others.

"Well, it might make me change my mind. I'd say, 'Is that all you have to show me?'" Leslie struck a sexy pose that made the girls howl with laughter.

"Leslie, it wasn't funny. This guy had me and he wouldn't let me go. I felt like I was being raped!" Leslie seemed to finally sense this wasn't material for comedy and fell silent. Sherry went on in a murmur. "I don't really want a guy right now anyway."

"That's what I was saying last month." Leslie took the bottle of whiskey as it was passed around. The taste caused her to make a loud hissing noise through her teeth while grimacing and shaking her head.

At about 11:00 the pot and alcohol were making Sherry feel drowsy and she was still depressed. She realized more beer wasn't going to help her enter into the spirit of the group, so she announced she was going to have to go, because she was behind in her homework.

"Oh, you're becoming too much of a scholar to have fun anymore! How're you gonna study after drinkin' and getting high?" challenged Gina, who had discerned Sherry's lie.

"I guess I'll have to get up extra early in the morning. See you guys," and she moved to leave. She saw Jean sitting with a vacant, depressed look on her face. Sherry slid behind her on the couch and, leaning over, hugged her. "I'm so sorry, Jean."

Jean nodded and patted her forearm appreciatively. "Thanks."

Sherry wondered, as she got into her car, whether Jean had any chance of avoiding self-destruction in a future relationship. She doubted it. Jean was so sweet, but she seemed to be one of those people who had a taste for dominating, exploitative men. On the other hand, she wondered, *What makes me think I'm any different?*

Later at home in bed, she reflected on the fact that she hadn't enjoyed the evening. She wished she didn't have such a negative attitude, that she wouldn't judge her friends so much, but she felt she couldn't help it. She felt muddled and almost in a stupor from the drugs. *I don't feel comfortable with this stuff anymore*, she thought, looking up at the ceiling.

Jack's incredible eyes suddenly reentered her mind, and she began to think about their encounter again. It had affected her deeply. She wasn't sure who was in charge during either one of their meetings. She wished she hadn't always tried so hard to control the situation by breaking off their talks. *He must think I'm really cold!* she thought. *I'm going to be nicer to him next time. I won't get involved or anything, I just don't want to close the door completely.*

Be careful, Sherry! she warned herself. *Don't get hurt again!*

Back and forth her thinking went until she passed into sleep.

10

On Thursday afternoon Sherry was sitting in Anthropology 651—
which was comparative religion—listening to Dr. Forsythe lecture.
She had been spending too much time with her new Bible and not
enough time doing the reading for this class, she realized as she looked
over the reading schedule. Dr. Forsythe was middle-aged with thinning
gray-streaked long hair. His brown corduroy jacket framed a black sweater
shirt in a fashion popular with much of the faculty. He paced back and
forth with animation as he lectured with a strong but high-pitched voice.

"One of the most influential tendencies demonstrated by religious
humankind is what we could call the 'objectification of religion.' It's also
one of the most universal features of religion. You'll be reading Dr.
Norbeck this quarter. As he observes,

> Great religions have indeed arisen as ethical or philosophical princi-
> ples for the guidance of man, but once they have become the
> province of multitudes . . . they have met a common fate of objectifi-
> cation; that is, of being cast into concrete form so that they may be
> actively appreciated by the eyes, ears, or other sense organs rather
> than remaining only abstract ideas and beliefs.[1]

"Today, many know the process Norbeck refers to by the name 'formalism.' Formalism means a focus on the outward forms of the religious
system. Eventually, the forms come to be the heart of the religion, and the
original abstract and inward spiritual principles are largely forgotten. For
instance, Taoism, one of the most abstract of all religious constructs in its
original form, today is usually practiced in shrines where sacrifices are
offered to wooden idols."

I bet this is true for Christianity, Sherry thought. *Maybe this is the difference I sense between the stuff in the Bible and the other stuff that bothers me. . . . Yeah, it's the outward forms that I have a problem with!* She
listened to Forsythe's lecture with growing interest.

"I'd like you to ponder this question this quarter: 'Why is formalism such a universal tendency?' As you do, consider forms such as rituals, sacred calendars, and sacred space.

"Sacred space refers to the universal tendency of religious man to identify space as sacred, and to delimit it from profane space. Once they mark off this sacred space, let's say, a shrine, a grove of trees or a temple, it usually plays a key role in their ongoing worship and religious practice.

"Identification of sacred space is critical to the development of formalism, and there's no *obvious* external reason for it."

Wow, this is it! Sherry thought. *This must be why the Christians make their buildings look different. This must be why they call their meeting hall a 'sanctuary.' Sanctuary means a sacred place, a holy place.* Sherry was disappointed by the insight, but she jotted down some of her thoughts in the margin of her spiral notebook. *I wonder whether Christianity's just superstition like the others,* she thought.

Dr. Forsythe went on: "Some scholars suggest that formalism is universal because most people aren't able to respond to abstract truths without some way to relate those truths to their senses. This seems to be Norbeck's view when he says, 'Most human beings respond poorly to words or ideas alone.' He also claims no religion can survive without a 'church-like organization and ritual of some kind in which adherents participate.'"[2]

I don't know about that, Sherry mused. *I find it easier to respond to the abstract principles taught by Christ than I do to the outward "church-like organization."*

Forsythe was still lecturing: "In your reading, Dr. Davies says,

It is as though abstract ideas need to be set within a symbol [like a ritual] before men can be impelled to act upon them. When any attempt is made to turn symbols into bare statements of truth, this vital trigger of the emotions can easily be lost.[3]

"The remarkable thing about these observations is that some of the greatest religions, such as Buddhism, Christianity, Taoism, and Confucianism, began with very little formalism. But they seem to have invariably developed it later.

"Sometimes these outward forms have even been *against* the teachings of the founder of a religion. For example, Muslims were not allowed to venerate pictures of Muhammad, but they quickly learned to venerate a piece of paper with his name written on it.[4] Likewise, within a few generations, Christ's declaration that people should worship God 'neither in this mountain nor in Jerusalem . . . but in Spirit and truth' was largely ignored in favor of older ideas of 'sanctuary' and 'the house of God' . . . that is to say, sacred space.

"Most scholars agree that the common man is not capable of handling pure abstraction well."

Sherry still had trouble with that point. *If people have so much trouble relating to abstraction, why did these major religions ever take root in the first place?* There was a lot to think about here.

Forsythe summarized his lecture: "Most religious people prefer to bypass the 'understanding' stage, and go directly, through outward forms and symbols, to a simpler relationship with the sacred."

Well, that's about as nauseating as anything I've heard for a long time, thought Sherry as she spat out her gum on the way home after class. She could feel a low-level headache coming on. *He makes it sound as if religious people don't even want to understand what they're doing! They just follow these rituals and go to their sacred places in order to get some kind of feeling-state. It's as if they're bypassing the mind and going directly to the brain stem!* She reflected for awhile. *I guess he must be right.*

Sherry flinched in revulsion. *I refuse to surrender my powers of thought for some mystical liver shiver!* But after thinking for a moment she thought, *Lisa isn't that way. She seems to understand everything about her beliefs.* Sherry remembered the statement Jack made outside class on Monday. Something about a lot of different ways to approach Christianity. *How can there be different approaches to the same truth? It sounds like you just interpret it any way you want.*

She began to think about Jack again. He was an interesting guy. She wondered why he hadn't tried to come on to her in some more definite way. *I wonder whether Christians get into romance? They probably have their priest or whatever choose a mate for them.* She snickered, but she found herself looking forward to seminar on Monday.

11

Sherry had one of the most successful Friday nights of work at The Bratcellar ever. When she counted her tips they added up to over $150.00. "Wow! Now that's how I spell relief!" she exclaimed to Carole, a fellow waitress.

It was after 2:00 a.m. before she left work, and she wound up sleeping in late Saturday. After a leisurely shower, she went to the library to catch up on her studies.

She knew there was a big party at a friend's apartment, but she decided to reserve the evening to rest and continue her reflections on the Bible. That afternoon, after enjoying a big homemade sub sandwich, she got a mug of fresh coffee and sat down in her chair with her Bible.

She turned to John 4 and began to read. As the story of the Samaritan woman unfolded, she again found herself intrigued by some of the statements of Jesus, but not always sure of the meaning.

Jesus told her He could give her living water springing up to eternal life. The water must be like a symbol for eternal life or something. He certainly lays it on the line. He wasn't squeamish about making claims for Himself. This man was either the biggest egotist anyone can imagine or . . . or I guess the alternative would be that His claims were true.

She read down to the point where the woman introduced the question of holy places.

Our fathers worshiped on this mountain, but you Jews claim that the place where we must worship is in Jerusalem.

There it is! She's talking about where people have to go to worship. This is what Forsythe called "sacred space." Now we'll see what Jesus thinks. She read on,

Jesus declared, "Believe me, woman, a time is coming when you will worship the Father neither on this mountain nor in Jerusalem."

Oh, cool! That's the verse Dr. Forsythe referred to in class!

You Samaritans worship what you do not know; we worship what you do know, for salvation is from the Jews. Yet a time is coming and has now come when the true worshipers will worship the Father in spirit and truth, for they are the kind of worshipers the Father seeks. God is spirit, and his worshipers must worship in spirit and in truth.

Now that sounds just like Lisa, Sherry observed. *That sounds like something God would say. He wouldn't care whether people prayed from one mountain or the other. Obviously He'd be more concerned with where they are spiritually than where they are physically.*

But that still leaves open the question of why there was such a thing as a temple in Jerusalem in the first place . . . and then there's the church. Forsythe claimed the church quickly moved to ignore these words. How did God ever lose control of the situation? Why would He let His own people go so far astray?

She read on,

The woman said, "I know that Messiah" (called Christ) "is coming. When he comes, he will explain everything to us."

That's completely off the subject. It sounds like she's trying to change the subject, thought Sherry. Then she read:

Then Jesus declared, "I who speak to you am he."

She laid her Bible down and sat back, looking out the window. Late afternoon shadows were beginning to lengthen on the lawn out by the pond. *Hmm, this is directly against what Professor Jennings said in Bible-as-literature class. He said Jesus never claimed to be the Messiah and that He even denied being the Messiah!*

It dawned on her that the textbook they assigned the students for that class contained only selected readings from the Bible. *I wonder how many other parts were left out.* She wondered what the motive would have been for distorting aspects of the Bible. *All I can think is they didn't consider this passage to be authentic.*

The phone rang. Sherry didn't ever answer it because she got too many unwanted calls, mostly from guys she didn't feel like talking to. Her answering machine was the perfect protection. This time, after the message, the recorder came on and stayed on, but no one spoke. Sherry reached over and fiddled with the volume control to make sure it was on. Someone was on the phone but they weren't saying anything . . . or was it that her machine was broken? She picked up the phone. "Hello? Is anyone there?"

Someone was there all right. But whoever it was, wasn't speaking. "Jim. Don't do this. I'm warning you. . . ." No one answered, but she could tell someone was there. "I'll call the police and they'll trace your call . . ." she waited again, but there was no answer. "I know it's you. I hope you don't think this scares me. You're such an idiot!" She slammed down the receiver in disgust.

It was quite strange to Sherry that the call upset her as much as it did. Once again, she was feeling violated. *He's trying to terrorize me without sticking his neck out. It has to be him.* She got up and went into the kitchen.

As she leaned against the counter drinking some ice water she reflected on whether Jim was stalking her. *If you look at this objectively, you haven't even seen or heard him at all! There's no objective evidence that he has ever given you a second thought since you warned him about the police. Lots of people get crank calls. That could have been anyone. And the other night you didn't see a thing . . . a moving branch! This could be all in your own mind. You've been traumatized. Just relax.* She tried to busy herself around the kitchen, but something still told her it was him.

She couldn't shake the feeling or memories of the terror and helplessness she felt when trapped in those vise-like arms. She decided to take a run, but she determined to take her mace in the pocket of her running shorts.

The phone rang again.

Sherry's nostrils flared and her eyes bulged as she stared at the machine, waiting for the message to end.

Her friend Sue spoke. "Sherry, are you there? C'mon, pick this thing up! I know you're there."

Sherry picked up the phone. "Sue! What's happening?" she exclaimed with a smile.

"The question is, what's happening with you? I go to the party and you aren't there. You haven't been showing up at things lately."

"I went over with the girls at the dorm on Wednesday, and I didn't see you either," she defended herself.

Sue brushed this aside. "Yeah, and the word was you were preoccupied and acting weird. Now don't try to cover up with me. What's going on with you?"

There was a moment of silence as Sherry was taken aback by Sue's directness. That silence gave her away. It was already too late to say "nothing."

"Well, I've been thinking about some things, but I don't feel like telling people about it yet." She played nervously with the coiled wire on the phone.

"You're thinking about something, but you can't tell anyone? What kind of thinking is that? You're thinking of suicide?"

Sherry realized it sounded a lot worse than it was. "No, I'm just trying to reason my way through some things, and I don't want people making fun of me or giving me a hard time right now."

"Oh, man! You've gotten religion!"

Sue was certainly fast on her feet! It only served to frustrate Sherry more. "That's a really bigoted comment, Sue. It's really kind of insulting. This is the kind of flack I feel I can live without." She began pacing in front of the window.

"Hey look, I'm not trying to put you down." Sue acted like she couldn't imagine what the problem was.

"Well, I'm pretty sensitive about the things I'm going through right now."

"What's his name? I bet it's a guy getting you into this, isn't it?"

"See, I don't feel like I'm getting any understanding." Exasperation filled Sherry's voice. "You're already psyching me out and figuring what the hidden motives are, and you don't even know what I'm talking about yet. This is why I didn't want to discuss it with anyone."

"Okay. What're you thinking about?"

"I don't feel like talking about it." She crossed her arms and stood glowering.

"Who's hassling who now?"

"Look, you can come over sometime and we'll have a serious talk about it if you want. I just feel uneasy about opening up with people at this time." She gestured with her free hand. "I haven't decided anything, and I don't need a lot of flack."

"What kind of religion is it? You're not getting into Krishna or some cult, are you?"

"Oh, for heaven's sake. . . ." She leaned her forehead against the window frame, grimacing.

"Well, some of these groups'll grab you and actually carry you away."

"I wish you'd give me some credit." She shook her head, still leaning against the window. "Do you really think I'm so ignorant? Give me a break!"

"Well, what is it then?"

Sherry paused, and looked out the window. She wasn't sure whether to open up or not. "I guess I don't feel like assigning a label to it for you. Let's just say I'm wondering about the meaning of life."

"Come on, we all wonder what the meaning of life is. You've already admitted you're getting into religion. Now what is it?"

"I didn't admit anything."

"I can't believe you won't even tell me what it is!"

"I said we could have a serious conversation sometime."

"You're just stiff-arming me."

"No, I'm just trying to avoid supplying you with a nice pigeonhole label to stick on me."

"You're ashamed. You don't want to admit what you're into."

"What I don't want is for you to brand me with one of your prejudiced names." She jabbed at the air furiously with her finger, as though Sue was there in the room. "I don't want to be called some label like 'communist'!"

"Get real, Sherry."

"Sorry, that's the way I feel about it. You don't want to take the time to understand where I'm at. You just want a name you can call me."

"Well, whatever it is you're into, it isn't making you a nicer person."

"How would you know? This three-minute conversation? You haven't stopped trying to make a snap judgment about me the whole time we've been talking."

"I feel like *you're* judging *me*."

"Well, I don't want to do that. You know I don't believe in judging others." Sherry was striving for self-control. "Just stop trying to push me."

"I'm going to get the girls, and we're going to come over there and get your head together."

Now Sherry was really boiling. "Sue, I'm going to be really hacked off if you go around to the girls telling them things about me. I want you to keep this conversation private."

"Well, you're asking a lot."

"If you think it matters how I feel, you won't go around telling people I've got religion or any other insulting summary like that, *and I mean it, Sue*."

"I think you're acting really strange, and you're even trying to control what I say now."

"If you hadn't forced your way into something I consider private . . ."

"I didn't force my way into anything."

"Oh, fine, just say whatever you want then!" Sherry slammed down the phone. She felt like steam was coming out of her ears as she threw on the top to her jogging suit and stormed out for a hard run.

12

Monday morning Sherry got up and immediately felt alert. Today was history seminar! When she came out of her shower she confronted her light brown dresser. Her eyes traveled over the clothes in the open drawer before her. She reached for a pair of nice-fitting, well-worn jeans. Then she got the white top with the V-neck off a hanger in the closet. It was tight-fitting and prominently displayed her slim but well-endowed figure.

As she looked at herself in the mirror, she broke into a grin. *Who are you trying to kid? I suppose these were the first things you could find?* She had stopped wearing tight-fitting clothes on campus over a year earlier because it caused too many problems. But she still had her things from earlier years, when she enjoyed the feeling that everyone was watching her. *Oh, so what!* she shot back at herself. *I can do whatever I want!*

She was thinking of Jack, of course. The night before, she had several times found herself thinking about seeing him in class. Her mounting feeling of alienation from her existing friends seemed to make her even more interested in new relationships. She realized now she had formed the plan some time ago to dress extra nice.

Sherry had a naturally pretty face, and she usually didn't wear much makeup—she didn't need to. Her dark eyebrows naturally set her green eyes off as though she had put makeup on. Today she carefully put on eye makeup, and even included a little lip gloss. All the while she felt like she had to defend her actions to some part of herself. Her objective side warned her not to get involved with another man and reminded her of her earlier determination not to. But the warnings didn't deter her from putting on her most dazzling look; they only made her feel frightened and a little excited. *I'm not necessarily getting involved!* she protested with a smile and a shrug in the mirror.

As she hustled across the sunny green and on into the heart of campus to class, her anxiety was rising. She realized she might be facing rejection if she wasn't careful. *He hasn't even asked me out or done anything overt. Yet I'm allowing myself to get excited about him. How do I know there's even any interest there?* she challenged herself. But after reflecting, *No. He's interested on some level,* she nodded to herself as she remembered their last talk. But she determined she was going to play it careful. *I'm not going to make a fool of myself.*

She was one of the last to get to class, and she took her seat with only a short glance and smile over at Jack, who sat near the window between two other students. *I should have gotten here early to see where he sat,* she thought. The class had individual desks pulled into a circle. She felt self-conscious as she took off her backpack and got out her notebook for seminar. She didn't want to look over to see if Jack was watching her, but she felt sure he was. She tried to look relaxed.

"Why don't you start the commentary on Rand's *Virtue of Selfishness,* Linda?" the professor said.

"I thought it was interesting and persuasive," said the redhead who spoke with a New York accent. "She seems to say that if I do what's best for me, I automatically do what's best for everyone. I think that makes a lot of sense. You know, how can it be wrong to be true to yourself?"

"The question is whether this rationale deserves the label 'ethic.'" Sherry looked around and saw it was Jack speaking. He shuffled in his seat as he moved from leaning back to leaning forward over his desk top. She had a clear excuse to look at him now. He gestured with his hands and a pencil. "The notion that the rationally selfish thing will always be the right thing is antithetical, I think, to the notion of moral right and wrong."

"Explain what you see here a little more," the professor prompted.

As Jack went on with his rather complicated explanation of the difference between moral norms and pragmatism, Sherry watched with growing admiration. The other students in the seminar challenged points he raised and he answered their complaints with a much more controlled, objective and friendly tone than Sherry had been able to muster herself the week before. He was so polite when one student obviously failed to understand what he was saying. She was impressed by his intelligence as well as his ability to communicate. *Mmmmmmm. Intellectually, he's head and shoulders above all of them*, she marveled. Then, with a little flash of jealousy she shifted in her chair. *He's probably above my level, too.*

At several points he was also humorous. She liked his clean powder blue cotton shirt with the sleeves partly rolled up. His shoulders were wide, tapering down to a slim waist. As she watched him in complete silence, she couldn't deny she wanted to know this man more—much more.

After class ended, she got up from her chair and began to gather things together while watching him out of the corner of her eye. She saw he was headed out, though she was closer to the door. She started out with him right behind her. She was hoping he would catch up to her again like he did the week before.

As they descended the front steps, she knew he was still right behind her, but he wasn't making a move. She decided not to take a chance. *It's my turn anyway.* She turned around and picked him out of the crowd pouring down the steps just a few feet behind her. She smiled and stopped him. "I thought you did a great job defending your position."

He smiled broadly with a little embarrassment. "Thanks. That's probably because you didn't decide to jump in there and waste me," he smiled.

"Ha! I wish I could do that well without getting angry or argumentative."

"Well, ethics is an area I've been thinking about for a long time," he said, looking down. Then he looked up into her eyes. "But I really appreciate the encouragement."

She smiled invitingly.

"So," he went on. "Are we still going to talk sometime?"

"Oh, yeah! I'm looking forward to that." She tried to look as interested as possible.

"Okay, well, I have to do something right now, so I'll have to see you later." He smiled apologetically.

"Sure." She acted like she didn't care. "Whenever." Suddenly, something caught her attention behind him and her eyes widened in instant terror. It was Jim Clemmons, walking down the sidewalk in front of the steps. He was looking right at her and Jack! He glowered angrily as he walked on by, his shoulders thrown back and his MSU T-shirt bulging with muscles.

Jack turned around to see what she was looking at. He turned back. "Someone you know?"

"Uh . . . yeah. I'm afraid he's a real creep, a nut case." She put her hand to the side of her face, feeling the hot flush, and groaned, "Oooooh, I can't believe that!"

"What? What's wrong?" Jack looked concerned.

Sherry was stunned by the way seeing Jim had instantly filled her with pure, raging fear. "Oh, my. That guy sort of attacked me a while back. I can't believe how scary it was seeing him! Was he waiting out here?"

"I don't know. It just looked like he was walking down the street. He didn't look too happy though. He's sure muscular!"

"That just sickens me. I think he's been stalking me . . . but I don't know. He would have known I had a class here. . . . Was he sitting over there with the others?" She pointed to a raised platform by the steps where a dozen students were sitting in the sun.

"I didn't see him until after you did. Listen, if this guy's bothering you, why don't you call the police?"

"I thought I was being followed the other night, and I thought he's been calling and, you know . . . just not talking. But I'm never sure it's him. This is actually the first time I've seen him. I haven't felt like I had enough evidence to go to the police."

"Well, what do you mean he attacked you?"

"Um, he grabbed me and tried to force himself . . ." she took a deep breath and blew it out, trying to relax, but her voice was still quivering. "He didn't get very far, 'cause someone came out. But it was scary. He didn't do much more than grab me and hold me against my will . . . he forced a kiss on me." Her face blanched, and she gathered her backpack to her chest and wrapped both arms around it as she looked down.

"I'm sorry." The tone in Jack's voice showed that her misery had registered on him. "That is a real bind. We really couldn't say we saw him following you today, even though he might have been."

"Yeah."

"Is there anything I can do?"

"I don't think so. Did he really go?" She was craning her neck to see if he had gone down the hill.

Jack was looking, too. "Well, I don't see him. But I think you should file a report with the police anyway, even if you can't show evidence. It'll be good if it's on record, you know, if something happens later."

"Yeah. That makes sense. I didn't call them that night because I just assumed that would be the last of him. Since then, I haven't been sure myself—I'm still not sure! But I think you're right. I'll have to call them anyway and get it on record." She looked up at Jack and smiled. "I'm sorry for dragging you into my problems. You must have thought I just witnessed a murder or something." She laughed.

"You went as white as a sheet. I felt like ducking—like someone was about to shoot us!" He chuckled, too. The release of tension was pleasant, and a moment of silence passed which suddenly was full of feeling. "I guess I'd better get going. Are you sure you'll be all right?"

She nodded, her arms still wrapped around her backpack. "I'm so glad you were here," she said with real sincerity, almost reaching out to touch his forearm, but thinking better of it. "I really don't want to meet up with him alone. Go on. Don't worry about me."

"Okay. I'll see you later." He smiled and turned to go.

Sherry checked the sidewalk again for Jim before heading up the other way from where he had disappeared. She was dejected because Jack hadn't shown more interest in talking, but he had seemed busy. *It's for the best anyway,* she told herself. The jolt of fear took some minutes to completely die away. *I must have gotten a serious dose of adrenaline!*

The rest of the afternoon, she kept thinking about the class and Jack's face as he made his points. She admitted to herself it wasn't going to be easy to avoid openly pursuing this guy, even though she was convinced she needed to avoid it in the worst way. It was a frustration she had felt often lately—knowing what she ought to do, but feeling helplessly compelled to do the opposite.

When she got home that afternoon, she went straight to the phone and called the police, using the number she kept on the phone. They said they would send an officer out to take a report.

When Officer Davidson arrived, he appeared very professional, about forty, with the usual close-cropped hair and a slight potbelly. He asked her to come out to the cruiser for the interview. Once there, he plied her with questions while writing on his clipboard. "So are you saying there was an attempted rape?" he asked.

"Uh, no. I couldn't say that. He didn't try to tear off my clothes."

"Did he strike you or in some way try to hurt you?"

"Not exactly. He forced a kiss on me. He wouldn't let me go."

"Have you been out with this man before?"

"Oh, yes, a few times."

"Have you and he been intimate?"

"Yes."

"Have you been with him since the incident?"

"No!"

"Why didn't you report this the night it happened?"

"Well, like I said, he didn't get very far, and I assumed that was the end of him. . . ."

There was a pause as the officer busily wrote notes on his clipboard. "Did anyone else witness the attack?"

"No, a lady in the building saw him there, but she didn't see any violence, because he quit when she came."

"Uh hum," he murmured, writing again. Then, after thinking for a moment, he looked up at her. "Well, you might have grounds for a complaint of assault, but it's doubtful you'd be able to make a case in court.

Do you wish to press charges?"

"No, I don't think I could make it stick, and it might just make him even madder. I don't want to antagonize him. I mainly just wanted this on record in case something else happens."

"Ma'am, we can't record every dispute people have, just in case something comes up. It's usually better to wait until criminal activity occurs, and then file a complaint." He must have seen her wince, because he again tried to help. "You said you think he may be following you."

"Yes."

"You've seen him behind you? What makes you think this?"

Sherry saw herself through the eyes of the officer: a spoiled girl who had a fight with her lover and now is paranoid and neurotic. She wished she had never called the police. "I can't say I've positively identified him, except today I came out and he was outside my class."

"Was he following you?"

"He might have been. I can't definitely prove he was."

"Hmmmm." He wrote on his clipboard again.

"But I believe someone was following me, and he has called me, and I believe he called again and just breathed into the phone."

He looked up. "How do you know it was him?"

"I don't *know* it was him, but I think it was. Look, the point here is not that I can prove he's following me or harassing me. The reason I called you is that I'm thinking, 'What if he *is* following me?' I wanted to document my concerns in case later I find him following me at night or something. Then it won't be the first time you've heard of the case."

"I see. Well, you definitely don't have a case for menacing at this point. You haven't seen him following you, and you're not sure who was on the phone. You saw him outside of your class, but he could have been there for other reasons. You really have no proof you're being followed."

She bowed her head and nodded.

"I've heard your story and made some notes. I'll keep them on file awhile, but I don't see a basis here for a complaint, and . . . you understand, I'm not saying he's not following you, or that you are in no danger. The best thing you can do is take measures to protect yourself."

"I carry mace."

"Good! These things usually die down. . . ." He went on to give her a short lecture on the subject designed to reassure her, but which she didn't feel she needed.

After he left, Sherry felt tired. She decided she needed to sleep awhile before going to her first Bible study that night.

13

After waking from a short nap, Sherry was groggy. She showered, and by dinner time she actually felt excited about going to the Bible study. *This is a lot more important than thinking about guys,* she told herself.

Without hesitation she called Lisa and arranged to meet her at her place. Sherry knew she was probably being overly paranoid by not revealing things such as her phone number and apartment location to someone like Lisa, but she felt the need to keep her defenses up. "Be sure to bring your Bible," was the only advice Lisa had given her.

After throwing a frozen hamburger in the microwave and eating it quickly, she drove over to Lisa's house, and together they drove to the study in Sherry's car. It turned out the Bible study was in a boarding house that was very close to Sherry's apartment, easily within walking distance. Of course Lisa had no way of knowing that, and Sherry left it that way.

She had planned to wait until the end of the evening before deciding whether to open up about her prayer experience. But instead, they hadn't driven more than a couple of blocks before she spilled the beans. "I think I might have had a religious experience the other night," she blurted.

"Oh? What kind of experience?" Lisa seemed to almost prick up her ears.

"Well, it's kind of hard to say. . . . I guess you'd say I tried to pray." Sherry laughed nervously. "I haven't tried to do that since I was a little girl," she continued, looking forward at the road.

"What do you mean you *tried*? Did you succeed?" Lisa pressed.

"Well, I don't know . . . see, I'm still not sure God exists."

"That must have been interesting!"

"Yeah," she chuckled. "I said something like, 'If You hear me . . .' you know, and well, I guess I didn't really have much to say. Do we turn right here?"

"Yes, then go straight for a while. So, you said, 'If You hear me . . .' what?"

"Uh, well, 'If You hear me, let me know You're there' . . . or something like that."

Lisa sat back and broke into a broad smile. "Well, I think that's pretty exciting, Sherry!"

"Why?" She shot a glance over at Lisa.

"Because I think God'll see the desire in your heart to know Him, and He'll answer your prayer."

"Hmmmmm," Sherry grimaced. "That's a little hard to imagine."

"Just watch for subtle changes. The Bible refers to the Spirit of God as a still, quiet voice. You may not be bowled over, but He'll let you know He's involved. You'll notice changes within yourself, in your perspective on things and people." She pulled down the visor and looked in the mirror. "You'll notice coincidences that seem to lead you closer to Him. You'll also have experiences when you read the Bible, or when you hear it taught. You may very well have one tonight; this guy teaching is really deep." She flipped the visor back up.

Sherry was thoughtful. *This guy lecturing must really be something to make her so positive all the time.* That sounded good. Sherry was ready to hear someone speak who made sense. Someone who could measure up to her professors at school. She didn't tell Lisa the whole story; that she felt she was already having experiences while reading her Bible. She began to review the past few days and wondered whether one could interpret her experiences as coincidental: the lecture by Forsythe, the crummy party, the debates in seminar, meeting Jack. . . .

Lisa must have been able to see the wheels turning in Sherry's head, and took a guess. "Do you already see some of those things?"

Sherry looked over at her for a moment and back at the road. "I don't know," she shrugged. "That kind of stuff's all a matter of interpretation."

"Yeah, but even your belief that I'm sitting here's a matter of interpretation if you want to be precise. You have to receive and trust your senses before you can say anything's real."

Sherry couldn't really disagree with what Lisa was saying, at least she couldn't explain why. "Yeah, but that's different."

"I know, but there's a similarity, too. You're the best judge of your own experiences." Lisa paused for a moment, but sensed Sherry wasn't convinced. "Your spiritual senses are just as real as your physical senses. Have you ever sensed someone was angry even though they didn't say or do anything that suggested anger?"

"Yes." She looked over at Lisa with a pained expression. "Don't tell me you think that's ESP or something."

"No, I'm just saying it isn't necessarily based on physical senses either.

There's a part of us under the surface, not strictly a part of the physical world. That's where you'll find your sense of spiritual things."

"Yeah." Sherry sounded doubtful. "Well, I'll keep an eye out, but I'm not going to try to fool myself."

"That won't be necessary. Before long, you'll probably have a strong confidence that God's there."

"I'll be amazed if that happens, and I don't think it will." Sherry shook her head in doubt. "I'm not that kind of person, Lisa."

"You *used* to be 'not that kind of person.' I'm afraid you've stepped over some boundaries that'll change all that. You've issued an invitation to the God of the universe to get involved in your life. Now He's going to show you the rest of the story so you can make the decision of your life. The second stop sign is where you turn right again."

Sherry kept staring straight ahead. Lisa was making her feel nervous. She wouldn't have listened to this kind of thing if she hadn't already come to admire and respect Lisa as a thinker. She wondered whether she was being swept away on some irresistible current. There was a tangible desire to run away before this current carried her over the falls. But another part of her was excited by the thought that she might be coming in contact with something spiritual that was real. The last light of day was fading as they arrived at the apartment.

They found a parking place, and got out. Now Sherry was feeling downright scared. *Why do I feel scared? I wasn't scared when I went to that church. Come on. These are probably going to be just some nice people having some kind of study.* She decided to ask. "Uh, nothing weird goes on at these meetings, does it?" she said as they walked up the sidewalk.

"No! It's just a Bible lecture, some discussion, and some prayer. Relax!" Lisa briefly touched Sherry's elbow in assurance.

Sherry still felt very nervous as they opened the door and a burst of rowdy party-like laughter, talk, and music greeted them.

Inside, the apartment was jammed with people milling around drinking coffee and pop. She recognized the REM tape they were playing. The people all appeared to be students, dressed in their normal clothes. *This seems more like a party than a Bible study,* she thought. But then she realized she didn't even know what a Bible study was supposed to be like! She guessed she must have expected a circle of people in silent meditation or something. Lisa introduced her to some girls who seemed welcoming and friendly. Sherry was still suspicious. *The people at the church were friendly, too, and I doubted the reality of that.*

At a certain point, someone yelled out, "Hey, let's go! Let's get it together here!" and everyone began to move toward a seat. Many had to sit on the floor. Lisa and Sherry were offered seats on the couch at the back of the main room, and it was clear a bunch of people were in the dining room also, which was on the other side of a large archway.

This was the part Sherry was waiting for. She looked down at her Bible and smiled inwardly as she anticipated some sort of stimulating discussion. She was eager to hear this "deep" teacher Lisa had mentioned. How could he be so great if he was just a student?

Someone turned off the stereo and the group began to quiet down. A coed with long blonde hair walked up to the stool in front of the fireplace and sat on it. "I'd like to welcome you to this home fellowship tonight," she said in a loud voice. "We like to just get together here and spend some time studying the Bible, and we believe we're getting to know the Author of the Bible a little better."

There were a couple of audible, affirmative murmurs. Sherry looked around to see who else had spoken. This was unusual!

"Before we study the Scriptures tonight we're going to have Ed Weaver come up here and do a number for us. Let's give it up for Ed!" There was a furious round of applause as well as whistles and calls from the floor. "Ed!" "Get down!" "The Edster!"

Ed ascended the stool. "Thanks, I'm going to sing a song tonight that's a spiritual song about when Jesus met this guy who was all messed up with occult spirits and changed his life. It's called 'Man of the Tombs.'" He started to play his guitar and sang beautifully with his clear tenor voice, and a sincere look of intensity on his face. At the end of the song, the group again applauded noisily, whistled, and hooted.

The blonde traded places with Ed, and said, "I'd like to lead us in some prayer before we study tonight." Everyone quieted down and bowed their heads. So did Sherry. "Lord, thank You for being here with us tonight. We ask that You'd help us to put aside the concerns of the day and focus our full attention on You as Your Spirit applies the words of Scripture to our hearts. In Jesus' name, Amen."

Sherry looked up and received a stunning shock. At the stool a man was trading places with the blonde. It was Jack Collins! ·

14

There was a rustling sound as people got out their Bibles or rearranged things. Jack looked around the room with a smile as he said, "Thank you, Carole." Then his eyes came to rest on Sherry. He broke into a bigger smile and nodded and waved to her. "Good to see you!" he said right out loud. Sherry smiled and nodded back, but inside she was exploding. *This can't be true! I've fallen into a trap! What's going on?*

She felt as if she was being pressed into her seat by a great force. *I'm losing control of my life!* she cried to herself, as she felt her face flush deeply. But forcing herself to show no lapse in her composure, she turned to Lisa and whispered, "This guy's in my history seminar!" Lisa lit up with surprise, but before she could respond, Jack began to speak in a resonant loud voice.

"The passage we're studying tonight is another of the 'signs' in the Gospel of John, which define Christ's mission and message in graphic ways.

"Let's read from chapter 5:

Some time later, Jesus went up to Jerusalem for a feast of the Jews. Now there is in Jerusalem near the Sheep Gate a pool, which in Aramaic is called Bethesda and which is surrounded by five covered colonnades. Here a great number of disabled people used to lie—the blind, the lame, the paralyzed.

"Now some of you may have versions containing part or all of this text which is in the margin in most versions:

And they waited for the moving of the waters. From time to time an angel of the Lord would come down and stir up the waters. The first one into the pool after each such disturbance would be cured of whatever disease he had.

"What we have here is probably a marginal note supplied by copyists which later was mistakenly included in some manuscripts. It's not found in the earliest manuscripts. So, whether this business with the angel and the stirring of the waters actually happened, or whether it was a superstition, we don't know. It could have been a superstition because the Bible itself never affirms that it happened, only that these people *believed* it happened.

"But there's a more important footnote here while we're on the subject of critical notes. Not long ago we could read naturalistic so-called Christian Bible scholars saying this pool not only was not visited by angels, but that it didn't even exist! They'd say this was one of the Jesus myths, almost completely imaginary, like the Land of Oz.

"These scholars argued that this kind of mythical material had slipped into the 'Johannine school,' which they believed wrote this book well over a hundred years after these events and in a different part of the Roman Empire. Clearly, they claimed, these second- or third-century Christians had no exact knowledge of what was going on in Palestine.

"Now, we don't read this kind of skepticism any more for one simple reason. The Pool of Bethesda has been discovered in Jerusalem and successfully excavated. I've actually stood right at the edge of this pool. And wouldn't you know it, it's by the Sheep Gate. And there are five porticos identified there. Not four, not six, but five.

"Well, this has certainly put a rather ridiculous cast on those liberal scholars. They arrogantly believed that because their limited study had not confirmed the existence of this pool, therefore it didn't exist! And there's a warning here for us as well. There may be other areas in the Bible that haven't been independently confirmed by scholars yet. But that doesn't mean we can declare them nonexistent either."

Jack was raising his voice, and his eyes flashed with anger. Sherry was seeing a new side of him. Until now he had seemed like a nice, polite, rather gentle guy. Here, he was displaying a passion and an aggressiveness that was intense and angry; not the bellowing of a TV preacher she had once heard, but a sane and plausible anger that she found stirring, even mildly exciting. Sherry realized this guy might be frightening if you got into the wrong situation with him.

Jack went on: "Well, let's read on in the story:

"One who was there had been an invalid for thirty-eight years. When Jesus saw him lying there and learned that he had been in this condition for a long time, he asked him, 'Do you want to get well?'"

Jack stopped reading again. "Now that seems a little strange to me. What kind of question is that to ask? They wouldn't be lying out there if they didn't want to be healed, would they?

"To understand the big picture here, we need to see that this story is real but it's also symbolic. It's a picture of what God sees when He looks down at the human race. Everyone's lying around sick, disabled, lame, and paralyzed. Of course, our sickness is mainly spiritual and moral.

"We don't like to look at ourselves that way. We say, 'I don't think I'm that bad off! I may have a crick in my neck, but I wouldn't say I am a cripple. I may have a little trouble walking . . . I may be a little lonely . . . I may not know exactly what the purpose of my life is . . . I may not feel much joy in my life . . . I may have a few emotional hang-ups . . . I may not be able to control this habit that's ruining my life . . . I may not be able to form successful relationships . . . *but it's not that bad!*'"

The group laughed heartily at this, and even Sherry chuckled. At the same time, she was hearing what Jack was saying in the deepest way. *Boy, I feel like he's been looking into my mind!* she thought.

Jack continued: "Well, it is bad. God says it's bad. God sees the whole human race as broken and helpless; just as helpless as this guy lying here on his cot. Our problems stem from our separation from Him. But before He does anything He has a question for us. It's the same question He asked this guy: 'Do you want to be healed?'

"That's right, God's saying He won't move in to help us until we agree. Jesus wants to come into your life tonight and make some big changes. He wants to heal you. But do you want to be healed? He won't force you. You're not a lawn mower to be fixed. You're a human being. You're a free-choosing agent. God has brought you to this place tonight so you can make a decision."

Sherry knew in her heart that she wanted to be healed, but she wondered what the price would be. Jack went on.

"Let's notice this man's response.

"'Sir,' the invalid replied, 'I have no one to help me into the pool when the water is stirred. While I am trying to get in, someone else goes down ahead of me.'

"Well, I'll tell you what. If there's anything stranger than Jesus' question, it's this guy's response. Jesus didn't ask how things were going with the neighbors. He just asked whether the guy wanted to be healed! I should think that a simple yes or no would suffice. I would expect this guy to say, 'Are You kidding? Of course I want to be healed!'

"Instead, when Jesus asks, 'Do you want to be healed?' the man says,

'Oh, you wouldn't believe what the people around here are like! For thirty-eight years I have stayed by this pool. Do you think when the water stirs anyone helps a poor cripple like me? Nooooooo.'"

The group laughed at Jack's facial contortions.

"This man's answer was not responsive to the question Jesus asked. But it reminds me of our reaction to God's call sometimes. 'What about these people around me? They don't care! They don't put me into the water. You think you have it bad? Let me tell you some things. . . . Nobody has any respect, even for a lame guy! I can't believe what things are coming to in this society! And then there were my parents! Boy, the way I was brought up, it's a wonder I can do anything at all!'

"I think I see a response here that's not unusual. God's making an effort to come to us and say, 'Hey, you have a problem there, don't you? Why don't you let Me take care of that for you?' And we're coming back with, 'You know, God, I have a lot of flaky people around me. I wish You could deal with some of them. And then there is my rotten situation! Why can't You get me out of this situation I'm in? And those people at work! They aren't normal!'"

Jack let the laughter die down.

"We want to talk to God about all the problems we have, about all the reasons things are bad. But we avoid the central question: 'Do you want to get well?'

"Well, it doesn't record the man's response, but Jesus did heal him, as it says,

Then Jesus said to him, "Get up! Pick up your mat and walk." At once the man was cured; he picked up his mat and walked.

"So I think this is a picture of conversion primarily, but it also applies to those situations where we, as Christians, have to specifically give God the go-ahead to heal us of problems in our lives. But let's not miss the very important statement at the end of this verse:

The day on which this took place was a Sabbath. . . .

"Uh, oh! Now we have a real problem! This becomes the focus of the rest of the story, and it brings up one of the main points I want to make tonight. Let's read.

And so the Jews said to the man who had been healed, "It is the Sabbath; the law forbids you to carry your mat."

"But he replied, 'The man who made me well said to me, "Pick up your mat and walk."'"

"So this begins John's account of the so-called Sabbath controversy. A modern reader might have trouble understanding why this issue takes up so much space in the Gospels. He might conclude that the observance of the Sabbath must be a really important issue, because they talk about it so much.

"But this would be the wrong conclusion. We should note that whenever the New Testament refers to Sabbath observance, it's always in a negative light."

A guy on the floor held up his hand. Jack stopped and pointed at him, asking, "Did you have a question?"

"Yeah, I guess I don't know exactly what this Sabbath thing is."

"Okay, let's take a minute for some background here. In the Old Testament there's a law that says the Jews shouldn't work on the Sabbath, which is Saturday. Now if you read it, you'd probably think this law is simply telling them not to go to work on Saturday. But under a legalistic mentality, the rabbis felt increasingly obligated to chop this law up, adding definitions, and they finally built up a legalism around the whole notion of Sabbath that's downright incredible. In the literature of the rabbis, there are hundreds of pages of legislation relating to this one law.

"For instance, you're not supposed to lift and carry burdens on the Sabbath. But what constitutes a burden? In their legalistic mentality, they felt they had to carefully define what constitutes an illegal burden to bear on the Sabbath. So, if you'd been sewing on your shirt and you left the needle in the cloth, you'd definitely be guilty of carrying a burden on the Sabbath, because you're carrying this needle around."

Sherry shook her head, smiling. *How strange religious people are!* Jack went on:

"If you handed someone some coins through your window, and he held his palm face-up so you could drop the coins in, that would be okay. But if you held the coins out palm up, and he had to pick the coins up from your hand, this would be work: not allowed! These breaches of the law could be serious. There were some severe sanctions and punishments that the community could impose on offenders.

"Now, Christ knew all about Rabbinic law. His actions and comments show He was well-versed in their teachings. Yet, when He healed this man, He also told him to pick up his pallet and walk. That kind of thing couldn't go unnoticed in Jerusalem at that time. Why did He do that?

"It was because Jesus was ready for a confrontation with the religious authorities over this issue. He was putting the religious leaders in the position where they'd have to challenge His legitimacy, even in the face of the most remarkable miracle, or they'd have to admit their rules were manmade and worthless.

"So we can imagine this man, walking down the street grinning. The authorities come up to him; what do they say? 'Why are you carrying your pallet? This is against the rules!'

"He answers, 'I just got healed from thirty-eight years of helpless paralysis!'

"They're saying, 'Hey, don't try to cloud the issue. Don't bother us with unrelated details. We're not talking about healing here. We're talking about a pallet, we're talking about the law, and we're talking about the law being broken!'"

The group was laughing vigorously. Jack also laughed joyfully.

"There's a strange mentality here. Jesus Christ was against this mentality! Christ was impaling these religious types on the horns of a dilemma. Their choice was not a pleasant one. Either they look directly at this healing, which was clearly the work of God, and say the one who performed it was evil, or they throw out their legalism as being misguided.

"When you read about the confrontations between Christ and the rabbis, you need to understand what's going on, or it will seem like Christ just had a chip on His shoulder. He's constantly deriding these people, and at the end of the book of Matthew He actually ends up calling them names in a public rebuke: 'Sons of Hell!' 'Brood of vipers!' 'White-washed tombstones!' 'Hypocrites!' and 'Fools!'

"The modern reader looks at these words of Christ and wonders, 'What's wrong with this guy? What's His problem?'

"The problem is that any time we have a thesis, we also have an antithesis. Christ came to present God's offer to us—a relationship with Him and eternal life, all at God's own expense, completely undeserved on our part. The religious mentality Christ faced here was the very antithesis of that message—not that God will give us *anything* for free, but that we must earn each blessing by prying it from His grudging, reluctant hands! We think we have to work until we become so deserving that He just about *has* to give us a blessing! This is why they thought the rules were so important.

"The issue here is not just the Jewish rabbis. It's the legalistic mindset, that says it's our observance of religious law that compels God to bless us. *That's* what bothered Jesus. And this same description would fit most world religions, including much of so-called Christianity!

"The controversy in the New Testament over the Sabbath is much more than a disagreement about how to interpret the Sabbath. It's a struggle between a relational approach to God, versus a rules-oriented approach."

Sherry sensed this was important. She had just assumed that her deeds, whether good or bad, were what interested God. Now lately, she was repeatedly hearing that God wasn't going to judge her by her works, but by her faith. The picture of God as a loving, personal Being who wanted to end the distance between Himself and her began to dawn. She felt drawn toward this understanding of God. By now she was relaxed and engrossed in the teaching. She could *feel* the truth in what Jack was saying.

Jack went on: "Also involved here is the struggle between true morality and what we might call pseudo-moralistic legalism.

"Let's remember, God wanted to define morality, and that's one reason He gave laws in the Bible. But to take the moral principles of the law of God and to split them into such particular rules has the *opposite* effect. When the legalist draws attention to the finest details of a legalistic system, he also draws our attention *away* from the main moral point of the law!

"This fascination with the finer points of legal observance is what Christ called 'straining out the gnat and swallowing the camel' in Matthew 23:24. It's a dominant feature of the religious mentality, and it's downright astonishing to see how universal it is. It's there in all the religious systems I've studied.

"Think about this carefully. What does it mean to 'strain out the gnat and swallow the camel?' We look into our drink at the picnic and see there's a gnat in it. We pick him out before drinking, right? But what if, after carefully doing this, we chug the drink down, failing to notice that there was also a camel in there? This is nothing but a complete lack of perspective! We've ignored the most important thing, while the unimportant has been scrupulously observed.

"In this passage tonight, a man was healed from a life of futility by God's power—that's important. Someone walks home with his pallet—that's unimportant.

"Now this is the vital thing to see here—mark this well. It isn't that the unimportant little rules are brought in *along with* the important, it's that the little rules are brought in *instead* of the important.

"We may think to ourselves, 'Boy, these people must've really been close to God! To be so zealous as to avoid even carrying a needle in their shirt shows they were in a very advanced stage of spiritual growth.' But no! It's just the opposite!

"Do you really think you'd avoid having a pin in your cloak because you love God so much? Because you want to be close to Him? Because you want to live His way? No. Just the opposite of that! It's so you can get *away* from Him! It's so the *real* ethical demands of the Scriptures—the ones that really hurt because you're failing to keep them—are covered over and camouflaged by a nice bushy build-up of ethical trash!

"You can look at your cloak and see no needle, and look into the mirror and say, 'Hey, I have it together!' People are literally hiding from God behind the cover of their homemade, ridiculous, external rules because they're afraid to face the awesome, absolute morality of God."

Sherry was fascinated. *Ooooh, wow! I wonder whether that's really the reason for some of those strange, picky laws in religion?* She remembered being disturbed in Brazil because the church expected women to wear long sleeves in the hot weather but never said anything about the fact that families neglected their children. She imagined Jack was probably right on this point. After tuning out for a moment, she listened further:

"Let's reason together about this. Why would anyone want to focus on something like a pin in their cloak? I'll tell you why. It's precisely because in the law there *is* real moral content. Now, when God says in the law 'you shall not covet anything,' *that* is moral! When you look over here and hate, *that* is moral! When you're filled with greed and self-centeredness, *that* is moral. When you fail to love others sacrificially, *that* is moral.

"These are the things we're failing at. But instead of admitting that, and honestly coming to God as failures in need of grace, this religious system allowed people to think they had kept the law, and there's no need to fall before God in their helplessness. This is why Christ was angry. Jesus put a point on it in Mark 7:8 when He said, 'You have let go of the commands of God and are holding on to the traditions of men.' And I must tell you, this critique applies to much of Christianity today, just as it did then.

"God's trying to care for people. He's trying to express His love for humankind. But His own words are being used as the basis of a religious system that's anything but loving. Isn't there a cold, harsh, and unloving attitude expressed toward this man healed of paralysis? How do you suppose he felt when they ignored his marvelous healing, and instead focused on his technical violation of some strange law? This story really illustrates the hardness and the lack of love in religious thinking."

Jack took a long pause as he let his words sink in. Sherry was flushed with excitement. How true this seemed to be! Jack was putting his finger on criticisms she had sensed about religious systems, but could never put into words.

He went on: "This is not a problem of the distant past, folks. Today, this same mentality is evident in varying degrees in the church. Many Christians wouldn't dare go to an R-rated movie, but they'd feel no qualms of conscience about living their lives for money. Many Christians wouldn't allow any alcohol in their house, but at the same time may fail to love those outside the church, and that violates the main commandment of Christ! Many Christians today feel as long as they have their devotional time and confess their sins, they're living for Christ, even though they may devote virtually no mental energy to living for Him during the rest of the day!

"When this is the case, we've found a way to contain God in a compartment, a cubicle in our lives, so we can live the rest of our lives apart from Him. This is the real purpose of legalism. This is the real purpose of formalism—when we focus on external forms and rituals in religion—as well. By focusing on the external forms of religion, we can divert our attention from the fact that the internal, our heart, is further away from God than ever! Legalism and formalism are brother and sister. They are the two grippers of the pliers. They're always seen together."

Formalism! thought Sherry. *That's what Forsythe was talking about. So this thing with forms might be a way to dodge the real issues! This might be the answer I've been looking for!*

Jack pressed the point. "One group might focus on the fact that they never go to movies or listen to rock music. Another group focuses on the fact that they attend regular, elaborate rituals. Neither of these ranks high in importance to God. You could be miles away from a life of Christian love even though you keep these disciplines. And you could be in there pretty close with God even though you didn't keep either one.

"So what's the solution? What are we supposed to do when we know we're falling short of true morality? First of all, don't try to pretend you're really doing okay. Don't try to cover the situation up. Come before God and admit your failure. This is exactly what God wants. When we admit our failure, when we come in humility, we can appreciate and accept the grace of God, whether it's for salvation or for growth. Our relationship with God takes on an authenticity that's tangible."

Jack seemed deeply excited about this description. His face seemed to light up with energy and a smile of enthusiasm as he went on.

"Nothing could be further from the religious mentality we've been looking at. We don't need the pretense anymore. We're free to relate honestly to God and to others. Real love becomes possible, and this is the true path to maturity, not outward fussing over religious rules!

"In 2 Corinthians 3:6, Paul says we are servants of a new covenant, 'not of the letter but of the Spirit; for the letter kills, but the Spirit gives life.' The 'letter' in this passage refers to a focus on legalism—the letter of the law even if it's the Law of Moses. Paul says it kills because, as we've seen, this kind of legalism butchers any honest relationship with God and replaces it with phoniness. When Paul says the Spirit gives life, what is he referring to there? Mainly, a relational approach to God rather than a legal one.

"This is what God wants for you tonight. He doesn't want you to commit to keeping a religious discipline. He wants you to come to Him with empty hands and an honest heart, and forge a relationship with Him."

Sherry gathered her Bible up into her bosom and folded her arms over it. *"Tonight?" Forge a relationship with God . . . tonight?* As she admitted to herself that she was strongly considering it, she felt a surge of goose bumps pass over her skin. She rubbed her arms as she listened to Jack, a slight frown on her face. She was feeling an urge to cry for some reason she didn't understand. She steeled herself, determined not to break down like an idiot.

"His terms are simple: First, admit that you need to be forgiven. In Romans 3:23 God says, 'for all have sinned and fall short of the glory of God.' Second, trust that the death of Christ covers your shortcomings and opens the way to an intimate relationship with God, free from fear, and without any need to justify yourself with legalistic sleight-of-hand tricks.

"This is what Jesus is referring to in verse 24 of John 5:

"I tell you the truth, whoever hears my word and believes him who sent me has eternal life and will not be condemned; he has crossed over from death to life.

"Will you believe in Christ tonight? Will you accept this gift before you leave here tonight? If so, I'll give you an opportunity to pray in your heart in a minute. If not, I hope you'll at least come next week when we study the passage at the end of this chapter, which shows how the Bible itself supplies us with powerful evidence that the claims of Christ are true."

As Jack finished his teaching he asked if there were any comments or questions. There followed a period of questions, answers, and free forum discussion that Sherry found very appealing. She was absolutely overwhelmed by the logic of Jack's presentation. This was the most common-sense discussion of religion she had ever heard. The Bible seemed to come alive, breathing with truth so obvious it was exciting. She felt like she could have listened for hours to such insight. Looking down, she realized the whole thing had taken only a little over half an hour.

Within a few minutes, Jack suggested the group pray. Sherry wasn't sure what to expect at this point, but she was pleasantly surprised. One person after another spoke up, praying out loud. Their prayers were in plain language and apparently from the heart. Sherry peeked to see who was speaking, even though she felt like she shouldn't. One of the people who prayed was Lisa. Sherry envied this woman who seemed to be more together than she was. Lisa seemed so friendly, and yet it wasn't the friendliness that desperate people sometimes exuded. There was strength in the way Lisa knew who she was and where she was going.

The rest of the group would murmur from time to time during the prayer, apparently in agreement with what was said. That part seemed strange to Sherry. Yet, she felt that these must be spiritual people. They seemed to have something in common that Sherry suddenly wanted very badly. Why wasn't she able to enter into this spiritual fellowship they were all sharing? Why did she always have to look at the question of God from the outside? She remembered her struggle to pray earlier in the week. These people did it naturally and with ease.

Then Jack spoke up in prayer. He said, "Lord, there are some here tonight who don't know You in a personal way. They may believe You exist, they may have gone to a lot of church services. But the fact is they've never actually asked You to come into their lives and take over. Right now, for those of you sitting here who know you want God in your life, I want you to speak to God in your heart and say this with me. 'God, I don't have all the answers I need yet. I still have some questions. But tonight I'm ready to accept the death of Christ as my provision for sin. I'm ready to have Jesus' death apply to me, and I'm ready to have You personally come into my heart with the Holy Spirit. Grant me eternal life as Jesus said You would in this passage we read tonight. It's in His name that I ask. Amen.'"

To her own astonishment, Sherry had agreed with each line, just as Jack spoke it. Looking up as the prayer ended, she opened her eyes and glanced at the people getting up and moving around. She knew she had planned to wait much longer and investigate more fully. Instead, she had followed her heart. She sensed things were going to be different in her life.

15

After the prayer ended, people got up and began milling around again. The music began again as well. Sherry turned to Lisa. "Well, that blew me away!"

"Do you mean that positively or as a critique?" Lisa asked with a smile.

"Oh, it's positive, all right. In fact, it's extremely positive! I've never heard anything like that."

"What did you find unusual in it?"

"Well, I guess he seemed to be like a professor in the way he analyzed the text." She paused thoughtfully. "But I felt like he was talking to me directly. I guess I've just never heard someone teach from the Bible like that."

"I know exactly what you mean. I just wanted to see if you had the same reaction I did," Lisa said, as they struggled to get up from the comfortable but sunken old couch.

"You got started in Christianity from Jack's teaching?" Sherry wondered.

"No, but the other guy I listened to was very similar."

"Well, I just can't believe it. This whole concept of a Bible study is so cool! I like this a lot better than the church I went to the other day."

"That's because this is more suited to your cultural background. The church you visited was attuned to an earlier culture—that of our parents and our grandparents, and really, of people hundreds of years ago."

"Boy, no kidding. I just couldn't relate to what was happening there, although I don't want to sound like I'm judging those people. I guess I just felt it wasn't for me. Now this is another story."

"I'm glad to hear you feel there might be something here for you."

Sherry felt barriers coming down. "Oh, Lisa, you have been so patient. I want to apologize for acting so weird and everything."

"What do you mean?"

"You know, I wouldn't give you my number, I wouldn't let you pick me up, stuff like that. I've been treating you like you were some kind of salesperson or something."

"Well, I think you did meet me as a salesperson, and in a way I am one."

"What's your commission on this sale?" Sherry asked with a grin.

"I guess the satisfied feeling I have right now . . . the feeling that you've seen a form of Christianity free from a lot of the stereotypes you probably had. You've been walked through a section of Scripture and you've come away feeling like there are answers there. I imagine you'll be getting the same feeling one of these days when you turn one of your friends on to God."

Sherry's head tipped back a couple of inches. "That's interesting. I'm going to have to think about that. I don't know whether my friends would get into this kind of thing."

"Well, let's not worry about that right now."

They were suddenly interrupted as Jack arrived. Sherry felt tingling nervousness rise up her back as she turned to speak with him. She was now beginning to feel a little intimidated by Jack. He smiled as he held out his hand to her. "Well, so this friend who invited you to a Bible study was Lisa! I'm so glad to see you here!"

Sherry smiled and took his hand. "Jack, I was so shocked to see you up there I thought I'd die! I thought you said you weren't a preacher."

"A preacher's like a clergyman, right?" He shrugged, looking for sympathy. "Anyway, I don't accept the title of preacher, I just say I'm a Bible teacher."

"Oh, I see. . . . Well, I think you're a very good one." She was anxious not to seem accusing.

"You think so? I was hoping you'd be able to get into this story tonight." Now she was sensing that same chemistry again as their eyes met directly for a moment. She quickly looked down.

"Yeah, I feel like I got into it quite a bit," she admitted as she looked back up directly at him with her sparkling green eyes. "Anyway, it was . . . a surprise." Then, self-consciously she added, "I really have to watch my language."

"You don't have to worry about it," Jack chuckled. "We talk the same here as anywhere else. There's no reason for you to fake the way you talk."

"It seems like you guys are intent on keeping things relaxed here," Sherry observed.

"Well, I think we really are relaxed. You know, if you were getting together at our house for a social thing, you'd expect to see people relaxed and informal right?"

"Yeah . . ." she acknowledged tentatively. "I guess if it was a social thing . . . but it seems a little different if it's a religious thing."

"Why?" Jack asked.

"Well, I don't know. It just seems more appropriate, I guess." She seemed confused.

"I think you're just reacting to your past experiences with Christianity," Jack suggested. "I think that's what I would call 'attaching cultural baggage to the gospel.'"

"You're going to have to explain that." Sherry shook her head.

"Okay . . . it's like, religious systems begin to view a certain cultural anomaly as though it was sacred. Christians know the Bible says we should be different than the rest of the world, but they mistakenly look for difference in the outward, like cultural differences, instead of inward differences, like the fact that we love God and others instead of living for self. The next thing you know, a visitor comes to the church, and gets the feeling she has to change the way she lives culturally if she wants to be a Christian."

"I hear that!" Sherry smiled at the obvious reference to her recent experience.

"It's that way in a lot of areas. Religious leaders also look at elements of the secular culture and worry about what effect those elements might have on their members. For instance, religious teachers look at the damage done by alcoholism, drunk driving, drug abuse, and whatnot, and they think to themselves, 'Look, if there's such a danger there, we'd be safer if we just didn't drink at all.'"

"But you don't feel that way."

"No, I don't. The problem is, when we try to protect people in that way, by adding a few rules that aren't in the Bible, we end up creating some terrible problems. You know, it's like nobody says, 'You can never drink a beer if you want to be a Christian.' But on the other hand, in some Christian groups no one ever does. And, you know, people are smart enough to figure out what the rules of a group are whether they're written or unwritten. So the unspoken message comes across, 'Before you become a Christian, you're going to have to decide never to smoke, drink, or chew, or go out with boys who do.'"

Sherry and Lisa chuckled.

"So, the thing is, God may lead Christians to abstain from drinking, because it's a problem for them, but if we make it a new rule, not based on Scripture, but based on the judgment of our little subculture, it becomes sort of a cultural hoop people have to jump through before they can come to Christ. And that's a problem, because God wanted to offer a free gift to people, which is hard enough to accept without human pride. And now we're going to go and say you have to jump through these cultural hoops in addition to humbling yourself to God."

Sherry nodded thoughtfully. "Yeah . . . I can see a problem there."

"You bet it's a problem! God's standing here behind us as we construct our artificial barriers to Christ, yelling, 'Hey, I never said that!' It makes you wonder how we could *dare* change His terms for coming to Him." Jack had that passionate frown on his face, and he was becoming more animated as he spoke.

Lisa broke in, "Yeah, it's like God's there saying, 'Hey, I love those people you just frightened away from Me! I wanted them to come to Me, and you made it harder to come to Me than I ever wanted it to be.'"

"Hmmm. That makes a lot of sense," Sherry said thoughtfully. "I guess there wouldn't be any good reason for going with anything other than what's in the Bible, if it's going to make things harder for people."

Jack broke into a broad smile. "I'm so glad you came tonight, Sherry. I hope you'll consider coming back again."

"Oh, I really want to hear the rest of this study on John," she said. "I told you I was reading the Bible."

"Yeah."

"Well, the book I've been reading is John!"

"Oh, that's great! This should work out well."

"Yeah, I'll say."

Then turning toward Lisa, he said, "Lisa, you'd better take care of Sherry's questions, but don't get into a debate with her."

"Why not?" Lisa asked as Sherry let out a groan and rolled her eyes.

"Well, in intellectual history I think they call her the human meat grinder or something like that."

"Oh, that is such a complete lie!" Sherry couldn't help but laugh at Jack's teasing, but she also slugged him in the chest. "I can't believe you're still distorting that!"

"What?" Lisa demanded to know.

Jack covered himself from any more blows as he went on. "This guy in class made the mistake of crossing her, and he's been sort of wandering around in a daze ever since, trying to figure out what happened to him."

"Oh, so you really thrashed him, huh?" Lisa asked with a grin, turning to Sherry.

"No, Jack just likes to exaggerate so he can get my goat. You're just like my brother, Jack."

"Oh, oh. That doesn't sound good . . . but I'm certainly not going to debate you on it!" he laughed.

Sherry just shook her head, smiling. She could tell this was going nowhere.

Jack changed his tone. "Okay, I'm kidding. Look, I have to go talk to someone, so I'll see you in class or something. Okay?"

"Yeah, great seeing you," Sherry answered. Then, with a nod of his head and a final look into her eyes, he waved his finger and turned to move away through the crowd.

Lisa and Sherry spent another half hour talking to other people in the group, one or two of whom looked familiar to Sherry. She was happy with her ability to joke around and socialize easily. People seemed eager to talk, or was it that she was just in a good mood? Finally, at about 10:30, as the house was becoming empty, they decided to go.

On the way out, Sherry looked behind her and saw Jack talking with a couple. As he threw his head back and laughed heartily, she felt a strong urge to get into the discussion, to get his attention. But she turned toward the door and left with Lisa.

16

"Well, you were certainly a big hit!" Lisa commented as they walked to the car.

"What makes you say that?" Sherry asked.

"Oh, I just think your personality makes you easy to like and people seem to enjoy talking to you. I know I do."

There was silence for a few seconds. "I really appreciate that, Lisa," Sherry said from the bottom of her heart. She felt her own affinity for Lisa continuing to grow each time they interacted. "I really enjoy talking to you, too. I think you've been more help to me during the past couple of weeks than you may ever realize."

"I can sense you've been going through a lot."

"Oh, more than I can explain! This period in my life has just been crazy. I feel like the wheels have been coming off. I know I have to change my way of life. And this thing about God has been there in a big way. . . ." She was thinking of telling Lisa she had prayed along with Jack at the meeting, but decided to hold back. She told only half the truth: "Lisa, I was thinking about praying that prayer tonight, you know, the one about accepting God and stuff?"

"Well, why don't you?"

"I might." She didn't feel good about lying to Lisa, yet she didn't feel ready to go public for some reason.

"Look, Sherry. It says in Revelation 3:20 'If anyone opens the door, I will come in.' Now, if you go home and open that door tonight, then you have God's promise that He'll come into you right then and there."

"I hope so."

"No, you'll know so."

"Well, you seem a little more sure about it than I am."

They both got in the car, and Sherry began driving.

"Just ask God for assurance that He's forgiven you, and that He's now in your life," Lisa said.

"Okay. I'll probably try that. Boy, I just don't know. . . ."

"Well, I'm so excited about this I don't know what to do! I really get the feeling you're very close to starting a relationship with God."

They drove for a bit in silence.

"Lisa," Sherry paused.

"Yes?"

"About Jack. . . ."

"Yeah?"

"Well, does he date anyone there?"

"No, not at the moment. Jack's dated around a bit, but none of us feel like he's really interested in women. There have certainly been enough of us trying to generate some interest there. He had a thing going for a little while last year with Jenny, but it didn't amount to much. I honestly don't know if there's anyone who can get his attention."

Sherry felt she knew Lisa was wrong on this point.

"Why? Are you planning on trying?" Lisa added, looking over with a wry smile.

"No. I'm not into dating at this point either." Sherry looked ahead at the road with her jaw set.

"Well, you must have asked for some reason."

"Yeah . . . I, uh, guess at one point I thought he was coming on to me down at school."

"Ahhhh!" Lisa said, raising and lowering her voice as though she had just found a ten dollar bill. "He *was* acting a little strange with you tonight, wasn't he?"

Sherry just shrugged. "He didn't seem that strange to me."

"Well, you're certainly pretty enough to be the one that breaks through that shell, I guess."

"No. I mean it. I'm really not interested. And . . . well, even if I was, that has nothing to do with this decision I'm thinking about tonight. At least I hope it doesn't."

"I thought you said you weren't interested." Lisa was grinning as she discerned what was going on, and continued to bore in, looking for more information.

"Well, I'm not, in terms of getting into something. I just mean, you know, he is an attractive guy, and I just hope I'm not reacting to that when I . . ." her voice trailed off.

"I don't think you should question your motives too much. Lots of girls have admired Jack, but I can't believe you'd give your life to something just because an attractive guy told you to."

Sherry looked over at Lisa. "You'd probably be amazed to hear the things I've done because an attractive guy told me to."

Lisa was unperturbed. "I doubt it. You know, I didn't grow up a Christian. I've been around, too."

"Really?" Sherry hadn't ever considered that possibility with Lisa. "I'd like to hear your story, Lisa. I just get the feeling I'm a lot worse than the other people at the study tonight."

Lisa chuckled. "I doubt that very much. I was living on the street before I came to Christ. And I'm not anything unusual, either. There are a lot of us who've been around."

"You!?"

"Oh, yeah! I'm afraid I've been around the block a few more times than I like to think about." They had arrived at Lisa's house. "Why don't you come in and I'll tell you all about it?"

Sherry looked at her watch. She knew she could catch up on sleep the next afternoon. "Okay. I'd love to come in for a while."

They went into the rooming house, which Lisa explained was populated by Christian women from the group they had just visited. When Sherry asked where everyone was, Lisa explained that most of them probably had gone down to The Fireside restaurant for some fellowship. They got some pop and chips from the kitchen, which was simple but clean. The refrigerator and stove were ancient relics. Sherry became aware that the old cabinets and linoleum floor gave off a subtle smell. She knew she had smelled it before, but what was it? It was something like . . . like a rooming house!

They went up to Lisa's room, which had a mustard-colored easy chair, and a study chair at her very small wooden desk. Sherry settled into the easy chair, beside the desk, and Lisa took the chair in front of the desk. They used the corner of the desk as a table for their drinks and chips. Their talk lasted long into the night. Sherry found out Lisa was working for a couple of quarters to save money so she could go to graduate school in Microbiology. It was intriguing to think of this little woman as a scientist. But it hadn't always been that way. Lisa told her whole story; how she had bought into the street culture near the university as a teenager; how she had lived with a series of guys in a world of drugs, sex, and crime. Sherry gradually came to realize she had not experienced as much promiscuity and street living as Lisa had, by a long shot.

Lisa recounted the abuse she had suffered at the hands of unprincipled men; how she had gone to a house on campus similar to the one they had been to that night where they offered a meal with the Bible study. It was the meal that appealed to her more than the study at first. She recounted how she had continued to attend for months before finally surrendering to Christ; the struggle she had endured trying to accept the idea that a righteous God could love someone like her.

By the end of the night, Sherry was also opening up to a surprising extent. They talked about the problems she had been having with Jim Clemmons, and about the discouraging visit that day with the police. They eventually ended up discussing what was on Sherry's mind—her bankrupt love life. Sherry talked at length about her own experiences with men, which began to surface some real pain. "Lisa, I've been getting these flashbacks about some things I did . . . with guys, you know . . . well, it's really been bothering me. I keep getting the shivers when I flash on some of these scenes, you know?"

"Yeah, I do know."

Looking at Lisa, Sherry believed she did know. "There was this guy from art class. . . ." As she looked down, she winced so painfully that Lisa saw it clearly, and reached out over the desk to put her hand over Sherry's hand. Sherry put her other hand over Lisa's as she looked back up, now with moistening eyes and a quivering lip. "I've made a real mess of my life! I don't know whether it can still be fixed."

"Oh, yeah! It definitely can!" Lisa said with feeling. "When I remember things like that, I can turn to the grace of God."

"I don't know what that means."

"It means that who I am, the reason I'm important, is based on what God thinks of me. It isn't what I think, or what I did, or what others think. The final standard is God."

"I'm not too excited about what God thinks of me." Sherry had to wipe a tear off her cheek.

"That's what the word 'grace' means. God doesn't look at you based on what you've done. He places all your sin on Christ. If you come under the death of Christ, you can come to Him in total purity! You'd be as pure in His eyes as a little girl."

Sherry just blinked at Lisa, lost in thought about what she had said. It had been a long time since she had been a little girl. It seemed like several lifetimes ago.

By the time Sherry was ready to go, she knew she had forged a new friendship. She had never had an experience like this. She always thought it must be possible to converse deeply like they had that night. But she had to admit, as she was driving home, she had never really engaged in such a long, in-depth conversation with another woman in her life. *Come to think of it, I've never had such a deep talk with a man either.*

One thing she didn't open up about any more was the undercurrent of her interest in Jack. She felt the less said about that, the better, especially since Lisa and Jack were obviously good friends.

As Sherry flopped into bed, she knew she was entering a new phase in her life. But she had no way of knowing her actions earlier that evening had triggered a large-scale realignment of spiritual forces on the university campus.

Sherry had indeed trusted Christ, and in so doing, she had overcome her main doubts about God and the Bible. But there were many things she had not yet considered. She still hadn't considered the notion of a personal Satan, and she would have had problems believing in the Devil and demons if she had considered it. She would have been even more surprised to find that the forces of hell were not only real, but they were even at that moment reacting to her situation.

The university had been relatively quiet spiritually for nearly two decades. The evangelical Christian groups there were struggling to retain their strength and numbers, but most, small to begin with, were slowly shrinking in influence. There hadn't been an explosive awakening since 1972, and the overwhelming majority of students were leaving the university lost and without Christ.

The group at Jack's house, though small, had already been targeted as perhaps the most dangerous group on campus, largely because the evil spirits knew that Jack Collins was not average. His gifts were unusual, and he had been exposed to a form of Bible teaching almost eradicated earlier, but now alive and well in his teaching. He was proving to be unusually resilient under attack, bouncing back from depression more quickly than most Christians, and the evil ones had failed to gain large-scale inroads into his personal life.

An unusually consistent barrier of prayer interference had made it difficult to get at the group. There was also dismay at the development of several other Christian students in the group, such as Lisa and Jack's friend Ken, who were headed toward lifelong service of God. To date, evil spirits had to content themselves by pursuing a strategy of isolation and containment. Although the group posed a threat, in that it continued to win people to Christ, there was no reason to believe the situation was out of control.

Now a colossal error had been made. Sherry Martin was known to the faculty at the university as one of the most brilliant students on campus. The demonic leadership at the university had not missed this point either, and they had even used Sherry several times to undermine the faith of weak Christian students on campus. With her intellect, her beauty, her forceful personality, and her agnosticism, she had been an effective influence for evil. The last anyone knew, her glimmer of spiritual interest two weeks earlier had been suppressed during a visit to a dead church.

But during a short two-hour period without surveillance, she had met both Jack and Lisa, and bought her own Bible. Now within one week, all control had been lost, as she had taken a romantic interest in Jack, and had even attended his teaching. Her immediate response to Christ was totally unexpected, and the long time spent with Lisa after the study made it doubly unlikely she would lightly walk away from her new involvement with Christ.

As the servants of hell gathered that night, fury and threats dominated their discourse. The last thing they needed was one of the most powerful personalities on campus joining up with Jack and his crew. On the other hand, she was only one woman, and even if she was unusually gifted, it was hard to see how a single person, one way or the other, could change the spiritual equation all that much. Just to be safe, new assignments were made, and a general assault was planned.

17

Wednesday morning, Sherry ran into Becka at their mailboxes. "Oh, Becka, you wouldn't believe this thing I went to the other night!"

"Really? What?"

"Well, it was this group, a Bible fellowship group, and it was really cool. The people there are just like normal people, you know, they're just like students and stuff. And they get together at this house right over here on Sixteenth and this guy gave a teaching on the Bible—it was really interesting! And they just hang around and talk. It's not like a church at all!"

Becka looked thoughtful. "On Sixteenth? Is that Jack somebody?"

"Yeah! Jack Collins. You know him?"

"I know about him, if it's the same guy I think it is," she said with a noticeably negative tone.

"You sound like you think he's bad news."

"Well, those guys are pretty radical from what I hear."

"What do you mean? What's so radical about them?"

"I wouldn't want to repeat anything that isn't true."

"Oh come on, you've heard something," Sherry pushed.

"Well, first of all, I hear they don't go to church. They think they're okay just going to their home group. I hear they don't even like other churches."

"Yeah . . . I guess that may be . . . they didn't say they don't like churches. I don't know for sure . . . but so what if they don't? Do you have to go to a church, like a regular church?"

Becka frowned, seeming both irritated and surprised. "Yes! The Bible talks about the church. It says you should belong to a church."

"Wow! Where does it say that?"

"Uh . . . I'm not sure where, offhand, but I know it's in there."

"Well, this is the first time I've heard of this. If you find out where that is, let me know, okay? I'd like to study it and ask them about it."

"Sure . . . Arthur'll know where it is."

"Who's Arthur?" Sherry wondered.

"Arthur Barclay. He's my pastor; you heard him preach."

"Oh, yes! He was good, too."

"Thanks. I know the Bible talks about the church. But another problem is that those people don't honor the Lord's day."

"What's the Lord's day? You mean the Sabbath day?"

"It was the Sabbath in the Old Testament. In the New Testament it's the Lord's day; Sunday."

"Oh, I wondered about that. So it does say you have to worship God on Sunday?" Incredulity blanketed her face.

"Yes, I've seen it before."

"You wouldn't happen to know where that one is, would you?"

Becka exhaled impatiently. "No, but I'll get that one, too."

For a moment, Sherry stared in doubt, but she sensed she needed to be careful about questioning Becka's statement. "I'd appreciate it. I guess that confuses me."

"What does?"

"Why God would want people to come to Him on a certain day."

"Well, you're not limited to that day. You can come to Him any day."

"What's the point then? There must be something special about that day."

"Look, I just know God wants us to honor the Lord's day, that's all." She swept her hand across like a scythe, and looked up at her mailbox as she opened it.

"Hmmmm." Sherry wondered why Becka was so irritable. From the testiness in her voice it was clear something about this conversation was bothering her. But Sherry wanted answers. She decided to try again. "I'm pretty new in this, but don't you ever wonder why that is? It's like . . . I was really turned on by this notion of a personal relationship with God."

"Yes. That's right." She looked back at Sherry. "It's a personal relationship with Jesus."

"Well, this thing about a special day seems a little impersonal somehow. . . ."

"I don't see anything impersonal about it."

"Well, imagine if you were married, and your husband wanted to designate one day of the week as his day."

"I know couples who have a special day they reserve for each other."

"Yeah . . . you have to arrange to have time for each other . . . but that can be on any convenient day. Like, these guys at Jack's place have a pre-arranged time to meet, but they do it on Monday evening. The strange part of this 'Lord's day' thing is that, you know, I can't make it to a meeting on certain days because I'm busy on that day. But here it's *God* who's saying *He* can't make it to the meeting on that day. It sounds like He's too busy except on a certain day or something."

Becka stared with a frown on her face. "I don't look at it that way."

"How do you look at it?"

Becka paused, gathering her thoughts. "Well . . . I guess I just feel like God said it, and that's good enough for me." She smiled triumphantly.

Sherry didn't like Becka's approach to the question, but she knew better than to say so. "Yeah, well . . . I guess that makes sense. But it still seems like if He said it, He must have a reason." They turned to finish getting their mail. As they walked toward the door Sherry spoke up again. "You know, though, it's really hard to believe that group I was with is way off target or something. They just seemed so much like what I would imagine Christians should be like . . . of course the people at your church were really nice, too!" Sherry suddenly realized Becka might feel defensive about her church. "I just didn't get much time to meet any of them . . . except for you, of course, and you've been real nice!" Sherry felt awkward as she tried to dig her way out.

"Yeah, but you can't always go by how nice people are, Sherry."

The statement was patronizing, but Sherry knew she had left herself open to that impression. "Well, it's not just that they were nice. It was also this Bible teaching—it was right out of the Bible, verse-by-verse, you know. I'd have to hear some pretty good reasons before I could believe that teaching was no good." She held the door open for Becka.

"I guess I don't know exactly what they teach, but I've heard there might be some pretty wild stuff going on over there. I know a couple of people who used to go to our church, and now they go there." They walked out and stopped in the parking lot to talk.

Sherry almost said something, as she thought she sensed possessive jealousy again, but decided to be more careful. "Oh, I wonder why they did that?"

Becka must have seen something on her face. "I'm not saying there's anything wrong with people going to another church! But this group isn't even a church, and I also think the ones who went were pretty carnally minded."

"What does that mean; 'carnally minded'?"

"They weren't really walking with God. They had their minds set on the flesh."

"Oh."

"I heard the whole reason they went over there was because those people encouraged them to sin."

Sherry actually chuckled out loud. "What?! What kind of sin?"

"I don't know for sure. . . . I guess I don't want to say any more about that. It could be gossip."

"Becka, you're really making me mad!" Sherry pulled the keys out of her purse and slapped the leather flap shut. "I didn't see anyone being urged to sin there. In fact, I didn't see any sin at all."

Becka was hesitant, but she went ahead and asked, "Are you sure you'd know sin if you saw it?"

Sherry instantly realized the implication of the statement. She knew Becka probably was aware of her relatively wild lifestyle—at least wild compared to Becka's. It angered her to see Becka throwing her past up against her. This was something none of the other Christians she had met so far had tried. On the other hand, why shouldn't she? After all, the question was perfectly valid in a way. She tried not to react, although the slight tightening in her face was no doubt detected. "I don't know whether I'd know sin if I saw it. It's a concept I'm still getting used to. But I didn't see any of the things I would think of as sin."

"Well, I'm not saying you're deep into sin or anything. It's just that sin takes many forms. There might be sin there that's hard to discern."

Sherry tried to imagine what this might refer to, but gave up. "Maybe you should come and see what you think?"

"I don't know . . ." she looked alarmed by the suggestion.

"Oh, come on! They aren't going to grab you and attack you or anything! What're you afraid of?"

"I'm not afraid. I just don't know whether it'll fit into my schedule."

Yeah, I can see you must be pretty hard-pressed socially right now. Sherry bit her tongue to avoid getting in her own digs. "Uh huh," she said with skepticism.

"Hey, look, I'll come some time. It's just going to have to fit into my schedule, all right?".

Sherry hung her head, backing away from confrontation. "Yeah, that's all right. In fact, I'd really appreciate that." She looked up and smiled, trying to soften the tone of the conversation.

They said goodbye in a spirit that was outwardly reconciled, and went to their separate cars. Sherry reflected on the conversation while she drove to the grocery store between classes.

Becka's negativity had really thrown a damper on the excitement she was feeling after her experience at the Bible study. One moment, she was telling herself Becka's warning should be heeded. The next moment, she would swear out loud.

But the more she thought about it, the more certain she was that Becka would like it if she saw for herself. *Yeah, she must've heard some things, and it's given her a bad impression. We'll see how she feels after attending. Still,* Sherry warned herself, *it's probably best to go slow and be careful with these people.*

Before going into the store, she looked at her mail. It was nothing but junk and one letter with no return address. She opened it, and within a few seconds reared her head back as she realized the letter was from Jim Clemmons! She scanned the area around her car, looking to see if he was there, but realized it was farfetched to think he would have followed her car.

She quickly read the letter.

"Sherry, you didn't say I couldn't write. I just want you to know I'm sorry for coming on strong that night. I still can't stop thinking about you. I'd really like to talk. Please call me! I know what I did was wrong, but you were wrong to get into that guy I saw you with, too. I knew you must have gone out on me. I'm ready to forgive. Are you?"

It was signed "Love, Jim," and at the bottom he included his address and phone.

She crumpled it up in fury and got out of her car, striding quickly toward the store. She got ready to cast it into the trash bin in disgust, but she stopped. Looking down at the crumpled paper, she pulled it out straight. *Don't be a fool! This could be evidence some day. I know exactly what to do about this.* She stashed the letter in her purse and went on with her shopping.

After she got home and put her groceries away, she sat down and wrote a letter of her own to Jim.

"Jim—No, I will never forgive you for attacking me. I have your letter, and I am going to show it to the police. I already told them you are obsessed with me, and you're following me and calling me. I had an officer over here, and he said to give him any evidence that shows up. If you ever appear again, I'll have you on record already and they'll take me seriously. You'd better stay away from me forever!"

She smiled at the letter. *Now I'm actually doing something. This'll scare his pants off.* She ran it down to the mailbox on her way to an 11:00 class.

Around lunchtime the phone rang. Sherry's mother was calling about some books Sherry had asked her to send from home.

As they talked, Sherry told her about the "cool home Bible study group" she had visited on Monday evening. No doubt, her mother could sense the excitement in Sherry's voice as she recounted the meeting and her conversation with Lisa afterward—how different it was from anything she had ever experienced in church at home. It was unusual for Sherry to open up extensively to her mother. Their relationship was usually low-key; Sherry didn't like the way her mom judged everyone, so she held her mother at arm's length. She was usually more comfortable opening up to her more-reflective dad.

Her mother sounded less than enthusiastic. "Sherry, there are a lot of extremist groups on campus these days. How do you know this group isn't a cult or something?"

Sherry's voice was expressionless, as though she was reciting a litany. "Mom, I'm old enough to think critically. I think I'll recognize any far-out behavior if it happens."

"Well, what kind of church is it? Are they Methodist?"

"No. I don't think they're into some national thing like that. I just think it's a local group of students getting together. The guy who was teaching is a grad student here."

"So there weren't any clergy there?"

"I don't know . . . no, I don't think so . . . who cares about that anyway? You think you can believe someone because he's a clergyman?"

"Well, I'd trust a clergyman more than some student!"

"Well, I wouldn't trust either one. I'd rather listen to the content of what a person says!" Sherry was fired up.

"Oh, so you're going to figure out all about theology now."

"I won't need to 'figure it all out.' I'll just take it as it comes." She picked up a brush from the desk and started stroking her hair vigorously.

"Oh, that's great, Sherry. 'Just take it as it comes.'"

"Yeah, that's right. Mom, if you studied more history, you'd know clergymen have stood up for every kind of folly and evil imaginable! I can't think of any error the church hasn't fostered at one time or another . . . slavery . . . anti-Semitism . . . witch hunts . . . war. I can't believe you're judging this group when you haven't even heard what they teach!" She threw the brush back down on her desk.

"I'm just worried about these campus cult groups. It gives me a bad feeling."

"A bad feeling! Now that sounds like something I'd better watch out for."

"I want you to be careful, that's all."

"Well, don't worry. I'm a big girl now. I don't think I'm any more likely to go off and join a cult than you would be."

After she hung up, she cut herself while slicing cucumbers for her sandwich. *Ow! That's just like her!* She indignantly threw the knife into the sink. *She's always so opinionated, it's useless trying to tell her anything.* But the more she thought about it, the more she cooled down as she realized it was probably normal for her mother to be worried about a group of religious people meeting in a home on campus. *Boy, everyone seems to be eager to guard me from Jack's group,* she marveled. *I wonder why nobody ever bothered to warn me about some of the groups I've hung around with who were into drugs, sex, and crime? How bad can these guys be, anyway?*

She spent the afternoon going to class and studying.

18

When Sherry got home around dinner time, she was surprised by a call from Reverend Lowell Billings, who said he led a group called the "Campus Faith Community."

It seemed Sherry's old pastor at home had called Dr. Billings. Billings explained that her mother was concerned about her new religious involvement and had mentioned it to her pastor, who offered to do what he could about it. Sherry was disgusted. "This is ridiculous. So my mother's checking up on me like I was a teenager!"

"Well, I realize it can seem patronizing, Sherry, but you have to look at it as a sign of love and concern." Billings sounded sickly sweet to Sherry. "Let's face it. It's better than parents who just don't care what you do."

"Well, I think she can care without trying to *police* me."

"No, that's not what this is about at all. I just said I would call you up and invite you to the Wellness Group tonight. After all, it's only prudent to get an exposure to different expressions in the community of faith."

"What's a *wellness group*?" she asked with a negative tone, twirling her long silver scissors around her finger.

"It's Christian fellowship. Just an informal discussion on issues of interest to Christians."

"I can't believe this. I just told my mother about this today at lunch! Here it's the same day and I have a preacher calling me!" She slapped the scissors down on her desk.

"Well, I didn't realize that. Reverend Simpson called me half an hour ago, and since the group was meeting tonight, I thought I'd just go ahead and call," he explained.

"When does it meet?"

"At 7:30 in the United Center. Do you know where that is?"

"The big new-looking building up on Decker?" she asked.

"Yes, that's it."

"Look, I'll think about it."

"Okay, if you make it, be sure to introduce yourself to me. I'll be leading the discussion."

"Okay, I might see you." As she hung up, she continued to burn with indignation that her mother had not trusted her judgment. On the other hand, she saw that visiting this group might be a good way to get her mother off her back. *I'll go once, and then tell Mom to back off and quit fussing over me*, she resolved.

She had an hour and a half to stretch out and snooze before she had to get up and leave.

At 7:30, Sherry sat in a folding chair in the small circle of students in the United Center lounge. The lounge was carpeted and spacious. Light walls and plenty of oak trim gave a modern feel to the seemingly empty building. She was surprised at how few people were there—fewer than twenty—for such a large and expensive building. She figured there must be others there at other times.

Dr. Billings was easy enough to identify. He was wearing a white turtleneck under his gray suit jacket, and a gold cross hung around his neck. He was about fifty years old, balding, had somewhat long hair over his collar, and a goatee.

The subject for the evening was genocide on the Amazon. They were to discuss the plight of the Indian tribes in the Amazon forest. Billings passed around a set of photos as he described Indian religion and tribal practices. Most of it was not new to Sherry. She had spent time with one of these tribes during the summer she worked in Brazil. He argued that the Indian tribes were being threatened by two dangers: the encroachment of prospectors for gold and gems, and the even more dangerous cultural genocide perpetrated by fundamentalist missionaries.

The discussion was like many Sherry had heard in anthropology classes. She was surprised at how similar the reasoning was to that in her classes, especially the fact that Billings disapproved of missionaries. He quoted several authorities who deplored the fundamentalists' belief that the Indians are going to hell and must be "saved." Billings argued that missionaries view Western society as superior to the ancient culture of the Indians, and violate the tribes by introducing modern implements and medicines in place of the traditional medicines of the forest.

When it came time for questions and discussion, Sherry listened to a couple of comments. They seemed to agree with the points Billings had raised. Sherry, on the other hand, had always been bothered by the notion of cultural imperialism from a humanistic standpoint. She decided to challenge the thesis even though it was her first time there.

She raised her hand, just as high as her shoulder, and Billings called on her. "Yes?"

"Uh, well . . . I guess I wonder whether there isn't an element of racism in this notion of preserving tribal culture without Western influence," she said tentatively.

"How is that? Isn't it really racism to make them live like us?" Billings shot back.

Her question had clearly irritated Billings, but Sherry dug in with determination. "Well, these people are in deep poverty, and they're plagued by a number of serious social and medical problems," she began, holding her Bible on her lap and gesturing with her free hand. "For instance, the most common cause of death in some Auca tribes is murder by spearing. Their spearing raids are a terrifying thing to the children. Infant mortality is very high . . . and other diseases claim people's lives unnecessarily . . . they often live in appalling pain from curable conditions, including parasites and dental problems.

"Now, suppose we found a community of white people in Appalachia living in conditions like these—barefoot, naked, poor, uneducated, sick, and lawless. Would we feel good about building a fence around that community so no one would disturb their traditional way of life? And if we wouldn't do it for poor whites, isn't there an element of racism here?"

"I think that's a completely different situation," said a woman with short hair and spectacles. "People like those you're describing would have been frozen out of their own culture for a generation or two or three. These tribes have been living this way of life for hundreds of years."

Sherry raised her eyebrows as though discovering something. "So it sounds like it's how *long* they've been in that condition that makes a difference. How long does a culture have to live in these conditions before they reach the point where they should be left that way?"

The woman looked away and shook her head, disapproving, but either not able or not willing to answer. Sherry felt a little bad for arguing on her first visit, but she couldn't quit now. She tried to let the short-haired woman off the hook by addressing a question to the rest of the group. "Don't Indian mothers feel just as badly as we do when their children die? Don't abscessed teeth hurt just as much whether your culture is ancient or recent?"

But the spectacled woman wasn't finished. "These tribes were doing just fine without ever seeing a white man. Every contact with the white culture has been a disaster for them," she shot back.

"That may be," Sherry responded with a shrug of her shoulders. "But just because some people have exploited them in the past doesn't mean that we can't have positive contact with them now . . . including relief and educational and medical work."

"Educating them in the ways of Western white culture, in other words." The woman nodded and smiled knowingly as she spoke.

"Yeah! There are some things in our culture that would help them. It almost seems like we view them as an endangered species, and we want to preserve them like a big zoo, so we can watch them."

There were some angry murmurs and groans around the room as people shook their heads in dismay at what Sherry was saying. Billings shook his head also. "I'm afraid you just can't keep from looking at this from a Western, industrialized perspective. You're a product of your inculturation."

Sherry knew a "naming fallacy" when she heard one. "Okay, you've labeled my position, but you haven't answered any of my questions," she retorted angrily. "Will you respond to my position directly?"

Billings tilted his head and gave her a smile, like a father who knew he had to be patient with his children. "No, I think it's just best to leave it that we see things differently here. I'm sure our views are equally meaningful to both of us."

Sherry felt he was just playing the relativism card because he couldn't answer critically. She smiled and nodded while rolling her eyes in a way that showed she wasn't impressed. "Right. Then I have another question," she pressed on, even more angry now.

"Okay," said Billings.

"Now, you said this group is Christian."

"Yes."

"Then I don't understand why you're criticizing Christian missionaries for going to these people. Aren't they telling them about the truth?"

Again there was a subtle murmur and some meaningful stares between the members of the group. Sherry sensed she had said something very wrong. After several seconds of uncomfortable dead air, one of the guys spoke up. "Some of these native spiritualities are more ancient than the Bible. I think it's just as arrogant to insist on our interpretation of spirituality as it would be to insist on our mode of dress."

Sherry's mouth set in a frown. This was something she wasn't prepared for. Her mind went into grid-lock as so many questions rose that she didn't know where to start. She tried to recalculate aloud, holding a hand out as though fending off the guy who had spoken. "First of all, I can't see the connection between what someone wears and their view of

God. But what does what you said mean—the part about interpretation and spirituality or whatever?"

"I mean we all have our own interpretation of spiritual reality. I don't see how I can evaluate the sense of the divine in another when I haven't lived in his shoes."

This comment didn't help a bit. Now Sherry's head was spinning. She had heard this sort of reasoning often in party situations, but always from those who were not Christians. It was clear she had taken a wrong turn in her thinking. "I'm sorry, I thought everyone here was viewing this from a Christian point of view."

"I think we are!" retorted the short-haired woman again. "Nothing could be more Christlike than a loving and compassionate view of others, including respecting others' religious interpretations."

Several approving murmurs followed this, causing Sherry's eyes to flit around the group. She was backpedaling mentally in total confusion now. "But wait a minute. It sounds like you guys don't necessarily believe that Jesus is the way to God or whatever."

"Now, you have to be careful about reaching judgmental conclusions," admonished Dr. Billings.

"Okay, let me ask it this way. Do you guys believe that Jesus rose from the dead?"

"Of course," Billings chuckled. "We treasure the Easter faith," he went on in what was supposed to be a reassuring tone. "The Jesus story is central to our whole understanding of religious hope."

Sherry was not reassured. She felt like the language Billings was using was some kind of code. "Why are you talking that way? Why are you using strange phrases and stuff?"

"I don't know what you're talking about. I'm sorry if I'm not stating it in a language context you're comfortable with."

She noticed a couple of grins from other members. The realization was dawning on her that she was playing the fool at this point. Sherry didn't know what she was dealing with, but it was clear the rest of the group understood more than she did. She tried to extract herself gingerly. "Well, it's clear we're dealing with some kind of different orientation here," she suggested.

"Yes," Billings jumped in to help. "Offhand, it sounds like you are coming from a justification-oriented theology, while we are probably coming more from an incarnational point of view. It's all a question of how you interpret the Jesus story and related mythology," he shrugged with one hand out, palm up.

Sherry could feel a burning flush in her cheeks, and her sharp eyes sparkled in angry confusion. She determined she wasn't going to say any more. She felt like a soldier who realizes he has wandered onto a mine-field. For some reason she couldn't yet fathom, she felt real anger at this group of people, but she also realized she was in no position to do anything about it. After a short silence, she went on with a big smile. "Okay, I guess that answers my questions. Thanks." She hoped that would be the end of it.

"You seem unresolved," Billings pressed.

"Well, no, actually I feel resolved for now. I might have some more questions later if that would be all right."

This seemed to satisfy the group, at least they left her alone and went on with a few more comments.

Finally, Billings said it was time to break up. "I'd like to remind you that we're going to need full participation in order to pull off our twenty-four-hour liturgy this weekend." They all stood, and before Sherry knew what was happening, they held their hands out to each other. The girl and guy next to her held out their hands and Sherry took them, though she didn't want to. Then, moving together, the group formed a tight circle, with heads turned down. In unison they repeated a verse:

As he gave, I give to you
As she loves, we love you too
God in all, creation's call
Together, one, forever.
Amen.

There was a hand squeeze passed around the circle, and the group broke up. Within seconds, Billings was standing in front of Sherry, smiling, with his hand out. "I'm Reverend Lowell Billings," he said.

"I'm Sherry Martin." She forced a smile and shook his hand.

"Yes, I'm not surprised. I hope this conversation didn't disturb you too much, Sherry."

"No, I was a bit confused at points, but I wouldn't say it disturbed me much." She didn't feel safe enough to tell the truth, and she only wanted to get out of there.

"Well, there are differences within the community of faith, and that's what makes it so beautiful that we can come together in complete unity."

"Yes, I guess that is beautiful." Her eyes darted around, looking for a way out of the conversation; a way out of the building. But something made her try to be polite. "So, this is the Wellness Group meeting, huh?"

"Yes. Of course, we often focus on things of a more personal nature. But sometimes I like to think about our world."

"I hope you didn't feel I was too forward in my questioning."

"Absolutely not! I just hope you have the same critical questioning posture when you're with your fundamentalist friends up at Jack's place."

She looked up at him. "Oh, so you know Jack!"

"Yes, from the description that Reverend Simpson gave me I could tell you were going to Jack's place. There aren't that many groups in homes here that focus on in-depth Bible teaching."

"Why do you call them fundamentalists?" She was regaining her equilibrium.

"Well, it may be unfair to label those precious believers. I think you're right there, and I apologize."

"No, you felt the word 'fundamentalist' was descriptive and I'd like to know why. What does that word mean to you, anyway?"

"What does it mean to you, Sherry?"

"I asked first." She narrowed her eyes and set her jaw.

"Okay," he chuckled. "Boy, you really go for the jugular, don't you?"

"No, I just asked a simple question—that you define a term you used."

"Well, I guess one of the main characteristics of fundamentalists in all religions is that they interpret the original Scriptures literally."

"But you don't interpret them that way?"

"Well no, of course not. These metaphors are there for their religious content, not as a history or a science text."

"So, the Bible is not a science or history text, then it is . . . what?" she challenged.

"It is a record of ancient man's quest for God."

She thought about his statement for a minute as she put on her coat. "But it's not a record of things God has said or done?"

"Oh, it is! Whenever someone has meaningful oneness with God, that's revelation."

She stared for a moment as she again had to ponder what sounded like double-talk. "I see," she said, nodding and looking down with a grin that let him know she saw more, perhaps, than he wanted her to. She decided to change the subject. "I heard you refer earlier to the myths associated with the 'Jesus story.'"

"Yes, the mythology is the religious context out of which we must pull our spiritual lessons. But you have to remember, this book was written over two thousand years ago. You just can't start applying it directly to today. Things have changed in two thousand years."

"Yes, but God hasn't changed. I mean, He's still God, right?"

"Well, our understanding of Him has changed. In the times of the Bible, religious wars, capital punishment even for witches, slavery, and intolerance of homosexuals were all accepted as the will of God."

"And now?"

"Now we have entered the modern age. Christian theologians have often led the way in society by realizing new freedoms, new aspects of equality that God intended all along."

She finished buttoning her coat. "I see. For some reason, I keep thinking your *interpretation* sounds more like what my nonChristian friends at the dorm think."

"Well, I can't evaluate that."

"Yeah, well, I think I like the *interpretation* they hold at the Monday Bible study more than what you're saying. At least they come right out and say what they believe."

"That's what fundamentalism is all about, Sherry. Easy answers. Quick answers. But unfortunately, narrow answers. I'm afraid you'll learn how to judge others and view yourself as superior at that study group."

"Well, I certainly hope that won't be my fate . . . and I hope *you* aren't judging those people, either." She looked at him with one eyebrow cocked.

"That is not my intent. I believe their religious experience is real and precious to them, and that's something I can't look down on."

"Even though it's completely false and narrow?"

"I never said it was completely false."

"No, but you implied it was."

"You misunderstand! How can something be false when they feel the reality of it? It clearly has religious significance and truth to them."

Sherry broke into a broad smile and looked down briefly, irritated by his relativistic perspective. She picked up her Bible and purse from her chair. "Yes, I see. Well, it's been nice meeting you, and I really have to do some studying tonight. Thank you for having me."

"I'm sorry you can't stay longer." He reached out and put a hand on her shoulder, but she looked down at his hand in a way that said "get it off!" and he did.

"Maybe next time," she said as she turned to go.

"I hope I haven't offended you by the things I've said." Billings could sense she wasn't happy.

She looked back over her shoulder as she opened the door to leave.

"How could I be offended by someone sharing his true feelings?" And with a knowing grin, she was gone.

On the way home, Sherry replayed the evening's conversations over and over. *Why did that group bother me so much? The hand holding and the poem at the end made my flesh crawl; it seemed so false.* But there was more. She had a deep-seated feeling the people she had been talking to were not being completely honest. They seemed to view the Bible in a different way than Lisa, Jack, and their friends.

She decided she would bring it up the next time she saw Lisa.

At the door to her apartment, she again got the sense someone was watching her. Once safely inside, she looked out the window to scan the courtyard. In the dark distance between buildings she could faintly see a man walking on the sidewalk, but there was no way to tell if it was Jim. It could have been anyone.

You were standing in the very place where it happened. It's no wonder you thought about him. Your fears are irrational; you're just making this worse! she told herself.

She read for class for a change that night.

19

The sun was creating long shadows off the beautiful maple tree, already sporting a few pink and red leaves outside Sherry's usual seat in the library as she completed her assignment for Dr. Forsythe. He had assigned a short synopsis of an article by Dr. Anthony Wallis, head of the department of anthropology at the University of Pennsylvania. The paper gave his explanation for religious ritualism and formalism.

As she prepared to check her paper one more time before taking it home to print it, she was startled by someone touching her shoulder. She whipped around, but nobody was there. She looked quickly over the other shoulder and saw the perpetrator; it was Jack! He was standing behind her chair and had just tapped her on the shoulder opposite where he was standing.

"Gotcha!" he gloated.

"Oh, Jack! You almost made me jump out of my skin! Where did you come from?"

"I was setting up for some work over at my usual place when I saw you were over in *your* usual place."

She turned around and saw his books and things on one of the tables behind her. "So that's where you sit and spy on me."

"Yes, it is," he said unapologetically. "What're you working on?"

"Oh, this is just an essay for Comparative Religion."

He looked on the screen of her laptop and saw the title of the paper:

Wallis' Cognitive Restructuring Theory:
Summary and Evaluation
by Sherry Martin
Dr. Forsythe: Anthro 651

"Oh, cool! I know this article by Wallis! Can I read your paper?"

She was startled by his request, but didn't know how to refuse. "Well, it's not original or anything. . . ."

"Yeah, I know. I'll proofread it for you!"

"Well, I guess." He pulled up a chair and sat close to her. Sherry was nervous about having him this close, let alone looking at her work. She felt herself breaking out in a sweat.

He didn't try to chat or carry on with her at all, but turned right to the paper, reading out loud.

Dr. Wallis has written an essay about what he calls "cognitive restructuring." He claims that the underlying purpose for rituals and sacred space in world religions is to alter the thinking of the participants. Put differently, the goal of ritualism, according to Wallis, is the restructuring of people's mental outlook through the use of stimuli and suggestion. He calls this new way of thinking the "new cognitive synthesis."

"Well said!" He turned and smiled close to her face. "That's a good businesslike introduction, no wasted words, and a clear forecast of what he's going to cover."

"Thanks," she spoke meekly with a smile. She had never experienced someone she was attracted to looking at her work—especially with her sitting there! It suddenly struck her as strange that none of her boyfriends had ever shown any interest in her work.

Jack read on.

There are five steps involved in the process of cognitive restructuring according to Wallis:
1. First comes the step called "Prelearning." Before the religious system or leader can guide the worshiper into an altered consciousness, there must be advance teaching.[5] This teaching manages expectations while it prompts the worshiper for the desired effect, no doubt creating a form of subconscious pressure.

"Oh, well, I thought you said this paper wasn't original."

"It's not!"

"The point about prelearning is Wallis', but I don't remember him talking about creating subconscious pressure. That part must be yours."

"Well, I suppose it is. You remember the article that well, huh?" she asked with real surprise.

"Oh, yeah, I know this article pretty well. Forsythe had me read it several years ago, and we've come back to it since. He's my advisor you know."

"Oh." He had a fresh clean smell that made Sherry feel like burying her face in his hair. *Mmmm. He's something!* she thought.

Jack was reading again.

2. Next comes a very interesting stage called "Separation." The ritualist separates himself from normal "profane" living by one or more means of separation. According to Wallis, these means include "deprivation of sensory contact . . . through such devices as physical isolation, darkness, distracting noise . . . the use of drugs . . . the imposition of extreme physical stress . . . which restricts attention . . . by the presentation of monotonous and repetitive stimuli . . . which produce a trance."

Jack chuckled. "So what do you think about that point?"

"Oh! I think it's so true I can't stand it! I've seen this kind of stuff in Brazil, on film, the ceremonies of the American Indians, those African tribal rituals, even in my own visits to Christian churches—it's everywhere!"

"Yeah, you said it. Wallis is putting his finger on something here, isn't he? I really believe this is why these groups want repetitive chanting and singing. They want to achieve separation—an altered consciousness."

"I suppose," she chuckled. "It's like they have to take leave of their senses before they can enter the religious state! But you guys aren't like that. Your group seems to just get into things in your natural state. Your language and everything is so normal."

"Yeah, we don't believe in doing this stuff." He began to read again.

It is important to see Wallis is not suggesting that the worshiper is necessarily unconscious, as he explains, "The degree of separation of attention achieved by these methods can vary greatly—from . . . simple withdrawal to a quiet, 'sacred' place to the profoundly dissociative effect of drugs, complete sensory deprivation, extreme stress, or prolonged drumming."[6]

3. Wallis calls the third stage "Suggestion." Having reached an altered (dissociated) state, "the cognitive materials relevant to resynthesis can be readily recombined under the influence of direct suggestion."

"Boy, that's a mouthful, isn't it?" he laughed.

She nodded, grinning, and looked back at the screen as Jack read.

This suggestion can originate either from prelearning, or from a religious functionary, or guide, who is present for the occasion. For instance, in the case of Plains Indian vision-quests, the young men know they are expected to stay on the quest until they meet an animal spirit-guide.

"Wow, again, well said! You've done a great job of summarizing this stuff, Sherry! That section was really difficult, and you've just condensed it here without losing what he's saying at all. I'm impressed!"

She elbowed him as she smiled. "You're embarrassing me!" But she really loved it. *It's strange—he appreciates my mind, not just my looks.* He was reading again.

If neither pre-learning nor a guide is present, there can be a "spontaneous sorting out of dissociated elements." There may be a temporary, or even a permanent change in mood, or other personality traits (as in possession phenomena, or ritual ecstasies).

"Have you ever seen this stuff?" he asked.

"Oh, yeah, that writhing on the ground, the dancing around, the tears."

"Yeah, me too. You can tell Wallis is on to something." He kept going.

4. Next comes "Execution." After the achievement of resynthesis, "the ritual subject will be expected, sooner or later, to act in accordance with the new cognitive structure." The ritualism is intended to change behavior in a lasting way.

5. Finally there is the phase called "Maintenance." Wallis says, in cases of ritual possession, it becomes easier to attain an altered state after once having the experience. In some instances, the maintenance "depends on post-hypnotic suggestion." In cases where the religious leaders seek lasting change, it is necessary "either to renew, periodically, the ritual itself, or to provide the subject with tangible cues from the ritual experience which will serve to maintain the new structure . . . such as amulets, talismans, and medicine bundles . . . special ornaments and uniforms, and by public symbols (such as the cross)."[7]

"He really lumps Christianity right in there with all the others, doesn't he?" Jack observed.

Sherry nodded, wondering if that offended Jack.

"Well, I guess from what I've seen, a lot of Christians deserve it, but not always," he said, looking around and facing her.

"Oh, yeah, like I said, you guys didn't seem like this at all."

"I'm glad you noticed that," he smiled.

Boy, he was good-looking! That smile was intoxicating. She was so excited that he seemed to like her paper. Most conversations with guys on campus had to be either pseudo-conversations made up of meaningless banter, or a discussion of sports!

He read further.

We see that, according to Wallis, sacred space plays an important role in facilitating the process of separation (or dissociation). The temple, shrine, church, or mosque is set up in such a way that creates a sense of "differentness" which leads to a feeling of altered consciousness. A dark atmosphere is preferred, and there must be clear distinctions in architecture.

"You're going beyond Wallis again."

"Well, yes. I figured this must be the reason for the sense I had at churches I've visited. I've wondered why they insist on differentness in all areas. You know, like, why don't they want to be the same as the rest of life in our culture?"

He nodded with understanding.

She went on. "Now the Monday evening Bible study seems just like any normal gathering of people, even though you guys do focus on God and the Bible. And I have to tell you, I can't see anything wrong with that, in fact I thought it was a lot better than the other."

"So do we." He continued.

This sense of separation is further enhanced by other elements common to ritualism such as incense, unusual clerical robes, monotonous bodily gestures, and the almost universal use of highly repetitive sayings, songs, or chanting.

Finally, sacred objects and magic play an important role, according to Wallis, in the maintenance of the new mental outlook. The worshiper can take symbols of sacredness home to prolong the effects of the experience.

This analysis, which is not flattering to the ritualistic mentality, accounts in a plausible way for many of the features that are so common to religious practice the world over.[8] Altered voices, falling to the ground, the quivering seizure-like movements, rolling of the eyes: these all clearly indicate dissociation. And there can be no doubt the practitioners feel they are being altered in a lasting way from these experiences.

Jack went on to read the conclusion, but Sherry wasn't paying attention anymore. She was watching Jack's strong jaw muscles and sensitive eyes as he read aloud. She couldn't believe how much she wanted him. But at the same time, she knew she had to be careful. This was not an ordinary man.

"Sherry, this is an excellent paper. I'll guarantee you'll get an A for it."

"Thanks," she said.

"Did you like that reading by Wallis?"

"Yes, I thought it was very stimulating." She ran her finger along the edge of the keyboard.

"Here, if you like that reading, I have some stuff you can read that'll go a little further," he said as he pulled her notebook over and scratched something on a paper.

"I don't know whether I'll have time to do much extra reading right now," she warned.

"Why don't you tell Forsythe you want to do your paper on this?"

"Well, that's an idea," she said as she watched him finish writing. Written on the page were the titles of three books or articles with their authors. "Yeah, these sound interesting. You think I should ask him if I can do research on ritualism and formalism, huh?"

"Yeah, sure! He's real interested in that stuff, and he'll let you form your own conclusions, too."

She was putting the paper into her backpack. "I'll give it a try," she said.

"Hey, this was fun!" He turned and faced her. "How would you like to go for a walk?" he asked, leaning on one elbow and facing her. "Unless you have to go somewhere."

"Uh . . . yeah, I guess it's a nice evening out." She smiled and fumbled with the computer while shutting it down, trying not to seem too eager to go. He stood up beside her, and when she had finished turning the machine off and stowing her stuff in her backpack, she stood and put the strap of the pack over her shoulder.

"You might as well leave your stuff over there with mine," Jack suggested. "We'll get Ken to watch everything."

She hadn't noticed Ken reading a couple of chairs over from where Jack was studying. He looked up and smiled as Jack introduced him to Sherry.

As she took the pack off and laid it with his books, Sherry reeled with the feeling she was sliding down a steep mountainside without self-control. So suddenly had this encounter come upon her, she didn't feel prepared. Was it really possible that she was about to have a romantic experience with this man when she knew she needed to be alone right now? She could feel the awesome power her attraction for him seemed to have over her. She had already fallen for him to the point where it felt like she would have to give him anything he asked. *Well, it's too late to worry about it now. I might as well enjoy it,* she conceded. She was only determined that he would have to do the asking. *Heck, you don't even know what Christians do when they date!* she warned herself. *Besides, he might be toying with you. Remember what Lisa said!*

20

Jack came up beside her, and they walked toward the door to the courtyard together. Her head was swimming. Without her books, Sherry wasn't sure what to do with her hands, so she put them into the front pockets of her jeans. As they got outside, she had to stand alone while Jack held the door for another girl. It felt like several spotlights were on her. She was so self-conscious she had no idea what to do or say. She wondered what had happened to her usual confidence in dealing with men.

When Jack walked up and joined her on the front patio, he very deliberately held his arm way out and with a big smile on his face said, "May I?" She took his arm. He stuck the fingers of both his hands into the pockets of his jeans, and they strode out onto the sidewalk leading across the huge green.

Sherry could feel her blood pulsing in her temples. She hoped he couldn't see how flustered she was. He must have read her like a book to have done the thing with his arm. Touching him was exactly what she wanted to do. Yet, he had done it in a way that could be interpreted as either a meaningless, silly thing or an initiation of physical touch. He had broken a barrier without sticking his neck out very far.

As they walked in silence, she decided to just enjoy holding the arm of the guy she hadn't been able to stop thinking about. He was wearing a T-shirt, and she could feel the smoothness and warmth of his well-toned arm. He was more powerful than she had expected. She moved closer, so there was contact between their bodies, and held his arm firmly up against her in a way that let him know the light was green. In the excitement of the moment, Sherry stopped caring about her fears. She was ready to experience something with this interesting and charismatic man. The only thing left to see was how he would manage to take the next step.

They weren't talking, which was a little strange, considering their relationship. It almost seemed like Jack was assuming a level of closeness he had no reason to assume. Yet, he was looking around, taking in the fall evening as though she wasn't there. Sherry was determined not to break the ice—either he would speak or else!

He walked with her for some time before speaking. When he did speak, it was not what she expected. "I don't think the trees are at the peak of color yet, do you?" he asked.

"No. I wouldn't say so," was all she could answer.

"When they get to their peak, I'm going to go for a drive up to this ravine area I know. It's actually sort of a river. There's trout there."

"Oh, is this somewhere close?"

"Yeah, it's less than an hour's drive. You can rent canoes there and stuff."

"Sounds nice." Was he asking her out? There was another silence. She knew she should help him make conversation, but she didn't feel able to. A cat had her tongue. *Boy, I'm having left-brain meltdown! Just relax!*

"What's your favorite season?" He turned and looked her in the eyes for the first time as he asked this.

"I guess summer."

"Why do you like summer?"

She thought for a moment. "I like sitting out with friends and having a beer on a summer evening without feeling cold. I like the smell of life in the air on a warm summer evening."

"'The smell of life . . .' that's good!" he said with a grin.

As they walked on for another minute, Sherry stared entranced at the western sky, now green, fading into a spectacular sapphire color with the first star twinkling. Jack spoke in a warmer tone of voice, looking down at her as he did so. "It helped me to speak when I saw you there the other night."

"I was so impressed by the whole meeting, and your teaching, and the people, and just everything!" she beamed.

"So does that mean you're going to come back?"

"Oh, yeah, without a doubt. I had a great time with Lisa afterward. I really like her!" She was talking more easily now. They went on chatting about Lisa and the women at her house.

As they rounded a corner and took the path to the left, she realized they were heading toward the pond. It was the ultimate spot for romance on campus. *Oh boy! Here we go!* she thought as the pond came into view, with its solitary spout of water shooting up twenty feet or so in the middle. There was a bench by the sidewalk, and Jack stopped and motioned toward it. "Why don't we sit down?"

This was more like the script Sherry was used to. Finally, Jack was acting like a normal man! Her excitement rose as she sat down. But when

Jack sat down, he brought one foot up on the bench so he was facing her a couple of feet away. It looked like he wanted to talk, but he didn't say anything. This wasn't the way the script was supposed to read.

Sherry decided to roll with the situation, and she broke the silence. "Jack, I think I need to tell you something."

"Yes?"

"You know when you prayed the other night, and said the stuff about accepting God and everything?"

"Yeah."

"Well . . . I did it."

His whole face lit up with a smile. "You asked Christ into your heart?"

"Yeah, I guess."

"Oh! Praise God!" He reached over and grasped her shoulder. "You can't imagine how exciting this is for me! This is such an answer to prayer!"

Sherry's eyebrows wrinkled into a quizzical frown. "Prayer? What prayer?"

"Mine, Lisa's . . . all of the brothers at the house . . . I'm sure the girls over at Lisa's . . . everyone!"

That sounded so strange to Sherry. "These are people who don't even know me! You're saying you all sit around and say prayers about me? What are you guys getting from this?" There was an edge of irritation in Sherry's voice.

"Look, you don't understand yet." He raised his hand and gestured with his fingers spread and his palm facing down. "First of all, we don't 'say prayers'. That sounds like some impersonal discipline a bunch of weirdoes sit around and do. We don't 'say prayers,' we pray. That means we're sharing the things we feel deeply about with our Best Friend and Father."

Sherry stared at Jack with a questioning frown still glued to her face before looking down and playing with the long tassel on her belt. She was beginning to see Jack had a knack for phrasing things in a way that gave one a different perspective.

After waiting a couple of seconds for a response (and realizing none was coming), Jack scratched the back of his head before continuing. "You have to look at this from the believing Christian's point of view. I realize you aren't used to looking at things that way yet—you haven't fully realized all of the implications of what you believe yet."

She looked up with one eyebrow lifted. "And you're going to help me out a little bit," she offered, with a note of cynicism.

"Sure, if you'd like." He smiled.

There was another silence. Apparently, Jack wasn't going to say any more unless she asked for it. Sherry was having a hard time feeling she was in control of the conversation. She wasn't sure she liked his patronizing tone, but she really wanted to know what he had to say.

"Yeah, I guess I'd like to hear that." She decided to be nice.

"Okay. You know Christians believe in heaven." She nodded.

"And I'm sure you also realize we believe in hell."

"Uh, yeah . . . but I guess I still have some questions on that . . . but go on."

"Now here we are, a group of Christians sitting around having some fellowship. That's what we call our times of sharing what's happening in our lives and our feelings and spiritual things, stuff like that."

She nodded again, but the frown was still there.

"So one of the sisters, that's what we call the believing girls sometimes, shares that she met this cool girl at the bookstore who's really seeking. At the same meeting, a brother, that's me, says he's been talking to a girl in his seminar, and it turns out it's the *same* girl. They talk about how this girl's definitely not a Christian but seems to be feeling her need for Christ to an amazing extent, and it just *happens* that both of us have come into contact with her, and she comes to Bible study. You get the picture?" He paused, but she looked at him noncommittally. "We're really *excited* by the thought that your heart reached out for God, and He's responding to you, and that we're having the honor of being used by God to carry His message to you!"

"Yeah, I guess I can see that," she sheepishly grinned and looked down, a little embarrassed for some reason.

"Now that's not the end of the story. Remember what we believe. All of us there realize you're at a decision point in your life that could land you in eternal life with us, or could leave you lost and without hope forever. What do you think we should do at that point?"

Sherry felt like she should know the answer, but she didn't. She just stared in a puzzled way.

Jack helped her. "At that point, we pray!"

Her face softened with recognition. She looked down and thought about it. "Because you believe God would make me decide the right thing if you ask Him?"

"No. That's not what I believe. I believe God would reach out to you and give you a strong inner conviction. You know, He would show you your need for Him, and give you a sense in your heart that Christ is the answer. I think you still had to decide what to do, but God was making it possible for you to make the right decision." He paused for a moment. "Don't you think God's been doing things in your life lately to bring you to this point?"

She hesitated. "Yes, I do believe that . . . I think."

"Well, do you see why it's natural and good for us to pray for you as a group? We'd do the same for anyone in your situation. It's the only loving thing to do."

"I guess I understand that. I'm sorry for feeling suspicious."

"You're bound to have a lot of suspicions. You don't know us that well yet, and for that matter, you don't know God that well yet, either."

"I have a question."

"Yeah?"

"When did this prayer thing happen?"

"Last night, the night after the Bible study."

"Well, I'd already done it by then."

"Yes, you're right. But I know Lisa and I had been praying for some time before then. And of course, we didn't know you'd made your decision yet. Lisa had the impression that you hadn't actually decided yet."

She looked down. "I lied to Lisa. I told her I was thinking about it when, really, I'd already done it."

"Well, she won't care. It's not unusual to be shy about spiritual things at first."

"I feel bad about it." She played with the frayed cuff on her jeans.

"I'm telling you, Lisa's going to be so happy to hear about that lie, she won't have a single negative thought."

"I wish you'd let me tell her," Sherry said.

"Sure, fine. My lips are sealed. But I hope you won't wait too long. I don't want to be in the position where I'm having to pretend I don't know something when I do."

"No. I'll call her tonight."

"Oh, this is so great! I couldn't feel more excited than I do right now!" Jack stretched out with his hands behind his head and stared straight up. "I praise God! I just don't know what to say!" Then he got up and stood in front of her.

"I guess I feel pretty excited, too." She got up and stood close to Jack.

He immediately embraced her, but only for a moment. It was more a hug of joy than anything romantic. He put his hand on her back and, guiding her up the walk, said, "Let's go back."

He didn't leave his hand on her, or put his arm around her. He just walked beside her with his hands in his pockets, looking down. Sherry was dejected. Had she done something wrong?

She almost asked Jack whether Christian men got involved in romance, but she stopped at the last moment, remembering she didn't want to be too vulnerable with him. Instead, she decided to ask him about some of the things she had heard at the United Center. "Jack, would you consider yourself a fundamentalist?"

"Heck no. Who laid that on you?"

"Who says anyone did?"

"Come on, you've been talking to someone."

Man, this is weird! she thought to herself. *How does he know that?* "Okay, I went down and talked to this guy, a preacher."

"Who?"

"His name is Reverend Billings."

"Oooooh boy!" Jack rolled his eyes and shook his head as he uttered this groan. "So, how'd you like old Lowellster?" He leaned over and picked up an acorn.

"You know him! Yes, he knew you, too."

"I can't believe he had anything nice to say about me," Jack said with an inquisitive look.

"He said you were a fundamentalist."

"Yeah, that figures." He threw the acorn with a side-arm toss, missing the tree he had aimed at.

"What would you consider a fundamentalist, Jack?"

Jack frowned and seemed to gather his thoughts. "The term 'fundamentalist' comes from a debate in the early part of this century. It technically means someone who believes in the 'fundamentals' of the faith."

"Well, do you?"

"No. I think one in particular is mistaken. They teach that Christians should be separated from the world, which usually means they can't go to movies, bars—you know, anything where people are sinning too much."

"Where do they get that?"

"Oh, there's a passage about being separate from the world, but they're misinterpreting it. It says, 'Come out from among them and be separate.' The statement was from the Old Testament, but in context in the New Testament, it really refers to forming binding relationships with nonChristians . . . like getting married to a nonChristian." He picked up another acorn. "But that's not the real point."

"What is the real point?"

"The real point is that the word 'fundamentalist' is used like the term 'fascist.' It's a pejorative, bigoted label used to put down evangelicals. That's what I am. An evangelical is someone who believes the Bible but doesn't feel the need to be separated from normal society . . . from our own cultural things . . . music, movies, nonChristian social gatherings, parties . . . stuff like that."

"That sounds good to me." Sherry was glad to have a name for what Jack and the others were. "But why does he want to put you down? What is he, anyway?"

Jack exhaled deeply, seeming to gather his thoughts. "Lowell Billings is what I would call a 'naturalistic theologian.' Some people call them liberal theologians, but I don't use that term because it has nothing to do with liberal values like equality, justice, and compassion. It has to do with the fact that they don't believe the supernatural parts of the Bible, they're embarrassed by the supernatural, and yet they work as full-time preachers." He stopped long enough to heave an acorn again. This time he bounced it off the tree he aimed at.

"Oh, I can't believe you said that!" Sherry marveled. "That's just what I was thinking on the way home. They didn't seem to really believe the Bible. Oh, Jack, it was so weird . . ." she trailed off, lost in thought.

"What was weird?" He turned to look at her.

"The way they talked. They used all these terms that were real general, and I had the feeling there was more meaning there than they were saying."

"Like what did they say?"

"Oh, they kept saying 'the community of faith' and 'interpretations of spirituality.'" She grimaced pompously and shook her head as she parodied them.

"Yeah," Jack laughed, "it's called 'inclusive language.' These are code words. They refer to the fact that the group believes in relativism. They think any faith system is just as good as any other. The only thing that matters is that it's real to you, and really, it can't be so-called 'fundamentalism' either, because we're considered too narrow. We won't admit other views are just as true as ours."

"Man! I thought that's what they were saying. They said they were coming from an 'incarnational theology.'"

"Yeah, that's another code word, at least when he uses it. It means they focus on the incarnation of Christ—in other words, the humanity of Christ. In their case, it means they believe Christ was just a man."

"Then why do they call themselves Christians? Why do they pray? Who cares about Christianity if Christ isn't the Son of God?"

"That's the sixty-four-thousand-dollar question. I know there's a religious system in place . . . there's a lot of money involved. I don't know, I guess some of them might be humanistic idealists. I guess I think Lowell might be a convinced New Age-type believer."

"But it sounds like you're very suspicious of him."

"Well, there's no question he will lie at times. Lowell has twisted the truth at several points during the past few years, and he's an unyielding opponent of mine. He fights every effort I make to win others over to the biblical worldview. How did he get to you?"

"I told my mother about the study. She told our minister at home, and I guess he called Reverend Billings with my number. Oh! It was so creepy, Jack! You should've heard this stupid poem thing they did at the end! Boy, it was nauseating!"

Jack shook his head and chuckled again. "Yeah, I hate that kind of churchy stuff. It's strange, even though they reject conservative views of the Bible, they're as conservative as anyone when it comes to worship and ritual. When they get into their ritual thing, it's like the Middle Ages all over!"

"Yeah, they mentioned an all-day liturgy or something."

"Yeah! That's what I mean! It's like the truth basis for Christianity has been cut out, but yet they get into these long ritual things. . . ." Jack seemed to be thinking out loud. "I think they just get some kind of feeling thing, some kind of buzz from it. Well, it's like Wallis says. Dissociation. Right?" He smiled at Sherry. "It has to be something like that when you consider they don't really believe in the historical basis for those rituals."

Sherry thought about it awhile as they walked. "Yeah, it's fascinating to try to imagine going through a twenty-four hour ritual from their perspective. I just can't get into that." A moment later she added, "Speaking of church stuff, my neighbor's warning me about you, too."

"Now what?"

"She's the one I went to church with a while back."

"And she knows me?" He screwed up his face in a frown of surprise.

"No. She seemed to know your group, though. She did mention your name, I guess."

"Why? What did she say?"

"She said going to this group doesn't count because it's not a church . . . and you guys are pretty radical . . . there's too much sin in your group . . . you don't honor the Lord's day . . . and that's about all I can remember offhand."

He rolled his eyes and shook his head. "So this girl must be a regular church-goer."

"Oh, yeah. She's very regular at church."

"So, she's loyal to the institutional church, and . . . she's into honoring the Lord's day, huh?" His furrowed brow suggested he was digesting this.

"Yeah, she said it's in the Bible, you have to go to church on Sunday morning."

"That's nonsense. The Bible mentions the Lord's day, which probably was Sunday in the early church . . . at least in some cities. But there's nothing that says you have to meet then. Also, you don't 'go to church,' you *are* the church."

"Well, she couldn't tell me where it was in the Bible, but she also said you have to belong to a church, and this group is not a church."

"That's nonsense, too! A church is any group of Christians. The church is a spiritual entity—it's those who've been put into the Body of Christ. And I can prove that!" He jabbed at the air with his finger. Jack was agitated now.

Sherry smiled in amusement. She liked watching Jack get angry. "She couldn't tell me where it said that, either, but she said her pastor could."

"Well, she doesn't know what she's talking about. In the times of the early church, there were lots of house churches just like ours, and there's no distinction. We're a church just as much as any other group is! What church is this she goes to, anyway?"

"Uh . . . Edgewood Bible Church."

"Oh, yeah, you told me that. Man . . ." his brow was deeply furrowed, "it really bothers me that they're putting us down. We're both on the same side of the river. This is entirely different than Billings. He's not even one of us."

"But these people are?"

"Well, yeah. They believe in Christ and the Bible. They're probably different in the way they approach things, but so is Lee Carulo at New Life, and we get along great."

"Who is he?"

"Lee's a Christian leader, a pastor here in town. He really knows his Bible, and he's sort of been a coach and teacher for me over the past few years. His church is basically traditional, you know, compared to ours, but he isn't hung up on that. He realizes one approach is good for his people, and another is good for ours. In fact, he encourages us to stick with a more underground approach."

"He sounds cool."

"Yeah, we're really close, and our guys meet with his guys once a month for prayer. We go over there sometimes on Wednesday nights to hear his Bible teaching, too. He's really deep."

"Well, I was just thinking the other night, I don't know why everyone's so eager to warn me about your group," she shrugged. "They never cared when I got into things a lot worse than anything you guys are doing."

"Yeah," he chuckled. "Well like I say, Billings is an enemy. I know he hates us. But this other outfit, I don't know what their thing is. It sounds like they're into formalism, doesn't it?"

She thought for a second. "Wow. I hadn't put that together."

"Well, they're hitting you up about outward forms, the Lord's day, formal church membership, and all that kind of stuff."

"Yeah, you're right. They really are into rituals, too. That's what bothered me about going there. It just wasn't for me."

"I hope I get a chance to talk to this neighbor of yours. She sounds confused."

"Well, I asked her to come to a Monday night meeting, and she said she might."

"Good! I don't want all this controversy to spoil the joy I'm feeling about this huge decision you made the other night." He smiled and put his hand on her back, but only for a moment. "I just feel like God's been working so miraculously in your life, and this may seem farfetched, but I think the Evil One is interested in derailing you."

Sherry was also impressed by what appeared to be the hand of God in her life, but she was still struggling with ideas like the existence of Satan. She realized someone like Jack must believe in the Devil. The idea that the Devil was real, let alone that he might be involved in her life, was new. She decided to think more about that concept later.

As they walked along, she had a strong desire to discuss their relationship. She was dying to find out what he thought about it, what he felt about it. She looked up at him, but he was looking straight ahead. She decided it wasn't safe to bring it up.

As they entered the well-lit library again, Sherry rubbed her eyes adjusting to the different environment. Jack asked if he could get a copy of her paper for Dr. Forsythe on disk to keep in his research directory. "Frankly, it's a lot better than the one I wrote on that article," he smiled.

"Sure," she shrugged modestly.

"So what are you going to be doing tonight?" he asked as they came up to their table.

"Well, I guess I was thinking of going over to see some friends at the dorm I used to live in, but I don't know. I guess I'm not sure what I want to do." She felt sure he was going to ask her out, and she wanted to make it clear the night was free.

"Yeah, I have to be at work in a few minutes," he murmured as he helped her get her laptop out of the pack.

That news hit her like a blow to the face. "Where do you work?" she asked, being careful not to show her disappointment. She booted up her computer and focused her attention on copying the paper.

"I work up at the university computer center."

"Oh, what do you do there?"

"I'm basically on call to help students with the rental systems. It's mostly a case of freshmen who don't know what a computer is—there're so many yahoos at this university it isn't even funny."

"Is it a good job?" she asked as she finished copying the paper and snapped the disk out.

"Well, the pay's poor, but the hours have been pretty flexible, and I get to meet a lot of people there."

She finished packing her things into her backpack. Jack had packed up as well, and they walked out of the library without saying much. Sherry couldn't believe it was going to end this way. Frustration was welling up inside her as she realized they were going to part ways without coming to grips with what she felt sure was there between them. Was it possible she was imagining it? All of her experience told her she wasn't.

When they got to the green, Sherry announced her place was on the left, which she knew was away from the computer center. They stopped and faced each other. A look of intensity came over Jack's face, clearly visible in the light from the post-lamps on the green. "Sherry, I . . ." he moved toward her until they were almost touching, then hesitated, visibly struggling with himself.

This was it! Sherry turned her face up with wide, beckoning eyes, her lips slightly parted. "Yes?"

There was a silence that lasted for what seemed like a long time, and he seemed to move even closer. No more than inches separated them now. "I really enjoyed talking with you this evening."

She could smell his cologne. "Me, too. I feel like you've really helped me . . ." but she left the statement hanging, beckoning. She wanted to reach up and kiss him, but she steeled herself, determined not to risk too much.

Jack looked down at the ground. "Yeah . . . well, I really have to go. I guess I'll see you later." He reached up and gave her arm a squeeze and grinned in a friendly way before turning and quickly striding away.

Sherry was shell shocked as she watched him go. She stood still, half-expecting him to turn back and run to her, but he disappeared around the corner of the library. *You've got to be kidding!* she thought, seething with frustration. She viciously kicked a pop can by the side of the walk as she stormed home. She had never had an experience like it before. In her mind, they had passed the point of no return—a man had *never* come that close, seen and heard that "yes" from her, and turned away!

Where did I go wrong? Is there something wrong with me? There was no way it could be her! Her ability to attract men was undiminished, and she had thrown every look and nuance she knew at him. *This is some kind of Christian thing! Either that, or Jack's weird. . . . Maybe he's gay!* The thought struck her with terror. She remembered what Lisa had said about his not really being interested in women. *What have I gotten myself into here?*

A sense of fear and panic filled the pit of Sherry's stomach as she realized she was in uncharted waters. Somehow she doubted Jack was gay. He certainly was attracted to her on some level. Besides, if he was gay, wouldn't Lisa know it, or at least suspect it?

She opened the door to her building and walked gloomily up to her apartment. *There's something here I don't understand. I'm sure he desired me, but he turned away by force of will. Something prevented him from doing what he wanted to do.* When she got into her apartment, she threw her bag on the couch and headed for the kitchen, deep in thought. Either he was having some conflict with himself—the gay idea fit well here—or there was something or someone else preventing him. *He couldn't be married! This has to be some sort of Christian thing! Maybe he's taken a vow like a priest?* Sherry shivered with worry as she realized she had let herself get too emotionally involved with this man, even though they had never even talked about their feelings for each other.

She made a sandwich for dinner in a state of mind that was agitated and restless. She thought of going over to the dorm to see Jean and the others, but hesitated. *I know I'd really tie one on if I went over there*, she warned herself. Increasingly, she was feeling a dreadful sense of failure and hurt mixed with confusion. She sat holding a cup of tea and leaned her forehead on her other hand. Her tender feelings and her desire for Jack were increasingly mixed with reproaches toward herself for being foolish enough to fall for him in her mind without knowing more about him.

Each time she tried to do some reading her mind was distracted, and she would get up again and walk. Eventually, she accepted the fact that she was too distracted and upset to study. She poured a strong drink and walked back and forth between her desk and the window.

Standing before the window, she realized where her answers lay. Something inside her reminded her she was involved somehow with God. After a moment's hesitation, she turned to God in prayer.

God, please help me. I don't want to be hurt. Is there something about me that means I should stay away from this guy? What do You want me to do with him? I don't feel like I can make some kind of celibacy vow! I hope You see how much I feel like I need to be loved. I hope You can understand my loneliness.

She thought for a minute before turning back to God with a little anger. *I met this guy while I was looking for You . . . and he's supposed to be one of Yours!* She thought again, fingering the rim of her glass. *God, this is the first time I've come to You asking for help since I invited You into my life. I felt so sure You've been working in my life lately, but I don't understand what You want from me with Jack. My feelings for him are so strong, I can't get my head together. . . .*

Her prayer trailed off as a sense of resignation came over her. She decided whatever God was doing, there was nothing she could do but surrender to it. *You're my only hope*, she concluded. She didn't feel good, but the sense of surrender seemed to relax some of the tension she had been feeling.

The door buzzer rang.

Sherry almost jumped, she was so startled by the harsh buzz. She went over to the intercom. As she reached up to press the button, she hesitated. *What if it's Jim? What if he found me?* She wasn't expecting anyone. Pressing the button, she asked, "Yes, who's there?"

"Sherry, it's Jack Collins."

21

Sherry's mind reeled as she brought her hand to her face. What did she look like after so much fretting? How could he be here? "Come up, Jack," she said with the button pressed.

"Uh, I wonder if you could come out for a few minutes. . . . It's okay if you're busy, I can come back later or call or something." She could feel his awkwardness over the intercom.

"Jack, are you all right? I thought you were going to work?" She wondered what she was walking into.

"I just got off for a while. I wanted to talk to you."

"Uh . . . I'll be right down, just give me a minute."

"I'll be waiting."

She ran into her bathroom. She was surprised at how good she looked on the outside. She certainly didn't feel that good on the inside. She decided to throw on a little eye makeup. *He must have overcome whatever was holding him back!* she thought. *It's going to happen after all! But why wouldn't he come up? I wonder if this is You answering my prayer, God?* She set her makeup down and gave up any further efforts. Just as she turned to go, she grabbed her bottle of perfume and put on a little bit. *This won't hurt anything,* she thought as she grabbed her keys on the way to the door and ran out.

As she trotted toward the stairs, she reproached herself again. *A minute ago you couldn't believe you'd been so careless as to get involved with this guy. Now you're running to him again! All he has to do is whistle!* She determined to be careful, but she knew she wasn't really in control of the situation.

She slowed down as she hit the landing and approached the glass security door. There he was, sitting on the bench next to the entry patio. She opened the door and came out slowly, with her hands in her pockets. "Wow, Jack, I can't believe you're here. How did you find out where I live?"

"I called Lisa," Jack admitted as he rose from his bench. "I hope you won't be angry at her."

"No." She searched his face for clues about why he had come.

"Listen, Sherry, I can leave if this is inconvenient or unwelcome. . . ." He looked downright scared.

"No! I'm glad you came. I sort of wanted to talk to you a little more." She smiled cautiously.

He motioned toward the bench and they sat down.

"Why are we meeting out here?" she wondered.

"Well, I hope this doesn't sound too weird, but I don't feel like I can go up to a woman's room unless someone else is there." One of her eyebrows shot up in surprise. He tried to answer the question forming on her lips. "I'm a Bible teacher, remember? With all the scandal going on with so-called Christian leaders these days, I feel like I have to be extremely careful. It's not just you—I take this position with women in general."

Sherry thought people ought to be more trusting, but decided not to say anything. They faced each other, each sitting with one leg up on the bench. There was a period of silence as Jack looked up at her and down again, apparently struggling with what to say. Sherry let him struggle—she was determined to let him talk first.

Finally, he spoke: "So you said you wanted to talk to me? How come?"

"I think I'd rather hear your reason first."

"Yeah . . . I guess that's fair." He paused and looked down while breathing out heavily in a sigh. "Sherry, I feel like I have some explaining to do, and I need to apologize."

She raised one eyebrow quizzically.

"I'm just going to come right out and say that I like you . . . uh, a lot, and . . . well, what I mean is, I think you're very attractive. I suppose you've noticed . . ."

"Well, I've sensed feelings coming from you, Jack, but I don't know . . ."

"I know, I've been sending you mixed signals. I've been inconsistent in my actions and words."

She agreed, but she didn't like the way he was agonizing over it. "Well, I don't feel like you've done anything wrong."

"Well, I'm afraid I can't agree on that point. God is convicting me that I've done something wrong."

"What could be wrong? I don't understand."

"Oh, man. I really messed things up." Jack bent over and buried his head in his hands. He looked miserable. Sherry could see he was suffering pitifully. She slid over and put her hand on his back.

He looked up. "Sherry, I have to warn you. You shouldn't get attached to me."

She took her arm off his back. A deadly serious look came over her. *Oh boy, here it comes.*

"You see, Sherry, I'm not like a normal guy." She stared at him as she retreated back to her corner of the bench and waited for the worst. "I treat my friends with integrity. And I want you to be my friend."

"Are you gay, Jack?" she asked in a low, matter-of-fact voice.

"No! No! That's not it."

"Are you married?"

"No! It's nothing like that. I have no secrets. I am what you think I am."

"I thought you were a single grad student Christian guy who seemed to like me."

"That's exactly what I am."

"Then I don't understand." Her spirits were lifting a little.

"You see, I've been a Christian for some time, over six years. And you just became one. In fact, I was letting you know how I felt before you were even a Christian at all."

"So what? If I wasn't a Christian, God wouldn't want you to like me?"

Jack winced. "No. You're looking at it the wrong way. It's a matter of integrity. . . . You see, if we got involved in a relationship, it could either lead to something serious, or just a short romance, right?"

"I suppose . . . you haven't asked me how I feel."

"It doesn't matter how you feel—I mean it matters, but not from the standpoint of what's right or wrong for me." Jack was visibly dying from frustration.

"I'm lost." Sherry flopped her hand on her leg in a gesture of giving up.

"Okay. If something happened, and it led to a more serious relationship, I might not be able to come through with my side of the relationship."

"Why not?"

"Because I have a previous commitment. I'm not free to pick any girl I want and build a relationship or even get married."

"You're not? Because of God?"

"Yes."

"This is some kind of vow you've taken? A vow of celibacy?"

"No. It's integrity. It's just the desire to do the right thing for you. See, my first commitment in life is to God and to His calling for me. If I get deeply involved with someone who doesn't have the same commitment, it is going to lead to trouble. She'd come to resent my values, my way of life, my refusal to devote myself to the same priorities as she has. Whether it's sooner or later, there'd be big problems. We wouldn't have in common the very thing, the very One who's most important in my life."

"Well, I can see where there might be a problem there, but who's to say I have no interest in these values? It sounds like you're already judging me as far as what I'm going to base my values on."

"No. I'm not saying you might not adopt an outlook just like mine. I'm just saying I should have found out whether that's going to happen *before* I involve you in an emotional relationship that might hurt you if you choose a certain way. Don't you see? I'm just saying I should've made sure how you view these things *before* I let you know I cared . . . you know, romantically. Otherwise, I'm going to be in the position down the road of telling you, 'Either adopt my worldview, or I'll have to hurt you.'"

Sherry stared intently at him for a number of seconds, turning his words over in her mind, feeling frustrated—there was something wrong with what he was saying, she was sure of that. "Well, I did say that prayer to Jesus the other night, and it wasn't because of you. I feel like you're doubting my sincerity."

"I'm not questioning your sincerity. I know you prayed from the heart, and I really believe you. But there's more, Sherry. A lot of authentic Christians follow Christ to one extent or another, without ever coming to the point where they're willing to make the kind of commitment I have."

"What is this commitment?"

"Well, I've revoked all claim on the direction of my life. I've waived all privileges, all my rights, in order to have my life count for Christ in the greatest possible way. It could take months before you'll even understand what's involved in this kind of decision." Jack grimaced as he realized how arrogant his statement sounded.

"Well, I knew you were deeply involved in religion, Jack, and I feel like I have to take my own chances."

Jack's expression became tense as he struggled to explain himself. It was clear he hadn't done the job so far. "I don't feel like I can encourage you to feel affection for me when I realize I may have to reserve the right to get out under certain conditions."

"But you . . . if. . . ." Sherry shook her head, sorting out her words. "That's dating! You're saying you can't date unless you know you'll get married!" she pleaded with urgent frustration.

Jack had to stop. He was looking intently at her, but now slowly looked off into space. She could see from his face that what she said must have sounded plausible. He was visibly confused. Then he seemed to realize the answer as he set his jaw. "No. It's not that we have to know the relationship *will* result in marriage, but we should know that it *could*.

Otherwise we're making false promises by implication."

Now Sherry was thoughtful. This was really something different. After a minute she said, "I feel like you're asking me to make this decision about some commitment right now."

"No!" Jack was agitated. "That's exactly what I want to avoid!" He held his hand out as though fending off something unpleasant. "I don't want you to feel like I'm pressuring you to make some decision. In fact, I think you should decide right now you won't decide anything for at least a month."

"And you're not going to see me or talk to me anymore?" She couldn't believe this was happening.

"I don't know. I think it would be best for you . . . if we plan on not relating much." He hung his head down again.

"I don't see how you get that. You can't help what you feel, neither can I."

He looked up suddenly. He had correctly understood the meaning of the last phrase, and was clearly affected by her admission that she wanted him. With a deep, determined frown, he said, "I can't help what I feel, but I can help what I do."

"So you don't want to see me or talk to me?" There was a sad protest in her voice.

He looked terribly torn. "I'm not saying that I don't *want* to see you, I just think it would be better if you grew for a while without me there to confuse the picture."

"That sounds like maybe later you might want to try dating."

"I can't say that. It might have the effect of making you wait. You need to feel free from interference at this time in your life."

"So, in other words, you can't say it, but you *do* feel it."

"You're trying to make me say something I don't think I should say."

There was a lengthy period of silence. At first Jack continued to look down, but then he raised his eyes and met hers. They stared directly into each other's eyes. Hers reflected frustration and confusion. His were full of sorrow, but also of longing. Each of them could feel the desire of the other as their eyes said more than their words ever could.

"I feel like it's going to be hard for you to ever trust me," he said, looking back down.

She had to think about that one. "Well, I don't know. I guess if you're telling the whole story . . . this might be the first time I've ever experienced a man turning away from me for *my* good. Most guys save this discussion until after they've already gotten what they wanted."

"I'm not going to use you like that, Sherry. But I hope you realize I have weaknesses like anyone else. I'm telling you what I think's right, and what I think I should do, but I feel like doing the opposite. Still, in a way, I feel like what I'm doing here has a selfish aspect also."

"How's that?"

"Well, I know if I don't get in there and mess up your relationship with God, it'll give me the best chance of having a better relationship with you later. . . ." He shrugged his shoulders. "You know, whether we're dating or not."

There was another silence. Sherry suspected she had just received a veiled message. Seconds ticked by in silence as she tried to think of a way around this barrier. She finally said, "I'm so far outside of anything I've ever experienced before, I can't form any conclusions, Jack. I just don't know what to say. I guess I want to believe what you're saying, and I don't have any reason not to believe it . . . other than the fact that it's unlike anything a man's ever said to me before. I don't like it . . . on the emotional level. It seems very *unnatural*." She sat for a moment shaking her head reflectively. "I don't know. On one level, I can see from your viewpoint . . . and it looks like you're treating me really good, and I should say thank you . . . but frankly, I don't feel very thankful."

Jack smiled and nodded in agreement. "I don't think you have anything to thank me for at all. I've put you in a bad position. . . . I have a suggestion."

"I'm listening."

"Why don't you call Lisa and spill this whole thing to her? I really trust her judgment and wisdom, and I think she'll be able to explain things from the female point of view."

"Is this something you guys agreed on at the prayer meeting also?"

"Hey, I haven't said anything to her about it. I don't think she knows anything."

This was certainly a strange request! "Well, you've suggested something else no guy's ever said. You're a little strange, mister!"

"Sorry," he shrugged, smiling—a beautiful, handsome smile.

"Actually, I was planning to call her tonight anyway."

Jack stood up, and Sherry followed suit. This was going to be weird for sure! "Sherry, I want to continue to have a good friendship with you as your brother in Christ," Jack said with real feeling. "You're really important to me as a person."

She realized he was trying to say something nice, but she didn't feel appreciative. "Yuck! I already have a brother, thanks."

Jack hung his head in a way that showed he was hurt by her sarcasm.

She decided to try to end on a positive note in case he changed his mind. "Well, I guess you're in charge, Jack. You'll have to say what you feel comfortable with, because I'm not sure the word 'brother' is really an honest description of what you feel for me, or me for you."

"You might be right on one level, but . . . well, let me think and pray about this. I'll be seeing you soon, and maybe if something more comes to me, I'll let you know about it."

"Yeah, that sounds good to me, I guess," she answered with a clear note of disappointed resignation.

"I'm sorry I've complicated our relationship. I'll have to see you later, Sherry. I have to get back to work."

"Bye."

He turned and trotted off into the dark.

Sherry was alone.

22

As Sherry sat in her chair by the window she felt tremendous depression. *I knew it was religious!* she thought with disgust. It was no more than a couple of minutes before she picked up the phone and called Lisa. She began by setting the record straight about the fact that she had indeed received Christ at the Bible study. There was a lengthy period of excited rejoicing from Lisa, who, as Jack had predicted, wouldn't even listen to her apology for lying.

After they had talked for some time Sherry began to describe what had happened that night. Lisa marveled as she realized how deeply Jack must have been involved emotionally to say what he did.

"I just feel like he doesn't really believe in my sincerity," Sherry complained. "He acts like being attracted to me is some kind of sin."

"I can understand what he's saying," Lisa said. "I think he was out of line, not because he feels attracted to you, but because he showed you how he felt at a time when you were making big decisions. Your decisions should've been made without confusion from him. It would've been more loving to wait a while. I remember you told me you worried that you might be reacting to him romantically to some extent."

Sherry remembered fretting over that possibility while talking with Lisa. "Well, even if I was, there's nothing he can do about it. Whatever he feels, he feels, and whatever I feel, I feel. I just don't see why he thinks it's up to him to control the whole thing." She was walking around her living room with the base of the princess phone in one hand and the receiver in the other, gesturing with the phone as she spoke.

"He could be viewed as sort of leading you on if he makes eyes at you and stuff without telling you where he's at in his life."

Sherry thought for a moment. "So? Now he's told me." She shrugged.

"How do you feel about getting involved with someone who has that kind of prior commitment? Do you realize the woman who marries Jack won't be the most important person in his life?"

There was a pause. "Mmm. I'm not sure how I feel about that. Well, anyway, he might not be the most important thing in my life either!"

"Yeah, that's a good point," Lisa admitted. "And I'm not saying he would be. I'm just saying you really need to think about what your life priorities are, and whether you're willing to take a chance with someone who may not deliver what a lot of women want from a man . . . you know, this kind of guy is an idealist. He might not be around sometimes. He might not buy his wife a good house."

Sherry hadn't been thinking that far ahead. She went over and sat in her chair. "It seems like we jumped to the altar awful quick. I was just thinking about dating."

"I know, but I think you can see there's a lot to think about with this kind of guy."

Sherry looked out the window, momentarily carried away by a memory from earlier that evening. "Lisa, what would your reaction be to Jack's commitment level if you were in my shoes?"

"You mean if I had just become a Christian?"

"No, I mean as you are today, what if Jack showed up interested in you, and he warned you he had this big commitment thing?"

"Oh . . . well, frankly, I wouldn't be willing to get serious with anyone who *didn't* have that commitment. You see, I'm just like Jack."

"You've done this thing where you waive all your rights and stuff?"

"Absolutely. And, like Jack, I wouldn't be willing to get serious with anyone unless he could convince me that he felt the same way. It's just something I'm not willing to compromise on."

"Why? Why couldn't you have your commitment level, and your guy have his?"

"Because, for one thing, I wouldn't trust a man who wasn't completely sold on Christ. The only reason a Christian would refuse to sell out totally to God, assuming he's been growing for a while, would be that he was selfishly holding back for personal advantage. I think you either base a marriage on God, or you base it on the desires of each spouse to get the best advantage for self. That's why I want a man who's into self-denial for the sake of Christ. If two people come together under the leadership of Christ, they have the makings of a successful marriage. Otherwise, they're playing roulette with their lives."

This was something new. Sherry felt drawn to Lisa's words, but she knew she needed more time to think about them. "I guess if you were both under God, it might be pretty cool. Maybe that's the answer to my fears about men."

"I really think it is. I don't believe any man can be trusted unless he's surrendered his life to God completely. You know, even if an uncommitted guy was really sacrificial and sweet, it could all change tomorrow if the underlying basis isn't there. The only time nonChristian men seem to remain consistently sacrificial in relationships is when they're really dependent on their women, and I find that kind of guy suffocating."

"Oh, man, you said it! I want a guy who can carry himself, but decides to be committed to me—not because he has to, but because he wants to. I'm sick of guys clinging to me like helpless leeches!"

"That's because they worship and serve you instead of God. A guy like Jack isn't ever going to be that way, but I think that's good."

"It's sounding a little better, the more we talk about it." She watched her finger as it twirled in the coiled wire of the phone.

"Well, I've made my decision, and you'll have to make yours."

"I have to tell you, Lisa, I respect you when you say that. I guess it just sounds so much like you. You always seem consistent. You have so much integrity." Sherry's eyes widened as she realized she'd just used the same word Jack used earlier.

Like clockwork, Lisa answered, "So does Jack. That's the kind of guy he is. You really should respect this stand he's taken, too."

Sherry smiled and shook her head. This was just too weird. "Are there a lot of guys in the group who are like this?"

"Well, there are a few. Our group's young, and a lot of these people are relatively new Christians. I don't know how many of the guys there really understand why they should sell out completely to Christ. I know Ken has. Do you want my advice, Sherry?"

"Yes, I do."

"Just wait. You need to grow in the Lord right now, and you need to make your own decisions. If Jack's the guy God has in mind for you, he won't go anywhere. I sort of imagine he might weaken on this stand anyway. But I don't think you should try to make him weaken. Instead, focus on the same thing all of us single women need to focus on."

"Which is?"

"Which is becoming the kind of woman who is spiritually ready to go places romantically without losing her way; the kind of woman a really spiritual man would be interested in; developing her own convictions; getting to where she's not some guy's spiritual baby-sitting project."

There was a period of silence as Sherry pondered the challenge, and Lisa was content to let her think. Finally, Sherry responded. "Yeah, well, I guess I do want to get my own spiritual thing together, and I sure don't plan on being anyone's baby-sitting project."

"Then you're way ahead of a lot of Christian women. I'm afraid there are too many of us who are looking for a man to depend on. But the kind of decision I'm talking about takes investment and determination."

"What kind of investment?"

"Well, for instance, time. You could come to our study group."

"You didn't tell me there was such a thing."

"I didn't know you were a Christian until just now!" Lisa chuckled. "We usually don't invite someone to the group until they've been coming for weeks or even months, because it's not that good for new people."

"Well, what is it?"

"It's a group of women who get together on Friday nights to spend some time studying and getting to know each other. We go through books of the Bible or topics, and one of us will prepare the study, and we all discuss it."

"That doesn't sound too bad. I like reading and discussing things. But I don't know what sort of commitment I'm ready to make. I'm just getting into this."

"Yeah, well, it's not any big deal. It's just that we don't want people coming there who're still at the curious stage, you know, because we want to be able to have some pretty frank discussions without worrying about what this new person's going to think, especially if she's a nonChristian."

"Yeah, I guess that sounds reasonable. It sounds like something I might be into."

"Well, if you'd like to come and check it out, we're going to start a study of the book of Acts, which is right after John. If you decide you don't like it, no one'll mind if you drop out."

Sherry pondered again for a bit. She was cooling down as she talked to Lisa. There was something so level-headed about her. Finally she said, "I like the idea of getting my mind off Jack and focusing on moving ahead, and this sounds like a positive challenge. Count me in!"

Sherry knew she could switch with one of the other waitresses to work Saturday. By the time they hung up, she had a whole new outlook. Instead of being focused on what she didn't have, she was getting excited about her possibilities with the women at Lisa's place. As she wandered toward the kitchen, she saw there was hope for her life if she hung around with people like Lisa. Turning to God in her heart, she said, *Thank You, God, for answering my prayer. I sense You're with me in a big way. This is just too incredible to believe! I'm going to trust You with my life, and this whole area with men.*

She dumped the rest of her drink down the drain, realizing God could provide *real* security in her life.

23

In the weeks that followed, Sherry began to feel a great desire and need to grow spiritually, as Lisa had. As she started attending the women's study group on Friday nights she quickly found a strong sense of belonging. She enjoyed studying the Bible and having serious discussions with the women in the group more than anything she had done for a long time. Before long she found herself eagerly anticipating Friday nights. Their times of prayer were increasingly important in Sherry's mind also. She was growing in the conviction that God was answering her prayers. The Friday and Monday night studies soon became the high points of her week.

Although she didn't realize it, the others in the group already viewed her as the most exciting new member to appear for some time. They could see Sherry had unusual communication and learning skills and she was honest. She would never tell them something because they wanted to hear it, and she would plainly declare any problem she had with something they said. Yet she didn't seem petty, and was satisfied with answers when they were good. Her strong academic background enabled her to move quickly ahead in her ability to understand complicated issues, and analyze sections of Scripture. The women were all more interested in study and growth as a result of her probing questions and eager attitude. Sherry wasn't reluctant to join in during prayer, and she seemed to be developing a sincere love for God.

It took several weeks, but with regular invitations and a little pressure, Becka finally agreed to come to the Monday night Bible study at Jack's house. There were more people there than usual, including a surprise guest, Jean Tamerelli, Sherry's unhappy friend from the dorm.

Right after discovering the group, Sherry had described it to Jean, who seemed interested. Sherry had given her directions to the meeting, but she never appeared. She assumed Jean must have only acted interested out of politeness. But now she showed up carrying a funny little white Bible with a zipper, no doubt from earlier days in Sunday school. Sherry introduced her two guests to each other and to some of the others

there, including Lisa, whom Becka recognized from the Christian bookstore.

Jack taught on John 7, and his coverage of the four verdicts people
reached about Christ stirred and inspired Sherry. Several times she
glanced subtly over at Becka and Jean, both of whom were paying rapt
attention. Sherry felt a pang in her heart as she watched Jack and remembered the evening at the library. *Why can't we be together?* she lamented
as his joyous, life-loving smile seemed to spread to everyone in the room
by contagion. She mentally shook her head and refocused her attention
as his teaching came to an end. She had already agreed with God she
wouldn't question His wisdom on this issue.

During the sharing, one guy challenged Jack's conclusion that Jesus
was either Lord, liar, or lunatic. Jack knowledgeably answered the questioner's eastern mystical objections with his well-read understanding of
eastern religion. Yet at the same time, he was able to make the questioner
feel respected, by acknowledging it was a good question.

The time of prayer was the best Sherry had experienced during the
weeks she had attended. Many people prayed, and the atmosphere of
excitement was contagious as young Christians spoke their faith and love
to God. Sherry wanted to pray, too, but she was too inhibited to say anything in front of this group yet. She decided enough people had prayed
for that week anyhow, and maybe she would pray next time.

As they stood around afterward, Sherry grimaced when she saw a guy
named Warren walk up to Lisa and Becka. Sherry didn't like talking to
Warren because he stood too close to her and seemed to boast all the
time. He was tall and relatively good-looking, with curly brown hair, but
something about him bothered her. She knew he was trying to impress
her, but she wasn't interested. She was also vaguely aware that there was
some sort of tension between Warren and Jack, or was it between Warren
and Lisa? Before she had the chance to reflect on it, Jean got up and
Sherry's attention turned to her. She looked up at Sherry with a wide grin
on her pretty face. "So this is what's been changing you so much," she
declared excitedly to Sherry.

"I'm not aware that I have changed so much," Sherry smiled in
embarrassment.

"Oh, yes, you have!" Jean always stood closer when she spoke to
friends than Sherry usually did, and often she would even touch the other
person, like now. She put her fingers on Sherry's forearm every few
words. "We've all noticed it. You've been walking around . . . it seems like
you have a grin on the inside—like you know some great thing no one

else knows."

Sherry chuckled. "Well, that's an interesting way of putting it. I guess I can't deny I've been pretty excited about this. What did you think?"

"I've never heard anything like it," she shrugged in amazement. "In my church they read the Bible, but for some reason it never seemed to have much to do with me. Tonight, I felt like God was talking to me." She thumped her chest with her fingertips.

"What was He saying?"

Jean hesitated, looking down as she pondered. Then, looking back up again, "He was asking whether I plan to come to Him, I think. I really feel like something's happening! This is a little scary!"

"Do you think you might want to receive Christ?" Sherry asked, trying not to sound demanding.

"I don't know. I've always thought I was a Christian, but I heard him talking about this 'receiving Christ' thing tonight . . . and I don't know whether I've ever done that or not." She looked down at her little Bible, fingering the gold letters on the spine.

"Well, I think you'd know if you had. I know I sure hadn't. I mean, I went to church when I was a girl, but then when I heard the teaching of Christ here, and I was reading it too, well . . . this one night Jack said if you wanted to receive Christ to pray along with him, you know?"

"Yeah. . . ."

"And I did it. That's all. I just decided right there on the couch I was going to do it, and I did it."

"What did you do?"

"I just asked Jesus to come into my heart . . . to forgive my sins . . . I don't know, just sort of like he was saying tonight." She gestured toward the stool where Jack had been teaching.

"It sounds too easy! What about confessions? What about the priest?"

"I just don't believe in that stuff. I don't think that stuff's even in the Bible!"

"It's not?" Jean looked up in apparent amazement.

"No! From what I can tell so far, those religious things, those rituals and things like that, the priests, and cardinals—all that stuff came later. Around here, they just go with what's in the Bible, because they figure that's the part God gave. The rest is manmade."

"So you don't believe you have to go to church or to the priest?"

"Do you?"

Jean thought for a second. "No. I guess I've considered most of that to be nonsense since I was a girl."

"Yeah, I know. But I'll tell you what. This is real! I know I have God in my life now, and I didn't earlier. It's for real, Jean!" Sherry was speaking with real intensity now.

Jean stared Sherry in the eyes for a moment with a funny look on her face. "I want it," she announced. "I know you have something, and I want it."

Sherry realized she should do something at this point, but she didn't know what. She decided to get help. "Jean, let's talk to Lisa about it. She'll know what you should do."

"Okay." Jean seemed ready to do whatever she had to.

Sherry stepped over and interrupted Becka, Warren, and Lisa with her hand on Lisa's elbow. The expression on her face told Lisa it was important. "Lisa, could we talk to you for a minute? Jean has something we need your advice on."

"Sure!" She and Becka turned to join in a four-way conversation and Warren excused himself.

"Uh, Jean says she wants to get what I have . . . we've been talking about receiving Christ and stuff," Sherry said with a plea on her face.

Lisa smiled and looked at Jean very naturally. "Oh, that's great, Jean. Do you feel like you understand what it means to receive Christ?"

Jean said she thought she sort of did, but it was clear she wasn't sure. So Lisa launched into a detailed discussion of human sin, the cross, atonement, the resurrection, and personal faith. She covered God's plan of salvation for Jean including numerous illustrations and stories. Jean was all ears, her big, beautiful, dark eyes full of longing, as she stood with her head nodding periodically and the little white Bible clutched to her chest. Watching her, Sherry felt a surge of love for Jean as she realized this was exactly what Jean needed. It felt so good to finally be able to do something for Jean besides commiserate with her during her sad stories.

Finally, Lisa asked Jean if she wanted to put herself under the lordship of Christ, and accept His death on her behalf. She nodded eagerly.

"Would it bother you to pray with us, or would you rather do it alone at home?" she asked.

"I don't mind you guys being there," Jean said with an open, honest face.

"Well, why don't we go to Jack's room and turn to God for an answer to this prayer then?" Lisa suggested.

They all murmured agreement, and Lisa led them back to the entry foyer where Jack was talking with some guys. "Do you mind if we go up to your room for a few minutes, Jack?" she asked.

"No, that's fine! Just don't get into my underwear!" he laughed.

"We just hope it isn't spread all over the room!" Lisa rejoined over her shoulder as she hit the steps.

"No, not this time," he reassured them.

As they went up the stairs, Sherry felt scared, but excited. This was really strange! What were they going to do when they got there? *Lisa must know what she's doing*, she told herself. They turned in at the first room on the right when they reached the landing.

It was a tiny room with a bed, a student-sized desk, and a single chair. Sherry noticed several interesting modern art prints on the wall. Along one whole wall up to a height of six feet were his bookshelves. It was an impressive collection of books, but there was no time to look at them.

Lisa sat on the bed, and patted it, signaling for Jean to sit beside her. Becka sat on the chair, and Sherry sat on the floor next to Jean's feet. "I'm going to pray, and then if you still want to, I'll help you pray to receive Christ, okay, Jean?"

"Yeah." Jean's voice was thin, quiet, and timid. She looked scared now.

Lisa said, "Let's turn to God," and she bowed her head. "Lord, thanks for being here with us. We know You've heard this whole conversation, and You know Jean. We're really happy to come before You to introduce you to a new sister, and enjoy together the fellowship we have in You. This has been a really fun night! Now Jean has something she wants to say to You." She put her hand on Jean's shoulder, and said, "Just tell God what you feel in your own words. There's no certain way you have to speak," and she bowed her head again.

Jean looked down, but she didn't say anything. Sherry was really nervous now. It seemed like something was going wrong. She could sense a struggle on Jean's part. Instinctively, she reached up and put her hand over Jean's knee. Jean immediately put her own hand over Sherry's and squeezed. At that moment, Jean spoke: "Uh . . . God . . ." she fell silent again. Sherry felt her squeeze her hand again. Looking up, she sensed more than saw that Jean was crying. "I feel so lost!" she sobbed. "Please help me! I want to be like these girls . . . who are friends of Yours . . ."

She trailed off again into silence. Lisa whispered. "Tell Him about the part where you want to have Jesus pay for your sin."

"Yes, I want Jesus to pay for my sin. Please come into my heart, God, and let me know that You're there when I pray. Give me this closeness with You that Sherry has." She looked up and smiled through her tears at

Sherry, who met her gaze, and smiled back.

Sherry looked down and began to pray herself. "Lord, thank You for bringing Jean here tonight, and for bringing her to Yourself. We're so excited to have a new fellow-believer here to fellowship with. I just pray that our friendship will be closer than ever now that we both have You in our lives."

After a brief silence, Lisa said a few more words of assurance and thanksgiving before pronouncing an "Amen" that ended the prayer. Immediately, Sherry got up, and Jean stood up and embraced her. They held onto each other, now acutely aware of their new closeness. Tears burst from Sherry's eyes, as she felt a wonderful feeling so deep she couldn't express it. Jean was not the only one to have her life changed that night. Sherry had been used by God to lead a friend to Christ. She would never forget the gratification and joy she felt at that moment.

Jean hugged Lisa and Becka also before filing back downstairs.

When they got downstairs, they all decided to go out for a drink at a hamburger and beer place called The Fireside. Jack and his housemate, Ken, came along with a bunch of regulars.

The Fireside was a very large restaurant, but it was broken up into one main dining area and several narrow vestibules off to the sides which opened into more private cubicles. Heavy wooden beams, low lighting, and candles on the rough-hewn tables created a rugged but comfortable feeling reminiscent of Tudor England. It was a little overpriced for a campus hangout, but everyone liked the dark atmosphere, and the volume level of the music was low enough to allow conversations. It was becoming *the* place to hang out after the Monday night Bible studies.

They spent an enjoyable hour or more, talking to others at their table of eight, and as word spread about her decision, a couple of people came by and introduced themselves to Jean, welcoming her into the family of God. On the way out, Sherry stopped by the women's room. When she came out, she saw Warren talking to Becka again. He peeled off as Sherry approached and went to a booth. Just then, Jean came up and said she needed to go home.

After seeing Jean off in her little car, and promising to call her the next day, Sherry and Becka walked out to their car. Sherry was bursting with happiness. She felt Becka had seen undeniable spiritual reality. The love and zeal demonstrated that night had expressed more clearly than Sherry ever could, just what she felt was missing from the church where Becka had taken her over two months ago. She looked forward to hearing what Becka would have to say.

24

In the car, they talked about Jean's conversion for a couple of minutes, and Becka expressed happiness about being there for it. After several minutes, Sherry asked her how she liked the rest of the meeting. Surprisingly, Becka was a little slow to answer. After a distinct moment of silence, she said, "Well, it was very interesting. I thought the teaching was pretty good."

But Sherry had clearly sensed the reservation in her voice. "It seems like something's bothering you," she observed.

"Well . . . I guess I don't know what to think about a couple of things. But I don't want to be critical."

"What things?"

"Oh, I don't know . . . what do you think about people smoking in there? I mean, one of the smokers was also one of the guys who prayed, I'm pretty sure."

Sherry was perplexed. "I guess I don't understand what you're asking, Becka. I mean, I realize that some people in the group smoke. . . ."

"Well, how do you reconcile that with Christianity? Don't you think God calls us to holiness?"

Again, a fog of confusion was clouding Sherry's mind. This perspective was so alien to anything she had ever considered it sounded like a foreign language. "I . . . I think smoking is bad for your health. I guess they shouldn't smoke if that's what you're asking."

"And then at the restaurant, I saw people drinking beer, too!"

"Oh, yeah, I wondered about that, too, when I first came. But they pointed out there's nothing in the Bible against drinking beer."

Becka was silent for just a moment. "I don't know about that." She sounded skeptical.

"Well, they teach it's a sin to get drunk, but not to have a beer."

"If people see even the leaders drinking beer, who's to say they won't feel free to get drunk?"

Sherry had to think for a moment. "I don't have any trouble understanding the distinction there. There's a clear difference. Besides, if I wanted to get drunk, it wouldn't be because I saw Jack drinking a beer!" she chuckled.

"What about alcoholics? Won't they be caused to stumble?"

"Uh . . . I guess I hadn't considered that. I don't know. . . . I know there are ex-alcoholics in the group. But I haven't heard they have a problem there. I heard the leaders talked to one guy because he was drinking too much."

"I don't see how they can say anything to a heavy drinker, when he's seen them drink."

Sherry flashed impatience as she gestured with her free hand. "You're just thinking in black and white! Drinking a beer and drinking a bottle of whiskey are *not* the same thing. They certainly don't affect you the same way!"

"I wouldn't know." Becka seemed pleased to make the statement.

Sherry was amazed and off balance as she wrestled with a way of thinking that was new to her. She tried again. "Jack said we shouldn't add rules to the Bible. He said we should draw the line between what's sin and what's okay the same place the Bible does."

"Well, it seems too loose to me." Becka settled back in her seat. "Besides, I still don't think this is the same as going to church. You can't just meet in a home like that with no minister, with only your own friends, and think that's enough. What do they do on Sunday morning?"

"I suppose they sleep in," Sherry shrugged. "That's what I do."

Becka shook her head. "I just can't see that. That is dishonoring to the Lord. You should be honoring the Lord's day."

"I still want to know where it says that in the Bible," Sherry had a skeptical edge to her voice.

"Pastor Barclay says he would be happy to talk to you about it." After a moment of thought Becka went on. "And how could a group like this celebrate the Lord's Supper? Who would baptize their babies?"

"Well, we've had communion before in our women's study group. They just passed some bread around and a glass of wine, and we took it, you know, while we prayed."

"With no pastor there?"

"Right. I don't think you need that."

"Well . . . that really sounds radical to me. I just know I wouldn't feel comfortable."

"You mean you think you have to have a minister there if you have communion?"

"Yes, to bless the elements."

"I suppose that's in the Bible, too?"

"Oh, I'm sure it is! They definitely had pastors in the Bible." They drove on in silence for a minute. "And as long as I'm at it, I might as well share that I'm afraid some of the leaders there aren't very mature, Sherry. I heard one guy at our table say a dirty word. These people aren't as far along as you might think. I mean, it was a likable group of people, but they just aren't as holy as I think Jesus would want them to be."

Sherry felt a flush of anger rise over her face, but she just tightened her grip on the wheel and didn't say anything. She realized she shouldn't be defensive, but it was really hard to hear the things Becka was saying, especially after such a beautiful night. *Maybe there are things about the group that aren't as good as I had hoped.* On the other hand, there was something suffocating about what Becka was saying. Sherry saw the people at Jack's place as possibly sinful, but also fun-loving and committed. Becka seemed to require a form of Christianity that was better behaved, but also seemed cold and aloof.

They pulled into the parking lot of their apartment building, obviously not in agreement on the point they were discussing. As they pulled into a space, Becka spoke up, asking how things were going in school.

"Now wait a minute . . ." Sherry cut her off. "I'm a little confused, Becka. Are you saying that after attending that meeting and everything tonight, all you came away with was the fact that there were smokers there, somebody said a cuss word, and some beer was consumed? We just saw a girl's eternal destiny change! And there are another twenty or more like her, *myself included*, who've met Christ there during the past year!" Sherry wasn't hiding her anger now at all. "All these people were lost just about a year ago! Doesn't that count for anything?"

"I don't want to put your group down, Sherry. I just don't think we have to compromise in order to win people."

"Compromise what?"

"Holiness." Becka could clearly feel the frustration in Sherry's voice. "You asked me for my reaction," she shrugged.

"Well, I know, but it seems to me you've singled out some things to look at and you've missed the big picture."

"I'm not saying God hasn't used the group in people's lives," Becka was defensive now.

"No, but that part doesn't seem to matter to you," protested Sherry.

"I just don't feel like I would be comfortable there based on some of the things that go on."

Sherry's eyes widened, and her throat tightened as the shock of what

Becka was saying hit her again. They walked up the stairs in silence as Sherry again struggled to gain a sense of composure. *We're both Christians,* she reminded herself. *There must be some rhyme or reason. . . .*

They had reached their apartment doors now, and Sherry decided to try once more. "I can't say there aren't some bad things there. It just seems like there's a lack of any sense of proportion in what you're saying."

"I can see I've offended you, and I'm sorry."

"No, that's not the point. I'm just trying to understand." Sherry fell silent in seething frustration. "What was Warren talking to you about? Do you know him?"

Becka looked at Sherry for a moment with some sort of discomfort in her eyes. "Uh, yeah. I knew him from church."

"Oh, you mean he was one of the guys that left the church to come to this group?"

Becka hesitated, carefully picking her words. "Yes, he left for a while, but I guess he's going both places now."

"So did he tell you about all the sin he's been learning in our group?" Sherry asked with a snide grin.

"No, but don't worry, he sees some things, too."

"Like what? What'd he say?"

Becka looked very uncomfortable. "I'm afraid I've already said too much."

"Come on, Becka!" Sherry had real menace in her voice.

"Let's just say he doesn't trust this Jack guy as much as some of the women do."

Now Sherry's eyes spread wide in curiosity. "What's that supposed to mean? What're you saying?" she demanded.

"I'm just not free to talk about his problems with the group, Sherry. You'll have to ask him about it."

"Well, you can bet I will!" She looked down and shook her head before looking back up. "Becka, if you know something, you'd better tell me. I think you're obligated to say."

"I don't know anything definite. All I got was that he has suspicions about Jack. Look, we only talked for a couple of minutes."

"Yeah, I suppose. But what's this thing about women?"

"You're just going to have to ask him!"

They stood for a long moment looking at each other, both determined. Sherry backed down first. "I guess I just need to think about what you're saying . . . and I don't want to react . . . but I am going to talk to Warren."

"Sure! He may have some interesting perspectives for you . . . and you know, I'm not trying to suggest this group isn't good for you. I'm just saying *I* wouldn't feel comfortable there."

"Sure, I understand. I'm glad you came out and saw it though." She decided to be gracious and break off the conversation.

"Oh, I was happy to come, and I'm really happy about your friend, Jean. I'll see you later." She turned to unlock her door.

Inside her apartment, Sherry threw her coat at the couch in disgust. She wondered if she was just being immature about receiving criticism, but that didn't change the deep-seated annoyance she felt about the conversation. *What is she?* Sherry marveled. *She seems like a totally different breed. I know she's a Christian, but how could our outlooks be so different?*

She decided to call Lisa.

Lisa had just walked in from The Fireside when Sherry called. She was so excited about the experience with Jean she could hardly contain herself. Sherry felt herself lifted up out of the confusion and depression she had felt after talking to Becka. The joy of being a part of God's working in reaching a lost soul, a close friend to boot, swept over Sherry's heart again.

Eventually, the conversation came around to how things had gone with Becka. "I don't know what to think, Lisa. She came up with all these things she didn't like about the meeting. I just couldn't believe someone, especially a Christian, could sit through the night we just had and not like it! The only things she picked up on were these problems, and I didn't know what to say."

"What problems did she mention?"

Sherry sat at her little desk and tapped a pencil as she ticked off Becka's complaints. "Well, she commented that people were smoking there."

"What did she think we should do about that? Order them to quit?"

"She just said something about us being called to holiness."

"Oooohhh!" Lisa let out a long descending groan of misery. "What else did she say?"

"She overheard someone saying a cuss word."

"Uh huh. That's great. And I suppose she wasn't crazy about people drinking beer after a Bible study either."

"No, she wasn't. I think that bothered her a lot."

"Yeah, well, remember this script because you're going to see it again and again. And I'll tell you what, it's always the same."

"I guess I don't understand."

"You see, Sherry, you're a converted pagan."

"Yeah," she chuckled. "I can't deny that."

"This gal must have grown up in some fairly rigid church."

"Well, I don't know what kind of church it was, but she's definitely always gone to one in her hometown and one here—Edgewood Bible Church." She ran her fingers through her hair.

"Yeah, you see, that's totally predictable. You have to be *taught* such a bizarre outlook. A new Christian would never get it naturally."

"Uh . . . I'm not sure I'm following you."

"Look, you were at the meeting tonight, and the time afterward. What did you think of it?"

"I thought it was stupendous! It was breathtaking, exciting!"

"You said it. God was at work there in a way so tangible you'd have to be blind to miss it."

"Oh, yeah!"

"Now how could someone, a Christian, sit through that meeting and come away with these observations you've mentioned?"

"Yes!" She slapped her hand on the desk. "That's what is frustrating to me. I couldn't deny some of her criticisms might have been deserved, but somehow she just seemed to miss the point."

"Precisely! That's what this kind of extremist religious thing's all about. You've studied this before."

"I don't remember studying that."

"Oh, sure. You were there when Jack taught on the man by the pool of Bethesda. Don't you remember how the Pharisees focused on the fact that he was carrying his bed on the Sabbath and didn't care that he'd just experienced a stunning miracle?"

"Oooh!" A big smile spread across Sherry's face. "That *is* sort of similar, isn't it? So what you're saying is that Becka is sort of a modern-day Pharisee."

"You got it."

"Boy, that seems a little harsh," Sherry said, but the smile stayed on her face anyway.

"Well, let's look at it this way. How long have you known Becka there at the apartment building?"

"I knew her a little at the dorm, and now for nearly a year here."

"And during that time, did she take up the issue of the gospel with you?"

"No. She never did." She was tapping her chin with the pencil now.

"So, it doesn't sound like she showed much concern about the lost state of your soul."

"Um, I guess not."

"Did she explain the gospel after you asked to go to church with her?"

"No. . . ."

"So even though she knew you were interested, she hasn't really demonstrated much concern, has she?"

"Well, no. But I may not have been very inviting either."

"I think you were remarkably responsive. You were spiritually hungry."

"Yeah, I guess. . . ."

"Now, since you've been a Christian, you've already shared with several people."

"Sure, a few. . . ."

"Do you think Becka's been sharing with people?"

There was a moment's pause. "I doubt it."

"Or even if she isn't sharing the gospel, is she showing the love of Christ in other ways?"

"I guess I don't know, but she doesn't seem very active in spiritual things, other than going to her church."

"So this is probably a sin of omission, isn't it? You know, she omits caring, she doesn't love."

"Yeah, if you want to look at it that way." She was running the pencil through her hair now.

"Well, how would Christ look at it? What did He say is the greatest law—loving God and then loving others, right?"

"Right."

"So this is what I mean. We all fail in various ways. I'm not suggesting Becka is some kind of far-out sinner or something. I'm not saying she's any worse than anyone else, only that she's the same. The problem is that violating the second greatest of all commandments according to Christ hasn't bothered her, but someone smoking and some people drinking are so bad they spoil one of the greatest movements of the Spirit she'll ever see! Do you see how it's really straining out the gnat and swallowing the camel?"

Sherry nodded her head reflectively as clear vision dawned. "Oh, I do! You just put a point on what I've been feeling." She used the pencil as a pointer now, jabbing the air. "That's why I keep getting this feeling of injustice in what she's saying."

"This is the whole secret to understanding these religious perspectives. They focus on sins of commission because those are outward. The sins of omission are just as serious, even *more* serious sometimes, but they're inward. Nobody can see when you're guilty. That way, you can feel self-righteous, even though you're no different than anyone else. Now let's take another area. Becka's overweight, right?"

"Yes."

"Well, that can be a health hazard, just like smoking. It dishonors the 'temple of the Holy Spirit.' It's an addiction like smoking, too, and Paul says, 'I will not be mastered by anything.' Why isn't she a little more worried about that?"

"I don't know."

"It's because overeating hasn't been singled out by churches as a 'biggie,' but smoking has. The whole thing is a cultural tradition—it's not based on God's Word. How would she like it if we told her at the door, 'Uh, we're sorry, Miss, we don't allow overweight people here'?"

"Oh, no way!" Sherry laughed at the ridiculous image.

"But that's what she seems to suggest we should say to smokers and cussers."

"That's so bizarre! But are you saying she's out of it for being overweight?"

"No. I'm saying she has a problem there, just like the smoker she was judging. You can't say either one of them is 'away from God' or 'not holy enough' just because they have these weaknesses. That's so self-righteous! The problem here is in the judging and comparing that makes her feel superior."

"Oh, that's so obvious." Sherry shook her head in dismay. "She's no more holy than anyone else!"

"Right. But she *thinks* she is, and this is the problem. Now that you see it, remember it. It never fails to shock me no matter how many times I see it, but it's always the same. I just have to pinch myself and say 'this is just a bad dream.'"

"Well, Lisa, there was something else that really bothers me."

"Yeah?"

"Uh, she talked to Warren, you know? And he told her something bad about Jack, I think."

There was a strange moment of silence. "What did he tell her?"

"I don't know exactly. Something about the women in the group trust Jack more than he does."

"Why did he say he didn't trust Jack?"

"Becka wouldn't tell me. She said I'd have to ask him."

Again there was that silence. Lisa seemed to be at a loss. "That's so disgusting!" she finally burst out. "He's really getting out of control!"

"What? You sound like you already knew about this."

"He has an attitude problem, I think. He's been a big critic of Jack's lately, but it's a lot of veiled, subjective stuff. I think he has a big chip on his shoulder!"

"Well, did you realize he came from Becka's church?"

"Yeah, I never knew that until tonight when we were talking there. He has some of the same views she does. He's always talking about drinking like that's some big deal. I just think he's jealous of Jack, to be perfectly honest."

"Jealous of what?"

"Uh . . . just the fact that people look up to him and stuff. You know, he does the teaching and all that."

They talked for a while, eventually resolving that they needed to ask Warren directly what his problems were with Jack. Eventually, they decided they had better get to bed. Sherry felt a lingering disturbance in her spirit about the encounter with Becka and the negative commentary from Warren as she lay in bed. She spent time with God and He showed her how to care for Becka. She began to see that Becka was the product of a religious tradition she had accepted unquestioningly. Slowly, her heart moved from anger to compassion as she imagined ways she could bring the issue up to Becka so she would understand.

25

As fall quarter progressed, the leaves, having turned to gold, orange, pink, and red, fell off the trees in early November. Fall began to slide into early winter chill as skies darkened earlier in the evenings. Sherry's life was undergoing transformation as she grew in her comprehension of the love of God. Lisa, as study group teacher, steadily fed Sherry's hunger for knowledge with reading, and spent time answering her questions and praying with her. During their lunches and evenings together, a friendship was building that Sherry increasingly treasured.

Lisa was pleased to find out Sherry was also a regular runner, and they shared time running together three times a week in the evening. To Lisa, it seemed that Sherry was cheating with her long legs, but Sherry stressed that Lisa had it easy because she was lighter. Lisa's rooming house had three showers, and after running, they would shower and sit down before dinner and talk about what God was teaching them. Lisa was stimulated by Sherry's powerful mind as she probed and questioned every point and eagerly consumed books on Christian living.

Sherry was also continuing her studies on the subjects of sacred space and formalism. She felt a growing certainty it was formalism, not true Christianity, that turned her off earlier. She also knew she probably wasn't the only one. She felt a sense of outrage when she reflected on the fact that formalism may have turned off millions of others as well.

These were happy weeks for Sherry, partly because, for the first time, she had a cause she believed in. No longer were her studies just for the sake of idle curiosity and impressing the professors. Now, as though her instinct for acquiring knowledge had caught fire, she ravenously consumed books and articles as she strove to understand the Bible, the Christian worldview, and religion.

Like many in the group at Jack's house, she and Lisa sometimes visited New Life Community Church to hear Lee Carulo teach. Sherry was impressed by the sense of mature love and understanding he emanated as he unfolded the Scriptures. She felt that he was talking about a close friend as he discussed the ways of God. She also noticed with a smile that some of Jack's mannerisms and phrases had apparently come from Lee. No wonder Jack enjoyed studying and praying with this man!

Lee was burdened that the church should not become what he called a 'spiritual ghetto.' He worried that Christians might just build a community pleasing to themselves, and ignore the needs of the lost masses outside the church. There was such contagious passion in his pleas for prayer and concern for missions and for outreach in their own community.

They also visited Edgewood Bible Church where Becka went. Sherry was realizing that formalism was truly a matter of the heart and the mind, not of externals. New Life Church sang hymns, and met on Sunday morning just like Edgewood. But the spiritual vitality seemed so much more real at New Life, and Sherry wondered why. For one thing, the people at New Life were excited about evangelism, and there were usually new people at their meetings. The fact that the church was moving ahead and reaching lost people seemed to infuse everything with an urgency and enthusiasm that was exciting.

During their visit to Edgewood, Sherry and Lisa sat with Becka, observing the Sunday evening service closely. They knew Pastor Barclay was planning to talk to them afterward at Becka's request. In the lobby after the service, Lisa and Sherry waited while Becka went over to remind Barclay of their conversation. He strode up to them, a large man in his green silken robe with yellow tassel, his salt-and-pepper hair neatly combed back. After introducing everyone, Becka prompted Barclay, "I was trying to remember where the Bible teaches people should belong to a church."

"Well, nothing is any more important in the New Testament than the church," Barclay smiled. "There are many passages stressing the church. For instance, Ephesians 5 says Christ 'loved the church and gave himself up for her.' So, if you're into Christ, you should be into His church."

Lisa spoke up, "Yes, but I guess my question would be, 'What constitutes the church?'"

Barclay turned and looked at her with eyes that were surprised to hear someone questioning his statement. Becka reminded him Lisa was a leader in the group at Jack Collins's house on campus.

"Ahhh, yes." Barclay's head reared in recognition as he turned back to Lisa. "Well, theologians agree that the marks of the true church should be present. The government of God, the proper administration of the ordinances, God-honoring worship, and the ministry of the Word are all marks of the visible church," he said with a musical voice and a mechanical smile that annoyed Sherry for some reason.

Lisa wasn't done. "Are you saying unless these things are present, a group is not a church?"

"Well, of course no group of people can simply gather one day and call themselves a church."

"Why not?" Lisa seemed genuinely confused by his answer.

He seemed a little confused as well as he coughed and collected his wits for a moment. "Young lady, the church is both an organism and an institution. I know groups of people form new churches all the time, but here at Edgewood, we stand in the center of the reformation position— that the marks of the true church are the necessary signs of God's approval for any visible church."

"Yes, but didn't that view lead to the persecution of Anabaptist house churches? Surely you're not suggesting a return to that mentality?"

"Some of those groups were dangerous extremists!" He raised his bushy eyebrows and held his big hand out. "Besides, I don't see any connection between a proper definition of the visible church and persecution. It was common in those days to use compulsion. That was before the concept of separation of church and state took hold."

"Well, the connection in my mind would be that the established church refused to recognize the legitimacy of these house churches."

In the momentary silence occasioned by Barclay's confusion, Sherry spoke up. "I have a question."

"Yes?" Barclay turned to face her, imposing in his big silk robe.

"These 'marks of the church'; is there a Bible passage where I can study what they are, and why they're required for a group to be a church?"

Barclay smiled. "Well, this isn't the sort of thing you can find in one passage. These are the conclusions of great theologians after years of Scripture study. This material is spread throughout the Bible."

"Well, I know you can't give me all the material on it, but I was just hoping for one or two examples I could study. For instance, Becka was saying that you have to have clergy before it counts as a church."

"Yes, the proper government for the church is one of the marks of the true church. The whole book of Leviticus and many other passages in the Psalms and the prophets are concerned with the priesthood and the proper direction of public worship. Then in the New Testament, they always appointed elders and deacons. Without those, you just have a disorganized rabble, not a church. First Timothy 3 and Titus 1 both discuss appointing elders and bishops."

"Oh, thank you." She was writing the passages down on her notepad. "And do these passages make it clear that you can't be a church without these offices?"

"Yes."

Now Lisa spoke up with a reluctant-sounding voice. "I hate to dis-agree, but I've studied those passages, and I can't see where the defini-tion of the church ever comes up there. Besides, what about the com-ment in Acts 14 that Paul and Barnabas appointed elders 'in each church?'"

"Precisely, they appointed elders." Again he held his big hand out toward Lisa, palm up.

"Yeah, but they did so 'in each church.'" She spoke each of the last words slowly in a staccato for emphasis. "That means these groups were already considered churches before the elders were appointed." Sherry was shocked at Lisa's ability to dialogue on this level. She turned to Barclay to see what he would answer.

"Yes, well, that may be the view of a small minority of theologians. . . ."

"It sounds like you're evaluating it on the basis of a majority vote by theologians, but I'm just saying the syntax of that statement implies they were already churches." Lisa shrugged her shoulders helplessly.

Barclay looked angry. "I'm afraid you're putting yourself up as the equal of the greatest theologians in history, and that's a mistake."

Sherry saw this as a dodge, and she didn't like him putting Lisa down, so she jumped in again. "So then, are you saying this is more a matter of theological tradition than anything in the Bible?"

"Theological tradition is *based* on the Bible, my dear," he smiled with a forced tolerance, his patience fraying. "I think it's a bit naive for your new group to suggest you exist in isolation from the historic Christian tra-dition. These efforts to return to the primitive church usually end up in extremism and elitism. Understanding the Bible is always a matter of text *and* tradition. You would need a thorough theological education before you could understand this fully."

Sherry pressed on, trying to seem as nonthreatening as possible. "What did the readers in the first century do without any opportunity to get this theological education?"

"Men such as Paul and Apollos were well-educated in theology, you can rest assured. Even John and Peter had three-and-a-half years at the Jesus Christ Seminary." He beamed openly, happy with his use of the last phrase.

"Well, I'm all for education," she agreed with a smile.

"The point is more than education," he went on. "The point is that the church embodies a tradition which, while it may evolve, cannot forget its own historical roots." His head seemed to bob with each word of this pronouncement.

"I guess I have a problem with that," Sherry was more direct now.

"Yes, I'm sure you do," his smile showed he was becoming smug now.

"Yes, I do. You're looking back at incidents, actually whole patterns in the history of the church, and saying 'That's not the way we are now, they were mistaken then,' like with the persecution thing. But at the same time, you're saying we can't move out apart from the tradition of the church. It's obvious you're picking and choosing which aspects of this 'tradition' you accept."

"Of course," he agreed.

"Then it's clear the tradition has no authority, because you carry over only those parts you agree with. What I'm wondering is, what is the yardstick you use to decide which parts are bad and which parts are good?"

"We use our developing understanding of the tradition."

"But you don't use the Bible."

"The Bible is part of our understanding."

"But you just said we can't take the Bible without the tradition. We have to understand the Bible through the tradition."

"That's not a contradiction. There has to be a balance."

"Well, in your case it sounds like, and please correct me if I'm wrong here, neither the tradition of the church nor the Bible is authoritative. It's just your professional balancing that's the final authority!"

"Young lady, people have been bashing the clergy for centuries, but the majesty of the church is still a reality you have to deal with. You can't merely sweep away two thousand years of history with your backhanded observations."

"I don't want to bash anyone. It's just that, although I'm not an expert, I know enough of that history to get the feeling we'd all be better off if we *could* sweep it away."

"Yes, I'm aware of the revolutionary point of view popular on a lot of our campuses today—iconoclasm, low church, lay leadership, anti-sacerdotal, communal, etc., etc., etc. When you get a little older, you'll probably be embarrassed about the hard-line stand you took as students."

"Well, there you have it," Sherry gave up, looking over at Lisa. "I guess we're all going to be pretty embarrassed someday!"

"I'm sorry to be the one who has to give you that warning," he said with a lofty smile that was outwardly kindly.

The atmosphere was uncomfortable, and it was clear they weren't headed toward agreement. "Well, Reverend Barclay, we appreciate your taking the time to talk to us," Sherry said as she held out her hand.

He took her hand and Lisa's and said, "I guess we just don't see things exactly the same. You're both welcome to study with us in our Catechism class on Wednesday evenings."

"Thank you. That sounds like it would be challenging," Lisa said with a smile. But as they filed out of the church and got into their car, both Lisa and Sherry were as angry as hornets in a rainstorm. "Boy, that guy was a real creep!" Lisa spat out as she slammed the car door.

"He was insulting! He basically said 'you girls have no business raising questions when you could never understand the answers,'" Sherry agreed.

"That's exactly right! That was his whole rap!" Lisa was flinging her hands up in agitated gestures. "When you really shake it down, he was just banging the tambourine for the status quo while he hid behind his stupid degree and his robe! I wonder what it would be like to live that man's life!"

"Yeah, what's he so afraid of? What's he really defending?" They drove for a moment in silence, lost in thought as they wondered about Barclay's motives. "I wonder if it's all a question of money?"

Lisa shook her head. "I don't know. He just had no interest in anything outside his *tradition*. Do you realize he still knows *nothing* about what we're into? He had us labeled, packaged, stamped, wrapped up, and in the mail before we ever opened our mouths!"

"Yeah, what a difference between him and Lee Carulo! It's hard to believe those two could be in the same line of work!"

"Well, it's obviously not necessary to be territorial and reactionary just because you're in the ministry."

Sherry giggled. "I thought I'd die when you hit him with that thing in Acts! His face looked like you'd reached out and slapped him!"

Lisa chuckled back. "You should talk! I think you gave him a lot harder time than I did. He was just seething when you kept asking for references in the Bible." They laughed and joked for a time, enjoying some merriment at Reverend Barclay's expense.

Sherry grinned. "You know what would really blow him away? We should show up for that study group he invited us to."

"Oooooh, and we could bring Jack and Ken!" Lisa giggled. "Oh man! Could you see the look on his face when we walked in and took our seats?"

They laughed together as they imagined crashing a meeting with their friends. But after having fun for a while, Lisa pointed out Jack would never agree to do something like that.

"Really? Why not?" Sherry wanted to know.

"Oh, he doesn't want any trouble with Christian churches. He'd probably say we were being carnal for having this argument tonight."

"Oh, man, he's a stick in the mud! I don't see what harm it would do." Sherry waved her hand as if sweeping the objection away.

"Well, I'm sure if this guy got mad enough he could bad-mouth us to area churches and get us into real trouble."

"What could they do to us?" Sherry wondered.

"I don't know, but I don't want to find out. I know we've had several students who've been dissuaded from coming back by their pastors. In fact, churches have been the main source of opposition we've faced."

Sherry looked over, stunned by what Lisa said. She pondered the amazing statement as they drove on. How could churches be the biggest barrier to what seemed to be so clearly a work of God? She realized the opposition must have been considerable for Jack to be unwilling to argue with area pastors.

She thought about Jack again. Her relationship with him had become more guarded during the fall. She avoided initiating too much interaction, as did he. It was just too awkward and painful to spend time talking when both sensed there was more there to say than either of them dared. It was clear there was too much magic there for them to carry on a normal friendship. However, they still chatted briefly once in a while, especially when they discussed what Sherry was reading and her research paper on formalism. Their talks were always filled with a tension that was pleasurable on one level but miserable on another.

As time passed, she was growing to appreciate increasingly how good-looking and masculine he was. He had the kind of good looks that seemed to be living and caring, not like a mannequin in a window. She could still sense clearly the fascination he had for her. Sometimes she thought she caught him looking at her, and he would try to act like he wasn't.

At the same time, she knew her admiration for Jack was emotionally risky, and she tried to keep him out of her mind. It wasn't easy when she saw him so regularly in one of her classes and during his teachings at the Bible study on Monday nights.

On several occasions during the weeks following their night at the library, she felt painful pangs of jealousy when she saw him talking to other women. She wondered whether he had any of these others thinking he liked them. It seemed doubtful from what she could see. But it took all of her willpower to avoid going over and openly competing for Jack's attention during those episodes.

The main thing holding her back was her sense that doing so would be counterproductive. Somewhere within herself, she still had an underlying confidence that, by biding her time and cultivating her own maturity, she would get the last word. Instinctively, she knew better than to crowd a man like this one. He was too strong to accept being pressured. He was too desirable to put up with a woman who seemed hard up. Besides, as Lisa regularly reminded her, God could be trusted to meet her needs.

As the weeks had turned to months, Sherry's perspective on her past with Jack had gradually changed. Her own spiritual growth was helping her understand the reason Jack backed away from a romantic relationship with her. There was more to Christian growth than she ever realized. Grudgingly, she was coming to the inner conclusion that Jack may have done the right thing by refusing at the time to get involved romantically. But she remained unsure, and still wondered if it was possible after all to avoid following one's heart when love struck. Even with the undercurrent of pain she felt about Jack, she was no longer feeling that sense of lostness and total emptiness that had hounded her earlier.

That night after attending Edgewood, when they reached Lisa's home, Sherry could see Lisa was thoughtful and distracted. "Hey, what's up?" she challenged.

Lisa seemed to snap out of her thoughts. "Oh, it's just this thing. It's nothing."

"Well, which is it? A thing? Or nothing?"

"It's nothing important."

"Come on, you're not getting out until you tell me what's on your mind."

"Oh, it has to do with Warren."

"Yeah! I was wondering what you found out there." Sherry was instantly tuned in.

"I have to admit, I'm really losing patience with him. I'm getting tired of his putting people down!"

"Who did he put down this time?"

"There was this guy at the house he lives in with some of the other brothers. I guess he shouted this guy down for smoking and burning the rug over there—they say it was really harsh. I know Billy, the guy he attacked. They say Billy was reduced to tears because Warren came down so hard. That's hard to imagine. . . ."

"Warren sounds like he needs to get his head together. How often does he get into these judging episodes?"

"A lot, if you ask me." Lisa bobbed her head angrily. "Way too much. I think we ought to get some people together and confront him—demand that he back off on the negativity. He needs to show some more grace."

"Well, did you ever find out what his problem was with Jack? I haven't forgiven him for messing with Becka's head."

"Yeah . . . but you're not going to like it." She had a slight smile on her face. "I wonder whether I should even tell you."

"You have to be kidding!"

"Okay, if I tell you, you have to promise not to react to it. You can't go make a fuss over it, okay?"

Sherry had to pause for a moment. She didn't feel like promising anything. "I'll promise that anything I do will be appropriate. How's that?"

Lisa knew it was too late to get out of saying what she knew. "Okay, we've already dealt with it though, so you don't have to go talk to him."

"If you already dealt with it, I'm sure I'll be able to see that, won't I?"

Now Lisa had to think. "Yeah, I guess so." Then after a moment she went on. "I guess he told Becka he suspects Jack uses his position as leader to get in with women in the group. The implication was pretty foul, actually."

"Oh, I'm sure! I thought you said everyone knows he rarely dates women."

"Well, not exactly. He doesn't seem to get very *serious*. But he has dated around a bit."

"Well, it doesn't seem to me like he's dating anyone at all lately."

"Right. I don't think he is."

"So what's he referring to?"

"You."

"Me? I've never done anything with Jack!" A bright flush of anger rose over Sherry's face, invisible in the moonlit car.

Lisa let out a sigh of exasperation. "I guess Jack was over with some guys, and he confessed this episode where he had been flirting with you, and you guys had taken a walk and he felt like he had led you on. I guess he felt really bad about it."

"So what? We didn't do anything. I don't see why it's such a big deal."

"I don't think it was a big deal. That's the whole point. Warren's blowing it into a big deal when it's really nothing. Jack may have felt bad about it . . . I think he did feel pretty bad about it, but I felt like he explained himself that same night, and I don't see what the big deal is."

"So what's Warren saying? Is he trying to imply something happened?"

Lisa had to think about that question. "Yeah, I think he may have left that impression. In fact, knowing him, I'd almost bank on it."

"That's really disgusting!" Sherry was going ballistic now. Her voice was loud and full of fury. "Where does this dumbbell get off talking about things he knows nothing about? I'm going to give him a piece of my mind!"

"Now see, you promised you wouldn't be rash." Lisa pointed her finger at Sherry, who tried to compose herself.

"Okay . . . okay, I'm going to keep my cool." She was holding her hands out in front of her, palms outward, as though holding something away. "I know what his problem is."

"What?"

"I think he'd like to go out with me himself."

"Oh, there's no doubt about it. He told Amy he thought you were really hot and all this stuff."

"Yeccchhh! There's no way! I'd like to bust him right in the chops!" She shook her clenched fist.

"Now you have to control yourself."

Sherry turned to Lisa with eyes of fire. "I don't know whether you realize how bad this is! My problem here goes beyond what he did to my friend, Becka. There's also the fact that I still like Jack! I haven't given up on getting together with him sometime."

"I realize that. . . ."

"Well, this is going to make him feel really reluctant—he's going to feel like he's confirming these suspicions if he asks me out or something!"

It was clear Lisa hadn't considered that possibility. She was thoughtful. Then she spoke calmly. "Jack knows he didn't do anything with you, and so does everyone else. Warren's the only one who's suspicious like that, and I don't even think *he's* suspicious. I think he just says stuff like that to get back at Jack because he's jealous."

"I'd like to get my hands around his neck!" She pounded the dashboard with her fist.

Lisa went on unperturbed, with a calming voice. "Sherry, if Jack feels the way is open from God's end to date you, he won't worry about what Warren says. Believe me. Jack is very strong. He isn't scared about what other people think."

Sherry felt somewhat calmed by Lisa's words. But she was still boiling in her heart.

Lisa laid her hand on Sherry's forearm and went on. "The reason I told you about this, is that I think you're going to have to go to Becka on it and set her straight. You're the only one who has any contact with her, and I hate the thought that she thinks Jack is using women in our group, or that you're here because of some sex-bondage thing. I just think that's a really vile impression that has to be refuted."

"Don't worry. It'll be corrected, all right."

They talked on for some time, eventually turning to God together in prayer. There, Sherry's eyes were opened to the importance of trusting God with her reputation and future. In her mind, she knew her life was in His hands, and she didn't need to worry about what others said. But her feelings of anger and hurt still came in surges. By the time Lisa patted her shoulder and got out of the car, Sherry was at least mentally resting in the Lord. She knew she would have an ongoing struggle with hard feelings.

While she drove home, she remained in unbroken fellowship with God. Her times with God were strangely comforting, and she reflected on how her new relationships with Christian women were more satisfying than any she had ever experienced with women before. She appreciated Lisa trusting her with the dangerous information about Warren's slander, and she was determined not to betray that trust by attacking Warren rashly—even though she longed to retaliate. *I'm just going to have to avoid him like the plague for a while, or I'll lose control,* she told herself.

26

The more she grew in the Lord, the more Sherry desired to share the truth with her friends. Already, she had appeared at the Monday evening study with several friends. Jean and Leslie were coming steadily and Jean was on fire spiritually. The other guest was more surprising: Sue, the one Sherry had argued with on the phone, had come the last two weeks.

Not long after making her decision for Christ, Sherry called Sue back. Sherry had little difficulty apologizing for her tone of voice and evasiveness during their angry conversation on the phone. "I realize now how suspicious and weird I was acting, Sue. I want you to know I have my head together now."

"Well, this is amazing! I'm not sure I've ever heard you eat crow like this," Sue marveled.

"Sue, I'm changing. You won't believe this group of people I've been hanging around with. I'm really learning some things. . . ."

The conversation turned quickly and naturally to a discussion of the truths Sherry had been learning. Sue was resistant and reserved at first. She even expressed open scorn at several points. But Sherry's enthusiasm was contagious and overpowering.

Sue referred with distaste to her experiences as a girl going to Mass, which indicated to Sherry that Sue, too, had problems with formalism. She longed to see Sue exposed to the truth of the gospel, unfettered by manmade forms. After listening to Sherry talk for several weeks, Sue heard that Jean and Leslie had gone to the same group and really liked it. Finally, she had reluctantly decided to come out and see what the ruckus was about.

Although Sue walked into the meeting with all her defenses up, the teaching that night was so interesting her face gradually showed an intensity and interest she couldn't hide. She didn't say much about it afterward, but she did admit it wasn't as bad as she thought it would be. "I can see how some people might have their needs met by this kind of thing," was her verdict.

"Well, what did you think about the points Jack made about the grace of God?" Sherry asked when they were outside on the sidewalk.

"I don't know anything about God, and I'm not sure he does either," she retorted with a wry half-smile, and trundled off to her car.

Later, when talking to Lisa about it, Sherry suggested Sue would probably not return. But Lisa cautioned her not to conclude what a guest was feeling based on initial outward reaction. "People sometimes put up a hard exterior to keep Christians from engaging in a hard sell," she explained. "Other times, they might react negatively at first, and later the Spirit gets in there and breaks down their resistance. After all, do you realize how negative you were at first?"

Sherry had to admit she had tried to hide her interest at first, but she was still shocked when she walked in the next week and Sue was already there, sitting on the couch, talking to Lisa. Again, she didn't indicate any positive response to the meeting, other than one observation: "That Jack guy is a pretty good speaker." But they were all hopeful now that Sue was responding to the gospel more in her heart than she was showing on the surface.

Sherry told the women at study group that Sue was influential and very strong. With Sherry's natural desire to reach out to others, it was instinctual to think of how she could show all her friends what knowing God was all about. She could imagine Sue joining up with her, Leslie, and Jean to follow God. She thought they might be able to win most of the group they hung around with at the dorm. The women in the study group prayed earnestly for Sue and the other women in their group of friends.

Already, there had been several exciting, and sometimes heated, discussions about religion at the Wednesday social gathering at the dorm, which was certainly a new feature. One week, Sherry took Lisa along to the dorm, and she hit it off wonderfully with the others. Sherry was surprised to see Lisa in this new setting. Her humor and ability to mix it up with the others showed she had been in many of these secular gatherings before.

During those weeks, it didn't strike Sherry as odd at all to be defending her views about God while her friends passed the water pipe around. She wasn't having much trouble passing the pipe on without using it either, not because she was never tempted, but because she was on record now as a Christian. The last time they partied at the dorm, Sue had spoken up during a discussion about God to say she felt one of the girls should be more open-minded about Christianity. It was the first clear hint she was doing more than just watching the Christians at Jack's house with amusement.

Sherry thought leading her friends to Christ was thrilling. There was a sense of adventure as she saw God opening opportunities to speak, and she felt the power of the Holy Spirit move through her when she shared. She never knew what to expect next. It was some of the greatest fun she had ever experienced.

She was also getting the same sense of thrill when the Spirit used her to build up her new Christian friends. During the weeks that followed, Leslie or Jean or both had several times come over to Sherry's place and enjoyed long conversations. It was clear by now that Leslie also had made a firm decision for Christ. They were feeling more ability to share what was really happening in their lives. Sherry wasn't getting the fake feeling she used to get during their conversations. They were still able to enjoy some jovial banter, but now they could also talk about real things.

One unusually warm evening in November the three of them had gone out by the pond behind Sherry's place with a sack of pretzels. After an emotional talk about Jean's feelings of hurt over her abortion four years earlier, Sherry suggested the three of them try to pray together. Although Sherry was used to praying with others by now, it was quite a step for the other two unchurched girls to pray out loud in front of others. But God blessed the time and they found a new level of closeness as they opened their hearts before God together.

That night as Sherry got ready for bed she felt a sense of joy in her heart that was something new. She realized her joy had been growing steadily over the past weeks. *This must be what Lisa and Jack mean when they say "abundant life." I'm really seeing that You love me, Lord! You're taking such great care of me!*

She fell asleep with a smile on her face.

Not far away, evil spiritual forces were again congregating. "Well, isn't that nice?" the leader smirked. "They think they're learning how to take over the campus for the Crucified One. Pretty soon they'll be talking about taking over the world!" He clenched his fist and shook it. "Within weeks, we'll have them wondering if they can even *survive!*"

The gathering broke out in robust laughter and cursing.

The leader addressed a dark face, hardly visible at the edge of the group. "Is your man ready?"

The dark specter spoke quietly, deeply. "My guy will act, and he will be effective."

"How far will he go?" the first demanded.

"He'll go all the way. He'll kill if he has to."

Satisfied murmurs and chuckles sounded around the group of demons.

"But he won't be able to go any further than we have clearance—they're praying."

"We know that, stupid! Right now, he's nothing but a decoy. You don't have the real hammer. Is he ready?" He faced a group on the other side of the gathering.

"He's more or less totally under control now," another spirit replied. "I hope we're all on the same page."

"Don't worry about us. We'll have our people and their leader ready. Just do your job! We'll deliver. I don't want anyone moving before we're ready. These guys are about to find out what real power is all about!"

Again, they enjoyed some eager, leering laughter.

27

It was Friday night, and the women at Lisa's house were meeting for study. There was a special topic on tap. They had decided to read and discuss together the latest paper Sherry had written for Dr. Forsythe. Jack and Lisa had suggested some extra readings on the subject of objectification of religion—Dr. Forsythe's term for formalism. Forsythe told her to focus on reasons for sacred space, sacred time, sacred words, and other marks of formalism.

Lisa got the women seated around the big dark-brown wood table in their living room, and started talking. "Okay, guys, I've asked Sherry to bring in this paper we've all been praying about and let us go over it with her."

"Yeah, it better be good, Sherry!" Amy jested. With her freckles, outgoing personality, and friendly face, she was a natural comic.

"Thanks!" Sherry gave her a sardonic smile. "Seriously, I don't know. It's the best I could do in a few weeks," Sherry pleaded. "Be gentle, you guys!"

"Okay, Amy, why don't you pray for us before we start?" Lisa asked. They prayed, and passed out copies of the paper to most of the women, though some had to share. Then Lisa said, "Jordan, why don't you start out and read that first section down to page two?"

Jordan read,

Formalism in Religion: Separating the Sacred and the Profane
A research paper presented to Dr. Forsythe
Anthropology 651
by Sherry Martin

According to Mercea Eliade, man has always set apart areas as sacred:
> The enclosure, wall, or circle of stones surrounding a sacred place—these are among the most ancient of known forms of manmade sanctuary.[9]

Why do religious people separate the sacred from the profane?

Jordan stopped reading and asked, "What does 'profane' mean, Sherry?"

Sherry looked up. "Uh, profane means 'common,' so, it's like, sacred things are special, or spiritual, and profane things are common. They're not spiritual, they're not religious."

Jordan nodded and read on.

Why are religious buildings, religious songs, religious words and religious deeds recognizable as different from the rest of "profane" society, no matter where or when they appear?

Eliade observes that the most common mythology explaining sacred areas relates to some encounter with a god that occurred in that spot.[10] When holy men "encounter" the sacred in a vision, a miracle, etc. they mark the place and that place becomes sacred. This claim is plausible in the case of many, but not all, holy places.

Lisa interrupted her. "Okay, Jordan, we thought this part might get too heavy, so why don't you skip down to the second paragraph on page three?"

"Sure," Jordan said as she found her place.

Eliade goes beyond this however, to assert the intriguing idea that,
The [sacred event] therefore does not merely sanctify . . . space; it goes so far as to ensure that sacredness will continue there. There, in that place, the [sacred event] repeats itself. [11]
Here Eliade is saying people mark space out as sacred because they are attempting to invoke a new sacred event. In other words, the holy place is not there simply to explain (or objectify) abstract concepts, but to enable the worshiper to provoke a spiritual event or blessing not available even one foot outside the sacred space!

Jordan stopped. "Whew. Sherry, where did you learn to talk this way?"

"That's just the way you're supposed to write for these guys," she explained, sweeping the comment aside with the back of her hand.

"What do you guys think so far?" Lisa asked.

"I think it's interesting, but it doesn't explain why churches are considered sacred space, you know. I can see this in some Mongolian shrine or something, but nobody has had a vision in a church."

"Yeah, that's a good point," Sherry answered. "That's why I said it doesn't apply to all sacred places. I do touch on churches later in the paper. For one thing, a lot of churches actually have a service where they consecrate their building as a house of God."

"Now wait a minute," Leslie spoke up. "Are you saying churches are sacred spaces?"

"Well, I don't believe there's such thing as a sacred space," Sherry answered. "But yes, people do consider churches to be sacred places. Haven't you ever heard a preacher refer to a church as the house of God?"

Leslie spoke slowly and reluctantly. "I might've heard that. . . ."

"Well, you've certainly heard the meeting hall referred to as a sanctuary, right?"

"Yeah."

"Well, that's what sanctuary means: A holy place."

Leslie had a frown on her face. "I've never heard that it means that."

"I'm going to have to agree with Sherry on that," Lisa jumped in. "The word sanctuary comes from the Latin word *sanctus,* which means 'holy.' I know because I looked it up when Sherry told me that, and the dictionary said sanctuary means a holy place."

"Wow, I guess I never knew that," Leslie admitted.

"Okay, let's read on," Lisa said. "Kerry, why don't you continue?"

This must be why many prefer to pray or worship in a church rather than simply doing so at home. Sacred places are locations where the divine is more responsive. In a sense then, the notion of sacred space implies an attempt to regularize and perhaps to control sacred events—to control God. [12]

Eliade points out that, in addition to the idea of provoking an encounter with the sacred, there is the notion of *protection* from the sacred.

(The dividing structure between sacred and profane space) . . . also serves the purpose of preserving profane man from the danger to which he would expose himself by entering it without due care. The sacred is always dangerous to anyone who comes into contact with it unprepared, without having gone through the "gestures of approach" that every religious act demands. [13]

"Oh, that's creepy! That's what they did in my church!" Kerry interjected. "You had to cross yourself all the time, and do this thing called 'genuflecting.'"

"Yeah, mine too," Jean agreed. "I always hated that!"

Kerry went on:

This clear boundary between the safety of the profane, and the danger of the sacred amounts to containment of the sacred, along with limitation and control. Sacred space not only enables religious practitioners to approach the deity more easily, it also enables them to leave His presence after the encounter.

"Yeeccchhh!" Kerry wrinkled her nose. "It really bothers me to think about this stuff! But I know it's true. Why are people so weird? Why do they relate to God that way?" There were some murmurs around the table.

"I think this is the tip of the iceberg when it comes to this kind of superstition," Amy offered.

"Well, let's check out this next section before we get too far into that," Sherry suggested.

Magical Elements in Formalism

Controlling, approaching, and avoiding spiritual powers: these all suggest the practice of magic. Parrinder says,

> Religious and magical beliefs are intertwined at most stages of culture, and indeed a case can be made out for banning the word magic and including it all, however crude, under the heading of religion; for these strange practices all depend upon spiritual conceptions and largely work by faith.[14]

"Are you saying magicians are bad?" It was Leslie again.

"This isn't magic like at a magic show," Sherry explained. "This is real magic. This is like casting spells, healing, cursing people, and making things happen like making your crops grow . . . you know, stuff like that—like what a shaman or a wizard would do."

"Oh, I guess some people believe in that."

"Oh, yeah! A lot of people do! Things like crystal good-luck charms and tarot cards are magic."

"Man, there's a lot of that stuff in the dorms, I think," Kerry jumped in.

"Yeah, I guess if you mean that kind of stuff, I see your point," Leslie said, and Kerry read on.

In the same vein, it is probably not merely coincidence that, as Eliade points out, the rocks, springs, caves, and woods venerated from the earliest historic times are still, in different forms, held as sacred by Christian communities today.[15]

"There you go right there! The Christians have just baptized native superstition in the name of Mary!" she couldn't help commentating angrily as she read. She went on:

It is likely that some Western thinkers are reluctant to admit the presence of an outlook for so long considered "primitive" in the heart of Western culture. However, the evidence shows that the underlying concepts behind sacred space and time are similar to religious magic.

The paper went on to show the connection between concepts found in formalized religion and those found in the most primitive beliefs such as fetishism. Finally, Mary read the section on exuvial magic.

Most of the great cathedrals, temples, mosques, pagodas, and other shrines the world over, have been built around a part of a human body. Whether some hair, bones, breast milk, teeth, or whole body of a saint, the shrine receives its identity (and, we must suppose, some of its sacredness) from the presence of part of a dead human body.[16]

Students of oral societies recognize this practice as a form of contagious magic called "exuvial magic." Norbeck explains,

Exuvial magic . . . involves the use of human exuvaie, hair combings, teeth, nail clippings, excreta, spittle, placentae, and the umbilici of newborn infants.[17]

Exuvial magic is a form of contagious magic, which holds that the exuvaie will transmit some of the characteristics of the saint. Here then, we see a striking parallel between modern Western religious practices and supposed early ideas of contagious magic.

"Yes, they did that in my church!" Jean blurted out. "When they built a new church, we had to go, and they brought this bone from someone, and we had a service and that's what got the new sanctuary going. So they do that in other religions too, huh?"

"Yeah, that's pretty much worldwide, too." Sherry nodded.

"Man, I can't believe that!" Amy marveled. "That's sickening! How could they possibly get into that in the modern world?"

"It's the idea of contagion . . . that bringing something—whether sacred or profane—into contact with something else spreads the spiritual essence like disease spreads." Sherry explained. "Let's remember ancient man believed disease was caused by demons. Even evangelicals today worry that if you contact something of the world, like a song, you might be spiritually contaminated."

The girls continued to read through the next several pages which detailed all kinds of close parallels between magic, fetishism, and the practices and ideals of developed religions. The girls were increasingly amused by Sherry's deadpan descriptions, all detailed in footnotes, which more and more set Western religion in the context of magic. Finally, Lisa was reading.

> It is observations such as these that lead scholars such as Norbeck to comment,
>
>> *Sacred objects of the great civilizations differ not at all in their general nature from those of primitive societies. Protective talismans, many uses of the cross, holy water, and the sacrament may all be objectively viewed as implying power which, although interpreted as bestowed or derived from a man-like deity, become the qualities of the acts or objects themselves.*[18]
>
> Perhaps this is a workable framework within which to understand the separation of sacred and profane: not a further development of the major religions, but the first step in returning to a way of thinking and believing that is as old as man himself.[19]

After citing several other authorities she concluded:

> These scholars all agree that formalized religion and magic are very difficult to differentiate.

There was another section detailing the theory advanced by numerous scholars that people simply aren't able to respond to the abstract and need tangible symbols. But Sherry suggested they skip that and talk about the notion of formalism and Christianity. They discussed it for a few minutes, and all seemed to agree formalism was a major barrier to a true understanding of what it meant to know God.

"Every time I try to talk about Christ with my friends, they keep thinking Christianity is like their experience in some formalistic, dead church," Amy lamented. "I think this stuff is really important." She started to thump the table with each word. "We have to get the idea out there that you don't need all this formal stuff!"

Sherry suggested they look at her conclusion and decide whether she was being too overtly Christian for a secular professor. They had gone around the table, so it was Jordan's turn to read again. As they read, one of the women would find and read each of the biblical passages mentioned.

Summary and Conclusions: A Christian Perspective

As one who has recently taken an interest in religion, I feel personally challenged by these findings. I hope it will not be out of line to discuss the synthesis I have worked out between the views of these scholars and my understanding of biblical Christianity.

Looking at the question from the Christian perspective then, what do we see? How does the Bible, which I have concluded is the revealed Word of God, relate to the issue of what some Christians call formalism—a focus on the outward forms of Christianity?

First, it seems that some outward forms are appropriate for most people, because God Himself included these elements in the Bible.

The Old Testament is rich in outward forms, ranging from sacred space in the temple, to a detailed cultus surrounding that space. One reason for this may be the illiteracy of the population at that time. For oral cultures, lessons contained in ritual and symbol would communicate, while a printed page with abstract truths could be problematic. Of course, even oral cultures memorize stories and teachings, so, at best, this is only part of the answer.

In the New Testament, we find this level of outward formality radically reduced, though still not eliminated altogether. For instance, there is no provision in the New Testament Era (which I take to have begun at Pentecost in Acts 2) for any form of sacred space. Paul, Christ, Peter and the author of Hebrews reinterpret the provision for sacred space in the Old Testament. They all teach that the temple now corresponds to the assembly of true believers in Christ. (Paul did so frequently, but most clearly in 1 Corinthians 3:16, Jesus Christ did so in John 2:19-21, and Peter in 1 Peter 2:5.) The early Christians met in the temple court, and may also have continued to relate to the temple ritual for some time, although this is condemned in Hebrews and elsewhere. (Hebrews 8:13, 13:10-14; Acts 7:48-50.)

Likewise, there was no claim made in the area of sacred time, or a religious calendar. On the contrary, in Colossians 2:16-17 Paul directly declares that the idea of a sacred calendar is obsolete. In Galatians 4:9-10 he says a sacred calendar is among the "weak and worthless elemental things," and the Galatians' observance of these things is the proof they have not understood Christianity correctly. Even

175

though Paul allows "weaker brethren" to observe "one day greater than another," he clearly views this outlook as unnecessary (*see* Romans 14).

"Man, this goes directly against my church," Jordan commented. "The sacred days were the high point of the year, and a lot of people never even came except on those days."

"Yeah, likewise." It was Jean. "I wonder what they thought when they read passages like that one in Galatians or the one in Colossians?"

"They probably didn't read them too much if it was like my church," Amy observed.

Sherry shared. "Lisa and I talked to this preacher here in town a few weeks ago, and he was arguing all this stuff. He didn't base most of his interpretations on the Bible. He based them on the tradition of theologians . . . you know, what 'experts' say. He cited the Old Testament a lot as referring to the church, and I got the feeling he believed the church existed in the Old Testament times. It was sort of like the Jewish people were the church then."

"Yes, that's the view of that school of theology," Lisa said. "And it's led to a bunch of problems. Like Sherry said, there was a lot more ritual in the Old Testament, and if you think that's basically the same as the church, you can see how it would lead to a high acceptance of ritualism, priests, holy days and all kinds of stuff."

The girls nodded as they comprehended this idea. "But just believing the church existed in the Old Testament period is not the whole problem. For instance, Jesus preached in the period before Pentecost, and that's essentially the Old Testament period, and He was against formalism as they already practiced it. He got down on their ritualism, their washings, their Sabbath thing, their ritualistic prayers, and things like that. So I don't think Reformed theology means you're into formalism."

"Do you know anyone who's like that, Lisa?" Sherry asked.

"Oh, yeah. Lee Carulo for one."

"He's a Reformed theologian?" Sherry seemed surprised. "You mean, he believes the church existed in the Old Testament?"

"Yes. I'm sure he does. But he believes all that ritual stuff was translated into different things at the time of Pentecost. You know, it's sort of like, you can say the people of God in the Old Testament were the Jewish people, by and large, and yet you can still leave open the question of the role of ritual and forms in the church."

"Wow! Well, Jack doesn't believe the church started in the Old

Testament, does he?" Sherry pressed.

"No. He and Lee don't agree on that point. But they've agreed their view on formalism can be the same even though they have different views there."

"I think that's really cool!" Sherry said and there was a murmur of agreement from the others.

"Yeah, me too. Why don't you read on?" Lisa said.

Human Priesthood was also abolished in the New Testament period. Priesthood is attributed primarily to Christ as our high priest, and secondarily, to all believers, making a formal priesthood obsolete. (Hebrews 5–8 decisively limits the intercession of the high priestly role to Christ, as does 1 Timothy 2:5. At the same time, Peter refers to all believers as a nation of priests in 1 Peter 2:9, because we are able to intercede for others.)

On the other hand, there are two specific outward forms in New Testament Christianity—water baptism, and the Lord's Supper.[20] However, these ordinances are very simple in comparison with the elaborate ritual of the Old Testament. Baptism is only practiced once in a person's life. And the New Testament gives no instruction on how often to celebrate communion. It only says "as often as you do it. . . ." This is a striking contrast to the Old Testament forms which were spelled out in exacting detail.

From the time of Pentecost on, the Bible teaches that the universal indwelling of the Holy Spirit enables people to remain faithful without many outward forms like in the Old Testament period. In place of outward forms, God provided for a more personal avenue of relationship. This is why He dispensed with the "shadows" or "elemental things" that had served as a tutor before (see Hebrews 7:18, Colossians 2:18).

Yet, even then, God allowed some outward forms, for the sake of the special kind of fellowship possible through these ordinances. While recognizing the value of symbols, the student of Christian history is also acutely aware of the spiritual dangers of formalism.

"I'm glad you said that, because I really like communion," Lisa spoke up. "I think communion is a beautiful way to remember and reflect on the Lord's death. In fact, I think it's time we had communion again here. Why don't we line up some wine and bread for next week?" They agreed they would, and Kerry read on.

In the Old Testament period, the people often tended to look to the symbols themselves, rather than to the reality they expressed, and this was a mistake. Amos laments that the people love to give offerings, but they have not drawn close to God in their heart (*see* Amos 4:4-5). God goes so far as to say He loathes their sacrifices because they are merely outward formalism (*see* Amos 5:21-26). In Isaiah 29:13 Gods laments,

> *"These people come near to me with their mouth and honor me with their lips, but their hearts are far from me. Their worship of me is made up only of rules taught by men."*

Likewise Norbeck, speaking from an entirely secular perspective, says,

> *Religious acts tend to become goals in themselves. Histories of religions provide many examples of rituals rendered meaningless by the passage of time but which are nevertheless tenaciously retained. Empty of their original significance, the rites themselves have become goals.*[21]

"Boy, you said it!" Jean moaned. "My mom has no idea why she does what she does. We've had a couple of discussions about religion, you know? And, I swear, she can't answer any of my questions! I say, 'Why do we do that?' and she just keeps saying, 'That's a stupid question,' or 'I don't know, why don't you ask the priest?' I mean it, she doesn't know why she does anything, and yet she tries to strictly observe all of it! Why are people like that?"

"It's sort of mysterious, but I think that's the trap of the religious mentality," Lisa answered. "People feel they are all right with God because they go through these practices, but they really don't know what they're doing, and often, they really don't know God."

Lisa looked down and shook her head in frustration as Sherry continued reading.

Many modern observers (myself included) find little in common between the simplicity of early Christian church life and the heavily formalized rituals of many modern churches. Therefore, we must conclude that, from the Christian perspective, there are benefits and dangers in having outward forms. I personally believe Christians should not introduce new outward forms not authorized in the Bible, unless they carefully and repeatedly explain the distinction Jesus made between the "wine" and the "wineskins" (Luke 5:36-39).

"Okay, why don't you explain more of what that means, Sherry?" Lisa interrupted.

Sherry read the passage about wineskins and then said, "This passage in Luke 5 teaches that the important part was what God was doing—the wine—not how people packaged God's program. Jesus was ready to overthrow the rabbis' religious system, because it interfered with what He was trying to communicate. Also, it was too stiff and unable to change, like an old wineskin."

"Well said," Lisa smiled. "Now, what should that mean to us?"

Sherry went on. "Well, I think it means we should be ready to throw over any aspect of our ministry that starts to interfere with our message. Instead, we usually start to view our traditions as though they were sacred. That preacher Lisa and I were talking to kept saying the 'tradition' of the Christian church was just as important as the Bible itself in a lot of ways."

"What would be an example of a situation where the wineskins are being viewed the right way?" Lisa pressed.

"The best example I can think of is the partnership we have with Lee Carulo and New Life Church. The skins are totally different, but both seem appropriate for the group being ministered to, and neither group seems uptight about getting the other to be like them."

"Excellent! That's a perfect illustration, I think," beamed Lisa.

They discussed the idea awhile longer before reading the end of the paper.

> The notion that people are not responsive to the abstract is suspect to me. It is too easy for clergy to assert that the "great unwashed masses are not as smart as we are." On the contrary, common folk often respond vigorously to the abstract, both now and at various times throughout history. The New Testament is very lean on outward forms, and long on abstract truths. Yet, the authors address their letters to the rank and file of the church, not just to the leadership.[22]

"Yeah, well I guess that preacher at Edgewood can eat his heart out! These simple rank-and-file Christians were able to understand Paul even without a 'thorough theological education!'" Lisa boomed the last part out with a deep voice like Barclay's, or at least as close as she could come in her little frame. They all laughed before going on.

> Also, in the case of Christianity, formalistic thinking has led to the exclusion of the laity from ministry, and from access to the Scriptures.

The overall effect of formalism has usually been to create and sustain an intermediary role for the clergy which usually precludes lay initiative in the vital areas of spiritual life. It also replaces a sophisticated understanding of the truth claims of Christianity with an over-simplified knowledge of some formal observance. The rank and file grow more ignorant under formalism.

Finally, we have noted magical aspects in formalized religion, ranging from containment of the sacred, to outright exuvial magic. I am unable to avoid the conclusion that humankind's craving for control and regulation of the sacred has played a major role in efforts to formalize religion.

Herein lies the greatest danger in formalism. Magic is an impersonal and mechanistic way to relate to God. Magic represents the bare attempt to manipulate the supernatural, or at least to avoid trouble with it. Such a relationship is analogous to most people's relationship to the Internal Revenue Service. It is a legalistic relationship where we do the least we can to stay out of trouble. There is certainly no personal love aspect to such a relationship.

Kerry jumped in. "Okay, there you have it. Man, Sherry, you're pounding away here right where it's needed! That's what I see at the dorm. The girls there believe in God, but they don't want to know Him. They just want to know how they can get favors from Him, like good grades, or a boyfriend, and then make Him go away and leave them alone! It's no wonder formalism is so popular in modern churches. It gives people what they want, but not what God wants."

Most of them agreed. Formalism leads to an arm's-length relationship with God that leaves the human in control. At last they finished the paper.

While these explanations account for most types of formalism in religion, they also account for the trend in the Bible away from outward forms and toward the personal and the abstract. Indeed, many Christians today and throughout history have enjoyed a walk with God almost completely free from formalism—a tendency that will continue into heaven itself:

> *I did not see a temple in the city, because the Lord God Almighty and the Lamb are its temple (Revelation 21:22).*

Sherry sat back and grinned, as the women gave her a joking round of applause. "Come on, you guys. Give me a break!" She shielded her embarrassed smile.

"No, I think this is a super paper, Sherry. I just wish I could write like that," Jordan beamed, as they all murmured their agreement. "I'm so proud of you!"

"You're turning into a champion for informal, personalized faith!" Lisa smiled. Then, turning to the rest, "I think we've all seen an example tonight of what we can do as we go to school. I especially liked the way she kept her research separate from the section on her own opinion. That's probably going to be the difference between an A and the respect of the professor versus a C for preaching in a research paper."

"Well, it's interesting that Jack studies under this same professor, and he's been witnessing to him subtly," Sherry said. "Maybe God can use this paper a little bit."

Several of the women thought Sherry should teach on the subject at Monday night Bible study sometime. They ended the evening praying God would use the paper in some way. Sherry knew Jack would read it, too, because he had offered to print her paper on the university's laser printer, which would look better than her dot-matrix copy. She was eager to see what he would say about it.

28

Sherry had a dentist appointment in the morning, so before she left that night she gave the disk containing the paper to Lisa who would be seeing Jack the next day. "Tell me what Jack thinks of it," she requested.

The next morning, Jack looked up from Sherry's paper with a slack jaw, shaking his head. He frowned in amazement at Lisa and Amy who were sitting at the table with him peeling oranges and eating the segments while he read. Lisa had suggested he come over and read it before taking it up to the computer center to print. She wanted to hear what he thought of it. "I just don't know where to put this in my mind!" Jack marveled. "What kind of person are we dealing with here?"

Lisa waved her knife in Jack's direction as she spoke. "I've never seen better insight than this, even from the most mature women in our Bible study." She spat out a seed. "It seems like we have some kind of a theological Joan of Arc here!"

"Well, you have to remember she's been studying history, anthropology, and sociology for a number of years now," Jack observed, as he accepted one of the orange pieces from Amy. "I guess she was already considered a gifted student in her own disciplines before we met her, and a lot of this stuff is based on anthropology, and on readings we gave her. . . . Still, she's seen the heart of the issue more clearly than I could have imagined." He shook his head.

Amy chimed in, "We're definitely dealing with an unusually gifted mind. This is just not normal! I couldn't write that paper even after three years as a Christian. I wonder if we're really equipped to handle this kind of person? Maybe we should send her to some school or something?"

"Yeah, it might be a good idea for her to go on to further study somewhere," Jack mused. "But God's sent her here for now, not somewhere else. That means He wants us to equip her for now." The question on all of their minds was the same: Should they be trying to teach Sherry something, or asking her to teach them?

"Well, this isn't the first brilliant paper she's shown me," Jack went on.

"I even talked to Dr. Forsythe about her. I was afraid he'd think she was cheating, you know, because I'd mentioned I knew her."

"Well, what did he say?"

"He said he knew the stuff was hers. He said the history faculty already had her picked out as an exceptional intellect, and they've determined they're going to find a way to help her in grad school in order to keep her here. She's already been privately assured she'll have a teaching fellowship next year!" Jack was getting up and putting his things in his briefcase. "It's true what he said. . . ."

"What?" Lisa pressed.

"He said they were impressed because she didn't just have the kind of intelligence where she could remember things and get good grades. He said they were impressed with her analytical skills; her ability to see the heart of the issue; to think for herself . . . to communicate complicated things."

"It makes you wonder what God could do with somebody like that," Amy reflected out loud.

"No kidding. You ladies must be doing a marvelous job teaching in your women's group. I know I didn't give her most of this stuff. Keep up the good work!"

Lisa smiled. "With this gal, teaching is so easy any moron could do it. I think we're all reading more than ever just to keep ahead of her."

"Well, we have to somehow keep her encouraged without swelling her head. I think you guys are right on target so far."

Amy spoke up. "Thanks, Jack."

"I'm surprised she's still around after you got through messing things up," Lisa chided Jack with a slight grin.

"Aw, come on, Lisa. Can't you see how a guy might lose it for someone like this?" he pleaded.

"I still think you should have waited until she was grounded at least."

"I know I should've! I just blew it. I lost control." He seemed to be pleading for understanding.

"Yeah, I'm just giving you a hard time," she smiled. "But I'm afraid you won't get as much slack from Warren."

"Boy, you're not kidding! He's been going around to everybody. He seems to imply something really bad happened."

"I don't like his attitude." Lisa shook her head. "I get a bad feeling when I talk to him. He seems to have it in for you. Why don't you guys go and rebuke him?"

"Rebuke him for what?"

"For his attitude! He even went and put you down to a first-time visitor at a meeting. How long are we going to let him spread his negativity?"

Jack let out a low groan. "I don't think you can just go getting down on people for something subjective, or for hearsay. What did he tell this guest?"

"Oh, he implied you messed around with Sherry. That you use your position to get women."

"To a first-timer?" Jack's incredulous look spoke eloquently of his own sickened heart. "Man, that *is* bad!"

"Yeah! It was Sherry's guest he said it to!"

They sat in silence for a period of time, obviously depressed by the negative note in the midst of the group. Jack finally spoke, staring vacantly down at the table. "Maybe I'll say something to him. The fact is, I did let her know how I felt. . . . I messed up. I was just dazzled by her when she spoke in our seminar, and then I had a couple of conversations with her. . . . See, I've watched her before at the library, and . . . I thought she was beautiful . . . I had fantasized about her when I didn't even know her. And when I heard her speak up in seminar, and talked to her and stuff . . . her personality was so much more interesting than I ever thought it would be . . . and then she came to a Bible study, and was getting into Christ! I don't know, I guess I just sort of lost it for her . . . and it does have the appearance of evil."

"I don't think it does," Amy retorted. "I mean, it would have looked evil if you'd gotten into something at that point, but you dealt with it, and that was months ago. I just think Warren wishes he could get into Sherry."

"Yeah, there's the truth," Lisa agreed.

Jack smiled and nodded. "I've suspected that before."

Lisa reached out and put her hand on his forearm. "I think you're just getting intimidated by this accusation, Jack."

He smiled weakly, but looked down thoughtfully, clearly struggling with something.

"What is it? What are you thinking?" Lisa pressed.

He looked back up with strained eyes. After hesitating for a moment he spoke haltingly. "I think I should level with you guys . . ." there was silence while he breathed deeply. "I really like this girl. I . . . I'm trying to stay away from her, but . . . I don't know, I guess . . . I just really like her. Sometimes I just want to run over to her and tell her how I feel, you know? If she showed up with another guy I'd just die! You guys should pray for me." He looked down again, obviously in inner misery.

After a moment of dead air, Lisa spoke up, "I think we all know you like her Jack. I think she knows it, too."

Jack looked up suddenly, as he realized they must have discussed it.

"At least she *suspects* it," Lisa corrected. "Anyway, I think you've been doing a good job giving her room to grow on her own. I just think every week and every month that goes by without you and her being involved is a step in the right direction. You should wait as long as you can."

"I'm trying, but I think about her all the time. I watch her whenever she's in the room. I just feel like I'm going to pop sometimes if I can't open up to her."

Lisa realized Jack was trying to warn them something might happen soon. She didn't want to be in the position of opposing their relationship, so she hastened to reassure him. "I don't think anyone would blame you if you did open up to her, Jack. But you're doing a good thing by waiting."

Jack gave an appreciative smile and nod, and gathering his things, he got up and headed for the door. "I appreciate your understanding attitude," he said at the door. "I'd better take this paper up and print it now." They waved as he ducked out the door.

Lisa and Amy looked at each other and shook their heads. He wasn't going to last long, and they both knew it. It was a little hard to take, and they both had struggled with pangs of jealousy toward Sherry at times, especially Amy, who wished Jack would notice her.

For a couple of years, everyone in the group had accepted the idea that Jack couldn't be reached by any woman. Then, when Sherry came around, it seemed like he had taken interest in one of the least mature members of the group. No one could deny she was beautiful, or that she was suited to Jack because of her interest in academic research. But when it came to light that he may have been flirting with her even before she came to know Christ, people were shocked. There had been several terse conversations at the time as some of the committed members of the group had called Jack to account for what he was doing. There was no doubt Jack's image had suffered in the eyes of some.

Gradually both the men and women in the group had come to accept that Jack was human, too, and they forgave his weakness—except for Warren. But some of the women still had to confess their feelings of jealousy to each other, and judge those feelings before the Lord. They had often talked about how they wanted their fellowship to be different than sororities or other groups where jealousies ruled the social climate. Most of them had spent several years learning to recognize and control jealous urges.

The process of healing was made easier because they found Sherry so

likable, and in her own way, completely innocent where Jack was concerned. They also appreciated the fact that Jack had admitted the problem on his own without getting "caught." Though Sherry didn't realize it,
women in the group were watching her to see whether she would try to
lure Jack in. Her steady refusal to give in to urges to flirt created the
impression she really wasn't that interested.

Of course, Sherry knew the real reasons, and so did Lisa. But neither
of them said anything about it. Lisa and Amy had both reached the point
where they could honestly pray for Sherry's continued advancement without jealousy.

29

J ack was walking down Main Street in the early afternoon. He knew Sherry was pretty consistent in her schedule, and she would probably be sitting by the window at McDonald's. He also knew that, with the quarter ending, her schedule would be changing. He didn't want to miss the opportunity to talk to her without a roomful of people standing around. He had to give her the paper he printed for her, and he couldn't see any danger in a short talk. Besides, he wanted her to read his paper and needed to explain it.

As he came into view, he tried to look as natural as possible while scanning the windows for a glimpse of her. She wasn't there. As he walked up to the door, he stopped and, after a moment's hesitation, decided to go in and matter-of-factly look for her, instead of pretending to run into her.

He entered the noisy dining room, his piercing eyes scanning the tables, most of which were occupied. There she was, sitting by the wall, at one of the little tables for two, a couple rows back from the picture windows. How beautiful her face was in the light of the huge windows! Her perfect bronzed complexion and flowing hair looked like they belonged on a magazine cover. He couldn't help admiring her elegant figure, either. He felt himself wavering as he turned away and went to the counter to order lunch. How he longed to reach out and feel the smoothness of her beautiful face! He actually felt childish as he sensed his pulse rising and a flush warming his face. *Man, this girl has me tied up in knots!* he marveled to himself.

He tried to look confident as he strode back to her table with his tray. "I can't believe someone like you is sitting here all alone."

She looked up from the book she had been reading, and a smile of recognition spread over her face. "Oh, Jack! You look like you need a place to sit."

"Yeah, do you mind some company?"

"Not at all." Her voice was musical and full of life. "I'm delighted to have some company. I've been working alone all day again."

He waited for her to finish clearing her books away from his side of the tiny table and, placing his tray down, took his seat. He laid his briefcase on the floor, and then his eyes came up and met hers. He almost gasped as he took in her radiant, smiling eyes but quickly looked down at his food and began fumbling around. He had felt this before; it seemed like all his confidence deserted him when he was with her. He felt like he was all thumbs as he fussed with his ketchup packet, tearing it too far down so that ketchup gushed out over his thumb. He stuck his thumb in his mouth, looking up to see she was smiling at his misfortune. "I hate it when that happens!" he laughed. Her quiet chuckle hardly eased the tension he felt. He pressed on the best he could.

"Well, Sherry, I just have to say, that was one of the most perceptive and even brilliant papers I've ever read, especially from an undergrad." He grimaced slightly, feeling like an idiot for adding the last phrase.

"Oh, thanks. I think you're exaggerating a little." He saw a distinct blush pass over her face as she looked down.

"No, I'm not," he continued. "Your analysis of formalism was so right-on, so . . . I don't know, it just isn't normal to be able to write that way, Sherry. You have a real gift. In fact, reading your paper has really set me free."

"What do you mean?" she frowned.

"I've been stuck on my thesis for days now. You know, I have the details . . . the sections, but I was having trouble putting it all together. I couldn't get the pattern down into words. After reading your paper, I just sat down and it all fell into place, especially the exegesis of the main passage I'm starting with. My ideas just flowed out, you know? In fact, I have the first section here if you're still interested in reading it."

"Oh, yeah! I'd love to read it." She was almost too eager. Jack felt somehow reassured by this manifestation of her heart. She still liked him, and she couldn't hide it.

He reached into his case and brought out his paper and hers, handing them to her. "Here's your paper as well, freshly printed on our best laser printer," he added, handing her another bundle.

"Oh! Thank you so much, Jack. This really looks great!" As she went to put them both into her backpack, she stopped and looked at his paper, tapping it with her long, slender finger. "I'll try to get this back to you as soon as possible."

"No, I ran that copy for you. Just toss it in the trash if you want, unless you have some comments you want to write on the text. I'd like to hear what you think about it. I put my number on there, and I was hoping you'd call if you find any parts confusing or faulty. I really need critical feedback." He was glad it was working out this way, because he wanted to be sure she had his number, anyway.

"Oooh, 'Strange Details in Stephen's Defense,'" she breathed as she scanned the title page. "Boy, you said it! This sounds interesting, Jack. I read that speech by Stephen after you said you were writing on it, and I have to say, it seemed strange to me. I just couldn't see why he said the things he did, you know, or what his argument was."

"Yeah, I know. I'll give you a clue: it has to do with your stuff on formalism. I think you're going to like this paper. It gets right into the area of your interest in formalism versus inner growth." Jack chomped his burger and beamed as he watched her brilliant green eyes quietly look over the sections of the paper. It felt great to be able to share his academic work with a woman. Most of the women he had dated tried to act interested, but really seemed confused when he got into the details of his research. He sensed Sherry was not only going to understand, she would probably be pressing him for advancement before long.

To Jack, the idea of a brilliant woman who was so beautiful was doubly appealing. As he watched her read, he wondered whether her passions ran as deeply as her thoughts. He had a feeling they did. What would she be like if she wasn't acting out of her cool intellectualism? He had seen deep feelings from her at certain points. But of course, he had never dared to enter into her full ability to express love.

She was still scanning the paper, and finally she looked up. "Well, this really looks good! I've been looking forward to this paper, Jack, and I'm going to enjoy reading it." She put the paper in her backpack. "Everything you say seems to make so much sense." She paused and looked down. "I don't know whether I've ever really come out and told you how much I appreciate your teaching. I feel like God has used you to change my life, and I don't know where I'd be today if it wasn't for you."

Jack's heart was throbbing with a warm inner glow. "Well, I'm sure God can work without any help from me."

"Yeah, but you sure don't hurt things any. How did you get all your stuff on the Bible, anyway?"

"I was fortunate to sit under a marvelous Bible teacher for several years, an older guy. . . ."

"Who was it? Where is he now?"

"Oh, you wouldn't know him. His name was Jim Leffel. He was with a campus group here, trained in a Baptist seminary, I think. Anyway, he wasn't working as a preacher when he was teaching here. It was just a campus student ministry. I've never seen anyone who could divide the Scriptures . . . who was deeper than he was."

"Where is he now?"

"He ran off with one of the girls in our Bible study group." He paused with a slight grin as the shock registered on Sherry's face. Then he answered the question forming on her lips. "His wife and two kids didn't appreciate that too much."

"Oh, Jack! That's terrible! How could that happen?"

"It happens more than you might think. The guy I studied with after him went weird, too. He joined a group that's essentially a cult. Believe me, you have to base your walk on God and His Word. If you base it on men, you're sure to be disappointed. I told Lee Carulo a couple of weeks ago I was waiting for him to show up as an embezzler or something."

"Lee really seems mature. We've been listening to some of his teaching. I just think it's so cool to see someone in the traditional church who has priorities like his."

"Yeah, you said it. Lee took a lot of flak for some of his righteous decisions early on, but he has his church on his side now. The guys we meet with over there are deep and committed. He doesn't just preach to people, he equips them."

She could see how deep Jack's feelings of respect and love were for Lee. "Yes, I don't believe he'll ever lose it."

"That's what I said about Jim Leffel."

"Well, I haven't been disappointed in you so far."

"I'll guarantee you it's only a matter of time." Jack was insistent.

"I'll have to remember that. I guess I shouldn't trust you so much?"

Jack didn't answer. She looked up from the straw she had been fiddling with and into Jack's face, which had longing written all over it. He lowered his eyes after a moment that was a little too long and mumbled, "Yeah, I guess you shouldn't trust me too much."

"What's wrong, Jack? I hope I wasn't offensive with that crack."

"No, it's not that. I guess it's just hard. I guess I want you to trust me on some level . . . I don't know. . . ." Jack was finding this conversation suddenly difficult. He couldn't decide what to say.

Sherry jumped in urgently, "I *do* trust you, Jack! I think I trust you more than any guy I've ever known!" Sherry sat back suddenly in her seat, and brought her hand up over her mouth, shocked that she had revealed more of her heart than she had meant to. Jack looked at her, uncertain what to say.

"Oh, man, I can't believe I said that," she said with wide eyes full of alarm and embarrassment.

Jack smiled broadly. "Why? Because it isn't true?"

"No, it . . . it just sounds really stupid."

Now Jack was suddenly intense. "I don't think it's stupid at all. I think it's one of the nicest things anyone's ever said to me . . . and I really appreciate it."

The conversation ran into a brick wall suddenly, and in the awkward silence that followed, he looked down, feeling the strong surge of emotion that her accidental vulnerability had called forth. There was a prolonged silence as they each struggled with what they both knew was there. Without planning to, they had reached a point of communication where each of them not only knew what the other was feeling, but also knew this knowledge was mutual. As Jack stared down intently at the floor next to their table, he wondered whether to continue to pretend they were just "buddies." He realized there was no longer anything to conceal.

He brought his eyes up to hers, and she returned his gaze. This time they stared into each other's eyes, trembling inwardly in the grip of what they both sensed had been coming all along. Neither of them had the slightest doubt they were spontaneously crossing a major threshold. They sat sealed off from the busy restaurant as though in their own bubble.

Thoughts raced through Jack's mind at the speed of light, seeming to almost come out in words but passing by. His eyes probed deeply into hers, so like emerald oceans. He wanted to warn her, to assure her, to openly declare his love for her, but as he stared into the depths of her eyes, nothing seemed important enough to risk breaking the spell that gripped them helplessly in its power.

Jack leaned forward over the little table that separated them, and she leaned forward as well. She seemed to think he wanted to kiss her. But he didn't. Their faces were close enough that he could smell her sweetness. Her eyes, upturned, seemed to plead to him for answers, for action, for assurance.

He brought his hand up, trembling, and slowly touched her perfectly smooth cheek. Sliding his hand back along her cheek, he pushed her hair back until he held the side of her face with his hand. Caressing her beauty, he marveled at the sheer fortune he felt. She covered his hand with hers, and pressed it closer. Instinctively, his other hand found hers across the table. Oblivious to all else, they swam in the dizziness of discovery. Fear mingled with eagerness.

Sherry broke the silence. "Are we doing something bad?"

"I don't see anything bad going on," he smiled.

Sherry was deeply frightened. They had come near this point before, only to have Jack's scruples rise up and dash her hopes. Could she trust this man? She realized it didn't matter, because it was too late to do anything *but* trust him. Like someone who regrets getting on a roller coaster, she knew events had taken control of her. She felt helpless, but excited.

"Would you like to go for a walk again?" Jack asked.

"Well, I didn't really like the way our last walk ended. . . ."

"That was a long time ago."

"Okay," she grinned mischievously. "Let's take a walk!"

30

The afternoon had a hint of chill and a December gray sky. As they came out of the restaurant onto the street Jack matter-of-factly reached over and drew her body next to his, his arm holding her waist firmly. She slid her arm around him and, putting her backpack over her other shoulder, wrapped both arms around him as they walked.

They strolled across campus clinging together and leaning heavily against each other. Periodically, Jack put his head down and pressed his cheek against her forehead. At other times they looked into each other's faces, as if to assure themselves that this was really happening. They walked silently, almost in reverence at the feelings surging through them. *This can't be wrong, Lord!* he breathed to himself. *She is so pure, so open. Don't let me mess her up!*

She seemed to fold into him, as though they were one person. He sensed the urgency in her arms around his waist as she pressed her head against his chest. The sweet smell of her hair filled his nostrils.

"Mmmmmm, you smell good! Do you have to be anywhere?" he asked her.

"I don't have to be at work until 3:00," she assured him. "Where are we going?"

"In here," he said, as they turned up a sidewalk toward the student union.

"I'm surprised."

"I have a place in mind," he said.

As they passed through the glass doors and into the spacious walkway, they passed people silently walking toward them. Nobody seemed to notice them much, which struck Jack as odd. It seemed like everyone should be able to see what was happening.

At a certain point he turned her to the left, and they entered one of the study lounges. This one was small and had a fireplace with a glimmering fire at one end. Jack guided her toward the couch in front of the fireplace. They were both glad to see it was deserted.

"Oh, this is a nice place," she murmured approvingly. "It's romantic."

"I think that's appropriate," he grinned, as they dropped off their coats and books at one end of the little couch. They sat down, arm in arm, and rested their heads together, the flickering of the fire playing on her face. He drew his head back a couple of inches and brought his hand up to her smooth, youthful face. "Sherry, I don't feel like I deserve to be here holding you like this."

She bent her head over toward his hand and stroked her face against it like a tabby cat. No answer was necessary.

Looking down, he saw her full and partly opened lips. He drew her forward, hesitating for a long moment, their lips only an inch apart. He could feel the warmth radiating from her face onto his own. Finally, he kissed her longingly and tenderly—she responded eagerly. They threw their arms around each other in a fervent embrace and expressed their feelings to each other through touch for an unknown length of time.

"Mmmmm," Sherry whispered in his ear. "I've wanted to do this so often." She seemed to drink in the sensation of holding this elusive man in her arms at last.

Jack buried his face in her wonderful fragrant hair as he clasped her desperately to himself. "I've been obsessed thinking about this moment. I can't believe I'm finally holding you. . . ." He felt water on his cheek and quickly drew back. Sherry's eyes were brimming with tears. She pulled him to her again and seemed to be holding on for dear life.

Sherry was lost in an ocean of feeling. This was like nothing she had ever experienced before. She knew what it was to be aroused . . . but what was this? She felt such a depth of caring, such an utter sense of rightness, along with a frightening level of arousal: It was confusing, almost sacred. She drew back and looked Jack in the eyes again as if in disbelief. "Is this the way it always is for Christians?" she asked in all honesty.

"I don't think so," he breathed with a frown. "I know I've never had an experience like this."

"What comes next?" she put the obvious question.

"I don't know. But I get the feeling we need to be careful."

"Why do you say that?" she frowned.

"Because you are the most important person in my life, and I don't want to hurt you."

"You mean you might have to break this off again?"

"No . . . no, I don't mean that," Jack said, staring slightly cross-eyed at his finger running delicately down the side of her smooth neck. "I wouldn't have come this far if I wasn't here for real. I'm not going any-where. I just mean . . . it seems like it's up to us what we want to make of this."

"This is your integrity thing, isn't it?"

He seemed to be considering whether he wanted to submit to her verdict. "I hope that's not a problem."

She paused and thought about it, a smile spreading across her face. "Far from it. That's why I'm sitting here."

"Sherry, you're the most beautiful person I've ever known. And I mean that inwardly . . . as well as outwardly." He looked into her eyes. "You're going to have to realize I don't know what I'm doing. See, I haven't had much experience with women, and I've certainly never expe-rienced anything like this."

Sherry looked down. His reference to lack of experience with women made her feel sad. She wished she could say the same thing back to him. She looked back up quizzically as she realized that the twenty-five-year-old man she held might even be a virgin. That thought filled her with awe, but it also made her feel unworthy. She decided to tell the truth. "Jack, I'm afraid I've been around more than you."

"You mean with guys?"

"Yeah."

"Sherry, that was when you were a nonChristian. Don't you remember the verse from the other night? You know, 'If anyone is in Christ he's a new creature, the old has passed away, and all that stuff?'"

"Yeah . . . but I guess I thought that means like, you know, to God."

"Well, it does. But there's also the part where He says, 'We don't rec-ognize anyone according to the flesh anymore.' You're starting over. What you're experiencing now is completely different than before."

Her face softened, and she pressed her cheek into his. "That's so kind," she purred. "With you, I get the feeling we can work things out." She felt there was somehow a great deal of truth in what he had said, but she still felt troubled. Jack was wearing a thick zip-up sweater over his T-shirt. She unzipped the half-open sweater the rest of the way, and sliding her hands around his chest, drew him close. She could feel his breathing close to hers.

It was wonderful to experience holding his body in her arms, not just the person she had dreamed of so often, but his tangible warm body. *Yes! This is what I've been craving!* Jack finally seemed like a breathing, living man . . . not just an idea. Her own body cried out for more of him, but she knew it wouldn't happen, at least not now. She ached with desire to show him even more how deeply she loved him.

She looked up and suddenly kissed him again passionately on the mouth, the cheek, his ear, his neck. . . . What a glorious thing it was to finally pour out her love on him and to sense his longing response!

It seemed like only a few minutes had passed when, with a groan, Sherry said she was going to have to start on her way to work soon. She sat back in the couch a little and relaxed, curling one arm up on the back of the couch. She laid her head down on her arm and stared at him. Jack did likewise. With their faces only inches apart, they wandered aimlessly through the depths of each other's eyes, sharing a knowledge of their feelings for each other that no one else could know. There was neither past nor future, but only the intensity of this moment, as kind, knowing smiles of love broke out on both their faces. They were truly in a world of their own; a new world, waiting to be explored and experienced. They sat at the gate to that world . . . searching into each other . . . savoring the moment . . . not in any hurry to go further for now . . . only wanting to enjoy the realization that they were there—together.

Jack reached up and touched below her eye where a tear had left a streak earlier. "You're so beautiful," he marveled.

She just smiled as he tenderly explored her face with his finger . . . her eyebrows . . . her thin nose . . . her cheekbone . . . her lips. . . . "I'll walk you over to work," he said very quietly. "I don't want you to get in any trouble."

"I don't know if I can go to work," she protested. "I want to stay here with you!" She kissed his finger as it passed over her lips.

"I'll meet you after work. I have to go to a meeting with Forsythe anyway."

"Okay," she said with resignation, as she sat up and reached for her things. "I guess I'll feel better later if I show up for my shift."

As they traversed campus again, they both felt like they were different people. A sense of awe held them in its grip as both of them realized that their emotional world had just been utterly transformed. Long minutes of silence passed as they walked along, pondering what it meant. Finally, as they neared The Bratcellar, Sherry spoke. "I'm worried, Jack."

"So am I."

"What are you worried about?" she asked in a surprised tone.

"I've never felt such a loss of control over my life. I feel utterly vulnerable, I feel like I'm at your mercy."

"That's exactly what I feel. I don't know what's going to happen and I'm afraid I'm going to be hurt."

"I think we have to try to trust God here, Sherry. He's our only ultimate security." They turned the corner and saw the restaurant just ahead.

"I guess I don't exactly know how to do that yet."

"I'm not sure I do either . . . maybe we should talk about that after your work?"

"Okay, I get off around 11:00."

He kissed her deeply again. "I'll see you then." They held each other.

"I really have to get in there," she pleaded, and grudgingly he let her go. She smiled and, turning, she ran up the steps.

Jack walked off into the late-afternoon grayness.

31

Sherry was so happy at work she drifted through the afternoon and evening. With hardly any customers to worry about, she had the luxury of numerous opportunities to lounge around the enclosed waitress station thinking about what had happened with Jack. The rest of the time, she floated around, working as though she was in a dream. Even as a schoolgirl she couldn't remember ever feeling so good. *Thank You, Jesus! Protect me! Guard me, Lord!* she breathed to herself over and over again as she worked.

She realized Jack must have "run into her" at McDonald's on purpose, not by accident as she thought at first. How else could he have just happened to be carrying a copy of his paper with his phone number on it? She wondered how much the whole thing was unfolding according to his plan. She decided to find out, even though she realized that, on one level, she didn't care.

She thought about the copy of his paper in her backpack. It was exciting to have some part of him with her. Especially intriguing was the thought that she had somehow contributed to his thinking in the paper. She wondered what he meant by that.

As the dinner business began to slow down even more around 8:00, she couldn't resist looking at the paper. She got it out at the servers' station and looked at it, wondering whether she could read it between trips to her tables. She realized she wouldn't be able to look at the paper objectively any more because she was too involved with the author. *Who cares?* she thought to herself, and began to read.

Strange Details in Stephen's Defense: A New Accounting
by Jack Collins

She read his opening comments about how difficult it was for many commentators to understand Stephen's speech. He quoted some of their cynical comments. It was surprising to see how many commentators openly admitted they had no idea why many of the details of the speech were there. Then Jack gave his own view of the speech:

I think this speech is the linchpin in the transition between Christianity as a localized ethnic religion, and a universal body. Stephen the Hellenist was able to see the implications of the gospel to an extraordinary degree.

Later, she went on to read what Jack thought was the key to understanding the speech:

The key to understanding why Stephen includes seemingly irrelevant detail is that these details deal with geography. He actually seems overly concerned with geography, and with the people's and God's relationship to it. Stephen is not only responding to his accusers' reverence for the temple but also to their fixation on the more foundational concept of sacred space or sacred land.

Mmmmm, Sherry thought to herself. *Geography. How strange. I guess I didn't get that. I can see why he thought my paper related to his. I can't believe I didn't catch this when I read it!* She walked over and got her Bible out of her backpack and, as she brought it back to the station where the paper was, opened it to Acts 7 so she could read along with the paper.

She found her place in his paper again, remembering his face and his keen eyes. A feeling of excitement rushed over her as she realized he would be waiting after work. After covering a couple of customers, she went on reading.

Jack explained that the holy land of Israel was part of the religious vision of the Jews in Stephen's day, and how they were scandalized when Stephen suggested the holy land wasn't important any longer. Jack argued that this attachment to the land was also connected to an emphasis on sacred space—on formalism. One section said,

At the heart of ethnic-religious worldviews are the twin values of "Race and Space," or to put it differently, "Blood and Soil." These values are hardly unique to first-century Judaism. Scholars have used the same terms to understand folk religions from shamanism to Nazism. Unfortunately, these values would adequately summarize the ethos of much of modern Western Christianity as well.

By demonstrating God's ability to work apart from sacred space, including the sacred city and sacred land of Israel, Stephen's speech lays a firm ideological foundation for the book of Acts. This foundation explains God's shift in focus away from both the temple and the land, outward to the rest of the world.

He went on to go through the sections of the seventh chapter of Acts, demonstrating his thesis. He showed that in each era of Old Testament history, Stephen proved that God was perfectly able to work outside the land of Israel, outside Jerusalem, and outside the temple.

Mmmmm, I get it. Sherry reflected. *So God's thing was often happening outside the land of Israel, and often with rejected spokesmen just like Jesus. God was getting ready to move the gospel outside of Israel again in Stephen's day. That's really cool! That's why Stephen brings this stuff up!* She envied Jack's insight into Scripture.

She wanted Jack for her own. What would it be like to have a guy, and be able to ask him about the Bible any time? *We'll know that soon!* she rejoiced. *Thank You, Jesus! I praise You for the chance to love this man. Please guard me! I'm worried! But I'm excited!*

She decided to read on. Reading Jack's words was the closest thing to having him there at work with her. She continued to plow through the thirty-some-page paper, finishing just as Carole, the other waitress on duty that evening, approached her. "Sherry, are you all right? You're letting your customers wait too long, and I'm having to cover for you."

"I'm sorry, Carole. I shouldn't have put that off on you. I've been so involved reading this paper by a guy I know. You wouldn't believe how interesting some of the stuff is that I've been getting into lately. . . ."

They talked on and off when they had a few minutes during the rest of their shift, Carole becoming more and more curious as she sensed Sherry's excitement. She even expressed interest in checking out Sherry's new group sometime.

32

As Sherry came out to the bar area around 10:30, she saw Jack there, nursing a drink and watching a game on TV. She wasn't sure why, but she felt hesitant to go up to him. Maybe she was afraid he might have changed his mind? After taking a deep breath, she went directly to him and leaned on the bar next to him. He looked around suddenly and a broad smile covered his face as he saw her. His eyes traveled down her body and back up. "Wow! You look great in that uniform," he observed.

She hadn't thought about her skimpy outfit, and she felt a little chagrined. Something about Jack was making her feel as modest as a teenager. "Well, I'm getting out of it in a minute." Neither one of them spoke for a moment, as they grinned at each other like two embarrassed conspirators. The magic was still there, and she felt a strong urge to wrap her arms around him for a lingering, loving hug. Instead she looked around to make sure no one was looking before leaning forward and kissing him lightly on the lips.

"When do you get off?" he asked in a low, soft voice.

"Well, I just have one table left, but they're taking their time. I could leave if it wasn't for them," she explained.

"Don't worry about it, I just came over because I didn't have anywhere else to go. I'm perfectly happy watching this basketball game."

"Oh, you wouldn't believe what I've been doing tonight." She lit up with mystery.

"What?"

"I've been reading your paper! I've been getting in trouble with the other waitress because I'm too distracted from my work."

"Wow!" His smile showed he was pleased. "I'm amazed you could read a heavy paper while you're working."

"Well, we haven't had much business tonight. I would've been standing around gossiping with Carole if I wasn't reading." She gestured toward the waiting station.

"How far did you get?"

"I'm done! I just read the last page of that section you gave me. Boy, guys like Stephen were the radicals of their day," she suggested.

Jack sat back in his chair. "Yeah, they seemed to have been the first ones there when it came to seeing it God's way."

"Jack, your paper's dynamite! Where are you going to go from here?" She was leaning forward on the bar, as eager as a puppy.

"The main thing with the rest of the paper is the history of interpretation. It's pretty boring compared to this part."

"Well, I just loved it. Thanks for letting me read it. Hold on for a minute." She left again to check on her table, and this time, she ran into Carole at the waiters' station. She couldn't resist telling Carole to check out the guy at the bar. Carole went out and returned shortly. "Wow! He's about as sharp as they come! So this is what one of those Christians looks like, huh? What's he like?"

"Oh, he's so sweet, Carole," Sherry beamed. "I'll introduce you to him when we have more time—he'll be there Monday night if you want to come."

"Are there any others like him there?" she joked.

"Well . . . I don't know about 'like him,' but there are some cute guys there. I think you'll like the group. The girls there are really nice, too."

"Sounds cool. Go on now, I'll save your last tip in the bottle."

"Thanks, Carole."

She stopped by Jack's seat. "Just let me clean up some stuff and change real quick. Carole agreed to close tonight, so I'm off."

He nodded, and she turned to finish her work.

She could feel her heartbeat rising as she hurried to the restroom. They had little lockers there, and she quickly changed clothes. She checked herself in the mirror. *I have to be careful not to jump all over this guy!* she reminded herself. She had put on some eye makeup earlier for the occasion. She felt a little insecure about spending time with Jack, but she realized her appearance was as good as she could make it.

"Can I buy you something?" Jack offered as she came around the bar to where he was sitting.

"No, thanks. I'd rather go somewhere else if that's all right with you."

"Sure."

As they walked out, she asked whether he would like to come to her place. He was silent for a moment, which piqued her curiosity. "What's wrong?"

"Well, I'm a little worried about going to your place."

"Oh, is this that thing you told me once about not letting someone see you alone in a woman's apartment?"

"Uh, yeah . . . I guess that's part of it. . . ."

"What's the other part of it?"

"Don't you think if we were alone in an apartment we might get a little carried away?"

"Well, not unless we wanted to," she suggested with a salacious smile.

Jack's eyes widened and he looked away as he took a deep breath and blew it out. "I guess that's the point. We might want to, but that might not be right."

This was new ground for Sherry. Her rule until now was that if both wanted to do something, it was automatically all right. Of course, she had heard teaching on why fornication was wrong. She had heard the line of reasoning that sex should be reserved for marriage, and that the failure to do so usually amounted to exploitation more than it did to love. But this seemed different. This was the first time she had experienced the trial of voluntary sexual abstinence. She inwardly resisted the restraint she felt as she realized she and Jack were not *allowed* to have sex. It made her feel a little rebellious. "Boy, this is different for me, Jack. Exactly what's considered fornication, and what's not?"

Jack answered slowly, appearing to choose his words. "I think you have to consider it from the standpoint of what's the loving thing for the other person." He shot her a sideways glance to see if she was receptive to his words—she wasn't.

"I think you can express love physically," Sherry pouted.

"Of course. I agree. But unless there's a commitment there, I don't believe we have any business actually moving toward . . . you know . . . actually getting it on."

Sherry felt a vague sense of rejection in what Jack said. In her mind she knew he was right; that he didn't intend it as a rejection of her. But it irked her to hear it anyway. She was frowning and thoughtful as they walked on. He seemed so calculating.

Jack must have sensed there was a problem. He put his arm around her as they walked. "Look, it's very frustrating to get aroused and eager, only to have to stop and go home, right?"

She nodded reluctantly. *He could always stay and sleep on the couch*, she thought to herself.

Jack struggled on. "That's why I think it's just more loving . . . more considerate of the other person if we draw the line long before that point. . . ." He looked down at her, but she wouldn't return his gaze. "Now, I'm not saying we can't show physical affection for each other. It's only a problem when we begin to deal with real, you know . . . arousal."

Again she didn't answer, but she knew he was right on one level. She wondered how could they show physical affection without becoming aroused.

Jack was almost pleading now. "Sherry, there's nothing I'd like more than to really show you how I feel. I think it'd be unbelievably exciting to get really intimate. But that's the whole point. I want it so badly that I realize the danger there. I don't want to even come close enough to that fire to get burned."

Sherry looked up with an acquiescing half-grin, and slid her own arm around him. She showed she knew he was right, but she still didn't like it. She remembered how she had felt about her heavy sexual past when they were together earlier that day; how she envied Jack's ability to say he was inexperienced with women. Now she was experiencing the other side of that restraint—the frustrating side. "So what do Christian dating couples do with themselves?" she asked the obvious question.

"I'm not sure how to answer that. I know I've really enjoyed studying things together, and I really like being with you. . . ." He thought for a bit. "I think maybe we should just spend some time talking deeply. I feel like I'm close to you on one level, but I want to be a lot closer . . . to know a lot more, on another level." He was gesturing with his free hand again, which he liked to do whenever he was arguing a point.

"Yeah, me too." She sincerely liked his suggestion.

"I guess part of the key is that we focus on the part we do have, not on the part we can't have yet."

Sherry focused on that last word. It sank into her fully for the first time that if she ever wanted to make love to Jack she would have to marry him. At the same time, she realized marriage was a definite possibility. She had turned down several proposals in the past, partly because the crowd she ran around with wasn't much into getting married. She always assumed she would get married some day, and she knew she wanted to have children, but she had seen so much failure in marriage she was quite wary. Right there on the spot, she began to look at marriage in a different light. It was a whole different calculation now.

She had determined long before that the biggest barrier to marriage for her was that in marriage, she would have to trust a man. Based on her experience, that didn't seem like a very good idea. But now walking with Jack, she thought, *Here might be a man I could trust.* Why did she think that? She wasn't sure.

Maybe it was what Lisa said. He didn't seem to be living for himself, or seeking personal advantage. In her mind, marriage still stood for the dangers she had witnessed in the lives of her friends and their parents. But now it also stood for this man she wanted, and any hope of a sex life. She decided to ask Jack a question that occurred to her at that moment. "As Christians, how do you know if you're compatible, you know, sexually?"

Jack grinned. "I don't know." Then after thinking for a while, "I wonder what that means, anyway?"

"Well, you know, there might be a different rhythm for different people," she suggested.

Jack grimaced, as though struggling with her comment. "Don't you think that kind of thing's dictated by how the relationship's going?"

"Oh, yeah, that's a big part of it."

"That's the problem I have with the idea of trial marriages or whatever. You're going to mess up the trust and the security in the relationship, because you're saying you might dump the person if you're not happy with how she, or he, performs in the bedroom. That'd make me a little nervous."

Sherry remembered the last time she went to bed with Jim. "Yeah, it's not very comfortable, actually."

"I'm told by some married friends you can tell all you need to know without having sex . . . in fact, I was recently reading a research study showing those who have trial marriages are twice as likely to be divorced."

"You're kidding!"

"No, this is for real. It was in a study done at Johns Hopkins and the University of Wisconsin. They showed that cohabiting couples are twice as likely to get divorced if they ever get married, and they showed that the longer they cohabit, the more likely divorce is. I thought that was really interesting, because it's just the *opposite* of what you would expect if you believed the nonChristian rap."

"Yeah, that really is interesting." Sherry was lost in thought. "I guess sleeping around hasn't helped my friends who got married. But I don't have anything to compare them to either."

"Well, I've met some pretty cool Christian couples, but I don't really base it on that. I guess I just feel like I'm going to do it God's way, and trust it'll be the best way. . . ." They walked on for a bit, both thoughtful. Then Jack asked in a soft voice, "Sherry, do you agree we should try to do our relationship God's way?"

"Yes," she said without hesitation. "I'm just having to adjust here to a new way of thinking."

"I'm glad . . . because I feel like we could lose the good thing we've started if we aren't really careful." Jack was obviously warning her there were boundaries that must be respected. Then he went further. "I'd like you to help me maintain whatever standards we decide are right, okay?"

It seemed like a reasonable request. "That sounds good to me," Sherry nodded. "But you're going to have to let me know what you're thinking on this."

"Fair enough." He gave her a squeeze of assurance as they walked on. They had been heading toward Sherry's place without necessarily planning to. As the building came into sight Jack suggested they warm up in the entry lobby before he headed home.

They pulled around one of the cheap couches in the tiny lobby so it faced the full-length window looking out onto the lighted courtyard. The view wasn't exactly awe-inspiring, but it was pleasant enough. A few snowflakes began to float around under the arc-lamps illuminating the yard and garden, and as always with the first flakes of snow for the year, Sherry got a special feeling watching them fall. Something mildly sad and nostalgic came over her as the snow signaled the passage of another year. They sat and began to try to understand each other in a deeper way by sharing about their pasts.

She found out Jack's parents were still together and had lived in Guatemala for the past five years, working with a U.N. community development task force. Jack's dad, Ned, had been a builder in Ohio until Jack and his two older brothers were all out of the house. It was then that his mom, Katie, had talked Ned into selling the business and going into a life of travel and social service. He was constructing water systems for the villages in Central America while Katie taught in the village school, and used her nursing degree to provide primary medical care to the poor villagers. Jack respected his parents' values deeply, and he told Sherry he hoped to see them come to Christ one day. So far, they had taken a cautious but respectful position toward Jack's faith.

When Jack plied Sherry with questions about her past, she opened up completely about her life. She talked about what it was like to be a little girl growing up on Lake Shore Drive . . . her adventures in Saugatuk . . . including Bruce Jager . . . her ambivalent feelings about her parents. "I'm not looking forward to going home for Christmas, because I know my brother, Doug, and my parents are going to grill me big-time. I just don't know whether they'll be able to accept the kind of view we have."

"Well, don't jump to that conclusion. The main thing is to avoid setting goals and expectations too high for the visit. You know, they probably won't fall on their knees and worship God, but if you handle it correctly, you might be able to get them to take a more neutral or even positive view of what you're into."

"Will you tell me some things to say?"

"Sure." As they talked, Jack had a knack for asking questions that showed he was a careful listener who wouldn't let her continue until he understood. He had an empathy that made Sherry feel secure even when she related some of the most terrible parts of her past.

"So you were pretty heavy into acid and grass then?" he asked.

"Yeah, what about you?"

"I did weed for a while in high school, and I did acid twice. Then I got into college and found Christ my freshman year through this Bible study Jim Leffel led in the dorm. Once I started to walk with God, I put drugs down."

"I'm sure there must have been a lot of opportunities with women in the partying crowd there at the dorm."

He smiled and looked out the window, visibly uncomfortable with her question. "Well, some, but not as many as you might think. I was sort of awkward and shy in high school and as a freshman. There was one girl in the dorms who was after me in a big way."

"Well?"

"Well, she scared me too much," he laughed.

"Oh, come on! You're trying to tell me you let her intimidate you that much?"

"I was just afraid of aggressive women." He shook his head in embarrassment. "And I guess I was afraid that . . . if she asked me out, you know . . . I guess I was afraid to go to bed with her."

"She must not have been very pretty, huh?"

"Not real pretty, no. But she had a great figure." He smiled wickedly.

"You weren't a Christian yet, so you must've been afraid of getting her pregnant or catching something."

"No, it wasn't that." He furrowed his brow, trying to find the right words. "I was inhibited," he shrugged. He saw Sherry staring at him, apparently trying to understand. "I really didn't feel safe dropping my drawers in front of a woman, and I felt sure this girl would've called for that. She was scary! I guess I was just intimidated," he shrugged again.

Sherry nodded thoughtfully as she watched Jack feeling uncomfortable. He was elusive, and he was strangely timid. It was odd that he was able to act so bold during his public teachings. She wondered what he would be like if he ever really let loose.

He went on. "You know, even as a nonChristian, I believed monogamy was where it's at. I never felt comfortable with the idea of just getting it on with a girl, even though I didn't really love her. And of course, once I started walking with God I realized that was His plan, too. I messed around some with a few girls, but I always knew I wouldn't be satisfied with anything less than a lifelong love." He turned and looked at her. For a moment it seemed like he was wondering whether he had found that love. "So let's get back to you. It sounds like you got even wilder after you came onto campus."

She began to describe some of her important romances and increasingly wild party life. She was shocked at herself when she twice began to cry as she recounted the points at which she had further hardened herself in order to bear the burden of a lifestyle based on self. The moral contrast between her story and Jack's was painful. Strangely, she talked without pain about Duchan, her longtime lover, but she lost it as she described running around with the other guys after breaking up with him. Jack didn't press her for details on this part, but she decided to open up anyway. She wanted to know whether he would still accept her if he knew her past. Shame welled up in her throat as she reviewed the shallow sexual experiences she had allowed herself to explore.

Jack reassured her. "You're like this beautiful princess who's been deeply hurt while wandering around lost." She could feel his compassion as his hand massaged the back and sides of her slender neck and played with her hair. Sherry even looked up at him to see if he was in tears. He wasn't, but he had a pained look on his sensitive face—it was as though he wished he could have been there to protect her.

"Tell me about this guy we saw outside class. The one you said attacked you."

"Oh, brother. It was so sickening! I was telling him to get lost, you know? And he grabbed me and locked his arms around me, like that was going to change my mind or something."

"He's muscular."

"Yeah, he's on the wrestling team. Anyway, I'm squirming, shouting, beating on him . . . and so he sort of corners me and just socks this gross kiss on me. Jack, my lips were *bruised* afterward! He was trying to hurt me."

"Oh, man," Jack winced. "That's sick!"

"Yeah, it was like I had a sense of what it feels like to be raped. He was getting back at me; it was pure, violent hate."

"Has he given you any more trouble?"

She thought for a minute. "I don't know. I made out the police report like you suggested. The cop seemed to think I was dreaming the whole thing up . . . and of course, I couldn't point to any definite evidence. Jim did write me a couple of days later, but I wrote back saying I'd reported him to the police and I was going to show them his letter. I said they wanted any evidence that came up, you know, like there was an investigation going on. I thought that would scare him."

"Oh, yeah! Why, you don't mean he's still following you?"

"No. But I get these calls once in a while where no one speaks, even though I can tell someone's there."

"And you think it's him?"

"Uh . . ." She shrugged her shoulders. "I can't say it is. I get the feeling it is, but that's probably natural, considering what happened."

"Yeah, I sure would think the thing with the police would be effective. And you haven't actually seen him, right?"

"Right. I'd call the police if I saw him hanging around."

"Well, I think you should be careful. You shouldn't walk around on campus at night."

"I don't! I carry mace, too."

"That's a good idea. If you have any more problems with him, let me know, all right?"

"Why, so you can go over and beat him up?" She grinned.

Jack chuckled and shrugged. "No, just so I can know you're having trouble."

They finally wound up in each other's arms silently drinking in the joy and excitement of holding each other. At 2:30 a.m. Jack kissed her and said he meant it this time, he was really going to go home. Before he left, he suggested they try to pray with each other. "Would that make you feel too weird?" he asked.

"No, I pray with my girlfriends. But it'll be the first time I've ever prayed with a date!"

"Well, this is one of those things I mentioned earlier. I feel like we'll do better in general if we learn early to pray together and sort of . . . you know, make it a habit."

"It sounds good to me," she said, and before anything more could happen, Jack bowed his head and began to pray.

"Lord Jesus, I just want to thank You for bringing this beautiful person into my life. Please let us relate to each other in a way that keeps You in the center. Let us focus on being the best thing that ever happened to each other." He shot her a glance and a grin, before looking back down. "Keep us from selfishness and carnality. I pray, too, that our dating will be a blessing for others also, not just for us."

He fell silent. Sherry felt more nervous than she thought she would. But she spoke up with a simple prayer.

"Dear God, I thank You for all the things I've learned since Jack came into my life. I thank You for this great chance You've given us to have something together, and with You. I pray I can learn a whole new way to do . . . like, a dating relationship, and I just pray this won't interfere with my growth as You and I get closer. Amen." She looked over at him and they smiled at each other, happy that they had verbally brought God into the center of their relationship.

They got up, and Sherry handed Jack his briefcase as he put on his jacket. He leaned over to kiss her and quickly left, taking one final look back over his shoulder.

She watched his form disappear from the edge of the lighted area in the courtyard and turned to go to her room. Undressing in a mood of drowsy delight before going to bed, she sat on the side of her bed for a few minutes. *Lord, I thank You and praise You for this whole pattern of blessing You've laid on me. I pray I won't blow it with this relationship! I agree with Jack, Lord. We need to do it Your way no matter what. I'm not going to try to control where this goes, God. I'm going to trust that You'll continue to bless my life as You have so far. . . .* She trailed off, as there didn't seem to be anything more to say at that point.

She decided it was time to go to sleep.

33

Winter is cold in Michigan. As fall quarter came to an end, the first early winter storm roared in later than usual, but just in time for Sherry to go home for Christmas. Most of the snow fell at night, but as Sherry prepared to leave the next morning, the wind had shifted and was coming out of the north. The temperature was falling rapidly.

She worried as she threw some things in the car, knowing her parents would want to talk about her experience with "religion" as they would put it. Jack and Lisa had given her some ideas about how to communicate effectively with her folks. She was also loaded up with several good books, and a few tapes of Jack's teachings given at the Monday night Bible study.

As she drove westward into periodic snow squalls and a blustery wind that shook her little car, she listened to the tapes of Jack, a couple of which she had never heard. Several times she sighed: How deep he was! How funny! How caring! How passionate! Wouldn't it be great if he was in the car with her right then, and she could look over into his eyes! She felt blue as she realized she was driving the opposite direction from what she wanted. *Oh, well, I'm only going to be there for a few days,* she reminded herself.

As she turned off the freeway near Saugatuk and headed out to the beach, her eyes flitted from one familiar thing to another. *How odd it is to come home! This gives me the strangest feelings.*

Her eyes fell on the gas station she walked to for pop as a girl. There was the orchard where she had received her first kiss. Jumbled feelings attached to every detail of scenery came rumbling back all at once, producing a confused traffic jam of emotion. There was something welcoming and comforting along with a melancholy sense of something lost.

The line of dunes along the western shore of Lake Michigan was visible now, and Lake Shore Drive ran across the tops of a number of dunes that had been leveled off. The result was an impression that one was driving along the top of a cliff over the lake. There were big old trees planted between the road and the edge of the bluff, with houses on the other side of the street only, so that the driver is right out next to the lake. Seeing this vista was always impressive, especially now that she didn't live next to it anymore, and only saw it a few times a year. She was transfixed by the angry, white-capped endless surface of the powerful Great Lake beyond a line of trees. She pulled her car over and watched the waves for a few minutes in the fading light of the still-overcast early evening. Bursts of wind shook the car as she admired the large breakers rolling in.

Dinner and a warm fire are going to feel great tonight, she reflected. *Lord Jesus, protect me, and use me to reach out to my family. You know I hate it when Mom blusters around. . . . I pray Doug will shut up!* She smiled and shook her head. *I can tell my attitude isn't right. I feel defensive already, and I don't even know what they're going to say. Just help me, please!*

Finally, she turned into her driveway. The big frame house had been built seventy years ago, rising up with a commanding view of the lake between several large maple trees. Sherry couldn't believe how she felt eagerness to see her family at the same time she felt fear and reluctance. *It's just fear of the unknown,* she reassured herself. *Just be nice and everything will work out fine!*

Her mom came running out without a coat and hugged her at the car. Dad came outside to the front walk and waited his turn. They went in together, and spent the evening finishing dinner and catching up on their now separate lives. No one seemed eager to talk about anything too serious right away.

After dinner they sat in the comfortable family room by the wood stove, which burned brightly with the door open. Her brother, Doug, hadn't come home yet, and she was glad for an opportunity to talk to her parents without his sarcastic voice there to disrupt. She went ahead and suggested they probably were interested in hearing more about what she had been going through in the area of religion. They began to talk.

Her dad was very negative. "I can't believe you've looked at this critically, Sherry. You're too bright to believe that trash!"

She felt blistered by his characterization. "What *trash*, Dad? What specific *trash* did you have in mind?" She was already struggling to keep her cool.

"Well, it bothers me to think you've thrown everything I taught you about the scientific worldview out the window," he lamented. He must have sensed her hurt, because he was obviously trying to tone down his rhetoric.

"How do you figure that, Dad?" she looked puzzled.

"Well, I'm assuming you don't believe in evolution, and that you believe in all those miracles. Where's the place for actual observation and the facts of science?"

Her mom jumped in at this point. "Now Dave, Erik Lindstom is a religious man, and he's certainly a brilliant scientist. I've heard you say he is."

"Yeah, that's true . . ." he acknowledged, still trying to control his negativity.

"I know a number of the students in this group are in science at the university, including my best friend there," Sherry protested. "She's planning to go into research in microbiology. Dad, this isn't some hare-brained thing, and you don't even know what I'm into yet. If you believe in 'actual observation' so much, why are you already jumping to conclusions when you haven't *observed* anything?" She was jabbing her finger at him accusingly. "You're the one who's forsaking your own method here!"

Her dad seemed to hear what she was saying. He held up a defensive hand. "Okay, I think that's fair. I'll admit I haven't studied the data yet."

"Are you guys willing to listen to the tapes I brought?" Sherry asked as she got up and went to stand by the fire.

"Oh, why do we have to listen to tapes?" her mother seemed irritated. "Why don't you just tell us what it is?"

Oh, that's so much like her, Sherry thought with frustration as she stared into the fire. She picked up the poker and jabbed at a flaming log, collecting her composure. Then, in very deliberate, measured tones she said, "I will tell you, but you ought to hear the thinking and the tone of these lectures for yourself. I think there's a lot there I can't explain. Remember, I've only been into this for a few months. I brought some reading, too."

Her mom seemed to ignore what she said. "The thing I don't understand is, if you want to get into religion, why don't you just go to church? Pastor Simpson says Reverend Billings is a reliable man." She was leaning forward in her rocker, pleading with her hands. "He knows him from some pastors' thing. And Billings warned him this group you're into is extremist."

"Oh, Mom, that guy was a total creep! He and his little group of pseudo-intellectuals were the most pompous, fake group I've ever seen! All they did was sit around and do their double-talk with each other."

"Oh, that's a nice way to talk!"

"Look, those guys believe all religions lead to God. If that's true, I don't feel any need to go out to their meetings or anyone else's either. They didn't have anything different to say than any of my professors. When I took an interest in religion, I was looking for some answers, not just a lot of posturing and sloganeering, and that's what they were into."

"So this new group has you feeling you're better than everyone else, huh?" Her mom was going into attack mode.

"No. I wouldn't say that at all. We went to another church that was really great. The pastor knows how to teach the Bible in a living and exciting way, and that's something I don't ever remember from our church."

"Pastor Simpson taught the Bible!" her mom protested.

"Well, I can't remember a word he said about it." Sherry turned to face her mother and bobbed her head confidently as she uttered these words.

Her dad spoke up. "Yeah, I can't remember anything either, Clara. He always seemed like he was talking in circles. I thought he was a bag of wind."

"Oh, you just never wanted to go to church, Dave!" Clara was offended now.

Sherry jumped in. "I don't see why you're defending that church, Mom. You haven't gone there regularly for years yourself."

"That's because it was too much trouble to get Dave and your brother up and moving when they didn't want to go. I just gave up."

"That doesn't bother me at all, Mom. I'm not saying you need to go there. All I'm wondering is why you're so defensive about the traditional church when it hasn't done anything for our family?"

"My parents took us to church, and that's the way it should be! At least the church isn't going to launch out into some kind of cult thing. Who knows what these people you're with could end up doing?"

She was getting more emotional now, and Sherry could read the warning signs. She restrained her response for several seconds as the big antique clock on the wall slowly ticked and the fire crackled. She tried to sound as deadpan as possible. "Mom, we have those far-out groups on campus, too, but it's really easy to tell the difference between them and the kind of group I'm in."

"I don't like it. These people aren't qualified. Who says they know anything? Who said they could be preachers?"

"Who says anyone can be a preacher?" Sherry gave the fire a last jab, hung up the poker, and went to her seat.

"These churches have been established for hundreds of years. They aren't just some Johnny-come-lately splinter group!"

"They aren't now, but they were at one time! Don't you realize every church was once a 'splinter group'? And the established church has fought against new religious movements every time they arise." She sipped her hot cocoa. "It's not because the groups are always bad either.

It's because it's the 'haves' versus the 'have-nots.'" She waved her hand in a backhand gesture that seemed to sweep them all away.

"I trust the church!" Clara sat with her arms folded now, angry and determined.

"Well, I don't!" Sherry rose up to her mother's anger like she had so many times before.

Dave stepped in to diffuse the situation. "Okay, you two don't agree on that point." Then in a pacifying, pleading tone, "Clara, why don't we listen to the stuff Sherry brought home with her? Remember, we said we weren't going to get into a fight over this."

"Fine!" was all she would say. Clara was quiet and sullen, and clearly angry for the rest of the evening. She always had trouble shaking off anger once she reached her boiling point. But later, she tried to be pleasant as she went out to get the chocolate brownies she had made for the occasion. The undercurrent of tension was clear, as it would be for the rest of the visit.

When Sherry's brother, Doug, arrived the next day, things took a turn for the worse. "How ridiculous! I can't believe my sister's gone into fundamentalist religion!" he scoffed as they ate lunch at the kitchen table.

"I can't believe anyone would care what her ignorant, out-of-touch brother thought," she snapped back before thinking.

"Look who's talking about ignorant!" he laughed. "The fundamentalist! Have you handled any snakes yet?"

"Okay, you two," Dave intervened again. He seemed determined to keep the home peaceful during the holidays. "If you can't talk about it civilly, then drop it."

They were silent for a few seconds as Sherry arranged her pickles and slapped the top on her sandwich. "You can look at the stuff I brought if you want to do anything more than name-calling." She tried to sound like she was calmly taking the high road. But she didn't get the feeling he would do what she suggested.

After the initial exchanges, the family didn't have much to say about religion for the next two days, but the tension was palpable. They went to a movie, and out to the best restaurant in the city of Holland for dinner. The rest of the time, they hung around in the large old house, and out in the glassed-in porch overlooking Lake Michigan, where Sherry had a black padded chair she had identified as her favorite many years before. In the summer the glass came out and screens went in, so they could even hear the sound of the surf, which is usually substantial on the eastern shore of Lake Michigan.

Sherry didn't feel like pressing the issue of religion, and she was a little relieved it wasn't brought up again. During those few days, she spent many hours resting and reflecting, often in prayer, as she stared at the cold, beautiful waters of Lake Michigan beyond the fringe of trees, and read her book by C. S. Lewis. With the relatively warm fall, the lake had not yet frozen.

She marveled that no matter how long one watched the lake, it never got dull. It was like watching a fire, or watching the clouds. She couldn't explain exactly what new thing she expected to see there, but the constant change was hypnotic, seeming to carry her away from daily struggles.

Christmas fell on a Monday, and that afternoon, after presents had been exchanged, Sherry was sitting in her favorite chair on the porch, reading. Faintly but distinctly, she heard the sound of Jack's voice. Shocked, she jumped up and spun around. It was her father, listening to one of the tapes up in his study at the top of the steps. Sherry broke into a big embarrassed smile as she sat down in her reading chair again. She was so happy someone in her family was taking her new discoveries seriously enough to investigate.

Again, after dinner her dad disappeared, and she heard Jack's voice upstairs. It was unusual for her dad to miss the news, but he didn't show up during that family ritual, even though Clara called up and told him it was on.

Several times that day, her brother had made sarcastic comments, trying to get her goat. At Christmas dinner that evening, he said in musical tones, "Maybe Sherry should pray for us."

Sherry said, this time with more composure, "If you're worried about your lack of prayer, maybe you should take care of that yourself!" as she went ahead and dug into her turkey.

By Tuesday evening, it was just warm enough to walk down Lake Shore Drive as the sun set over the water. Beautiful red haze spread out over the orange setting sun, which looked as big as a basketball. Sherry strolled down the street in her heavy coat, burdened by the thought that her family might never understand her again. A new feeling of distance had settled over their time together.

She faintly heard someone call her name. Looking back, she saw her father emerging from the house a couple hundred yards away. He was coming to walk with her. As she waited for him to jog up to her, she considered how rare it was to see him run.

She took his arm as they walked along, happy she still felt a certain closeness to her dad, and appreciative that he had taken the time to listen to the tapes. He had to catch his breath for minute, and then brought it up directly. "Sherry, I've been listening to those tapes you brought, and I'll just come right out and say it; I'm very impressed with this Jack Collins."

"No kidding?"

"Yeah, he's a real clear thinker, and he obviously understands the Bible a lot better than anyone I've ever listened to."

Sherry's heart soared with joy. "Oh, Dad, I'm so glad to hear you say that!" She threw her other hand up and held onto his arm with both hands. "I've been feeling like an outcast here for the past few days."

"Well, I don't think you've been cast out by your mom or your brother. They just don't know what to make of this new thing you're into. I felt the same way." He used his most soothing tone of voice.

"I know. I tell myself that, but it doesn't feel much better. I'd especially like to bust Doug's mouth, he's such an arrogant jerk sometimes."

"Your brother's just pulling your pigtail to hear you yell. By getting angry, you give him what he's looking for." He grinned at her.

"I know, I know. I need to keep it together."

"I've also been reading that book by Mooreland, what is it, *Scaling the Secular City*?"

"Yes. What do you think about that?"

"He's really sharp! I'll tell you the truth Sherry, you have me rethinking this whole area of the existence of God. You've really found some provocative thinkers. Jack talks a lot about this notion of grace."

"Oh, yeah. That's the missing part, Dad. I don't think we ever heard it here at church—it just seemed like you should be a nice person, and things will work out. I think the grace thing answers a lot of questions."

"Yes, I can see where it might. . . ."

"I'm leaving tomorrow, but I'll send you stuff as long as you want it. Let's write each other about this."

He hesitated. "That sounds good to me. But I don't want you to be disappointed if I decide there still isn't enough evidence for me. You know, I may not believe . . . and I worry you'll really be hurt if I come partway on this but don't want to go the distance."

"Dad, you've already been more fair than anyone else in this family. If you decide you're not into it, at least you'll understand what I'm into."

"Yes, well, my respect for what you're into has risen considerably after listening to those tapes. Who is this guy anyway?"

"Well, he's just a student there, a grad student. He's finishing his master's in religious studies . . . so, I suppose that puts him in a similar position to most pastors. He's twenty-five."

"And you're dating him?"

She looked at him, startled. "Why would you ask that?" She almost asked if someone had been talking to him, but she didn't.

"You didn't answer." He had a big smile on his face now.

She blushed deeply as she looked down. "I don't see why you'd think that."

He laughed merrily. "So, I'm right! You're not ready to put the old man out to pasture yet!"

She broke into a smile and gave him a slug with her free hand. "I want to know how you knew!" she laughed.

"Well, I just figured if this guy was the main guy in the group, you'd just go up and snap your fingers and land him."

"Oh, Dad, it was nothing like that. He was one of the ones who got me interested in God. He was in one of my classes."

"So he must be awfully good-looking."

She smiled and looked down. Dad had some discernment all right. "Yes, he is. He's really good-looking. But I didn't get into God because of him, Dad." This last statement was uttered with her most authoritative voice.

"I thought you just said you did."

"No, I said he was one of the ones I was talking to. I mean, there were things he said . . . I thought were really convincing. And . . . he was also . . . sort of a model of a Christian that I thought was impressive. We were in this seminar together, and well . . . like you said, he's awfully sharp. But there's this girl who's also sharp, and I've really dealt more with her than I have with Jack. She's something. She leads this women's study group I'm in, and I just admire her totally."

"But you *are* dating Jack."

"Just last week we sort of got involved. But I'd been coming to the group for several months by then." She looked at him with a frown.

"I'm not suggesting there's anything wrong with your dating this guy," he shrugged. "I'd kind of like to meet him sometime."

"Well, I'm not ready to bring him home yet, if that's what you're suggesting."

"No. Not yet." He smiled again.

"We're just going out a little! It may go nowhere!" She slugged him again.

"Yes, well, you kids can get hold of me if you need help financing your first house," he kidded.

She smiled and shook her head. During all the time she had lived at home, her dad had never discussed one of her boyfriends with her. She wondered why, but before even asking, she remembered it was because she wasn't willing. She had frozen her parents out of her love life early on, and never let them back in again.

"This thing with Jack is really important to me right now, Dad. I like him . . . more than any other guy I've been out with for a long time."

"Well, he couldn't be any worse than that Duchan guy. He was a real strange ranger."

"You only met him once."

"Are you saying he was okay?"

"No. He was a creep."

They turned and started walking back. The sun was down and the temperature was falling rapidly. Sherry knew her dad was the most credible thinker in the family. Although her mom wouldn't take his word for anything, she would probably at least soften her stand some. By the time they got home, they were both glad to see Clara had made hot chocolate.

34

Sherry was speeding as she drove back eastward toward Lansing and school. Her spirit was filled with happiness about the trip home. When she left her parents' house, she had managed to speak civilly to Doug. "You know, you really owe it to yourself to check out the stuff I brought home," she mentioned as they walked out to her car.

"I'll think about it," he said as he kissed her on the forehead after helping her load her things into the car. "I'm just giving you a hard time," he reassured her. She figured her dad had probably laid a guilt trip on him about his sarcasm and prejudice.

Clara just talked about Sherry's clothes and the food she was sending back with her. Sherry was happy to get as much food as possible now that she had a kitchen.

She gazed at the scenery on both sides of the sunlit highway—the many shades of brown and gray in farmland and woods with no leaves, and the road signs she now had learned to predict from driving this highway so many times. Her emotional focus turned from behind her, in Saugatuk, to in front of her, at the university. She could barely stand the several hour wait before she would see Jack. She was also anxious to see Lisa and the other women.

As she drove, she communed with God, reflecting on her family. Though they were all older than she, and had lived in various cities during their lives, none of them had ever before heard the message that had so intrigued and attracted her father. Even now, her mother and brother had still not heard this message of grace, unadorned with traditional trappings. Before God, she pressed the question, *How is it possible that intelligent adults have never heard a cogent presentation of Your gospel, Lord?*

The only clear answer she got was the realization that the little group she had fallen into was special. She felt God was urging her forward, not to be more cautious as her mother suggested, but to be even bolder. She knew she should remind the believers in her group that they had something rare, a stewardship they must spread to the oceans of lost people all around. Within her heart there was a sense this group of students was going to become something very important—some kind of movement. She wondered whether she was being recruited by God to play a future role in this group.

All her life, teachers and parents had reminded her she was unusual because of her intelligence. On one level she sensed she was different, but she never knew why. *Maybe this is my destiny. Maybe You've made me what I am . . . You've given me this personal power only so I can use it for Your glory.*

Sherry's inner self glowed with pleasure at the realization that God was opening her eyes to see things from His perspective. She felt certain God was summoning her to fulfill a mission—a mission she would fully discover later. *You're talking to me!* she smiled. *You're calling me, aren't You?* In her mind, she stepped forward and accepted His call. She imagined herself up in front teaching like Jack. She felt certain she could do it. She knew she really wanted to, and she told God so.

When she got to East Lansing she drove directly to her parking lot. She took a load of her things into the apartment, and immediately called Jack. He said he would be right over for a few minutes before work. Sherry began unloading her car, full of happiness and anticipation. It was so wonderful to have a man to love who could be trusted, so wonderful to be a believer with her future destiny assured. All seemed well, but it wasn't going to be that easy.

35

As she gathered her second load, Jack arrived and saw her unloading her car. He took her in his arms and held her for some time, assuring her nothing had changed while she was gone. It was exciting, but also a little awkward when he agreed to go up to her apartment for once. He said since he had to go within minutes there was no harm in coming up for a look, and besides, she still had things to unload and carry up.

As she warmed up some tea in her apartment, he strode slowly around the flat, studying her pictures, her plant arrangements, and her books, commenting periodically. "I love Salvador Dali!" he smiled as he stood before her huge print of Dali's *Time*. He breathed deeply, smelling the spicy scent from the potpourri she often boiled, and the more subtle scent of her plants, which hung everywhere.

"Yes, I'm aware of your tastes in art," she said, coming out of the kitchenette and leaning on the doorjamb.

"How's that?" He looked around.

"Remember when you let us go up to your room to pray with Jean?"

"Oh . . . yeah." He acted a little shy, having trouble finding things to say. She gestured for him to come, and he ambled over toward her as she led him into the kitchenette where teacups sat ready at the little table.

He started plying her with questions about her trip home as they sat and had tea. He was intrigued that her father had been responsive to his tapes, and that he had guessed the two of them were dating. "I'd like to meet your dad sometime."

"Well, I suppose that might be arranged," she said as she stirred her tea. She was apparently thinking of something for a moment before she looked up, suddenly more serious. "Jack, do you believe God still speaks to people . . . I mean, not with words necessarily, but . . . like, in your heart?"

Jack finished his sip of tea before replying. "Yeah, I think that's part of what it means to have a personal relationship with God."

"Well, I feel like God was showing me something on the way back."

"Really? What?" he looked up expectantly.

She hesitated. "It's not easy to put into words. It was basically that we need to realize what we have here. Your understanding of Scripture . . . and Lisa's . . . your ties with Lee, that's part of it . . . the people we have coming. . . . It's just not ordinary, Jack. This kind of thing is not going on very much elsewhere, I don't think."

He leaned back in his chair and stretched his legs out beside the table. "I think you're right as far as things just like this. Of course, there are a lot of things going on, God's doing a lot of things. . . ."

"Yes, but this is special! I think God has a combination here He likes. That's what I thought He was showing me."

Jack smiled a deep, knowing smile and took a sip of tea. "You're saying you've copped a vision for our ministry."

"Yeah . . . I guess you could say that. I have a vision that we're in a position to do something really big. . . ." She leaned forward with intensity flashing in her eyes. "Jack, I mean *really* big! This might be the best-kept secret in North America!"

As she spoke Jack's smile and the twinkle in his eye only seemed to deepen.

She suddenly felt self-conscious. "Are you laughing at me?"

"No." He lifted his cup and took a sip.

"You think this is stupid, don't you?"

"No! Nothing could be further from the truth!" He put his cup down firmly.

"Then what are you grinning about?"

He took her hands in his. "Sherry, God's granted you something really important here. And I'm so excited about it, I don't know what to say."

"Because . . . you mean you believe what I'm saying?"

"Oh, it's more than that." He nodded as he spoke.

"I don't understand."

"I don't want you to take this wrong . . . but you're seeing something I've also seen . . . already . . . before."

She stared at him, weighing what he was saying. "Explain what you saw."

He thought for a moment, looking up with a grimace. Then he went on very deliberately. "I believe I've been shown by God that this group of Christians has a mission to perform. We're not just a home Bible study. God has shown me we're the nucleus of something so big, He won't say what it is."

Her eyes widened. "Ooohhh! That *is* the same! When did you get this?"

"Over a year ago, and I'm not the only one."

"Lisa?"

"Yes."

"How many others?"

"Well, I don't know . . . no one else has told me God gave them a special . . . sort of, uh, message like this, except for you and Lisa. But there are several others who believe the same thing."

"What . . . ?"

"Because we've told them."

"And they believed you?" she asked.

He nodded.

"Like Ken?"

He nodded again.

"Amy?"

He nodded.

"Jordan?"

"I don't know about her." He shook his head and frowned.

"Why didn't you ever tell me?" she wondered.

"Well, I feel like I have to be really careful who I tell this kind of thing to. It would be pretty easy to interpret it as some kind of boastful thing, you know . . . or even as a manipulative thing." She was nodding as he spoke, realizing how right he was. "And besides, if God wants people to know this, won't He show them? For that matter, if it's true, won't everyone know it eventually?"

"I don't know. You've been dealing with this longer than I have, but I get a pretty strong urge to tell others."

"I did that, and you don't always get the response you expect. Some people really take offense. They probably believe it's some kind of self-aggrandizing thing."

"Yeah, I can see that. But you told Ken."

"Yes, I don't feel God's said not to tell anyone. He's only shown me I have to be careful. This vision is for me, to keep me going in the face of opposition . . . and for certain others who're in the same position, like you, I guess."

Sherry sat back and stared at her teacup, pondering what they were talking about, and Jack let her think in silence. He studied her perfect lips and eyes as he had so many times before. She was glimpsing something that made her pulse rise. "Jack, are you saying this for my sake?"

"See," he chuckled. "Even *you're* suspicious."

"Yeah, you're right." She laughed at the irony that she had just done the very thing Jack suggested. "Man, this is really wild! I still get the feeling you view this as . . . sort of a secret."

"Well, like I said, it's not really secret . . . I'd say it's . . . uh . . . inside information. I tell people about it on a 'need to know' basis."

"Who else knows?"

"Well, one other guy knows, I think, even though he's never put it in exactly these terms. . . ."

"Who?" she demanded impatiently.

"Lee Carulo."

"Oh, that figures! That really figures . . . but what makes you think he knows?" She poured him another cup from her fat, little blue teapot.

"He's said things to me like, 'Jack, no matter what happens, no matter who else quits, never turn aside from your calling,' and he says things like, 'You don't realize how different your calling is, Jack,' and 'You don't realize how unusual this group and your teaching gift are.' Stuff like that."

"Oh! That just gives me goose bumps!" She was rubbing her arms. "What do we do with this?"

"We do what a lot of saints have done from the earliest times," he said with a smile.

"Yes?"

"We 'wait upon the Lord.' Lee says, 'If you're into the Lord, you're into waiting.'"

"Oh, man, I hate waiting for things." She put her elbow on the table and propped her head up with her hand. "But I get the feeling I'm willing to wait for this. This thing, this mission . . . if it's as big as I sense, we need to be ready. We wouldn't want to get into a position where we weren't ready."

"Yeah, I hear that."

"Jack."

"Yes?"

"I feel God's saying I'm going to be a part of this, too."

"Oh, I've been getting that feeling all along! I thank God that He's confirming it in you!" A surge of love feelings rose in Jack's heart, as he reveled in the joy of knowing both Sherry and he were chosen—chosen for a mission of great importance. But a mission they couldn't describe or even name. All they knew was, it was going to begin with their group at Jack's house.

They decided to spend a few minutes in prayer together, but as they got ready to address the Lord, Jack was hesitant. "Uh, there's something we need to pray about," he said ominously.

"What?"

"Well, while you were gone, this thing happened at the house."

"Yeah. . . ."

"You know Warren lives a couple of blocks over on Simmons."

She nodded.

"Well, he's been coming off pretty strong with some of the younger brothers."

"Yeah, I heard about that. I also heard he slandered the heck out of you and me to my friend Becka!"

"Uh-huh, did you get hold of her?"

"Yes. She acted like she didn't quite know what I was talking about, but I could tell she did."

"Well, this past weekend, he came down on this one guy pretty hard because the guy was dating a girl who wasn't into the Lord. And, it's been happening pretty often . . . he's been in several shouting matches with guys around the house. A couple of people have brought up some objections before, but we didn't feel like we were getting anywhere. So, Saturday, it finally got to the point where Ken and I decided we needed to sit him down and talk to him."

"Yeah?" Sherry could see this really bothered Jack. He seemed to grimace as he thought of something. "I know Lisa felt someone needed to get him under control a while ago."

"Yeah, she thinks we've been too patient, but it's hard to say. Anyway, Ken and I told him we wanted to talk to him, and we got together . . . things didn't go well . . . he wasn't hearing any of what we had to say. I started to press the case and got pretty hot and sort of lost it." He looked up at her. "I sort of cussed him out!"

"Oh, man! That's hard to imagine, Jack. He must have been pretty provocative. Was he cussing you out?"

"I suppose he was. But you can't let yourself get caught up in somebody else's immaturity like that." Jack sipped his tea with a deep frown. "While I was talking about his harshness, I went ahead and told him I knew what he was telling people about me and you and women and stuff."

"Yeah! What did he say to that?"

"He said the word was that you and I were openly into it now. I said, 'Sure, we're dating. But we never did anything before this past week.' And, you know, he just laughed. He said something about believing in Santa Claus, and claimed he knew there were other women and stuff. That's when I let him have it. So there I was trying to admonish him for his bad temper and harsh ways, and I go ahead and do the very thing I was criticizing!" Jack was silent, staring at the table, apparently remembering.

"Sounds like he had it coming. So how did it end? Where did you leave it with him?"

"Well, he said we should basically mind our own business, and he continued to maintain I should take my own moral problems in hand instead of worrying about his."

Sherry slapped the table in disgust, hard enough to rattle the teacups. "Man, he makes me sick! He has a lot of nerve!"

"Ken finally spoke up at that point and said he viewed the thing where he's slandering me as serious. I could have used a little more verbal support from Ken. Anyway, we warned him we weren't going to let him mess up the atmosphere in the group. I said it was okay if he came on strong with someone like me, but we didn't want him scaring off new Christians who haven't learned how to walk yet. I apologized to him for losing my cool, but I also said he couldn't teach our men's group again until he agreed to ease up on people."

"Wow, I didn't know he was teaching your men's group."

"Yeah, once in a while. Ken or I teach it most of the time."

They sat in silence awhile, both with their own thoughts. Sherry found herself not only angered, but strangely depressed by the news. It was the first time she had been confronted with unseemly conflict in the Body of Christ and there was something defiling about it. She felt torn between the desire to go and give Warren a piece of her mind, and the desire to stay out of a fight she couldn't win. "I'm definitely going to go and tell him nothing happened between you and me back in September," she nodded to herself.

"Sherry, you can go if you want, but I'm absolutely *certain* he already knows that."

"What?" She looked up with shock.

"When I first mentioned the incident back in September, he believed me. He was saying, 'Boy, Jack, I would have gone ahead and taken what was offered,' or something like that. He said he really admired me for the stand I took. I'm sure he knew I was sincere."

"When did it change?"

"Frankly, I'd say it changed when he met you a couple of times."

"I knew it. He has some kind of thing for me, I can feel it. That's what this whole thing is."

"There's more bad news."

"Now what?"

"Friday, he went out with Sue, and I guess they really hit it off."

"My Sue?"

"Yep."

"Oh, no. What could she see in him? This is really bad. I know Sue. It wouldn't be smart to tell her he's a flake. She'd just hold on tighter. I'm going to have to be really careful."

They finally managed to pray, calling on God for protection. They also thanked Him for including them in His plans, and for bringing them back together.

At 5:00 he stood up from the table and said he was late for work. He again took her and kissed her, holding her face and telling her how much he had missed her. She stood holding him close, feeling his heartbeat, breathing in his wonderful fresh masculine scent. Then he was gone.

Since she didn't have to work that evening, Sherry decided to call Lisa, and spent the rest of the afternoon and evening with her friends at the women's rooming house. She didn't get a chance to talk to Lisa alone, but she told her she wanted to discuss "this calling thing and the thing with Warren" when they had more time.

She was glad to be back.

36

When Sherry got home from her evening at the rooming house, there were still a couple of things in the back of her hatchback to take up. She smiled in drowsy contentment as she gathered the last of the food her mother had sent. *Tuna! Four cans. Yeah, I can get into that.*

Suddenly, she stood up and looked around like a deer in a clearing. *Oh, no! I'm getting it again!* A sickening chill ripped down her spine. *That feeling! Someone is watching me.* Her eyes searched the buildings and bushes all around her. No one was in sight. She shook her head in dismay as she leaned back into the rear of her car and picked up the bottle of salsa that had fallen out of the bag. *I've been back less than a day, and I'm already paranoid. I wonder if I'll ever be free from these irrational fears?* she wondered. *All the time I was home I never felt this.*

She walked up to the apartment, unable to shake her feeling, but determined to walk slowly and deliberately. She didn't want to be running into her apartment the rest of her life. *I have to overcome this,* she told herself, gritting her teeth. She pondered how fear could dominate people's lives. Some of her friends suffered from anxiety, but Sherry had always found it hard to be patient with people who worried too much. Now she realized they may have had traumatic pasts that left a residue of fear, just like her trauma with Jim had left her thinking people were following her.

She got to the apartment, and leaned against the door to stabilize the sack of groceries while she found the key and opened the lock. Something caught her attention down the hall—IT WAS HIM! Running straight at her at breakneck speed . . . silent, deadly, he was already halfway down the hall!

She threw her groceries onto the floor in her apartment and jumped in, ready to slam the door in his face. She grabbed the heavy metal door and threw it shut, but his hand was caught at the jamb. "Aaaaagh," he cried as he threw the door open and strode into her apartment, holding and massaging his hand and scowling at her as he closed the door behind himself.

"GET OUT!" Sherry screamed hoarsely, running for the phone, and immediately dialing 911. *"NO! GET OUT OF MY PLACE!"* She was screaming hysterically.

He stumbled on a can of tuna as he careened toward her, grabbing the phone from her hand and hanging it up—no one had answered!

Sherry backed up now, wide eyed, almost paralyzed with fear, her hands out in front of her in a defensive posture. She could smell whiskey all over him. His eyes were bleary and drunk, crazed looking. He came forward menacingly, and in a lightning quick move, grabbed her arm and instantly drew her toward himself. "You messed me up real bad, Sherry," he slurred. "I'm off the team thanks to you . . . you thought you were too good for me . . . the know-it-all."

She cried out, "Let me go!" as she twisted away from him and pulled out of her coat, leaving him holding an empty heavy winter coat. Now she was just in her flannel shirt and jeans. He threw down her coat and instantly peeled off his letter-jacket as well, revealing the bulging, menacing muscles under his T-shirt. "Fine, I don't mind if we get more comfortable," he slurred sarcastically. He lunged at her and caught her again, locking her in the same painful, viselike bear hug. His powerful upper body controlled her completely.

Sherry's mind was screaming as she struggled to free herself from his grip. She sensed his viciousness could be deadly. There must be something she could do! "Wait! Hold on. Okay? Let's talk, Jim." She tried to sound as if she were giving in, deliberately relaxing her body. "Can't we just talk a little bit?" she pleaded, her voice quivering from her terror.

"Ha!" He blew rancid whiskey fumes in her face. "I'm gonna let my fingers do the talking, babe!" He brutally reached up with one hand and tore her shirt wide open. She tried to dart away in the moment he loosened his grip, but he was too fast. He locked her again in his steely arms, savagely tearing her shirt backward, and off one arm. Sherry began screaming again. "No! Aaagh. *NO! STOP IT!*" She clawed and thrashed desperately, without any effect whatsoever, her arms now again trapped helplessly beside her.

"Mmmm. You always were sweet lookin'!" He leered at her as he grabbed the front of her bra and jerked it. She was sickened as he pulled her tight against his sweaty T-shirt-clad chest. She lurched so heavily they both crashed back against her desk. He continued to struggle, trying to tear off the rest of her clothes.

Suddenly, her left hand came to rest on something—it was her silver scissors! Carefully, she got a solid grip, sliding her fingers through the large loop handle. She knew this could be her only chance to save herself. Continuing to struggle, she aimed the pointed end at him just below his ribs and with everything she had, she drove the scissors upward at his gut! With a distinct *pop*, the scissors broke through his abdomen and slid into his body!

Crying out and grimacing in pain, he grabbed her hand that held the scissors, but his grip was already weakening. "Ugh!" she shrieked. She didn't dare pull the scissors out for fear he might turn them on her.

He staggered backward until he ran into the half-wall between her kitchenette and living room. Leaning against the wall, he stood bent over, clawing at his stomach, glowering at her. The bloody scissors fell to the floor with a thud.

Sherry pulled her clothes back around her. Her face was glowing red and moist, her shoulders heaving as she gasped for breath. She leaned with one hand on the edge of her desk, and bellowed warnings at him. "You move one step and I'll let you have it!"

He said nothing. He just stared, breathing heavily. Looking down, she was stunned to see a river of blood pouring out between his fingers. His jeans and the beige carpet under him were already covered with blood. She looked down at her own hand. It too was completely drenched in warm, sticky blood.

Sherry suddenly exploded with vomit. Helplessly, she retched, bending over slightly. Wiping her face with her clean arm, she continued to stand, leaning on the desk, gasping, her nose and throat burning, already sobbing, but still watching, alert, ready to strike if he moved.

She couldn't believe he was just standing there glowering with hate. Surely, he was going to do something. "I swear I'll *kill* you if you move a muscle!" she breathed between gasps.

He looked down and saw the blood that was still flowing at an amazing rate. "Aaaahh!" he moaned, and looked up at her in amazement with an expression that seemed to wonder why she had gotten carried away.

"Oh, you just thought I'd be a nice little friendly *rape,* right?" She spat out the word *rape* with ferocity. "Don't you *dare* try to reproach me, you *coward*!" she screamed.

After staring at her for another moment, his eyes rolled up, and falling to his knees, he keeled over sideways on the floor.

"Oh, my Lord!" she cried, her hand over her mouth. Carefully, she reached over him for the phone and quickly picked up the scissors, away from his reach. Sobs were coming uncontrollably now, but holding the phone in the same hand as the blood-soaked scissors, she managed to dial 911.

"Police! Help! I stabbed him! I think he's dead!" She gave her address and pleaded for speed before dropping the phone and staggering into the kitchen. She looked back at the motionless body on her floor before dropping the scissors into the stainless steel sink. Running cool water over her blood-covered hand and forearm, she shook with hysterical sobs. With her other hand she grabbed a cup and scooped up some water from the tap to wash out her mouth. She tried to put the sleeve of her shirt back on, but it, too, was covered with blood. She tore the shirt off the rest of the way, and threw it against the wall where it left a grisly mark. She looked and saw Jim still in a heap on the floor, but she grabbed a long carving knife from her knife block before approaching the passage into the living room.

Trembling, moaning, and whimpering, she reached over him and again grabbed the phone. She pressed the hang-up button and immediately called Jack. The phone rang and someone answered—it was him! "Jack! Jack! It's him! I killed him! I stabbed him! Help me! Please!"

"Where are you, Sherry?"

"At home," she sobbed, as she heard a police siren. "I called the police, and they're coming."

"I hear the siren! Are you all right?"

"I . . . I think so . . ."

"I'll be right there!"

The phone went dead as he hung up. She dropped the receiver, and slumped into the corner of her couch. Across the room, his body lay motionless. Someone knocked at the door. It was a woman. "Are you all right in there?"

Sherry was too stunned to move. She stared straight ahead at the body on her floor. Breathing heavily, but no longer weeping, she began to float into shock. Her jaw hung listlessly as she drifted into a semi-conscious stupor.

"We called the police. You'd better leave her alone!" The voice was scared, and sounded as if she was standing away from the door.

Sherry sat and watched him, the long knife still laying across her lap. Some time passed, but she wasn't sure how much.

Suddenly, there was a heavy pounding at the door. "Police!" a deep voice called. "Open up please, this is the police!" Sherry stared at the door, now too far away to consider trying to reach.

The door burst open, and two officers flew into the room with their revolvers drawn. They saw the body on the floor and looked over at Sherry's blood-streaked body, laying back into one corner of the couch. She stared at them without expression, oblivious to the fact that she had no shirt on. "Are you all right, ma'am?" he asked. She nodded weakly, but didn't answer.

"Let's see if anyone else is here, you check the bedroom," one of the officers ordered the other. They parted ways and probed the rest of the apartment with their guns drawn.

Suddenly, Jack burst into the room. He saw the body, and then looking over, he beheld the woman he loved, blood streaks across her unclothed abdomen and bra, her hair tousled. He ran over and, falling to his knees, he took her into his arms. She had just enough strength to throw her arms around him as he gathered her tenderly to himself and held on for dear life.

The police officers came up behind Jack, their guns lowered at him. "Sir, step back please," one of them ordered. Jack ignored them, clinging to his loved one, his arms wrapped protectively around her body.

"Sir, back away NOW!" the officer barked, finally getting Jack's attention. He looked back, and slowly laying Sherry back in the couch, he began to turn around. "GET YOUR HANDS UP!" the officer shouted. Jack obeyed. "Now lay on the floor, face down!"

He lay on the floor as one officer reached down and frisked him for weapons, his gun trained at the back of Jack's head. The other officer was talking on his walkie-talkie.

"He's my boyfriend. He's okay," Sherry peeped weakly.

"Okay, sir. You may get up. Please move over to that chair and have a seat," he commanded, pointing to the chair at Sherry's desk as he sheathed his gun.

The officer went over and examined Jim, feeling his throat for a pulse. Jack stared bug-eyed at the immense pool of blood that had spread out over the carpet. "I'm not getting anything here, Larry. He's code blue!" A siren howled in the distance, as he pulled his walkie-talkie out and began to talk into it. The older officer began to work on Jim, trying to revive him.

Sherry continued to drift deeper into shock. When the younger officer asked if she had inflicted the wound on the man on the floor, she could barely nod in response, staring straight ahead.

"How did he get in, ma'am?" he asked, as he took the knife from her lap and laid it on the floor. She stared ahead blankly. "Ma'am, how did he get past the security door? Did you let him in?"

She stared ahead, her lip quivering slightly.

"Okay, I hear the ambulance, we'll get them to the hospital and then worry about what happened," said the younger officer.

"Can't you put something over her?" Jack asked. "She's half naked. She may be in shock." But the officer was already headed for the bedroom to get a blanket. They wrapped her in the blanket, and got her to lie down on the couch, just as the paramedics ran into the room. Two men went to work on Jim on the floor, and another went over to Sherry.

The officers questioned Jack while the medics prepared Sherry and Jim to go. "She called me after the attack," he explained. "She said she stabbed him, and . . . uh, she pleaded for help. I live just a couple of blocks over, so I jumped on my bike. It only took a minute to get here. I came in after you were already here."

"How did you get past the security door?" the officer asked.

"A woman was coming out as I came up. I got through the door before it closed. You know, Sherry told me this guy was stalking her."

"Yes, fine. What did you say her name is?" They set about getting their report, as first Jim and then Sherry were carried out.

37

Sherry was given liquids when she got to the hospital, which had the desired effect. By 1:00 a.m., she was lucid and even agitated. Near-hysterical tears began to flow as she relived her nightmare again and again. She began to insist they let her go, so she could be with Jack, but they refused. Finally, her doctor administered a sedative that put an end to her struggles and she fell asleep.

At 10:00 a.m. she woke up to see her parents looking down at her from the right side of her bed. Dave and Clara had arrived at 7:00 that morning, after receiving a 2:00 a.m. phone call from the East Lansing Police.

Patting her hand and stroking it, they spoke words of reassurance and care. Yes, they explained, Jim was indeed dead. His liver had been lacerated so severely that he bled to death. He had never revived. Sherry was surprised to see both her mother and her father shedding tears as they fussed over her, passing their hands over her as though assuring themselves she was really there and safe. After anxiously talking and reassurring themselves she was all right, finally they all fell silent and just held on to each other's hands.

To lighten his daughter's mood, Dave laid his free hand aside Sherry's face and said in a very quiet voice, "Sherry, I met him."

With the sedative befuddling her mind, she had to think for a moment about what he said. Then a smile spread slowly over her face. "Jack? You met Jack?"

He nodded somewhat excitedly, like a co-conspirator, an insider. "He's everything I imagined, and even more! You're going to get over this, and you have a wonderful life waiting for you."

Sherry smiled and squeezed his hand in appreciation. She was so glad her parents were there. The horror of the night before seemed like an unreal dream. For some reason, her love for her parents seemed more tangible at that moment than she could ever remember.

"I liked him, too, dear." It was her mom. "He seems so sweet."

"Where is he?" Sherry asked.

"He's been here at the hospital all night," Dave said. "We sent him down to get some coffee and a bite to eat. He'll be back any minute."

As if on cue, someone entered the room. It was Jack! He came up next to her on the other side of the bed. She held her arms part way up to him and he bent over to give her a yearning hug. "Mmmm." He kissed her repeatedly on the forehead, cheeks, and lips. "I'm so thankful you're all right," he rejoiced. Before long, he backed away, conscious of her parents.

He asked her how she felt, and ascertained she was okay. She shared how surprised she was by the fact that she didn't feel worse after killing a man. "I feel like I should be moaning in agony or something."

"Well, those sedatives have a way of creating euphoria, you know. And, as horrible as it was, it was self-defense," Jack observed.

"Yes, I think you're right." The voice of a man spoke behind him. Turning around he saw Dr. Gordon, who had already been by earlier. "Those sedatives make things seem unreal, but she'll have deep emotional turmoil to deal with later, I'm afraid."

They interacted for a few minutes until Dr. Gordon informed them they would all have to leave so the staff psychiatrist could talk to Sherry. "We may be able to get her out of here this afternoon if things go well," he said.

They all said goodbye and ambled out to the lobby.

Later that afternoon, true to Dr. Gordon's prediction, Sherry was released. Her parents took her to the hotel where they were staying; a Guest Suite Hotel with a living room and a fireplace. There she called Lisa and asked if she would come over, and within ten minutes Sherry and Lisa were reunited in the living room of the suite. They embraced one another for some time. Lisa didn't want to let go, as though she could never risk being away from Sherry again. As they sat down with Sherry's parents, tears rolled down Lisa's and Sherry's faces so that Dave had to get them tissues.

For several minutes, Sherry recounted what had happened. Her voice was halting, and she forgot her place twice. Lisa urged her not to go into it right then if she didn't want to, but she shook her head, and continued. Except for a visible shudder of disgust at two points, she wasn't openly emotional, because a general tiredness and depression was settling in, making it hard to concentrate.

"What did the psychiatrist say, dear?" her mom asked.

"Not too much . . . he asked me what happened . . . he said the fact that I could talk about it was a good sign . . . he said I was probably suppressing my feelings about it, and I have to go back next week."

"I want you to stay with me at the house," Lisa said a few minutes later. "I have an extra foam mattress in my room, and there's no way you can go back to that place, at least not for a while."

"We think you should come home for a week or two," her mother volunteered.

"That won't work," Sherry shook her head.

"Why not?"

"I don't want to go home. I want to be here for the start of the quarter Monday. I really feel like I can somehow carry on with my life."

Her parents weren't happy about it, but they knew there was no point in trying to get Sherry to do something she didn't want to do.

There was a knock at the door.

Dave Martin walked slowly to the door and opened it. It was the police! "Is Sherry Martin here?" one of the two officers asked.

"Yes, what do you need? She's just back from the hospital."

"May we come in?"

"This isn't the time for police work," Dave protested. But the officers were insistent. "We need to speak with her."

He let them into the room. They weren't the two officers who had come to the apartment the night before. Looking at Sherry and Lisa, the heavy one said, "Which one of you is Sherry Martin?"

"I am," Sherry offered.

"Miss, I'm afraid we're going to have to ask you to come with us."

"This is an outrage!" Dave yelled. Clara and Lisa were complaining at the same time. "Can't you see she's just been through hell?"

"She's been cleared by the psychiatrist at County Hospital, and we have been sent to bring her in for questioning, sir."

"Well, she won't go! Just get out of here!" Clara blustered.

"Ma'am, she's an adult. She can decide for herself." He held a quieting hand out at Clara.

"I'm not going," Sherry said. "I'm with my family and friends, and I'm staying here."

The heavy officer looked at the other one, who gave a barely perceptible shrug. "Okay, I'm placing you under arrest for suspicion of voluntary manslaughter. I want you to know that you have the right to remain silent. Anything you say, can and will be used against you in a court of law. . . ."

Although everyone in the room was protesting at once, the officers went ahead with their work, even insisting on using handcuffs because it was "regulation." Sherry stood quietly, staring straight ahead as they helped her on with her coat and cuffed her. She looked back at her father, a tear now running down the side of her nose.

"This is about the most ridiculous thing I've ever seen!" Dave was really boiling now. With both parents and Lisa yelling at them, they led her out to their cruiser.

"Don't say anything, Sherry!" her dad warned. "There's no way you can talk to them without a good lawyer present! I'll get one!" She didn't respond, but she looked back at them again as the officers ushered her into the back of the cruiser. They drove away.

Dave went back inside, spitting curses, and spent an hour calling friends to find a competent criminal lawyer in town, but couldn't reach any. He tried to call Darik, professor of physics, who was one of his business associates in town, but couldn't reach him. As he called law firms from the phone book, they were all closed. Finally, he sank down in an arm chair, resigned to the realization there was nothing he could do now to help his daughter.

As darkness fell, Clara, Dave, and Lisa were pacing the suite and fuming over Sherry's arrest. Dave tried to comfort Clara, who was sobbing uncontrollably. They got ready to go down to the police station to see if they could get in to see her. Dave was determined to press a complaint to someone. It was inconceivable to all of them that she had actually been arrested. How could this happen? The whole episode was beginning to seem like a story by Kafka.

Half an hour after the arrest there was another knock at the door. It was Jack, showing up with a copy of the evening paper. They told him Sherry had been taken away and had to relive another rage episode as Jack viciously slapped the folded newspaper in his hand against the kitchenette wall and stormed around the apartment. Lisa had never seen Jack so uncontrolled. "Well, I know why they did it!" he exclaimed as he held the paper out and shook it.

They gathered around the table and looked at the evening paper. There on the front page was a prominent story about the killing, under the large title: "Varsity Wrestler Slain in Coed's Apartment." The reporter had done his homework. As Jack opened the paper, they were horrified to see on the bottom of the front page a picture of Sherry and one of Jim Clemmons! The reporter had found a copy of the picture from the year before when Sherry had won the Gladwell research award for one of her papers.

With sinking hearts, Sherry's parents and Lisa read the account, which was factual enough. It quoted a neighbor, saying the woman who did the "slaying" claimed she was attacked by the victim. The story then gave biographical information about both the victim and the accused.

It turned out Jim Clemmons' mother was chairperson of the East Lansing Chamber of Commerce and had served a term on city council! His father was a former star linebacker at Michigan State University, and owned a car dealership. The reporter quoted Jim's mother as saying, "We're going to make sure we find out why our Jimmy is dead! There's no way he would attack anyone! He was a model boy!"

"There you have it," Jack said. "This guy was the son of an influential couple. I bet they pressured the police to bring her in." He looked at the faces of the other three who were comprehending the seriousness of the situation. "When we were in the apartment, I heard the officer ask her how he got past the security door and how he got into her apartment. He asked her if she let him in."

"Well, what did she say?" Clara asked.

"She couldn't answer. I think she was in shock."

"She just told us a few minutes ago that he was already inside the building," Dave said.

"That figures, because as scared as she was of this creep, there's no way she would let him in." Jack shook his head.

In growing dismay, the four of them stood in silence.

"I sure hope this never comes before a jury in this town," Dave spoke the fear they all felt.

38

J ack and Dave decided to drive to the police station, having convinced Lisa and Clara to wait at the hotel in case Sherry called. They drove in silence except for Jack's instructions about where to turn, each absorbed in his own feelings. After several minutes' driving, Dave suddenly began to cry. "My baby! My little girl!" he burst out as painful sobs of agony seized him. "My sweet little girl! How could this happen to you?"

Jack's eyes also welled up. He laid his hand on Dave's shoulder, and the two men both openly wept for the woman they loved.

Jack wondered what the police were doing to her. Would they make her take off her street clothes and stay in jail overnight? After what she had been through, the thought was unbearable. Jack silently prayed, and as he did so, his eyes were opened, as he saw the hand of Satan lashing out at this young Christian woman. He felt led to speak aloud, "I rebuke you, Evil One, in the name of Jesus Christ! I command you to release her! Be gone from this Christian woman, you have no authority here, she belongs to Christ!"

Dave looked over in shock and back at the road again. He was visibly shaken by Jack's words. "So you think that's going to get her out." He shook his head, wiping tears from his face. "Where has God been this whole time? Seems like He's forgotten one of His people here!"

"There are two sides to the spiritual equation, Dave," Jack answered. "I realize you're not a Christian, so there's no reason why you'd believe in someone like Satan. But if you want my view, Sherry's been realizing some things recently, and the hand of God is on her. That makes her a target of the Evil One, and he's been after her from the day she believed."

Dave shook his head in disgust. "So everything is explained in terms of demons and spirits!"

"No. Not everything." Jack was annoyed too. "I believe in cause and effect just like you do. But I also believe it's possible for God to intervene in history—or for the other ones to intervene. This thing could be one of their schemes."

"Uh-huh. And so what happens now, Kemosabe? You say the magic words and she walks out free, right?"

"No, I'm not saying that'll happen. But if it's a spiritual thing, they'll have to listen to my rebuke. They'll lose power in this situation."

Dave let out a scoffing snort and shook his head again. "I liked your lectures, Jack. But I'm sure not ready to jump into the kind of thing you're talking about. That just sounds weird. I'm sorry, but it does. I feel like I should get out a tambourine and play it while you say that stuff! Maybe I should shake a rattle?"

"I can understand your feeling," Jack said, content to leave it at that. The last thing he needed right then was a theological debate. "Turn right here at the light." They drove on in silence for another five minutes.

As they pulled up and walked to the station entrance, Jack continued to pray in his mind. He knew God might want to mature Sherry through this testing, but a deeper suspicion told him he should contend with the Devil for her, in the name of Christ. The Third Precinct headquarters was a small building, and from the front desk they saw her, sitting with her back to them next to a desk.

"Sherry!" Jack called out.

She turned around and immediately jumped up, picked up her coat, and came running out to them.

"How did you get here so fast?" she grabbed one of each of their arms as if to go.

"Wait a minute," her dad said. "You're going to get in more trouble if you just walk out of here."

They looked up and saw a detective emerge from some back room and approach them.

"I'm free to go! Didn't you get their call?"

"No. Nobody called us."

The detective walked up and held out his hand. "I'm Detective Botti. I missed you at the hotel. You'd already left." He was introduced to both Jack and Dave before going on. "We didn't book Sherry. There's a police report on file, which I just located with Sherry's help. It's from October and was filed by an officer who's been on vacation this week. It indicates Sherry complained that this young man was stalking her at that time."

"Praise God!" Jack cried out—though he immediately felt self-conscious.

"Well, maybe God has been watching out for her," the detective went on. "If Sherry's story is true, this was a remarkable case. The young man was a powerful athlete, and I know few women would have been able to defend themselves against him." He held up his hand. "But we're not going to close this case yet. I'm letting Sherry go tonight, because there's insufficient evidence to hold her. I would like her to stay in town while we finish the investigation. I'll be interviewing a list of people she has provided me with, who she says will testify she has had nothing to do with the deceased during the past several months. If they check out, there'll probably be nothing to worry about."

"Well, I can tell you right now!" Jack piped up. "I'm dating her, and there's no way she's been seeing him! I also saw him in the street back in October, and he scowled at her. He looked really mad."

"Okay, I'll be getting your statement later. I think we've all done enough for tonight. Why don't you all go home and get some rest?" Turning to Dave, he said, "I'm sorry the officers handcuffed her. They didn't know what the story was. They were just told to bring her in, under arrest if necessary."

"C'mon you guys! Let's get out of here," Sherry pleaded. "I'm tired of talking about it."

They went out to the car, and enjoyed a minute of hugging and rejoicing before getting in.

Sherry wouldn't let Jack sit in back in the bucket-seated Buick on the way home, so she sat on his lap with her knees facing sideways, clinging possessively to him. She nuzzled her face into his neck, drawing deeply of his wholesome, clean scent. Tears began to flow as she let down her guard and melted into the secure arms of the man she loved. Dave drove in silence for several minutes before he began to open up. "Well, Jack, I guess I need to recalculate my equation, don't I?"

"I'm as stunned as you are, Dave," Jack admitted humbly. "There's no way I was expecting that!"

Sherry sat up and wiped her eyes. "What are you guys talking about?"

"On the way up here," Dave began, "Jack here suddenly starts barking out these curses on the Devil. He just started speaking to Satan like he'd be listening, saying 'leave her alone' and 'go away!'—things like that."

She looked at Jack, who smiled sheepishly.

"Well, I thought it was absurd, and I told him so. I said, 'So I suppose we'll just walk in and take her out of there now?' and, well. . . ." He took a breath and blew it out. "We walked in and took you out! I still can't believe it!" He was holding the top of his head with his free hand, as though it might fly off.

Neither Jack nor Sherry felt led to say anything, partly because they could see Dave was already moving in the right direction without help from them.

After driving for a minute in silence, Dave spoke again. "It's really hard to believe that I might've lived my whole life without ever noticing there's a spiritual world! I just don't know. . . ." Then after thinking for another minute, "It could have been a coincidence. . . . I guess that's really bad to say, huh?"

Jack spoke up. "No, I wouldn't say it's bad. To be really honest, I think you have to admit it's *possible* this was a coincidence, but I don't personally believe it was. I felt inwardly that God was indicating I should take authority over evil spirits in this situation, and that's what I did. For a Christian, for one who understands spiritual warfare, that's no big deal. It's just one of those things you do in certain situations." He could see the incredulity still plastered all over Dave's face. "I know what it's like to doubt the reality of the Devil. I think Sherry's had trouble with that, haven't you?"

"Yeah, earlier," she said. "I've pretty much come around on that. But I'd still have trouble speaking out loud to Satan. That seems really strange."

"It *is* strange," Jack acknowledged. "But every year that goes by for me as a Christian, I grow more certain the Devil's not only real, he's pressing us a lot of the time. It's become more important to me to recognize his presence and take it to him directly . . . to take authority like that. That's how things work in the spiritual realm."

Jack and Sherry could see Dave's wheels turning as he marveled to himself in silence. "Dave," Jack said, "I can tell that you sense this episode was real."

"Huh? Oh . . . well, I guess I can't say it *wasn't* real," he admitted.

"Why don't you turn to God in your heart and ask Him to show Himself to you?"

"What? I'm not sure what you're saying."

"I'm saying, why don't you just tell Him that, if this stuff is real, you want to know more about it? What harm could that do?"

"Well, before I could do that, I'd have to believe in God."

"No," Jack said. "I think you can approach Him tentatively, sort of asking, rather than declaring."

"That's what I did, Dad," Sherry said. Dave looked over and turned back to the road while Sherry went on. "I didn't know whether He was real or not, and I told Him so. But I knew pretty soon after that that He was."

"I don't know," Dave resisted. "That just sounds like a leap of faith. I don't think I've *ever* prayed!"

Jack tried to explain. "Well, like I said, it doesn't have to be a strong statement of faith, but it does take courage to open yourself up to something you don't understand fully. I'm not going to press you on this, but it's something to consider. Maybe tonight when you get some time to think, you ought to give God a chance."

They were pulling up to the hotel, so there wasn't any time to discuss it further. As he turned off the car, Dave looked over, nodded, and said, "I'll give it some thought, Jack."

They all ran up to the room, and there followed a time of unbelievable joy and love—as though the three of them had returned victorious from a battle. As they all settled down, their thoughts turned to food. Sherry said she felt too weary to go out, so they ordered pizza.

For the next three hours, the five of them sat around the little fireplace in the hotel suite watching sawdust logs burn while they talked. Dave and Clara were marked by that night, as they saw and felt for themselves the wholesomeness of the friendship these young Christians exhibited. This was something to which Clara especially was responsive. She didn't have to analyze what she saw, she could feel goodness emanating from the three students as they shared and cared for one another and for her and Dave. Neither of them would be able to lightly shrug off Christianity after that night.

39

The next day, around noon, there was a knock at the door of the hotel suite. It was Sherry's brother, Doug. He gave Sherry a heartfelt, protective hug. "I've been pretty worried about you," he admitted. He stayed for a few hours, but had to leave before dinner that night. Before leaving, he turned at the door and faced Sherry again. Reaching into his pocket, he pulled out a little gift-wrapped box. "I thought you might like this," he smiled sheepishly.

She took the gift and opened it. It was a beautiful silver, turquoise, and opal cross on a chain. Sherry knew how much Doug had to humble himself in order to get the expensive piece. "Oh, Doug . . ." she said as she hugged him gratefully.

The next day, Sherry's parents went home, after getting a list of things to pick up from the apartment and taking them and Sherry over to Lisa's house. Sherry insisted the stay would only be temporary, but she was happy to spend the nights with her best friend.

As winter quarter began, Sherry was happy the doctor had given her a few sedatives to help her sleep. Nightmares of the attack troubled her even with the sleeping pills. She also had to face the daily hardship of attending classes and working in the Michigan winter. People seemed to get used to the harsh conditions after a few weeks, and Sherry, who had grown up in Michigan, had less trouble than most. The busyness of a new quarter helped take her mind off her trauma.

Sherry's friends at the dorm and at the Bible study were extremely kind to her during the days following the killing. At the dorm, the girls hailed Sherry as a hero—an avenger of male oppressors. They praised her for showing him and the other men on campus what a rapist could expect.

Sherry knew it was easy for them to extol the killing because they couldn't possibly understand all that was involved. They didn't have to contend with the memories of taking another person's life. She remembered with a sense of shock, her own brutality during the struggle and afterward, as he stood dying. The counselor at the hospital had made her face that scene more than once, and her deeper feelings of horror and even guilt had surfaced in floods of tears during her therapy. She knew the probable significance of the fact that Jim had not regained consciousness. She felt like she had probably sentenced him to something much worse than capital punishment.

Privately, she had to examine her own belief in hell. Would she stand at the judgment day and watch him being led away to everlasting damnation? It seemed too awful to contemplate. But when she considered what the alternative would have been to striking him down . . . that seemed too awful to consider as well.

Jack said God wouldn't have let him die if he had in his heart any desire to come to Christ. Sherry wasn't sure what his scriptural backing for that position was, but it was such an appealing thought she decided it must be true. Jack also said it was wrong to speculate about whether he was lost or not anyway. "The fact is, we don't know, and nobody knows. That's the way we should leave it," he insisted.

Within a couple of weeks, her friends' kindness began to wear on Sherry. She wanted to be treated as a normal person again. They all seemed to think she was going to shatter like a porcelain doll. One by one, her friends told her the police had called, and they had confirmed that Jim Clemmons had not been in contact with Sherry as far as they knew.

✳

The forces of hell were not happy with the way things had gone. "Your flunky hardly made a ripple in the water!" the leader rebuked the dark-faced spirit. "Killed by a woman!"

"She had some kind of protection! We couldn't go into the room with him!" he pleaded.

"Then explain why the police didn't take her! She should be in jail right now! What kind of diversion is this?"

"Jack broke through our cordon. There was some report from months ago—it wasn't even official!"

"In other words, you missed it. You didn't do the work. You blew it!"

"We still have the parents. The mother is responsive."

"Ha! If she's like her son, we'd be better off without her. He was so ineffective, that girl even has her parents coming her way! We're worse off now than we were! I'm just glad I never trusted your plan in the first place."

The failed spirit hung his head.

"Get out of here, you idiot!" the leader bellowed. Turning to the others, he gathered himself. "Now, just like we thought, we're going to have to stake everything on this revolt to hold them until we can get our guys organized for a public attack. I want total coverage. . . ."

Big changes were evident at the Monday night Bible study.

Within a few weeks, many new people began showing up at the meeting. The excitement in the group seemed to rise as people sensed a work of God happening in their midst. By the fifth Monday of the quarter, the crowding was severe at Jack's place.

The first Monday night in February, not only Carole from The Bratcellar, but also Jean's new boyfriend and two more girls from the dorm were there. Leslie brought a guy from one of her classes. All together, Sherry's circle of friends at the meeting numbered eight. Sherry was annoyed to see Sue sitting with Warren on the couch. Their romance was now an established fact, and to no one's surprise, Sue had begun making some negative observations about Jack during the past couple of weeks.

Ken Long, the tall, super-friendly guy who lived with Jack, taught.

Sherry knew Ken and Jack went back together all the way to high school, and she was intrigued by the idea that he probably knew Jack a lot better than she did. Ken was an engineering student in his fifth year, so he had to be pretty smart, but he wasn't verbally expressive most of the time, except for the periodic, very funny little comments he poked into conversations. As a result, Sherry had never realized how deep he was until this night.

He did an excellent job teaching from the end of John where Jesus repeatedly asked Peter if he loved Him. Ken's unusually deep voice and excellent, dry sense of humor made it easy to listen, and his straitlaced, perfectly groomed good looks seemed to fit with his large vocabulary and warm manner. Sherry gained a new respect for Ken, while she also understood the story of Christ's challenge to Peter for the first time.

Sherry noticed other people had taught at the last couple of meetings, and it made her wonder. Earlier, when she first started coming, Jack nearly always taught. Lately, he seemed to be taking a back seat.

Toward the end of the meeting Sherry was immediately electrified when Warren suddenly spoke up with a louder-than-usual voice. "I think it's interesting that only after asking Peter whether he loved Him did Christ suggest he feed His sheep. It really makes you wonder what Jesus thinks of those who presume to feed His sheep from other motives. I wonder what Christ's attitude will be to those who stand as shepherds for their own *selfish* reasons?"

Something about the way he said it made Sherry feel sure it was an indirect shot at Jack. She looked back up to Ken with fear in her eyes, wondering how he would answer.

"Yes, well, we all usually have a mixture of motives a lot of the time. Probably the best thing to do is ask God to show us where our motives may be bad and take them to Him at that point."

"Shouldn't one who's a shepherd for the wrong reason step down from that position until he gets his motives right?" Again, there was that angry tone in his voice that sent shivers down Sherry's spine.

Ken frowned and looked slightly frustrated. "No, not necessarily. I think God can work with our sin areas while we serve Him, as long as the problem isn't too bad. Some things might be disqualifying, while others might be so common that there would be no reason to resign."

Someone else spoke up at that point, and Sherry looked back behind her and found Jack's face where he was sitting with a friend. Looking her in the eye, he subtly shook his head, showing that the meaning of Warren's words were not lost on him. Although the time of prayer seemed normal on one level, Sherry felt unedified by what she saw as a divisive note. Something burdened her spirit in what Warren had shared. She wondered during prayer whether she was judging him unfairly out of anger over what he had said about her and Jack.

Both guys visiting for the first time were quite interested. Sherry and Lisa spent the evening talking to them and other new people. As usual, most walked down afterward to The Fireside restaurant in twos and threes.

At The Fireside several exciting and challenging conversations came and went during the course of the long evening. Sherry sat at a table for six and got to hear Jack interact with Jean's boyfriend about religion. As he moved into a stirring explanation of the gospel of grace, his gift for communication was unmistakable.

Bob was obviously hearing the message in a new way. "Well, this evening's given me a lot to think about," he admitted. "I feel that if I'd been confronted with Christianity in this form earlier, I might've been more willing to consider it."

As the new guests trickled out around midnight, some of the more committed Christians moved over to the table with Sherry, Lisa, and Jack. Finally, only Lisa, Jack, Sherry, Ken, Leslie, and Amy were left together at the table. They shared stories and savored the excitement of seeing people meeting Christ. But eventually they began to discuss the crowding problem. "We're going to have to do something," Jack lamented as he shook his head. "The place is full, and we're going to be restricting what God wants to do if we don't find a solution."

"Let's move the group to a larger place. I keep telling you the student union is ideal," Lisa said.

"I'm reluctant to leave the home environment," Jack replied. "I think there's really something special about staying away from an institutional setting. People relax in a home."

"They wouldn't relax in the crowd we had tonight," observed Amy.

"Why don't we do both?" asked Sherry. "We could move the main group to the union, and split up on another night in two homes or apartments. We could use my apartment for one of them if you want."

Jack and Lisa looked thoughtful. A moment later Jack said, "That would mean three meetings a week for people who're also in a study group. That's going to be too many meetings for a lot of people."

"We could meet one week at the union and the other in houses," Sherry rejoined.

Jack grinned, enjoying Sherry's quickness. "Who would teach the home groups?" He gave her a hard time.

"Well, I can't give all the answers, I'm new here," she bobbed her head as she looked at the others, shrugging her shoulders. "But I thought Ken did a great job tonight," she went on as she saw him at the end of the table. Ken grinned and thanked her for the encouragement.

"Yeah, Jack," Lisa spoke up. "You know very well we've been getting other teachers up there for exactly this possibility."

"I know, but we hadn't planned on needing to move this fast . . . and we hadn't considered the idea of having a meeting at Sherry's place. I think that's an interesting idea when you consider how many of her friends are coming."

"Yeah, no kidding," Lisa agreed. "There must've been six or eight there tonight, and they're really responsive. We should get up a team and send them out like a mission group to go over there and reach all these people's friends."

"I think I should go," said Jack.

"I was going to say I should go," rejoined Lisa.

"You can both come!" Sherry urged.

There was a moment of silence as the friends at the table realized they would not be seeing as much of each other if they were meeting in different houses.

Amy finally vocalized what they were feeling. "I don't want you guys to go away!"

"Well, it's not like we'd be going to Chicago or anything," Lisa reminded her. "We'd see each other at the meeting at the union, and at our women's study group."

After going to the rest room, Sherry returned to find that Leslie had left the table and those sitting around had strained looks on their faces. "What's going on?" Sherry asked.

"We have some problems," Lisa said. "Warren is openly challenging the legitimacy of Jack's leadership, for one."

"Oh, I know! I was sure he was talking about you tonight!" Sherry looked at Jack.

"Well, that's nothing. You should have heard him Friday at our study group. He challenged everything I said. He's really angry. I don't think he's over the confrontation we had with him at all. He just seems to be probing for any opportunity to criticize me."

"It's just sickening," Lisa thumped the table, "especially to bring his problems into the middle of a Bible study!"

"There wasn't actually any proof he was directing his comments at Jack," Ken observed. "Let's be fair here. We may be falsely judging the guy."

"Baloney!" Lisa squinted. "I know what that guy's up to. And anyway, he's not our only problem." She looked back to Sherry. "We've also got a situation where Joe Emery and Karen are basically living together and they won't quit."

"Hmmm. Has anyone tried to explain God's will to them?" Sherry wondered.

"Oh, yeah," Ken said. "We've been to him several times on it. This last time, Jack, Lou, and I went to talk to him, and he just told us to mind our own business."

"And Karen keeps lying to me about it," Lisa said. "But she admitted to Amy they get it on all the time."

"Man, I can't believe that," Sherry marveled. "If they want to have that lifestyle, why do they want to come to Bible studies?"

"Yeah, that's the hard part to figure," Jack agreed. "We feel like it's to the point where we need to tell Joe and Karen they have to decide whether to stop sleeping with each other, or stop coming around."

The look of shock on Sherry's face brought the conversation to a stop. "You'd tell these guys they can't come to the meetings if they're sleeping with each other?" she asked with incredulity in her eyes.

"Yeah," Jack nodded.

"That sounds like . . . I don't know . . . like you're forcing them."

"It says in 1 Corinthians 5 you shouldn't let a Christian who's living in open sin—not even trying to stop—go on in fellowship."

She stared with amazement. "How will he get over his problem if he can't come to fellowship and get built up?"

Lisa tried her hand. "The idea is, they've been coming to fellowship, and it's not doing any good. You've warned them. It gets to the point where some people are just fooling around with God. They use the fellowship to get a good religious feeling, and then they just spend the rest of the time openly scoffing at the will of God." She speared one of the last olives on her plate with a toothpick. "I think at that point, God says it's better for those people if you demand they choose either their way of life, or Christian fellowship."

Sherry looked like she was trying to assimilate this point of view, but it was clear she was having trouble.

Ken finished stirring the cream in his coffee and tapped the spoon before throwing in his point of view. "The hope is, if they get out into the world and don't have Christians holding them up, they have to face their way of life as it really is—you know, loneliness, emptiness, all that stuff." He wagged the spoon at her.

"But how do you square this with the idea of grace?" Sherry shook her head.

Lisa held up her hand as though holding off the wrong conclusion, a frown on her face. "They're still accepted by God. You're not sending them to hell or anything. You're just putting them under discipline— you're putting them in a hard position in order to show them where their way of life leads."

"And what if they change their mind?"

"Then they can come back. All is forgiven."

Sherry stared at Lisa with a wrinkled forehead, still not clear. "Why don't you throw people out when they cuss or something?"

"It has to be a serious area of sin, like the ones listed in 1 Corinthians 5. And it should be a pattern too—a way of life, not just a fall from grace." They all nodded and murmured agreement.

"And this is biblical?" Sherry still seemed unsure.

"Oh, yeah." Jack spoke up again. "And, we counseled with Lee Carulo on it. He felt sure we need to move, and I think he's right. These guys probably aren't the only ones in the group who are fornicating, but they're open and flagrant about it. I'll show you the passages on this stuff if you want."

"Yeah, I guess I need to look at those sometime. So go on. How are we proposing to do this?"

Jack went on. "Well, according to the passages on this, we have to get together with all the committed members, like, we're thinking of the study group members, and we have to tell Joe and Karen they're going to have to choose. . . ."

Sherry just continued to stare in disbelief. "Man, that sounds rough. They'll really be embarrassed!"

"Jesus says in Matthew 18, if someone won't listen, you should tell it to the church." Jack pointed out.

"Man, this is really hard to choke down." She shook her head. "I mean, I'm sure the Bible teaches it, but . . . it's really hard to get used to."

"Well, that's where we're at. And Lee thinks we should take care of it before long."

They agreed they would tell their study groups to get together at Jack's house that Friday for a meeting. Joe and Karen would be called on to come. If they refused, they would no longer be allowed to come to the meetings.

With a new note of fear, they agreed to pray about both situations—the crowding and their problems with Joe and Karen. They bowed their heads at the table in the now-quiet restaurant and submitted their plans to God. All of them agreed they were willing to do whatever God wanted.

As they came out onto the street, they huddled around in their heavy coats at the corner before splitting up and going in different directions. Sherry saw the anxiety etched on Jack's face. "Jack, are you all right?"

He took a deep breath, and blew it out in a cloud of steam. "This is the first time we've ever faced a case of formal church discipline. It really scares me for some reason. . . . I feel sure we're doing the right thing. These are both Christians, and they're really deep in their sin. . . . I guess, according to Lee, if we just look the other way in cases like this, our group will lose its spiritual power and become like a country club."

Everyone stood for a moment in silence. Sherry sensed she probably wasn't the only one who felt shaken by the sight of Jack wavering in fear. She laid her hand on the side of his upper arm. "Jack, if this is the right thing to do, we don't have to worry. We'll all be there, and God won't let us down, right?"

"Yeah," he smiled. He told her he would call her the next day. Then he put his arm around her and kissed her goodbye right in front of everyone. For some reason, Sherry again felt a strange sensation as the others saw them as a dating couple, instead of just members of the group. She was happy Jack was openly affectionate, but she didn't want it to interfere with the closeness she felt with the group.

As she waved to the others and walked off to her car nearby, she reflected on how it seemed that Jack sort of belonged to the whole group. She felt like others might not appreciate her having a special relationship with him. But she had dealt with jealousy before, many times. All in all, except for the negative conversation in the restaurant, it had been a fantastic evening.

40

At 6:30 Friday evening, Sherry walked into Jack's house with a sick feeling in her stomach. She had never been at anything even remotely similar to this meeting, and the fear of the unknown seemed to combine with something else. The intangible sense of horror and evil was so thick she wondered whether she could stand being in the room for long. She sat next to Lisa on the couch and took her hand, which was wet and clammy like her own. She leaned over to whisper, "It seems like you could cut some of the atmosphere in here with a knife and spread it on toast!"

Lisa nodded at her with a face so haggard and frightened it only served to heighten Sherry's own anxiety. Looking around, she saw Joe Emery was there without Karen. Across the room was Ken, sitting near Warren. A fresh chill of fear shot through Sherry the moment she saw Warren. Looking quickly away, she saw Jack taking his seat on the stool from which they usually taught. She guessed there were twenty to twenty-five people there.

Jack started to speak, asking the group to turn to God in prayer. He prayed for them, and then addressed Joe. "Joe, we're here tonight to talk to you about your way of life. We're following Jesus' instructions to tell your problem to the church because you wouldn't listen to us when we came to you privately."

Joe suddenly spoke up. "Jack, you might as well drop the phony talk, because I already know you've gossiped about me to everyone in this room."

"That's not true, Joe."

Joe waved his hand as if to dismiss Jack. "You're just a self-righteous ruler here, Jack. Once a person gets on your bad side, it's only a matter of time before you attack. You and your yes-men and women."

"Joe, you know that's not true. I've pleaded with you in love to stop fornicating, and you always tell me to mind my own business."

"Yeah, but you never do, do you?"

"You've admitted to people here that you and Karen are living together and that you've been fornicating, Joe."

"I want to know who authorized this meeting!" His tone was sharp and menacing now. "Where do you get the authority to tell me what God wants for my life?"

"My authority is 1 Corinthians 5:11. Paul commands that we not associate with any sexually immoral man. . . .'"

"Oh, and you would admit it if you ever fell, wouldn't you, Jack?" His skewed smile was full of sarcasm.

"I believe I would." Jack was serious. "I know I'd need to admit it and repent from it. That's what we want you to do here."

"Yeah, well, we stopped sleeping together weeks ago. How about that?"

There was a period of dead air as Jack and the others tried to adjust to this unexpected position. Much to Sherry's disgust, her left eye began to twitch in an irregular spasm.

Lisa spoke up. "Joe, Karen already admitted the two of you are getting it on all the time."

He rotated his head over to Lisa and said without hesitation, "Well, she must have lied. And she's not here anyway."

"But you admit you're still living with her?" Jack asked.

"Maybe. But that's none of your business, and if I did live with her, I would expect to be taken at my word as a Christian that we're not doing anything."

A negative murmur went around the room as people clearly rejected what Joe said. "That's not going to do, Joe," Jack went on. "We're demanding that you repent, and that means no more of this 'none of your business' garbage, and it means you'll get her to move out immediately. Are you going to do it or not?"

Joe tipped his head from side to side. "That's not going to do. That's not going to do. That's not going to do. Just who do you think you are, Jack? Since when are we here to be bossed around by you? Man, I'm not sure I care what you think!"

Suddenly Lisa spoke up with surprising anger. "Joe, you're trying to make this a thing about Jack when it's really about your sin! You're also lying to us. Why don't you just admit your sin and repent?"

Amy spoke up, talking about how Joe was harming her friend, Karen.

Before anyone else could speak, a booming voice broke in, full of anger. It was Warren. "Why don't you all just get in front of the mirror? Will you look at what is happening?! When I came to this group, I thought it was different because it was loving! I thought this group loved people, that we cared about people! Now look at us! We've become a bunch of self-righteous Pharisees! We've lost our first love and gone over to legalism. I can't believe this is happening!"

"What can't you believe, Warren?" Jack asked. "That we're obeying the Bible?"

Warren turned with fury and pointed his finger at Jack. "You! You are the one who brought us here. You are the one who is leading this group back under law! Your only thought is to maintain your control over us. Where is the *care*, Jack?"

"I do care, Warren." Jack was speaking with sharp intensity, but was still controlled. "I care for Joe enough to confront him for his own good."

"Yeah, like you cared for me! You guys should have seen him shouting cuss words in my face just a few weeks ago for breaking one of his rules. Now he's getting another brother. Where is it going to end?"

Amy spoke up, "Jack never shouted cuss words at you, Warren."

"Ask Ken," he challenged. "Ken, did he cuss at me or not?"

Ken was quiet for a moment, clearly signifying he couldn't answer no. "Well, you were cussing at him, too."

"In self-defense, yeah."

"No, it wasn't in self-defense. I believe you started it," Ken said.

"It was a sin," Jack spoke up. "And I apologized to you for it."

"You never should have been getting in my face in the first place!" Warren was still full of fury. "But that seems to be the climate around here now. Look at us! If Joe's having a problem, we should lift him up. We should pray for him. We should esteem him and love him, not bring him in here and pound on him."

"Oh, Warren, you're such a lying hypocrite!" Sherry was stunned to hear these words literally shouted from Lisa. "The whole reason they went to talk to you was 'cause you were jumping all over Billy for nothing more than a burn in the carpet! *You* were the one who was harsh! Now you come in here acting like you're the apostle of patience."

"See?" He held his hand out toward Lisa. "Gossip. That's what I mean. If I had a problem, why does she know about it? Answer me, Jack."

"She's a leader here, and we discussed whether I needed to go talk to you. I need advice sometimes."

"Oh, right. Advice." Warren was standing and leaning forward toward Jack. "You were just spreading your story so everyone would back you when you and Tonto here came over to rough me up. It was really because I dared to speak the truth about you and your own womanizing, wasn't it?"

Lisa spoke up again. "You know you were just jealous, Warren.

Everybody knows it."

He looked around, his eyes glowering with fury. Slamming his hand against the banister, he cried out, "Okay. That's it. I've about had it."

Now Sue spoke up through tears. "Leave him alone, you guys! He's right. This isn't a very loving group." She buried her face in her handkerchief and sobbed.

"Okay," Warren continued. "I'm leaving here and going over to the house on Simmons. Everyone who wants to be part of a fellowship group based purely on grace and love instead of the egotistical law of Jack Collins can come along." He reached over to pick up his Bible and held his hand out to Sue. To Sherry's horror, she took it and got up to leave with him.

"No, Sue! Don't go!" she called out, but they were already moving to the door. Joe stood to leave as well, and to the complete shock of everyone, several others rose to join them. Altogether, seven people—three guys and four women—left with Warren. The rest were left sitting in stunned silence. Several sobbed openly, instantly stripped of their illusory belief in the solidarity of their community. Sherry ran up to Jack, and he looked up with absolute defeat and misery written on his face. For the first time in the short history of the fledgling group, a full-scale division had begun.

41

During the days that followed, gloom hung like a blanket over everyone who was at the meeting when Warren left. Sherry was shellshocked as she went through the motions at work and spent some time with Jack on Saturday. Nothing they said seemed to help the terrible feeling of oppression hanging over them. Jack commented he was glad Ed was teaching Monday evening.

During the days that followed, several more people were said to have gone over to Warren's new group. Everyone who had any gripe with one of the existing leaders seemed to take advantage of the opportunity to get a new start. Lisa was inconsolable. She was convinced her lost temper had precipitated the break. Sherry and Jack both tried to assure her that Warren had been determined to create a division the first chance he got. Her words may have been unfortunate, but they weren't the cause of the division.

Sherry was inconsolable also. She couldn't accept the idea that Sue would defect to a dissident group. They had several conversations about it, which tended to be terse and short. Sue said things that hurt Sherry's feelings—that she had always wondered about Jack's motives, that Warren knew the Bible as well as Jack, maybe even better, and that Sherry should consider coming over to their new group. She said their first meetings had been spirit-filled like no other meetings she had been to. She felt the new group knew how to worship better than Jack's group. Sherry also had her hands full working with Leslie, Jean, and the other girls from the dorm. They were clearly disillusioned over the division. Some of them talked about going part-time to both groups in protest.

The only one who was upbeat was Lee Carulo. He spent time with Jack and the guys at the house, reassuring them they were doing the right thing, so they could leave the outcome in God's hands. He was worried they would draw the wrong conclusions from the experience and never risk disciplining anyone again. He pointed out he had experienced several divisions, and that there was nothing unusual about it. "If God is with you, they'll come to nothing, and your ministry will continue to grow and flourish after a brief setback," he insisted. "A lot of these people will come back after a while."

Jack agreed in his mind, but his mood didn't change for the better. Deeply depressed, he went about his work like a machine—faithfully carrying out his duties, but without joy or confidence.

Lee insisted they continue with their plans for a meeting at the union, even though the crowding at Jack's house was down a bit, with a dozen or more regular people missing. He said an outward focus would be the best thing for morale and faith. "When you take a hit like this, the enemy expects you to cower. Just keep marching straight ahead as if nothing happened."

Jack felt Lee knew what was best, and that his experience was more important now than ever. He completed the registration papers and paid the fee for the use of the Terrace Lounge through the end of the school year. Considering the condition the group was in, it seemed strange indeed to be paying for a larger meeting place.

During the following weeks, members of the group at Jack's house felt an increasing sense that they were beleaguered. They felt a sinking feeling that was the furthest thing from the confidence they had felt before. There were even some recriminations as some members accused others of precipitating the division. Most members felt a lack of energy which made it hard to witness or share.

During each of the succeeding weeks, more people went over to Warren's group. The numbers were never large—one here, two there. But the knowledge that up to fifteen or twenty of their members had left depressed everyone. The leadership of the group tried not to talk too much about what everyone referred to as "Warren's group," because it was too tempting to start hammering the people there for what they had done, especially Warren. At Lee's urging, they started a prayer meeting before each weekly Monday night meeting to fend off any demons and ask for protection for the group.

42

Sherry moved back into her apartment in February. The landlord had cleaned everything up, and Lisa went with Sherry to make sure there wouldn't be too much trouble returning to the scene of the killing. Sherry felt so awkward she asked Lisa to stay the night just to help her adjust.

That night as they lay in Sherry's oversized bed, Sherry broke down. "I can't believe what's happening in my life, Lisa," she complained. "Here I am trying to resolve the fact that I've taken the life of another human, and our friends are leaving right and left. . . ." She burst into tears. "Where has God gone? Why are these things happening? I feel so sorry for Jack. I can tell he's unhappy." They both ended up crying together as their trials seemed to weigh down on them like a dark cloud.

During the day, Sherry realized she was happy to have all her clothes back, and she carefully began nursing her neglected plants back to health. The brand-new dark green carpet and fresh off-white paint gave no clue that a man had recently been stabbed to death there. But as her eyes traveled to different parts of the room, vivid memories flew into her mind, making her shiver. After several nights, she felt she had adjusted fairly well, although every time she came into the building, a frightening wariness came over her.

That weekend, Sherry got off work Saturday night, and she and Jack went out with Lisa and Ken. Ken had finally asked Lisa out only a week earlier, after weeks of urging from Jack. Although Ken had said he thought Lisa was cute, he wouldn't ask her out, and Jack gave him a hard time, even jokingly calling him a weakling and a sissy. Ken would just grin and good-naturedly claim he was busy and just didn't have time for romance right then.

When he got around to asking her out, she responded enthusiastically. They enjoyed each other more than expected, and it was clear their friendship was moving in new directions. Both Sherry and Jack were encouraging them, because they loved the idea of being able to go out with their close friends.

That night they went to an inexpensive Thai restaurant with a great atmosphere. They sat in a secluded booth with high-backed bench seats that made it seem as if no one else was there. Under the circle of light cast by a hanging paper lantern, they spent almost three hours eating and enjoying friendly conversation. Sherry was temporarily exhilarated by the opportunity to go out on a formal date. She was beginning to feel freedom from her anxiety and depression over the killing and even the division seemed somehow distant.

Ken and Lisa looked funny when they walked into the restaurant, because he was over six-foot-four, and she was just a couple of inches over five feet. It seemed like she only came up to his waist, although it wasn't really that bad. Also, Ken's voice was unusually deep, and Lisa's was relatively high. Sherry and Jack got good mileage from teasing them about both things over dinner. "You seem like his daughter!" Sherry laughed, but Lisa and Ken would just smile good-naturedly and look at each other.

"He's a pretty nice daddy," Lisa beamed, laying her head against his shoulder in the booth.

Sherry had never felt so good about being out on a double date with another couple. Before she became a Christian, she always liked to have her man exclusively to herself. She now realized so much of her feeling in that area related to sex. It was somehow totally different in a Christian relationship.

Jack was at his best, full of humor and fun. It was the best mood Sherry had seen him in since the meeting with Warren. Sherry wore one of her favorite blouses: a festive yellow muslin piece embroidered by the Ojibwa Indians. She liked the way it hung on her body, especially when she tied a cord around her waist as a belt. Jack liked the way it hung too: He couldn't take his eyes off her all night long. With her dark complexion she looked like she could have been partly Indian. She had even braided two strands of her long hair in front and pulled them around to join behind her head like a headband. Jack thought she looked like an Indian princess.

After dinner as they sipped coffee, they began to talk about their problems.

"What I've been hearing makes me feel like there may have only been eighteen people who left, but everyone else's confidence seems weakened as well," Jack lamented. "There just doesn't seem to be that verve and thrill there."

Lisa nodded. "It seems like people doubt our leadership or something." She tapped her chopsticks on the table. "And I'd have to say my leadership ability should be called into question after that beautiful display of childishness I put on."

"Lisa," Sherry said. "You have to stop accusing yourself over your part in that meeting. You're doing the Devil's work for him."

"I think we really need the kind of strong input you give us, Lisa," Ken offered. "I think we tend to be a little too soft, and you were calling on us to do something about Warren weeks ago."

"Yeah," Jack agreed. "Maybe if we'd been a little stronger a couple of months ago when he started with the slander and stuff, we wouldn't be facing this division now."

"I don't see what that has to do with it," Lisa mumbled.

"It has to do with the fact that you're strong, and you're not afraid," Jack insisted. "You have good discernment and you don't operate based on a popularity contest. That's the kind of leadership we need. The fact that you let Warren get you angry in that meeting wasn't good, but it wasn't such a big deal, in my opinion."

Sherry nodded again. "Jack's right. What you said in that meeting certainly was not the reason those guys left."

Lisa considered their words for a moment. "Yeah, I can see that. He was just waiting for an excuse to lead a faction out. I guess we all contributed little errors that led to this."

"I don't necessarily agree," Jack argued. "I think if we had done everything right, they *still* might've left. I think you're implying their reactions are up to us, and Lee keeps stressing that's not true. He says that's a codependent view of ministry. He says we have to have the courage to do what's right and let the chips fall. The chips are God's business."

The waiter came and poured more coffee before Jack went on. "I'll tell you what I think our biggest mistake was. I think we should have gotten together with everyone for prayer before that meeting and reached one mind on the matter. We should have warned the people that some might react the wrong way, and we needed to decide whether we were ready to face that if it was God's will to discipline Joe and Karen."

Sherry agreed enthusiastically. "I'm sure glad you guys talked to me about it Monday night. I'd have hated to be going through the shock I felt Monday when I was right there in the meeting!"

"Yep," Lisa said. "We blew it right there. You're right, Jack."

"I think we're missing the real point," Ken suggested.

"What's that, Ken" Jack asked.

"The real point is that we have a terrific group of Christians who are still coming, still learning, still walking with God, and still winning lost people to Christ. Nobody's happy about what happened, but we can't just look at what we've lost. We have to also look at what we still have."

"What about the notion of the good shepherd leaving the ninety-nine and going out after the one lost?" Jack wondered.

"I've thought about that verse some. I think we should take any opportunity to try to talk to anyone we can. But there are two problems I have with applying that verse here. In the first place, I don't believe any of us are going to be able to go over there and get those guys to come back." They all nodded assent to that proposition. "Also, when Christ refers to the lost sheep, He's talking about God's heart for the lost. These people aren't lost to God, they're only lost to our group. We might not feel good about the group they've formed, but it's definitely Christian."

"That's a good point," Jack agreed. "Just because somebody leaves our group and goes to another Christian group isn't the end of the world."

Sherry shook her head. "Man, I still wish there was something more we could do!" She covered Jack's hand with hers and looked into his pained blue eyes with concern.

He smiled weakly but appreciatively. "I think there's a lot we can do. We can pray God will give our people the strength and discernment to resist these doubts. We can pray Satan will be bound."

After discussing the incident a while longer, they finally paid their bill and got their things to go. As they ambled out to Ken's car, Sherry was moved with a deep sense of how much the division had hurt Jack; of how deeply he cared for the friends they might have lost in the incident.

Until now, most of what she had seen in the group was fun and exciting. Now she was seeing another side to the leadership roles these young people had assumed. She wanted to reach out and heal the hurt she could feel in Jack, and she slid her hand up under his short coat and around his warm waist clinging tightly to him as they walked. He responded, holding her tightly up against him in the chilly night breeze.

They all decided to go to Jack's place and watch a video movie in the TV room the guys had set up in the basement. The old couches arranged around an area rug and an old TV were musty but comfortable. At about 1:00 a.m. Lisa and Ken abruptly got up and announced they were leaving. The couples said their goodbyes, and Jack and Sherry found themselves alone on the couch.

Jack had been feeling an aching desire for her all night as he had watched her move inside her Indian blouse and tight jeans. Her magnificent figure had been driving him crazy with desire to touch and hold her beauty, and his desire was only made worse by his own depression. Now, as they watched Ken and Lisa go up the stairs, they turned to face each other with the sudden realization they were alone in a place where they would not likely be disturbed. Her scent had a dizzying effect on Jack as she moved her face closer to his.

"We probably should go," Sherry suggested without much conviction, as she looked up into his face.

"Yeah, I guess we could wait a couple of minutes, though," he grinned as he pulled her the rest of the way into a passionate embrace. They heatedly kissed each other as feelings suddenly rose up and exploded in desire so fierce they could hardly control themselves. Jack felt that her lips were warm and saw her face flush as she responded to his thirst for her.

Slowly they began to sink back toward Jack's end of the couch, until Sherry was almost lying on top of him. There was an urgency in her kiss Jack had not experienced before. His mind was lost in a sea of emotion as his hand strayed over her body. Sherry offered no resistance and even eagerly gave herself up to his caresses.

Suddenly, Jack stopped. "Wait . . . no . . . we have to stop this," he whispered, still breathing heavily. Sherry gave a complaining moan as waves of frustration washed over her. It wasn't that she didn't agree they were getting out of control. It was just that she didn't feel like gaining control right then and there.

They sat up, and Jack looked down, leaning his elbows on his knees and resting his forehead in his hands. He sat for a minute, and then looked up at her. "I'm sorry, I shouldn't have done that," was all he said.

"Come on, *you* didn't do anything, *we* did something. I was right with you, Jack," she protested, rubbing her hand on his back.

"Well, I guess that's true, but it doesn't change anything. I feel really bad that we broke that barrier. This was something I wanted to avoid." He looked miserable as he reached his hand back and patted her knee reassuringly, but he was still bent forward and looking away from her.

"I guess it just didn't seem that bad to me, Jack. You were only showing love for my body. I mean, after all, we didn't even take our clothes off." He continued to stare at the floor in silence as Sherry wondered what to say. She was frustrated by his silence. "I just feel so jaded sometimes when I'm with you. What we just did was so small-time compared to what I've done before." She was getting quite depressed now in her own right as she pondered the contrast between her past and this episode. She wondered whether she would ever be able to survive under this Christian standard.

"Sherry, I don't think you're using the right standard here. You're judging the present by your past. I want to hold you in respect, and to me, that means having the self-control to treat you like a sacred sister."

She sensed he was trying to say something nice, but she didn't find it very appealing. A confused frown was on her face as he looked back at her. This time she wouldn't speak.

Jack tried again. "Look, our relationship is headed one of two ways in the end, right?" She didn't answer. "We either make it permanent, or we decide for some reason to get out of it, right?"

There was a pause before her unenthusiastic answer. "I guess."

"Well, either way, I want to act now so it'll be good then. You know, if we decide to get married, we'll be glad we waited to do anything until our wedding night. And if we decide we're not into it, I don't want you going off having been pummeled and used by me."

Sherry was rebelling in her heart against what Jack was saying but she didn't want to seem too resistant. "You may be right . . . I'm not saying you're not right . . . but I like you when you're excited. Maybe you'll think I'm just a tramp, but I feel good that, you know . . . you can have strong feelings or even lose control over me. I suppose that's really bad. . . ."

He looked at her and slowly broke into a grin. "I could lose control over you a lot worse than that," he warned. Then, forcing a frown, "I'm not sure you realize how easy it would be for us to get into deep trouble."

She admitted to herself she hadn't really been considering it from that perspective. "Okay, I agree, we need to be careful," she said with resignation.

They decided they had better get out of there. They grabbed their coats and drove to her apartment without saying much, deep in their own thoughts. When he walked her to her door, Jack took her once again and kissed her. He held on to her, his face next to hers as though treasuring her for one last moment. There was no reproach or any sense of distance in his language. But something was wrong. He left.

43

Jack came down from his room Sunday morning and made some coffee. He sat at the dining room table that stood before a big window looking southward toward the street. The sun glistened on a thin layer of fresh snow from the night before, and he sat watching the dust particles in the room float through the slanted beams of morning sunlight as he sipped his coffee.

The burden he felt was so heavy it filled his whole body with sadness. He was full of unresolved guilt that only felt worse as he repeatedly replayed images in his mind from the night before. The thing that bothered him most was the realization that he really wanted to do it again, and even more besides!

He bowed his head and rubbed his eyes, as if he could change what was on the screen of his mind. He felt trapped between his feelings for Sherry and his conviction that they needed to avoid rushing into a deeper commitment. The idea of breaking up with her in order to get control of the situation occurred to him, but it was unthinkable at this point. There was no way he would risk losing this love.

Once again, he remembered the sense of urgency he felt in her when they were on the couch. A shudder of desire went through him. How could anyone resist such beauty? He felt like crying as he realized how much trouble they were in. After crossing this threshold, there seemed to be no way they would ever control themselves again.

After he sat for nearly half an hour, Ken came into the dining room. Jack looked up with an expression on his face that made Ken do a double take. "What's wrong, Jack?" he asked as he sat at the table.

Jack opened up completely to Ken. He poured out not only the story of what happened the night before, but also how guilty and helpless he felt now. Ken listened and marveled for a time, obviously feeling deeply the intensity of Jack's struggle.

Ken had eyes of his own, and as he imagined what it would be like to try to resist temptation with someone like Sherry, he shook his head. "I guess I can see why a guy might lose it with her," he admitted. But then a different look came over his face. "Jack, you're going to have to take this to the cross."

"Man, I know God hasn't rejected me. I know I'm forgiven . . . but I feel like I've done irreversible damage to our relationship." Jack shook his head and moaned before burying his face in his hands. How could something so beautiful become so terrible? How could he have done this to her? "I know I let God down . . . but I know He can take it. His grace is infinite. But the thing that really kills me . . ." his lip quivered as he moved to the brink of tears, "the thing that really kills me isn't that I've let God down . . . because I know He can take it . . . it's that I've let *her* down!"

"Bro, I think you have to deal with this between you and God first. You have to leave off taking responsibility for her, and face the One you sinned against in the first place."

"I've confessed my sin and repented. I've already done that."

"Yeah, but you haven't believed His Word. You're feeling that she's been irreversibly damaged . . . that's unbelief, man!"

"Why? I don't get that."

"You're denying the power of God! You're denying the grace of God! You're trying to atone for this sin on your own. Can't you see that?"

Jack shook his head. "No."

"Your self-flagellation is a prideful rejection of the grace of God!" Ken insisted, and this time, his statement rang true to Jack.

Jack stared hard at Ken. Never had he heard Ken speak with such fervor . . . with such . . . truth. "I'm listening. I'm hearing what you're saying, but it's hard . . . I don't know. . . ."

"What don't you know?"

"I know what you're saying is right. But . . . why can't I feel it?"

"The ego always dies hard, man." Ken put a hand on Jack's bent-over shoulder. "Are you prepared to give up on this mess you've made, and hand it over to the sovereign power of God, or not?"

"You think that's what it is, huh?"

Ken sat back in his chair. "What are you asking me? Do I think God can handle Sherry Martin? Do I think He can handle Jack Collins? Is this what you want to know?"

Jack broke into a smile. As he leaned on one elbow looking at his best friend, his face was still tinged with sadness, but now with hope. "You're killing me. Have mercy," he pleaded jokingly.

"Hey, you know I'm right on this. Now, I asked you a question."

"Am I prepared?"

"Yeah."

"Prepared to what? Say that again." Jack really wanted to hear it again.

"Are you prepared to give up on this mess—to leave off paying for it, to leave off taking responsibility for 'fixing' it, and surrender it to the power of God? Are you ready to come to God on this with empty hands?"

"Oh, man, that's beautiful! Yeah, I'm ready."

They bowed together before the Lord of the universe as Jack renounced the luxury of self-flagellation, as well as the ownership of Sherry's well-being. His eyes were opened as he saw the selfishness in what he had been feeling. He stood as a naked, forgiven sinner before God.

Then Ken prayed, rebuking the accusations of the Evil One. He pointed out they were not ignorant of his schemes . . . that with the new student union meeting scheduled to begin soon, it was the perfect time for the enemy to try to unhinge Jack's confidence in God. "Lord, we need this servant of Yours standing up there next month strong in Your love and grace, not cowering under a load of guilt and accusation. Please protect him." Then he prayed for Sherry. "Lord, what this older brother has shown her is bound to be confusing. We wonder what effect it'll have. But we believe You love this girl more than either one of us. We believe You can bring her through this trial as You've brought her through everything else. We're going to actively trust You with her."

As they prayed together Jack felt the healing power of God flowing into his spirit, along with faith that somehow Sherry and he would find a way to control their desire for each other. Jack had never appreciated the steady reliability of his longtime friend as much as he did at that moment. Afterward, they decided to go out for a run on campus.

As Jack studied later that day, he was still melancholy, but the deep oppression had been lifted somewhat. However, visions of their time on the couch the night before continued to haunt him, drawing him repeatedly back into guilt and temptation. He realized he would be living with these temptations for some time to come.

44

Sherry had a full day and evening of work on Sunday. Her discomfort and worry about the tense scene with Jack plagued her the entire time. She couldn't exactly identify what she was feeling, but she knew that, among the jostling emotions troubling her, there was a clear strain of anger at Jack. She wasn't sure why. Was it because he was being a stick in the mud? A choirboy? Was it because she felt somehow put down by his reaction? Was it because she felt he was accusing her?

She was too busy serving to figure it out. She decided to wait until she got home.

Later than night in her apartment, Sherry bristled with bewilderment and anxiety. This was the first negative element to creep into her relationship with Jack. She knew the incident on the couch had hurt Jack in some way. She wondered whether it only bothered him because it contradicted the image he wanted to project: the 'man of God' who has it all together. She felt faint sensations of rejection, but she couldn't tell why. *He's so self-controlled, it's suffocating! Why doesn't he want me as much as other guys do?*

She knew she felt guilty, but she wondered if it was him making her feel that way.

She decided she would try to discern which it was at Bible study the next night.

That week there were fewer people at the group than the week before. The meeting was deflated, as people wondered whether still more people had gone over to Warren's group. Perhaps it was just that people were losing faith in the vision and leadership of this group. Whatever the reason, the meeting was unenthusiastic and almost depressing. Jack tried to plead his case from the book of 1 Corinthians, but Sherry felt she had never seen him so ineffective as a teacher. During prayer, people apparently didn't feel like saying much, and even when Sherry tried to offer an impassioned prayer she felt like her words were falling to the floor just past her feet. Somehow it was as though the spiritual energy in the meeting was being sucked out by a great vacuum attached to the window.

Afterward, for the first time, Sherry heard other members discussing whether there was something wrong with their group, suggesting that perhaps the Lord had withdrawn His presence from them. Fear, concern, and depression were evident on most faces.

Jack was acting distant and awkward. Twice Sherry came to stand next to him while he was talking to someone, and tried to get involved in the conversation. Both times he was polite but distant. He was called away from one conversation, and left to go to the rest room during the other. Sherry felt frustrated about her inability to connect with him. She wasn't seeing the special looks and eye contact they usually shared. She told herself there was no reason to believe he was avoiding her, but the way he did or didn't look at her, the nervousness in his mannerisms, and the things he said made her feel distant from him.

At midnight he came by Sherry's table at The Fireside and announced he was tired and was going to bed even though they hadn't had a chance to talk. She immediately stood and said she wanted to chat for a minute on the way out. As they reached the street, he walked two feet away from her. Now she was certain. "So, what's the problem, Jack?"

"What do you mean?"

"I mean, you're avoiding me, you're acting distant and weird."

"Oh." He didn't contest her perceptions. "I guess I'm . . . acting weird because I'm feeling weird."

"Is it because of the other night?"

He shuffled along, apparently reluctant to engage her. "Uh, that certainly hasn't helped. But I think there's more." Again he fell silent, looking steadily down at the sidewalk, taking stock. "I didn't feel good about my teaching tonight. I didn't feel good about the meeting. That really depresses me. I feel like I let the whole group down."

"You did your best! I didn't think it was that bad."

He tipped his head and pursed his lips in a way that said, *You're lying.*

Sherry said, "Okay—it wasn't your best."

"And I can't seem to get into talking to anyone tonight. I guess I'm really tired . . . and maybe sort of depressed. I'm getting the feeling we're on the losing team."

"I get that feeling too. There's something wrong. Some people are speculating God might have taken His power away from us."

"Boy, talk about a terrible thought." He shook his head in a way that made Sherry think he had toyed with the idea himself.

"Is that what you think?"

He thought a bit as they stopped walking at the corner where they would part ways and faced one another. His brow was a deep frown. "No. I think you have to be really careful about believing things like that. The Devil always suggests that. I just think I'm really messed up right now." He looked up and stared off into space, his hands in his pockets. "I think the things we've been going through are weighing down on me . . . for some reason, I haven't been able to trust God with them . . . and this thing coming up at the union really scares me. Here we are down to fifty or sixty people, depressed, disunified, and we're going out into a situation that's really going to be challenging. . . ." He hesitated awkwardly, staring over Sherry's shoulder. Suddenly Sherry was shocked to see his chin quiver. He was on the verge of tears! A moment later his voice broke as he had to force his words out through tears he couldn't hold back: "I don't know. I guess I feel pretty intimidated right now."

Sherry reached out for him, and seizing his jacket, she pulled him toward her. She wrapped her arms around him and pressed her head against his chest. She felt him sobbing as he threw his arms around her, welcoming the comfort. Tears of fear and hurt now welled up in Sherry's eyes as she felt Jack's pain. Never before had she seen him as a broken man. Gone were the vigor and the vivacious attitude of joy in the Lord on which she had been feeding for months. They clung to each other and wept.

He lifted her face and, after wiping his own eyes, he wiped her cheek where a tear had streaked it. He kissed her softly, reassuringly. He was back in control again. "I hope you can bear with me at this time."

"Of course I can, Jack. You know I'm here for you!"

"Yes, I know you are, but I feel like I'm hurting you."

"I want to hurt with you. I don't want you to hurt alone."

He looked sorry but determined. "I don't think you can help me right now. I wish we could work this out together, and I want to talk to you more about it. But I feel like I need to be alone awhile. I have to go home and get my head together with God, Sherry. I hope that's okay."

"I want to help you! I want to be with you!" she protested.

He was still determined. "I feel like I need some space. Sometimes I just need to be alone with God, okay?"

She looked disappointed, but tried to sound brave. "Yeah, it's okay. If you really need to go, that's fine."

"Thanks," he smiled, but it included sorrow. "I'll see you later. Don't worry about me. I think this mood will pass."

She nodded. He turned to head up the street, leaving her standing with an empty, helpless feeling.

At home, Sherry dumped her coat and raised her hands to feel her cheeks and face, which were burning with a deep flush of anxiety and turmoil. Her burden for Jack was so heavy she couldn't relax. She sensed his problems were within himself—not that he wanted to get away from her. The most disturbing part was the way his depression fit into the overall pattern of spiritual demoralization evident in the lives of all their friends.

Somehow the combination of factors was adding up to something greater than the parts. Sherry realized that, considering the state Jack and the rest of the group were in, they could well be facing a painful defeat in their bid to move to the union and plant a new group at her apartment. She went into her bathroom and turned to God. *What's my part in healing Jack and the others, Lord?*

Immediately, thoughts of their last night together on the couch came back. As she reflected, she understood that the passionate episode on the couch had wounded Jack's conscience. *Why does he have to be so conscientious?* she complained to herself.

As she undressed for her shower, she looked at herself in the mirror. Since high school, she had competed with other girls by taking advantage of her shapely figure and good looks. As she stood thinking, there was something going on inside her. Gently, but firmly, God showed her she had *wanted* Jack to lose control with her that night. His "self-control" stood as a challenge to her—a clear sign something was more important to him than his desire for her. She took a shower, still preoccupied.

As she finished her shower, her eyes were opened to see what was inside her. A wave of sorrow came over her as she sank down on the corner of the bed. *I've been waiting for the opportunity to go further with him. When the chance came, I jumped at it.* She saw that her opportunism came partly from the desire to satisfy her need to know that he couldn't resist her. She hadn't fully accepted the notion that their relationship with God must always supersede their relationship with each other. God spoke to her, letting her know she was usurping His place in Jack's life.

God also showed her something else as she sat on the edge of her bed. She had already seen that God had given her great intelligence which she was to use to glorify Him. Now she felt challenged that her beautiful body was also a stewardship from God.

You want me to use my looks for You? she wondered. Somehow, her looks seemed to fit into a different category than her mind. It was easier to see how her mind was something that could serve God. But it took only seconds for her to realize that her body was also a part of her—that God wanted her to agree that if she had beauty, it was from Him, and for His glory.

She turned to God in her heart. *Okay God, I realize what we did was wrong, and I repent from it. I want to continue to see this as an issue between You and me, not between me and Jack.* She thought for a moment. *Let me be the kind of woman who won't interfere with his relationship with You. I know You've given me a certain amount of beauty . . . and I thank You for that . . . and I want to learn what it means to use that for You. I don't want to be the one who damages this great guy.*

As she lay back on her bed, tears began to fill her eyes. It was all so sad! Their beautiful relationship . . . the oppression in their fellowship ever since the division with Warren . . . her horror at killing a man who may have gone to hell . . . Sue, lost and alienated . . . people feeling unable to pray . . . the broken state Jack was in that night. . . . *Oh, God, please help us! Don't let us lose everything You've given us!*

Gradually, God reassured her of His forgiveness as His grace flooded in. Even in the face of continued fears for the well-being of Jack and her friends, a certain peace that comes from resolving a conflict with God allowed her to sleep.

45

As the next few days passed, Sherry's spirits began to rise. The experience of receiving revelation from God about herself, along with a heartfelt repentance, had done wonders for her emotional life. She was hopeful again. That weekend, her work schedule conflicted with Jack's, so they weren't able to go out. But at work Sherry enjoyed unbroken fellowship with the Lord as she worked. Gradually, a certainty grew within her that she had the key to free Jack from some of his hard feelings. She called him after work Saturday, even though it was late. "How have you been doing today?" she wanted to know.

He answered slowly. "I'm . . . walking around wondering how you're doing, I guess." She could immediately tell he was still morose and defeated.

"Well, I'm doing great!"

Jack was annoyed. Was it possible she could have come away from their recent defeat without sensing the gravity of the situation, without conviction of sin? "I'm surprised," was all he said.

"Don't think I'm playing down what happened last weekend. The fact is, I've come right around on my view of the whole thing."

"Oh? How's that?"

"Well, I feel like God came in and dropped a bomb on my head this week." She wound the cord around her finger.

"Really?"

"Yeah. I was just standing there worrying about everything, you know? And, it was like the Spirit came in and opened my eyes. I've never had God bear down on me like that, I guess. Anyway, it wasn't burdensome or depressing even though I saw where I was wrong."

In the short silence that followed, Jack must have wondered how to respond. Finally he said, "Uh, where were you in the wrong, if you don't mind me asking?"

Sherry took a deep breath. "Okay. Well, this is a little hard to say . . . but, I guess the fact of the matter is that . . . in a way, I realize I was hoping you'd lose control for me last Saturday." Jack was silent again, apparently letting her words sink in. Sherry went on. "I'm sorry, Jack. I feel like things are going to go a lot better in that area after this."

Jack was still quiet even though it seemed like he ought to respond to what she was saying. He drew himself out of his reflection finally. "Wow, that sounds really far out. But I don't want you to think you have to be cooling me off all the time. You know, I don't want there to be . . . an artificial aspect there."

"I don't think that's what we're talking about. I think the point is, I haven't been in step with you on where we should be drawing the line physically. I think . . . man, this is really hard. . . ." She was struggling, but he didn't help her out. "I guess it's embarrassing to say, but I think I've been viewing this ability you have to turn away from . . . falling all over me as . . . sort of a challenge. You know, the guys I've dated in the past have all tried their best to get whatever they could . . . and you've been so different. This must sound really crazy!" She jerked her finger out of the cord she had been playing with and stood up with the phone.

"No, I can see where you'd get that."

"Well, I guess to be perfectly honest, I've almost felt a little sense of rejection because I don't drive you crazy enough. I know this is all really fleshly, really immature, and I can't stand saying this stuff, it's so embarrassing. But I just haven't been doing my part in the area of self-control, especially last Saturday."

"You know, as I hear that, I realize you must've had a deep dealing with God, but I want to resist it at the same time. I feel like . . . boy! Talk about fleshly thinking!"

"Come on, I told you what I was feeling."

"Well . . . shamefully, I have to admit that, on one level, I like the idea of your trying to seduce me, and I wish you'd do it again."

"Well, that's not so bizarre," she reassured him. "I think that's pretty normal in fact."

"Yeah. . . ." He seemed to be thinking again as some dead air hung between them. Then he went on. "I'm just so wiped out, I don't know. You shouldn't listen to me."

"You're really messed up over this, aren't you?"

Jack spoke very slowly and haltingly. "Yeah, I can't deny it. Ken came in and we talked it out Sunday morning, and I felt better. . . . Boy, what a brother he is! But I don't know, my head's just swimming."

Sherry was frustrated by the defeated sound in Jack's voice. "Jack, what we did was wrong. Do you hear me?"

"Yes, I know that." But the same sense of resignation and defeat permeated his voice.

"We've been forgiven, we've learned a lesson, and we're going to move on and do better. Okay?"

"You're going to have to help me, Sherry. I don't know whether you realize how desperately I want to . . . to go even farther than we did. See . . . I'm not just struggling with feeling guilty about what we did . . . I'm wondering how we're going to deal with temptation in our relationship in the future."

"It'll be different with me helping! I'm telling you, my perspective has been wrong here. I really think it's going to make a difference," she pleaded.

"You're giving me hope. You're like an older believer right now. I feel like you're so much closer to God on this. Where'd you get so much maturity?"

"If I'd been more mature, we wouldn't be in this situation right now." She began winding her finger again.

"Well, I don't believe it was your fault. I feel like I'm making my own choices here."

"A woman has a lot of control over these things, Jack. I can make it so tough you'd have to get away from me to control yourself. I think I can also make it easier."

Again, there was a silence as Jack seemed to process what Sherry was saying. She gave him some space, sensing it wasn't time to speak further. Finally, she was rewarded when he went on in a more resolved tone. "I feel really happy listening to you. You're the greatest. I love you so much."

Sherry smiled from ear to ear. "I love you, too. And I want you to stand up there Monday night knowing we've dealt with this thing completely and put it behind us."

"Okay, I feel like I might be able to do that now. Maybe you should share what happened with Lisa?"

"Yeah, I agree. I think that's exactly what I should do. That'll help me resolve this the rest of the way."

When they eventually hung up, Jack was a new man. He turned back to his books and tried to prepare for his teaching.

46

Finally, the time came for the last meeting at Jack's house as one group. There were more people there than the week before, but they had still never returned to the jam-packed conditions common before Warren and his people left.

After the group of a dozen leaders and workers met for prayer, people began arriving, and almost immediately it was clear that the people's morale was improved. Whether because of the extra time they had taken to bind Satan away from the meeting place or the fact that everyone knew the group had reached the end of one phase of its mission and was ready to jump into a new challenge was not clear. But there clearly was a sense of the old excitement in the air as tangible as crackling electricity.

After opening with prayer, Jack read the description of the church in Jerusalem from Acts 2:41-47:

> And about three thousand were added to their number that day. They devoted themselves to the apostles' teaching and to the fellowship, to the breaking of bread and to prayer. Everyone was filled with awe, and many wonders and miraculous signs were done by the apostles. All the believers were together and had everything in common. Selling their possessions and goods, they gave to anyone as he had need. Every day they continued to meet together in the temple courts. They broke bread in their homes and ate together with glad and sincere hearts, praising God and enjoying the favor of all the people. And the Lord added to their number daily those who were being saved.

With passion, he pressed the point that their group was no different from this one described so long ago. He pointed out the main similarities: "In the first place, they devoted themselves to the apostles' teaching and to fellowship. This is no different from what we do. We have the apostles' teaching in written form, and we meet here and in our study groups for fellowship. We have communion, and we pray together just as they did.

"We don't have our belongings in a common pool, because there's never been any need. But I would hope that, if people were in serious financial need, we wouldn't hesitate to lay our belongings on the line, just as we've laid our lives on the line for God.

"The togetherness, the glad and sincere hearts, taking our meals and living our lives together—these are the things we treasure, too!"

Heads nodded around the room and one or two murmurs could be heard, "That's right!"

"And then there's this sense of being 'filled with awe.' I don't know about all of you, but I can really identify with this. Now, when I was a kid, 'awe' wasn't how I would have described my feelings about church. Nothing could be further! I guess I remember saying 'Aw, do we have to go?'"

The group broke into laughter.

"But now I understand what this is saying. I've seen God do some things here during the past year that have caused me to feel a terrific sense of awe! We're going to hear from some of you tonight about changed lives. And I guess most of you feel the same way, but I know when I look at the changed lives in this room, I have to sit back and say, 'God, You're awesome!'"

Several spontaneous voices spoke up. "Yeah!" "You said it!"

Jack went on: "And what about this last comment? 'And the Lord added to their number daily those who were being saved.' You know, this whole description just wouldn't read the same way without that statement! We could have fellowship, teaching, prayer, and communion all for ourselves. But something's missing! What about the ocean of people around us who don't know God? I'm telling you, a group just isn't like this New Testament church without that last comment.

"You know, we may think our group has it together spiritually. But if no one's being attracted to the love of God, there must be more of a problem than we think!"

Murmurs could again be heard around the room.

"I could go on about this for some time, but we aren't here tonight to hear me. Let's just say we're committed to seeing this healthy growth and life continue. That's why we've all been talking about splitting this group into two groups. And of course, we've all determined to move ahead this next week. And we've also discussed getting together and bringing our friends to the student union, and we're ready to move on that.

"I realize this is something different, that we won't see all our friends in this home setting. This thing we're trying might not even work. But I think it's worth trying, because the stakes are so high. Tonight, I'd like us to remember how high those stakes are, so why don't some of you tell what God has done in your lives through the ministry here?"

One by one, those who had been converted or changed by God through the ministry of the group took turns standing and sharing what God had done in their lives. The stories were interesting and moving. As people from widely different backgrounds told their stories, there was the common thread of the grace of God changing lives. Several choked up with emotion as they thanked the Lord for what He had done.

Near the end, Sherry spoke up. Her explanation of how God seemed to have closed in on her from all directions brought approving murmurs from the group. Leslie and Jean both joined in with their own testimony, and in a surprise move, Jean's boyfriend spoke up and gave a slightly confused, but sincere testimony.

Finally, Jack called on the group to pray, and requested special prayer for the team going to Sherry's place to start the new home group. Prayer was long and enthusiastic that night, just as in earlier days. It seemed everyone wanted to speak up while they still had the chance to pray with all their friends together. There was an odd combination of melancholy and excitement in most people's hearts as they contemplated together before God the next phase of their lives and mission.

Jack closed the prayer session, and people got up to mill around. There were many hugs and heartfelt expressions of love that night as everyone seemed to sense God was going to use them to do great things in the future. Their recent sense of defeat seemed to have changed to one of victory, as they looked forward to breaking out of the house that had contained the group up to that point.

But that night at The Fireside, Sherry's spirit was dampened by more bad news when she stopped by the table where Jack and Lisa were sitting with a couple of others. "So, our buddy Arthur has started a new ministry in his church," Lisa said with an ironic look on her face.

"Arthur Barclay? At Edgewood? What ministry?"

"It's a self-help group for people leaving our Bible study!" Jack chimed in. "They're calling it 'exit counseling'!"

"Why, that bag of wind!" Sherry shook her head.

"The group is up to over twenty of our ex-members," Lisa added.

"Yeah, and guess who's helping him run the group?" asked Jack.

Sherry thought for a moment. "Not Becka!"

"No, much worse than that. It's Warren!"

Sherry's spirit was instantly dashed as though someone had splattered warm oatmeal on her face. "Oh, no! How do you know this?"

"They tried to get me to go," said Jerry, a newer member of the group. "Dave Merker told me this Barclay guy knew ten times as much as Jack, and that this group was sort of the last word on Christianity."

Sherry felt a sinking feeling in her heart as she listened to Jerry. It was so depressing to think of people in the city who were actively working against their ministry, especially when they were Christians.

"There's no way something he says is the last word on anything," she asserted. Then looking over at Lisa, "You don't suppose our talk with him would have led to this?" She felt sudden guilt and fear that she may have done something to jeopardize God's work through the group.

"I don't think so." Lisa shook her head. "Let's remember, Becka had a negative view of this group before she ever came. Someone had told her we were sinners and extremists."

"That's right. But I can't imagine our talk helped matters any."

"No, it probably didn't," Lisa had to agree.

"Do you guys want to tell me about this talk?" Jack asked the two suddenly somber women.

They spent a few minutes explaining to Jack and the others.

"Well," Jack said, "it wasn't smart to antagonize him, but if that's the reason he's doing this, I can only say, he must be pretty petty. How could someone jump all over another Christian group just because of disagreement on a few points? I mean, it's not like we went in there and tried to mess up his ministry."

"No, but there are a couple of guys here who used to go there," Sherry observed. "I don't know whether you realize Warren was originally from there."

"Yeah, I knew that," Jack nodded. "But what are we supposed to do if someone comes and wants to fellowship? Say, 'Oh, I'm sorry, you're already in a church, so you can't come here?'" he shrugged. "I realize Barclay might have felt menaced to some extent by the defection of some members. I wouldn't mind him critiquing our approach in his own church. After all, that's his role, to teach his people what he feels is right. I guess I just don't like the idea of setting up a group that has its purpose recruiting people from our group. That's really aggressive!"

After they talked about it a little longer, they decided not to say anything about it to the rest of the group. They hoped that by ignoring it, it wouldn't amount to much in the long run. Besides, with the return of decent morale in the group, nobody wanted to risk sharing more defeating news. They decided to go home.

47

When Sherry woke up the next Wednesday morning, the depression was back. Somehow her whole spiritual life seemed to be a big joke. The faces of those she had brought around to the group appeared in her mind. In each case, there was something that seemed futile, some reason why they probably would not go on with the Lord. She imagined the meeting coming up at the union that night and felt anxiety mixed with apathy. *Who do we think we are anyway?* she wondered. *What makes us think we have the answers to the spiritual needs of this campus? And even if we do, what makes us think anyone will want to listen?*

All through the morning the negative thoughts kept recurring in Sherry's mind. Usually when she felt this negative she just dealt with it herself, but today she was glad she was going to see Jack after her medieval history class.

When she saw him sitting on the wall next to the steps in front of Cummins Hall, she immediately sensed something was wrong. He was slumped over a newspaper with a deep frown on his face. As she approached and called his name he looked up without smiling.

"What's wrong?" she asked.

"This!" he spat out as he slapped the paper with the back of his hand. She took the paper and saw the heading of the front-page article.

"Campus Religious Groups Decry Freedoms"

With growing horror and fury she read the article, which was a piece of investigative journalism intended to unmask the menace of the new "fundamentalist underground." The article claimed there were a growing number of extremist groups appearing on campus, all sharing a "values system that, according to experts, threatens civil liberties and fosters racism and prejudice."

The reporter named three different groups, including a splinter group centered around a particularly obnoxious street preacher who made a habit of offending passersby on sidewalks, a campus Pentecostal group that required the women in the group to wear head coverings and long dresses, and Jack's Bible study group.

Some of the descriptions of Jack's group were more positive than those of the other groups, but pejorative comments were predominant. The meetings were characterized as "surging with fundamentalist fervor" and "simplistic treatment of ancient religious metaphors as though they were literal." The leader, Jack Collins, "admitted he views homosexuals as sinners."

Sherry shook her head in disgust as she read the unfair description and twice stopped to stomp her foot and complain. "Just having us lumped in with these other groups says it all!" she protested.

"Read on, it gets worse," Jack warned.

Then, as she read on to the next column, her hair bristled with fury even more.

"I'm afraid there is an irresistible appeal in the simple answers these groups offer to complex questions," observes Reverend Lowell Billings of the Campus Faith Community. "Unfortunately, this kind of simplicity often is tied to narrow paternalistic interpretations of culture and history. These theories are often similar to the seemingly informed answers the Nazis provided to Germany. The Nazis also studied history, philosophy, and the Bible. But everything was pushed through the grid of their narrow, prejudiced ideology. There was never the need to see things through the eyes of others. Those not complying, those who don't fit into the definitions of these groups, are targeted for ultimate persecution. Women, homosexuals, Blacks, and Jews are usually the first to suffer under these systems."

"This guy's two-faced!" Sherry stormed. "He prances around there with his little huddle of weirdos and extols accepting all views. Is this acceptance? It doesn't sound like we're all members of the happy family of faith!" She parodied the words as her green eyes flashed with anger.

Jack grinned at Sherry's angry denunciation. "You look beautiful when you're angry," he chuckled.

"Oh, shut up!" she elbowed him, a hint of a smirk on her face. She continued reading.

The article went on to cite the opinion of a priest on campus who agreed about the danger of anti-Semitism. He also suggested that mind-control played an important part in these kinds of groups.

"Racism? Anti-Semitism?" she looked up with a confused frown.

"Oh, yeah. They argue that when we say Jews need Christ too, we're guilty of genocide."

"I don't get it."

"You know, like, they become Christians, so they're not Jews anymore, and if that process continues the whole Jewish race would disappear."

"Why do they think they wouldn't be Jews anymore?"

"Good question. I guess the definition of a Jew is religious when convenient, and ethnic when convenient. All I know is, the believing Jews in our group know they're as Jewish as ever. They like to call themselves 'completed Jews.'"

"Where do the Blacks fit in? They make it sound like we have a problem with Blacks."

"I don't know. They probably put Blacks in for good measure. There might be a race thing in some of these other groups. I don't know."

"Boy, this must be the ultimate irony. Now we have a Roman Catholic pointing the finger about anti-Semitism and mind-control! I just came from medieval history!"

Jack pointed out the author was the long-haired guy Sherry had debated in ethics seminar several months earlier. "After several discussions with me he eventually came up to watch a Monday night Bible study. He left early and never returned. I remember he said he wrote for the campus paper." For several minutes Sherry and Jack sat and commiserated over the article.

"Man, first the thing with Edgewood Bible Church, and now this! How're you ever going to get up and teach tonight, Jack?" she asked with her hand on his knee.

He sighed. "I just have to keep my eyes focused on Christ. I can't let this intimidate me," he mumbled with little feeling of confidence. "I was already depressed this morning, and this article just makes me sick," he lamented.

"Oh, I've really been depressed, too," she jumped in.

"You have?"

"Oh, yeah, especially today, like you wouldn't believe!"

Jack thought for a moment. "Thank God!" he said with a broad smile. "I'm glad to hear that!" He reached for her hand.

"That's great, Jack," she said, pulling her hand away and looking at him flatly. "Nice to hear that you *care*."

"No, I mean it!" he went on. "I've been having the same kind of experience for the past couple of days. I mean, it's like someone threw a spiritual blanket over my head and proceeded to beat me with a baseball bat. I stare at a page of the Bible or my text, and it's like staring at death. I just feel so helpless. And now this article! And Jerry's thing about the exit group! It seems like everyone's against us."

"It's terrible, but I still don't see why you're so happy just because I'm suffering, too."

"Don't you see? If this is happening to a number of us, it's probably not natural."

"Oh . . . you mean you think it's some kind of spiritual thing?"

"It must be! After all, we're doing something potentially threatening to Satan's control of the campus, at least his control over the lives of a good number of students."

"Yeah. . . ."

"Well, I don't know about you, but this isn't normal for me at all. I mean, I get depressed sometimes, but this is really bizarre. And now I hear you're having the same problem! This article is some of the most poisoned journalism I've ever seen. It has to be an outright spiritual attack on the workers in this group."

"You sound like you're actually enjoying it."

"No, I don't enjoy it at all, but I do realize the significance."

After a short silence she prompted him, "Okay, so then what's the significance?"

"In my experience, the Evil One doesn't waste his efforts. If he's going around attacking our workers it means he believes God's going to do something really big through us tonight. You know, when you fly over the most strategic target, you get hit with the heaviest flak. This really bodes well for our ministry."

"Isn't there something we can do? I mean to cut down on the misery we're in? I think I'll go over to that Campus Faith thing and really give that Billings creep a piece of my mind! That might make me feel a little better."

"No, that's the wrong direction."

"Oh, come on. Stop being a choirboy! I think we need to kick this guy hard! We ought to sue him!"

"Okay, there're two reasons why you need to change your mind on this. First of all, there's the sort of colorful saying my uncle gave me when I worked on his farm. It's classic."

"Really?"

"He used to say, 'Never get into a pissing match with a skunk.'"

Sherry chuckled. "Okay, I'll give you that one. What's the other reason?"

"Well, Paul says, 'We wrestle not against flesh and blood.' This guy's just an agent of the real enemy. We need to get together and pray. Let's call the other workers and see if they're having the same problem. Then let's arrange dinner at the Union Grille at 6:00 and have a time of prayer together. I'll call the guys. Can you call the women?"

"Okay, I'll call Lisa and work it out. How're you doing on your teaching?"

"I don't know. It should be good. I have something to say. But I just don't have a good feeling about it right now. You can pray for me, starting right now."

"Jack, God's going to do something powerful through you tonight. Just hang on and trust Him fully."

Before they parted ways, they prayed together. With Jack sitting on the railing, Sherry leaning on his knees, her elbows resting on his legs, they bent their heads together and pleaded their case to God. Sherry went home and got out her phone book to begin dialing the other women in the study group. Several of them reported they were also suffering with unusual depression, and most of them agreed to meet for prayer. They all agreed they needed to fight with the power of God for the victory they sensed could be at stake that night. Across the campus, earnest prayers were offered for Jack and for the guests several of them were planning to bring.

At dinner, Sherry could hardly sit still, she was so tense and excited. She shivered with anticipation of what the meeting might bring. A number of key group members talked about the various kinds of spiritual attack they experienced that day. After eating, they leaned together over the table for an urgent session of prayer. Together they wielded the mighty spiritual weapons of God, seeking to bring the power of the Creator of the universe into the situation they had planned. Several had to leave early to pick up guests they were accompanying to the study. The rest sat back for a few minutes of nervous chatter before going to set up the lounge for the meeting. They had done all they could do.

48

The meeting itself was in one of the lounges overlooking the little green in back of the union. This large student lounge was bordered by hallways, shops, offices, and restaurants. They had selected the Terrace lounge because, although there were usually relatively few students sitting in the lounge itself, there were always hundreds circulating around the open hallways bordering it. They figured if students saw someone speaking to a group in the lounge some would come in and see what was going on. They felt this setting would feature the quality speaker they had in Jack while it allowed the rest of them to meet and converse with the new people who came.

No one was prepared for what happened that night. Even at their most crowded meeting at Jack's house there had never been more than seventy or eighty people. This night, though attendance had been down lately, there were already over eighty people there, fifteen minutes before the meeting was to begin. Lee Carulo and his wife, Tory, had come to watch. It was only the second time Sherry had been introduced to Lee, and the first time she had been able to meet Tory and talk to them both. Lee was about five-foot-ten, with curly black hair except for gray sideburns and occasional flecks of gray throughout. Tory was friendly looking, thin, with short dark hair streaked with a bit of gray, and had large glasses. Sherry sat with them, happy to meet them at last. She guessed they were both in their fifties.

Jack and Ken had arranged for a two-man music act to do some acoustic numbers before the teaching. People continued to drift in as the music played. Sherry wanted to take Jack in her arms and give him strength and confidence, but she had learned by now Jack didn't like being disturbed during the time right before he had to speak.

Finally, at about 7:40 Jack stepped up to the microphone, with the floor to ceiling picture windows behind him. With shock and delight, he looked out over a group of nearly 130 students!

With no podium, Jack held a small Bible in his hand and began to address the group on his subject for the first four weeks: "Satisfying

Sexuality." Beginning in a quiet but firm tone, he surveyed the relational bankruptcy of modern American culture. Citing statistics, he demonstrated that few people today are able to carry on lasting sexual relationships. He contrasted the secular theories of sexual relating with the biblical view, stressing the necessity of life commitment for successful sex, and love of the whole person.

As he went on, he warmed to his subject and gradually raised his voice. Sherry thought it was vintage Collins, as good as she had ever seen him—high in content and convincing, yet personable and likable at the same time. Looking around, she saw that more students were gathering to listen as they noticed the group in the lounge. By the time Jack finished, there were over 170 people listening.

He held back from giving a strong call for the gospel and simply called on people to come back and join them for the further development of this biblical line of reasoning. Then, as usual, Jack opened the floor for questions and comments. Quite a few Christians and nonChristians used the opportunity to raise questions.

One student asked about the legitimacy of the gay lifestyle. He wanted to know whether the principles Jack would teach in the series would apply equally to loving gay couples as to heterosexual relationships.

Jack unambiguously pointed out that, according to the Bible, gay sex was a sinful behavior, not an inherited feature like skin color or height. He tried to qualify his statement by observing that some might have a *tendency* toward homosexual feelings, but this didn't mean they were fated to be homosexual.

Before he could go on to cite the absence of research support for absolute genetic determination, the student and a friend called out an angry denunciation of Jack and the group. Jack reacted calmly, pointing out that they were not engaging in dialogue, and that name-calling would accomplish nothing. One of the two men hurled a curse as they headed for the exit.

Suddenly, a student from another campus Christian group wearing Christian buttons on his lapel stood up and cried out while pointing at the departing men, "The wrath of God is revealed against all ungodliness! He gave them over to degrading passions! Men exchanging the natural function of women and burning in their lust for each other! We will all stand before the judgment seat of God!"

The two men, now by the exit, turned to hurl obscenities at the group. Jack tried to smooth the situation over, calling out, "No, no, that's not the message we want. This brother is speaking for himself!" But the two men had already exited through the double glass doors. At that moment several others stood as if to leave, and a number of people looked nervous.

The student turned angrily on Jack. "Are you denying the inspiration of sacred Scripture, *brother*?" The emphasis on "brother" seemed accusing.

"No, I'm trying to communicate, not denounce!" Jack flashed with anger at the volunteer spokesman. "We have a certain demeanor we want to hold out here, *brother*. We want to project a certain level of openness for people, for all people."

"Oh, I understand. You want to sneak the gospel in without the offense of the cross! You're afraid to tell these lawless ones they're sinners!"

"No, I'm afraid the offense here is not the cross, it's your come-off, and lack of love! I just said they were sinners—that's why they left!"

"I take my stand on the inerrant Word of God!" the student uttered, looking off into the air over Jack's head, but there were audible groans and "boo's" from the group, and Jack shook his head disappointedly.

"I wish you'd take your stand outside this meeting if you don't feel you can control yourself, brother."

"You are ashamed of the gospel of Jesus!"

Now people called out saying, "Hey, why don't you just sit down and shut up?" Another cried, "No, we're ashamed of *you*!"

The brother gathered up his things and strode out of the room in the opposite direction as the earlier men.

Jack flopped down on a stool the musicians had been using. Still shaking his head, he spent a few minutes pointing out that people didn't have to agree with all of his conclusions, but that civil discussion was still an expectation if they wanted to attend the study series. At the end he announced he was going to pray and people were free to join him in their hearts if they felt like it.

He turned to God and prayed for the people who had left the meeting in protest. He asked God to give people in the group an opportunity to talk with the alienated people. Finally, he said, "Lord, some people are sitting here right now realizing that they've heard something tonight that's probably true. Some of us are sitting here realizing we don't have it together in this area of our sexuality. We've experienced a lot of pain in this area, and we're ready to hear what You have to say to us. Some of us are thinking we may want to hear the rest of the series. Some are even thinking we need to deal with our relationship with You. I ask that You'll reassure any here who are feeling this way, that it's safe to come back and hear more about the Bible; that it's safe to come personally to You, the One who's given us this revelation. I pray lives will be changed as a result of this series of studies, in the name of Jesus, Amen."

People got up and milled around, introducing themselves to each other. Many were shaking their heads, obviously deploring the situation that had broken out at the end of the meeting. Several new people came up and asked questions of Jack. Meanwhile, Sherry spent a few minutes talking to the Carulos.

"You guys have it made here!" Lee exulted. "This is so exciting, it makes me wish I was a student again. You're really on the front lines of battle!" Tory stood next to him smiling and nodding.

Sherry was still unsettled. "Oh, yeah, it was exciting. But what about those guys?"

"Oh, don't worry about them. That just shows you're scratching where it itches. People won't be influenced much by those kinds of incidents. They can see what you guys are all about. Jack was fantastic." He gestured up toward where Jack stood talking to several students.

"Wasn't he something?" Sherry beamed and nodded. "We haven't seen Jack like this for some time."

"Yes. He's taken some serious pounding from the Enemy. But that's good for growth. You have quite a guy there. Both of you really need to stay faithful to what God's given you. This is extraordinary! And I hear you're one of the main people bringing new guests."

"Well, I've had a few friends come."

"Do you enjoy bringing friends?"

"Oh, yeah! It's great when some party-friend finds Christ."

He put his hand on her shoulder and looked right into her eyes. "I hope you never lose that joy, Sherry. God and the angels feel that same joy, and it's a blessed thing."

"I don't think I ever will," she smiled.

"Well, you'd be surprised," he muttered as he bent over to pick up his coat. Tory was putting on her coat as well. "The aging process does some things to a lot of Christians, and they're not all good. There are a lot of old creeps like us around wondering what ever happened to that joy."

Sherry could only marvel at this statement. *How could Christians lose the joy of leading others to Christ? Was Lee saying he had lost that joy?*

They all started to amble out, and Tory came up beside Sherry as they walked. Tory seemed like a quiet woman, but something about her unusually deep but sweet-sounding voice exuded wisdom. "Lee isn't one of them," she said, leaning confidentially toward Sherry.

289

"One of what?" Sherry wondered.

"He's not one of the old creeps who've lost the joy of evangelism." Her kindly smile was inviting.

"I'm glad to hear that. He seems depressed."

"He's frustrated tonight because he's had a number of disappointing conversations with members of our church today. He was so depressed at dinner I suggested we come down here and get pumped up again. He just loves watching you kids—you're so vibrant, so excited. I think he gets his bearings here."

"Oh, that's sad." Sherry had never considered the problems pastors might face. "Are there a lot of people in the church opposed to Lee's views, like about evangelism?"

"No, but when you get older it gets harder to win your friends . . . of course, when you have a family, there's less time to make nonChristian friends, too." She walked thoughtfully for another moment. "I just think a lot of people get disappointed and they feel like quitting. Even good-hearted people lose the emotional energy to witness. And they often have a lot of problems they need to deal with in their own homes . . ." she seemed to trail off thoughtfully again. "Well, you kids have fun up at your restaurant." They were at the bottom of the steps, and the Carulos were getting ready to part ways, heading to their car.

"Oh come on! You're not going with us?" Sherry pleaded.

Lee came around next to Tory. "This is sort of a time for you and your friends," he suggested.

"Nonsense! We'd like you guys to come out and tell us some stories. We never get to talk to mature Christians like you."

After a minute of discussion, Lee and Tory looked at each other, and it was clear he wanted to come. She shrugged, and nodded in agreement, and Sherry and the others almost cheered. "All right!" she exulted as they started off toward The Fireside.

At the restaurant, Lisa came up to their table with a student she met at the meeting named Mary. It seemed Mary had been in one of Lisa's classes the year before, and she sat at the table along with the Carulos and Amy. They talked for some time about what the group was and what they were doing. Lisa even managed to get in a few words about the grace of God and a short testimony. They could tell Mary was very interested.

At one point Sherry looked around and saw the place was packed. People from the Bible study seemed to occupy most of the tables. By the time they made room for two more at their table, they were all crowded in together. "We need to find some other places to go," Sherry observed as she passed the peanuts around. "We're like a big flock of lemmings." Everywhere one looked, new people were sharing with members of the group.

Lee was vivacious and entertaining. He seemed to draw energy from the busy setting, and the students egged him on, laughing at his anecdotes and jokes. Tory contented herself with correcting him several times when he exaggerated, and telling him to tone it down. Each time, he would make a face like a bad dog that sags its ears. Sherry thought their friendly, policing relationship was riotously funny. She even wondered whether they had rehearsed it like a comedy act.

It turned out the Carulos had served nine years on the mission field in Mexico City before Tory's health had forced them to return home. Their doctor was worried about her liver after several bouts with hepatitis. Consequently, Lee had only been in church ministry for fifteen years, and only six of those were at New Life. Sherry could tell they missed the challenge of the foreign field from the way they talked about it. Their only daughter and her husband were studying at a seminary in Illinois, preparing for mission work themselves.

Later, Sherry ran into Jack coming out of the rest room. "I've never heard you be better than you were tonight, Jack." She looked up at him with a smile.

"I can't believe what happened. I just wonder whether anyone will come back?" he lamented.

"Are you kidding? I thought it was great!"

Jack looked at her with a wrinkled brow. "How could you think that was great?"

"Oh! It was so exciting! Those guys were such creeps, and you just stood out by comparison. Don't worry. It was plenty interesting. People will be back, I promise."

He smiled, and sliding his arm around her waist, he stood beside her looking out at the restaurant. He gave her an appreciative squeeze. "You really like a good fight, don't you?"

"Sure! Doesn't everyone?" As they stood and surveyed the dining room buzzing with conversation, Sherry was overflowing with excitement. "This is the most amazing thing I've ever seen!" she exclaimed. "I can't believe this kind of stuff was going on all the time I was an undergraduate here and I never noticed it."

"No." Jack shook his head. "There was never anything like this going on. If there was, I would've known about it. No, this is something I've never seen before."

As they stood together, the Carulos came by, now determined to leave. Lee held out his hand. "Jack, this was incredible. I feel like a new man!" He shook Jack's hand warmly.

"I was really glad to see you could make it, Lee. How are you this evening, Tory?"

She smiled broadly and took his hand also. "Great, Jack, we enjoyed this so much! And I've been charmed by your wonderful friend, Sherry!" She looked over at Sherry who took her hand as well.

"Jack was just saying he's never seen this kind of thing on campus before," Sherry said, fishing for a perspective from Lee and Tory.

"I haven't either, but I've heard of things like this," Lee offered. "It looks like you may be experiencing the beginning of some kind of spiritual revival."

"I've heard of tent revivals." Sherry looked confused. "What does it mean?"

He got a frown of concentration on his face and took a big breath. "Uh, well . . . an awakening, yes. I guess it has to do with the pattern people have noticed in how the Spirit works. It seems like the Holy Spirit doesn't always reach out in a steady, regular way. He seems to be pretty quiet at times, and then He moves at certain times in a very powerful way. I know of cases where huge numbers of people came to Christ all of a sudden. It seems like God brings all the factors together—all the people He needs—and He works in their hearts until things are right, and then *boom!*" He clapped his hands. "Everything seems to happen at once."

Lee helped Tory on with her coat and went on. "Man, I just wish we could get a piece of this with you. I wish we could get involved somehow, but I know it would be bad for a bunch of old people to start showing up."

Sherry and Jack were all ears.

Tory spoke up. "You need to spend lots of time in prayer . . . you and your friends. Satan won't let this go unchallenged."

"He's already challenging. Did you see the article about us in today's campus paper?" Jack asked.

"No. What did it say?" Lee asked.

"I'll bring it to you when we meet Friday. Man, it was a real stinker!" Jack shook his head in contempt.

"I've never seen such a bitter, one-sided slash job," Sherry said with disgust. "Do you know this Billings guy at the United Center?"

"Oh, yeah," said Lee. "He's a militant liberal. Is he the one who wrote it?"

"No," Jack said. "But he was quoted extensively."

"That's sickening. But don't worry. Nobody cares what those guys say anyway. It might even bring more people out to see for themselves."

"I hope so," Jack muttered. "And then there's that Barclay guy over at Edgewood."

"Arthur Barclay," Lee said knowingly. "What about him?"

"He's joined up with Warren and they're running a group in his church doing 'exit counseling' for people leaving our group."

"Barclay?" Lee and Tory looked at each other and shook their heads.

"Oh, Lee," Tory said. "You should call that stuffed shirt and tell him off!"

"I will call him," Lee said. "I bet I can get him to back off a little at least. Boy, that's shocking. He's an evangelical . . . although he's a hard-liner on tradition. I've never seen eye to eye with him."

Tory looked determined as she took Lee by the arm. "Lee, we have to get our church praying for these kids. That's one thing we can do to get involved." Lee nodded thoughtfully.

They eventually left, and Sherry and Jack were standing alone again.

"I just love them!" Sherry marveled at how deeply her feelings had gone out to the Carulos. "Did you know he's frustrated that his people are sort of . . . uh, defeated about evangelism?"

"Yeah, he gets impatient. But he has a great group of guys in that church who really have a heart for God. I just get the feeling it isn't easy to reach people when you're that age. I mean, they do it, but not like we can."

"Tory is so sweet! I just loved her. She seems so caring, but strong, too! I wish I could get a time to meet with her like you do with Lee."

"Well, I'll ask him if he would talk to Tory about working that out."

They talked for a few more minutes about what God was doing. Jack was reflective. "There's no telling how far this could go. Maybe God's beginning to unveil His purpose for us." He looked at her knowingly. But a moment later, breaking into a smile, "Of course, the whole thing could fizzle, too."

"That doesn't seem likely." She shook her head. "I got the feeling a lot of the new people tonight are planning to come back next week. The new girl Lisa and I talked with said she was going to bring her roommate. I think this is going to be really big!"

"Yeah, it feels good. Praise God . . . it feels really good!"

49

Within a few weeks, the Bible study at the student union was one of the biggest things happening on the campus. Hundreds of students and even some faculty members were coming to the meetings. A number of Christians from other groups were attending because of Jack's excellent Bible teaching and because of the electric atmosphere. Most of the new people, however, were nonChristians, or professing Christians who weren't involved in any fellowship.

The people from the Monday night Bible study group were ecstatic and shocked—even frightened. How could they have come from such oppression to victory in such a short time? None of them would have predicted such an overwhelming response. God was working at the meeting in a way none of them had seen before. It was already clear they were filling a special need by teaching at high content levels, approaching the subject of religion at a level similar to that found in campus classes on other subjects. The informality and the open discussions were very popular. Everyone wondered whether the trend of explosive growth would continue or disappear as quickly as it had appeared. No one felt confident.

By the fourth week, there were nearly five hundred people at the meeting. That week there was also a negative incident. After the lecture, Sherry noticed a number of people passing out pamphlets at the rear of the meeting. They were causing an audible ruckus as they moved among the people near the rear. Sherry quickly headed back to see what new group was proselytizing. As she drew near she was dumbfounded to see that one of the people handing out pamphlets was her old friend, Sue! Quickly, Sherry looked around at the others. It was the group that had left with Warren, about two dozen of them. And there in the middle was Warren himself.

A tiny cry escaped her throat before, with a burning heart, Sherry advanced toward Sue, reaching out and intercepting a pamphlet she was offering to a student. Their eyes met; fury in Sherry's, fear in Sue's. But immediately Sue smiled and held out her arms, taking Sherry in a hug.

"Oh, so glad to see you, Sherry! It's been so long."

Sherry was stunned into imbalance. Out of pure habit, she submitted to the hug and tried to be polite. But she was speechless with suspicion. She looked down at the pamphlet. It was an invitation to their class on Sunday nights, "Deepening Your Spiritual Walk." It met at Edgewood Church.

Sherry's face hardened. "Don't give me your phony hugs, Sue! I know what this is!" She shook the pamphlet in front of Sue's face. "This is your *deprograming* group. You guys are here to attack what we're doing!"

"Oh, that's so paranoid, Sherry. You really ought to come. You need some freedom from this martyr complex. It's so typical."

"You guys have a lot of nerve coming here," Sherry glowered.

"Why? Because you'll excommunicate us? It's public property, Sherry."

Sherry crumpled the pamphlet up and threw it on the floor at Sue's feet before turning and striding off to find Jack. Halfway to the front of the room, she turned around and strode back to Sue. "If you guys keep coming here, we'll get up a big group and come up to your stupid 'class' every week! You won't be able to get a single bit of propagandizing done with us there to challenge everything you say!" Again she turned and strode off.

By the time she found Jack, someone had just told him about the invasion by Warren's group. He was standing staring at them as they busily passed out their pamphlets, a look of utter dismay on his face.

Lisa was at his side, talking to him. "Jack, we have to do something about those guys," she demanded.

"What would you suggest? Call them out to a fist fight?"

"There has to be something we can do!"

"I'm not so sure. This is a public lounge. We may just have to let them operate and figure people either won't go, or if they do, they'll see that these guys aren't credible."

Lisa was furious. "Man, I can't believe you're just going to let them tear us up like this!"

"Hey, I already did something," Sherry interrupted.

"Now what?" Jack looked worried.

"I told them if they keep coming here, we'll organize a big group and all come up to their so-called class, you know? We could bring up more people than already go there. I said we'd make it so they couldn't do anything because we'd challenge everything they said."

Jack smiled and then broke into a laugh. "You told them that?"

"Yeah! Why not?"

Jack kept laughing. Lisa and Amy began to laugh also. "I can't believe you. How did you come up with that so quick?"

"We were imagining doing it way back in October when we went there. Of course they weren't attacking us then."

"It's beautiful. It's the perfect response. If they're passing out invitations, they must want us to come! I think we should go back and reiterate that threat. I bet we don't see them again. Barclay isn't going to want his church full of angry students."

"What if they don't go away?"

"Then we'll make good on the threat! Come on, let's go tell them."

They went to the rear and made their position clear. The group was already out of brochures, apparently having anticipated fewer students than were there. Within minutes they filtered out, each one having let slip a look of fear when they heard of the offer to come and take their group over by numbers. No one knew whether they would return to call the bluff.

In the meantime, the feeling of oppression and defeat rose up again in many of the young Christians' hearts. It just seemed too terrible that fellow Christians would launch an assault on their ministry just at a time when things were going so well.

50

The study in Sherry's apartment was also under way during those weeks. Each week, there had been two or three new people at the meeting, and, after an initial meeting of nine people, it had grown to fifteen by the third week. Sherry and her friends were having no trouble bringing other people to the meeting, partly because it was at Sherry's place.

Because of the size of the group and the adequate space in the relatively large living-dining room in her apartment, they decided not to go out after the meetings. They simply stayed in the apartment, sharing and discussing while enjoying refreshments. The times of discussion and fellowship were lasting long into the night. They began to leave the door to the hall open, and neighbors in the building would come by to see what the racket was about. Sherry or one of the other women would stand near the door and invite them in. Two had already returned for the Bible study on subsequent weeks.

One night after everyone else left, Ken, Lisa, Jack, and Sherry sat crowded around her tiny table in the kitchenette. Sherry noticed Lisa giving Jack a meaningful look, and saw him grin subtly. She challenged them. "Okay, what's going on, you guys?"

Lisa looked at her. "We think you should teach this group in a couple of weeks."

Sherry was stunned. She was accustomed to sharing points with the group, so there was evidence she could teach. And of course, she had been toying with the idea of teaching. But she assumed she might want to try it in a year or so. "I'm flattered, but this seems like it's pretty soon!" she challenged.

"Well, it would only be one time, and you have your formalism stuff down pretty well," Lisa pointed out.

Sherry looked at Jack, and he shrugged. "At least it isn't as soon as Paul did. He started preaching within days of his conversion. And there isn't a hint of doubt you could do it," he assured her. "Look at how many of these people are friends of yours anyway!"

"Well, okay, I guess if you guys think I can do it . . ." she agreed.

After discussing various options, the three of them decided she would teach on the story of Elijah and the prophets of Baal from the book of 1 Kings, a passage she and Lisa had studied together recently, which dealt with some of the issues discussed in Sherry's paper.

During the two weeks that followed, Sherry studied furiously and prayed often about the body of material she was planning to communicate to her friends. She was happy she could incorporate some of her material on formalism into the teaching.

A week before she was supposed to teach, Tory Carulo called her and asked if she and Lisa would be interested in joining her and two other women from her church for coffee, prayer, and fellowship on Thursday afternoons. They eagerly agreed, and that Thursday they spent several hours in the Carulos' breakfast nook sitting around the table with Bibles, brownies and coffee cups littering the surface. They had Sherry go over her outline and made suggestions for illustrations and cross references. Tory and her friends turned out to be a significant help to Sherry in developing her teaching. Every week from that time on, Sherry and Lisa had the advantage of an older woman who had a wonderful knowledge of Scripture and spiritual things.

Gradually, an eagerness to speak on her subject grew in Sherry's heart, partially replacing the fear that had been there. As the evening approached, she was struggling more with what to cut out of the teaching than anything else.

Two nights before she was to teach, Sherry came home to her apartment and found one message on her machine. She pressed the replay button and a woman's voice came on, thick and throaty. It sounded like a middle-aged woman in some sort of distress.

"Sherry? Sherry Martin? . . . Are you listening? I have something to tell you. . . ." There was a long pause as the woman seemed to be gathering herself. Then she went on, "You *murderer*! You butchered my son! I'll get you if it *kills* me. You got the police in your pocket but let me tell you, you little tramp . . . you're a murderer, and you're gonna pay!" The message ended abruptly, leaving Sherry staring wide-eyed and bewildered, her hand laid over her chest.

She reached out to push the erase button, but hesitated. *Wise up! Don't miss the signals this time!* she warned herself. She decided to call the police right then and there. Within a minute she was talking to Detective Botti. "I've just been threatened by Jim's mother."

"What? What did she do?"

"She called me. I just got home, and she had left a message on my answering machine. She threatened to get me if it killed her!"

"Okay . . . okay. She's been threatening us, too. Do you have the tape?"

"Yes, I didn't erase it."

"Good. Pull that tape out and save it. Would you like to press charges for menacing?"

"No, I wouldn't like to. But I will if that's the only way I can make her leave me alone."

"Why don't I call her and let her know we know about it and we'll press charges for menacing and assault if she calls again. I'll let her know we're watching, too. She wouldn't get anything but a slap on the wrist if we charged her right now, but if she ignores a warning, the judge will hit her hard to teach her a lesson."

Sherry thanked him and saved the tape. She wondered what Jim's mother could do to her. A pervasive sense of evil seemed to stick to her spirit like molasses. The experience had shattered her composure. Although she tried to focus her attention on her preparation, the only thing she could think about was the violent and bitter threat.

The call brought back all the feelings of dread and horror from the killing as vividly as though it had happened yesterday. Sunday evening, she spent time with Lisa and Jack talking about it, which helped some. But with the stress she was already under, this incident had left her in a jumbled emotional state so troubled she felt like she might fall apart.

Jack offered to take over the teaching for her so she wouldn't have to worry about that part, but she refused. "I'm not going to let the Evil One derail me from this ministry."

Lisa agreed. "That's all this is. Satan's just saying he's going to huff and puff and blow your house down. I don't think you should let him intimidate you. Nothing else he's tried has worked yet. You have your stuff down, you know what you want to get across, and you should stand your ground."

Jack shrugged. "It is true. This kind of thing happens with uncanny regularity just before you speak for God. I think it's called a spoiling attack. It's like Satan wants to beat you to the punch. It's probably a good sign when you think about it. I think you should start learning how to get up there by faith, not heeding your negative feelings, and trust that God's going to come through for you."

It was settled. Sherry would go, but she also decided to sleep on her old cot in Lisa's room that night.

51

As she and Lisa cleaned up her apartment for the meeting Monday evening, Sherry couldn't believe how nervous she was. She kept taking big breaths and exhaling with a shiver. She was far more nervous than she had been before any of the research presentations she had given in history seminars. The stakes were far higher now. People's eternal destinies were at stake. She was worried some about personal embarrassment, but even more that she might be spiritually ineffective; putting more of herself than of Jesus Christ into the talk.

Lisa had repeatedly stressed the need to put feeling into the material. "The last thing you want is a research report," she warned. Sherry prayed fervently in her heart that God would enable her to speak under the spiritual anointing she had heard Jack and others refer to when they taught.

That night, Jack and Ken showed up half an hour before the other people began arriving. Together at the kitchen table, the four of them prayed from their hearts God would continue to bless the ministry of the group and sustain Sherry in her first attempt at public Bible teaching. Sherry felt like a stammering idiot by the time the first person arrived at the door. With her head swimming in a fog of confusion, it took everything she had to act civil with the guests as they arrived. She was so preoccupied with the upcoming teaching that her usual ability to socialize seemed to desert her.

Over the next half hour, more and more people arrived. Word that Sherry was teaching had drawn many who knew her from the dorm. Unbelievably, by the time the meeting came to order, there were over twenty people in the living room. One of the last guests to arrive was a special shock for Sherry. Dr. Forsythe walked in, smiling, and came right up to her. "I hope you don't mind if an old guy comes to one of these meetings?" he asked mirthfully.

"Oh, Dr. Forsythe, I'm so nervous I feel like I'm going to puke! But I'm glad you're here," she lied, as she shook his hand, self-conscious about her sweaty palms. "You can set me straight on my material afterward, or maybe you should just set us all straight instead of me trying to do this teaching."

"That's ridiculous. I hear you're going to use some things from the paper you did for me," he said as he was peeling off his dress coat.

"Yeah, I figured that was an area I'd done some study in."

"That paper was sensational! You know how I felt about that."

"Yeah, you were generous. But I didn't know you were interested in things such as Bible studies."

"The Mrs. and I go to a church, but we're really unsatisfied there." He hung his coat over his forearm. "They never have much to say as far as I'm concerned. I really go for Anna's sake, I guess."

"No! I had no idea you were a church-goer."

"Yes, in fact, they even get me to teach Sunday school for the adults sometimes. You know, of course, I respect Jesus' teachings from an ethical standpoint. My only problem is where to go from there. Jack and I've had some interesting discussions. I think he wants to convert me."

"Well, I know Christ is much more than an ethical teacher as far as Jack's concerned."

"Yes, and I've been intrigued by some of his arguments along the way. His religious vision seems to avoid a lot of the pitfalls of other religions, and I respect that, so I was thinking of coming to hear him sometime. But when he said you were going to speak, I decided that was something I didn't want to miss."

"Oh, I'm so flattered!" She smiled, looking down with embarrassment. "But this thing has me so scared at this point I don't know whether I can even do it."

"Just relax and share what you know." He patted the back of her shoulder. "You're among friends."

Sherry felt almost like Dr. Forsythe was a Christian brother, although her mind told her this couldn't be true. As people moved toward their seats, Jack sat on the stool at the end of the room. "All right, let's all get a seat on a chair or on the floor. . . ." He said he wanted to open the time with a word of prayer, which he did.

He went on, "We're going to have a special treat tonight. We're going to hear from one of our own who I think is also one of the most interesting and original thinkers I know: Sherry Martin." The group applauded, which turned Sherry's face bright red. The next thing she knew, she was getting up and sitting on the stool in front of her first Bible study group.

"I can't believe you guys did that," she complained, shaking her head as she got her Bible and notes arranged on her lap. After greeting the group, she had them turn to Colossians 2.

"This passage reveals that the group in Colosse was in danger. Not danger from being arrested and thrown in prison or something—far worse than that. The danger threatening this group of Christians was like a deadly spiritual bacillus that could infect them forever! The danger is described in verse 8:

> See to it that no one takes you captive through hollow and deceptive philosophy, which depends on human tradition and the basic principles of this world rather than on Christ.

"These 'basic,' or 'elementary principles of the world,' these 'traditions of men,' what are they? These principles are a collection of notions *antithetical* to Jesus Christ, but so appealing people will actually be 'captivated' by them. These are dangerous counterfeits that could replace the truth of Christ. They might outwardly have some connection to Christ, but actually they're the farthest thing imaginable from Christ.

"The term comes up again in verse 20.

> Since you died with Christ to the basic principles of this world, why, as though you still belonged to it, do you submit to its rules: "Do not handle! Do not taste! Do not touch!"?

"Now we could do an analysis of this passage and find that the heresy in view in this passage was a Jewish-inspired asceticism with dualistic overtones."

There was a ripple of laughter at the complicated-sounding phrase.

"That wouldn't mean much to us, would it? But these elementary principles are much more widespread than that. We'll see the notions he's referring to are universal features of manmade religion. The details may differ, but the themes remain the same in this religious mentality. And if I get in trouble, I'm glad we have a professor here tonight who teaches comparative religion to set us straight. Meet Dr. Forsythe."

She waved her hand over toward his nodding and smiling head in the corner.

"I hope you'll back me up on some of these generalizations tonight."

He held up the OK sign. As she continued sharing her material, something came over her. Her nervousness disappeared as she felt a growing feeling of excitement for her subject. As she looked into the responsive, even eager eyes of the people watching her, Sherry was feeling her God-given gift of teaching being energized for the first time by the Holy Spirit.

She had no idea it would be so exhilarating to have the power of God moving through her.

"Okay. Let's read this passage starting in verse 16 and figure out what these elementary principles are.

> Therefore do not let anyone judge you by what you eat or drink, or with regard to a religious festival, a New Moon celebration or a Sabbath day. These are a shadow of the things that were to come; the reality, however, is found in Christ.

"So he says, 'Watch out for those who want to judge people based on things such as religious festivals and holy days, new moons, and Sabbaths,' in other words, *sacred time*. You know, it's like 'this hour is the holy hour, but that one's profane.' 'This season's sacred, but that one's just normal.'

"Isn't that a little bit strange? Have you ever wondered, if God created the whole year, why are some parts of it sacred and some parts profane? It's a weird concept when you really think about it.

"And then there's the brother concept to sacred time: *sacred space*, which is exactly the same sort of thing. With sacred space, we're going to mark out an area on the ground here, and say within this line on the ground one religious program's in effect. But just one foot outside that line, the space is profane, and another program's in effect. It really makes you wonder. Is God really this way? Is this really true?"

She saw Lisa and Jean, sitting on the couch, break into broad knowing smiles.

"Let's not make the mistake of thinking this is superstitious thinking belonging to the ancient world. This is modern Western religion, too. When people say, 'Kids, don't run in the sanctuary,' what are they saying? They're saying this is a *sanctuary*—that means a holy place. You can run, but not in the sanctuary. You can eat chocolate, but not during the sacred time of the year.

"Why is that? Why do people draw lines around space and time and call them sacred, and then judge those who won't observe their designations? This is one of the elementary principles of the world.

"I've been studying this in school, and for now, I'm just going to suggest both these notions have to do with rendering or interpreting spiritual things as external. It also has to do with localizing and controlling spiritual forces.

"Now, if we were in a more 'primitive' setting, we might go as far as actually making a spirit trap. To do this, a person puts the magic ingredients in a bottle and says the magic words, and the spirit or devil enters the bottle. Now if the bottle is hung around the neck someone would be healed by it. Or if a devil is captured, it could be buried under the step of an enemy, and every time he enters his hut, he gets zapped by that devil!"

She waited for the laughter to die down.

"Man controlling the divine. It's at the heart of the elementary principles of the world.

"And then there's the area of *avoiding* the divine. You have this building, this shrine, where God is accessible in a special way. That means you can approach Him there, in the sacred space, and you can also *leave* afterward. That's why people will light up a smoke in the parking lot, but never in the sanctuary. They talk differently outside the "house of God" than they do inside it. It's almost like they have God in a box! I remember my pastor actually used a special *voice* when he preached or prayed in the church!"

She acted out a few phrases to the amusement of the group. Then she went on:

"Unfortunately, when we make these designations, it implies a mechanistic relationship with God. It's sort of like going to see Bolo the gorilla at the zoo, or even like working a pop machine. I put in the coin and punch the button, and I get my result. I go to the shrine and do the ritual. It's not a real relationship. It's nothing like the kind of personal relationship we would want to have, let's say, with a close friend. It's nothing at all like the kind of intimate relationship God wants to have with us, where He is actually *in us*!"

Sherry's voice had been rising in intensity, and she left a moment of silence and gazed around intently as people reacted to her statement. She was surprised at how upset she felt as she argued against a view of God that had nearly frightened her and her friends away from Christ. But she pressed on.

"What we're looking at here is really pretty bad as far as God is concerned. Look at the exasperation in Paul's voice in this passage in Galatians 4:9-10—

Now that you know God . . . how is it that you are turning back to those weak and miserable principles? Do you wish to be enslaved by them all over again? You are observing special days and months and seasons and years!

"Do you see the choices before us? Either 'knowing God' and the freedom that comes with that, or the 'elemental things,' and the slavery that comes with that. And this sacred time thing is a dead giveaway."

People were nodding in agreement as they looked at the passage.

"There are other features of this religious mentality, these elementary principles of the world, as well. Let's read on in Colossians 2 at verse 17.

These are a shadow of the things that were to come; the reality, however, is found in Christ.

"Oh, so here's an important word of explanation. In the Old Testament we have things like a temple, and festivals, Sabbaths, etc. How do we account for these things in the Old Testament period?

"The answer's right before us: 'these things were a mere shadow.' In other words, when I stand in the sun, I cast a shadow. The shadow is shaped sort of like me, and you can learn something about me by looking at the shadow. But you'd be really mistaken if you think the shadow *is* me!

"Likewise, in the Old Testament period, God used some of these things to teach certain concepts about Himself and ultimately about Christ. For instance, the temple sacrifices prefigured the work of Christ. Like when the death of an innocent animal would symbolically pay for the sins of the worshiper, it prefigured Christ's death, which pays for our sins if we trust Him.

"But let's not miss the point here. The point is what he says here, 'the reality, however, is found in Christ.' Now that Christ has come, we don't need shadows anymore. It's now possible to have a level of intimacy they never had in the Old Testament period. It would be a big mistake to go back to the shadows now when the substance, the reality, is with us.

"Now reading on from verse 18 to verse 23 it says,

Do not let anyone who delights in false humility and the worship of angels disqualify you for the prize. Such a person goes into great detail about what he has seen, and his unspiritual mind puffs him up with idle notions. He has lost connection with the Head, from whom the whole body, supported and held together by its ligaments and sinews, grows as God causes it to grow.

Since you died with Christ to the basic principles of this world, why, as though you still belonged to it, do you submit to its rules:

"Do not handle! Do not taste! Do not touch!"? These are all

destined to perish with use, because they are based on human commands and teachings. Such regulations indeed have an appearance of wisdom, with their self-imposed worship, their false humility and their harsh treatment of the body, but they lack any value in restraining sensual indulgence.

"Okay, who can name another of the elementary principles based on this passage?"

Jean spoke up. "My version says 'self-abasement.'"

"Yeah, and I think that's a better translation, but notice also verse 23 where he says again, 'harsh treatment of the body.' This is self-abasement, asceticism. Does God say, 'I want to see you hurting. Then I'll think about listening to what you ask'? What sort of God are we implying here? This is one of the worst areas, and it's one of the most insightful, too. We'll talk more about it in a minute. What else?"

Eileen offered another answer. "It mentions the worship of angels."

"Right. That's one of the elementary principles. Religious man realizes his separation from God. He feels the need for an intermediary. Scholars have shown that these proto-gnostic heresies believed in angels as intermediaries between them and God. As a result, people prayed to an angel instead of God! It's similar to the way some pray to saints instead of God. You again sense the impersonal aspect here. 'I can't talk directly to God, I have to pass Him a note.' Okay, let's name another one."

There was a brief silence as people found their places. Then Ken spoke up. "It mentions someone taking his stand on visions he has seen."

"Good. So the religious man doesn't base his conclusions on something objective like the Word of God. These notions are manmade, and that often starts with someone claiming he's had a vision. A lot of these shrines are built where someone claimed to have had a vision. So the point is, it's manmade. Okay, there's one more."

This time Charlene spoke. "Well, there's this stuff about 'Do not handle. Do not taste, etc.' which sounds like some kind of serious abstinence thing."

"Exactly. Under this mentality, you have to avoid all kinds of things because they could contaminate you morally. According to Matthew 9:10-11, the religious leaders in Christ's day believed you could be contaminated if you went to a party where there were too many sinners. They believed evil contaminates from the outside. What's wrong with this? It's fundamentally false, and objectionable to God. Our problems with evil don't come from others, like a disease. They come from our own heart!

"All of their abstinence wasn't getting them any closer to God. They were fooling themselves as they judged others.

"All of these things suggest God is distant, hard to know, and hard to please. For some reason, they think He wants to see us do without. He needs to see us in pain before He's sure we're serious. There has to be a demonstration of effort on our part, whether it's doing without, observing some repetitive discipline, or actually damaging our own bodies. Only then will He grudgingly dole out blessing. I'm not surprised God has a problem with this way of thinking!"

As Sherry shook her head in disbelief, her broad, beautiful smile charmed the group so that they couldn't help but break into smiles with her. A few chuckles broke out as people realized how ridiculous the whole scenario sounded. A moment later, Sherry went on.

"Let's look at an example of this mentality from the Old Testament period in 1 Kings 18. This is the story of the confrontation between Elijah and Baal. In this story, Elijah challenged the prophets of this nature deity in order to show the people that Baal was no more than a figment of their own imagination. He said, 'Let's see your god light a fire without a match—just pray to him and let him light the fire, and I'll try the same thing with Jehovah God.' And they agreed.

"So a huge crowd gathers for this confrontation, not just of the prophets of Baal and those of Yahweh, but a confrontation between paganism and the worship of the true God. And, in Paul's terminology, it's a confrontation between the elementary principles of the world, and the true posture of a person before the Creator God.

"Okay, so the prophets of Baal were first. They prepare the sacrifice Baal was supposed to light for them, and then they go into their routine. We read in verse 26,

> They took the bull given them and prepared it. Then they called on the name of Baal from morning till noon. "O Baal, answer us!" they shouted.

"Well, when you think about it, it doesn't take several hours to say that phrase, does it?"

The group laughed.

"So, what were they doing during this several hour period? Obviously, they were doing what all religious people do. They were repeating it over and over again. We're seeing here a chant, or a prayer that's repeated many times over.

"Why repeat it? Can't God hear the first time? Why do we need to say it even twice, let alone a hundred or even a thousand times over? It's interesting to contrast this practice with the words of Jesus. He said in Matthew 6:7, 'When you pray, do not keep on babbling like pagans, for they think they will be heard because of their many words.' When we say something over and over, is it really a personal communication? Or is it really an effort to force the deity to do what we want?

"Let's imagine one of you guys sitting at dinner with your roommate. You look him straight in the face and say, 'How about some butter, buddy? How about some butter, buddy? How about some butter, buddy? How about some butter, buddy? How about some butter, buddy? How about some butter, buddy? How about some butter, buddy? How about some butter, buddy?'"

She paused as the laughter died down.

"That's impersonal! You'd never deliberately irritate someone by doing that. Wouldn't you say that's strange? Well, God thinks it's strange, too! If we repeat ourselves like this, the intent is no longer communication. The Buddhists in Tibet have taken this a step further. They print the prayer on a wheel, and let the worshiper spin the wheel. As it turns past a stylus, the prayer is repeated over and over again, each time building up credits with God."

Laughter broke out again.

"Oh, yes! It's a regular prayer machine! And at this point, we have a machine at both ends of the communication line, instead of only one.

"I can just see God sitting there; we've gone into the church and the priest has told us to repeat this prayer ten times. Here we go on number eight: 'Our Father who art in heaven. . . .' And He's sitting there shaking His head saying, 'You already said that. . . .'

"Why? Why do people feel the need to do this? Often they're trying to induce a 'feeling state.' They're taking leave of their normal perception of reality, and entering an altered state of perception they identify with religion. Scholars call this 'dissociation.'

"Another reason may be that they're tapping into the underlying *rhythm* of the universe. Especially in nature religion, where seasons and fertility cycles are important, you have to catch the rhythm of life like a surfer catching a wave. And they do this through rhythmic chanting and dancing.

"You may say at this point, 'But this is done out of devotion!'

"Well, it may be devotion, but it's confused. If you want to be devoted to Christ, do what He says. Avoid the repetition.

"Contrast their hours of chanting with Elijah's prayer in verses 36 and 37. It's just like, 'Okay, God, show these people I've been acting on Your word, that You're really God, and turn their hearts back.' And then *woooosh*! God just *flames* the whole area! No song and dance. No chanting. He heard Elijah the *first* time he spoke!"

There were several murmurs of discovery as people looked at the verse she mentioned.

"Let's go back to the prophets of Baal. Look at what else they did. Verse 26 comments that 'they danced around the altar they had made.' Why do this? Either Baal will hear them or not. Why do they think *dancing* is going to help?"

She wrinkled her nose in confusion as people chuckled.

"This is a ritual dance they're doing while saying the chant. You've probably seen this sort of dance before on National Geographic specials."

Sherry bobbed up and down on the stool with her arms moving in ritualistic motions. The group howled with laughter.

"We're saying at this point we're going to get our bodies into the act; actually *working* the prayer upward. These are the 'gestures of approach' scholars say are necessary before approaching 'the sacred.'

"Again, how different this is from the simple and straightforward prayer of Elijah down in verses 36 and 37.

"So anyway, Elijah mocks them in verse 27.

At noon Elijah began to taunt them. "Shout louder!" he said. "Surely he is a god! Perhaps he is deep in thought, or busy, or traveling. Maybe he is sleeping and must be awakened."

"'Call out with a loud voice. . . .' Obviously this god is not omniscient or omnipresent. His hearing is defective. He can't hear because you aren't talking loud enough! Isn't that the implication of what they were doing? This ritualism, this repetition implies a defective God who needs these things for some reason. The repetitions aren't doing the worshiper any good. So who are they for, if not for a needy god?

"Elijah says their god is either 'busy' or, as the NASB says, 'gone aside,' or 'is on a journey.' This pseudo-god can do only one thing at a time. You have to get his attention. He's preoccupied. When it says he's 'gone aside' it's an idiom that means he's gone to one side of the path to . . . you know . . . relieve himself."

The apartment was rocking with laughter.

"'He must be asleep.' Oh, yes! Their gods did sleep. These manmade gods were not the infinite-personal God of the Bible. They were over-grown human beings. They needed to eat and sleep according to the mythology of the day. And this is what Elijah was bringing home to them by taunting them. As he taunted them, he was actually giving them a sting-ing theological critique of their simplistic nature religion.

"But wait! We're not done! Look at this in verse 28:

> So they shouted louder and slashed themselves with swords and
> spears, as was their custom, until their blood flowed.

"What? Why cut themselves with lances until the *blood flowed*? What's going on here? Why cut your flesh? Where does this fit into religious ide-ology?"

Her grimace lasted for a moment as she looked around the room. From the faces she saw, it looked like she had succeeded in creating shock.

"At this point we're touching on something very deep . . . something *terrible* in the mind of religious man. It's similar to what we've already seen, but it's going further still. This is asceticism, or what Paul calls 'self-abasement' and 'severe treatment of the body.' Here the religious thinker is saying, 'God, look how serious I am about this!' And he cuts himself, or starves himself, or deprives himself to show he means business. We see the effort, the intensity coming from our side—from the human side—as we try to cajole blessing from this hard-to-please God.

"But wouldn't God be able to tell whether we mean business without this? What interest would God have in this kind of behavior?"

She raised her voice to a new level, her eyes flashing with fury.

"I tell you, He is not interested!"

She let her words ring around the room for a moment before going on. "There's one final comment that we should note in 1 Kings 18:29, 'But there was no response, no one answered, no one paid attention.' Why didn't Baal answer?"

She waited, but no one said anything. They seemed to be stunned.

"Oh, come on! It's because there's no such thing as Baal!"

One more time she had to wait for the group to quiet down. The obvi-ous point seemed to break the tension that had been building.

"That's right. It makes a real difference whether we base our beliefs on objective truth, or the wishful thinking of our own minds.

"Again, let's not make the error of thinking this sort of thing is limited to ancient religion, or to Baalism. These elemental principles have also been common in the history of Christianity, and in more sophisticated forms, it's still with us today. But so far from bribing God, or appeasing Him, this disgusts Him even more than it does us!

"Now someone might say we're getting too heavy in putting down religious people who've shown their devotion, which might have included a little asceticism. Maybe we need a little more understanding here and less judgment, right? Let me use an illustration to show why we can't back down on this.

"Let's suppose my boyfriend here, Jack, shows up at my door with his friends, Lisa and Ken. He holds out his arms to me, which he has slashed with a razor, and blood is gushing out of open wounds. He says, 'Sherry, look what I've done for you!'"

The group was silent in muted shock as she held out her bare forearms, palms up.

"Yeah, and what am I going to say to him? I'm going to say, 'What kind of monster do you think I am? What have you done to yourself?'"

She paused with a deep angry frown on her face to let the point sink in.

"Now if Lisa speaks up at this point and says, 'Sherry, Jack worked really hard at that, you know. Those cuts are really deep.' What's my response? Hey, I'm sorry. I can't find anything good to say about that. So what if the cuts are deep? Even more so, I'd have to say this guy is so confused about what I'd like, he just has to be crazy!

"And so, here we come to the bottom line. To appreciate the nature of true spirituality, first we must *reject* all these elemental principles of the world. We need a thorough critique of this wicked, misguided outlook! The elemental principles of the world, manmade religion, create a terrifying caricature of God. They must go before we can establish the antithesis, a true, loving relationship with the infinite, personal God of the Bible.

"Look at Paul's counter to these principles in Colossians 2:19. He says when they're into their elementary principles, they've 'lost connection with the Head, from whom the whole body, supported and held together by its ligaments and sinews, grows as God causes it to grow.'

"He's saying instead of following the elemental principles, we need to opt for an organic link with Christ. The term 'the head' refers right across the page to chapter 1 verse 18 which says Jesus is the head of the Body, or the church.

"This is your decision tonight. Not whether you'll start some new religious discipline. Not whether you'll join something. The question is, will you forge that union relationship with Christ tonight? He wants to give

311

you that relationship for free, at His expense."

She went on to explain the gospel and issue an appeal. She also warned the believers: "Some of us may be turning to the elemental things in our heart subtly without even realizing it. We may be dealing with God on a ritualistic basis in our mind. We'll think more about that possibility next week. Let's stop there for now. Are there any comments or questions?"

As she opened the floor for discussion, people began to share experiences from their pasts that reminded them of the religious mentality Sherry had described. They seemed excited by the insight Sherry had stimulated. The idea that one could know God in a personal way and dispense with the trappings of typical religious thinking was tantalizing to the new people in the meeting. Even the Christians seemed to be fired up by a deepened sense of the truth of God's Word.

One new girl recounted bitterly her disgust at the church in which she had grown up. She said the people seemed to be observing the outward forms without any sense that they even cared about each other or ever had a deep thought. She angrily described the guilt trip her pastor and others had inflicted on her and her determination never to come under that kind of threatening relationship again.

Several others chimed in with their gripes about the churches they had grown up in.

Sherry began to feel things were getting too negative. She tried to redirect the discussion. "I think a lot of us know how you feel," Sherry answered one angry guy. "The question for us now is whether we're going to let this negative experience from the past ruin our chances to know God in a new and deep way now."

Lisa jumped in and shared her testimony, including both the negative and the positive. Before long, people were taking turns sharing what they enjoyed about knowing God in the framework of His grace.

Finally, Sherry noticed Jack motioning toward his watch. Astonished, she looked at the clock on the wall and found that they had been meeting for over an hour. She suggested they pray.

The group bowed their heads and, after their usual fashion, began to take turns speaking in informal, conversational prayer. After several prayers of thanksgiving for the excellent teaching, the group was electrified when the new girl who had first complained about her church spoke up. "Uh God . . . I, uh, guess You know who I am. I've said some pretty bad things about You, and I've felt some pretty bad things. . . ." In the silence that followed, it was clear she was welling up with tears. Haltingly, between quiet sobs, she went on, "I think this was good, what I heard tonight . . . and I think I want to change things . . . I . . . I don't know what to say, really . . . just please help me."

She fell silent. Sherry's face flushed with emotion as she recognized this prayer—so similar to the one she herself had prayed months before. She decided to pray herself. "Heavenly Father, we thank You for the really honest prayer that was just prayed. I ask that You come into this woman's life in the same way You did mine when I prayed something very similar last fall. Just show her You're there and that You love her and want to have a relationship with her based on the work of Jesus on the cross. And we pray the same for anyone else here tonight who may be reaching out to You. Thank You, Lord, for what You've given all of us. We realize You could have us slashing ourselves, hopping around, and chanting. You had every right to require that if You wanted to. But You didn't. You've reached out to us as our Father. We rejoice in this security tonight. Show us if we're beginning to develop attitudes similar to these elemental principles You deplore so much. And we also ask for some great fellowship during the rest of the evening. We pray this in the name of Jesus, Amen."

The group murmured approvingly and began to stand and turn to each other. It was a time of high emotion as people broke up into separate animated discussions. Sherry moved right through the room to the girl who had prayed so movingly. They began a conversation that lasted for over half an hour. Her name was Kirsten Briscoe, and she attended a class with one of the guys in the group. There was an immediate meeting of hearts as Sherry first listened to her story, then shared what she would need to know to draw close to God.

When Lisa came up and joined them, Sherry challenged Kirsten to go over to the bookstore and get a Bible from Lisa, just like she had. Both of them could sense the beginning of an exciting friendship. Sherry reached out and took her hand before she left. "We're really glad you came here, Kirsten. I hope we'll see you again."

"No doubt about it. I think this is great!" She smiled. "And I'm sorry for being so weird when I tried to pray."

"That's ridiculous!" Sherry protested. "You gave the most honest and moving prayer we heard tonight!"

"Thanks, you guys are really nice," she said before gathering her stuff and leaving.

Just then, Dr. Forsythe came by with his jacket over his arm, ready to leave. He had been talking to Jack and Ken most of the evening. "Sherry, this is one of the greatest things I've ever been to," he beamed. "All my life, I've been interested in the spiritual side of life, but I've never found anything I felt I could commit myself to . . . and, I'm not necessarily saying I have now. . . ." He looked down and rubbed his chin as though realizing he had said more than he had planned.

"It sounds as if you're saying something like that." Sherry decided to take the direct approach.

"Well, I'm saying . . . it's exciting to see that you kids have found something."

"This isn't for kids, Dr. Forsythe. There are a lot of people older than you who've reached the same conclusions."

He looked at her with a thoughtful grin for a moment, still holding his chin. "Yes, I suppose there are," he said in a way that made Sherry think he might really be considering it. "I do feel like I'd be too old for this crowd, though."

"You don't like to hang around with younger people, huh?" Sherry challenged with a subtle grin.

"No! I like it. It's just that I don't think you guys would like it that much—having an old guy around."

"Why don't you let us decide that? I don't see anyone losing it because you're here. How old are you, anyway?"

"I'm nearly fifty, Sherry."

"Well, it doesn't matter to me. And I don't think it matters to anyone else. We're all going to be together for a long time in eternity in the future, and I doubt anyone's going to care whether there were ten or twenty years separating us when we found God."

Forsythe smiled. "Your vision of religion is plain and refreshing. You've given me a lot to think about tonight."

"Well, I guess that has to be good. Does that mean you will come back?" she asked.

"I might come again sometime," he said warmly.

"How about in two weeks, when we meet again?"

He hesitated a moment, then said, "Yes, maybe I will." Soon he left.

It was 11:30 before all the guests left except for Jack, Lisa, and Ken. As Sherry poured herself a Coke, strong arms encircled her from behind, and Jack held her close with his face next to her ear.

"So, a new era dawns!" he whispered.

"What are you talking about?" she giggled.

"The Sherry Martin era."

"Oh, Jack, don't be weird."

"I was so proud of you I wanted to die! You're an unbelievable communicator. I don't think things'll ever be the same."

She leaned her head and her shoulders back so that she was pressed close up against him, and wrapped her arms around his. She stood for a moment enjoying the closeness. "I feel so happy," she breathed quietly.

"Okay, that's enough of that!" Ken said as he and Lisa came into the kitchen.

Jack and Sherry just looked over and smiled. "I told you she could teach," Jack offered.

"No, I told *you* she could teach," Ken came back. Sherry turned to come to the little table in the small kitchen, and pulled out a chair. The four of them again sat crowded around the tiny table and poured Cokes. "That was a marvelous teaching, Sherry," Ken went on.

Lisa beamed at her with obvious pride. "You were greatly used by God," she said. "Your gift is exceptional."

"Oh, you guys, thanks. You know I got everything from you, anyway."

"I've never even heard some of that stuff!" Ken protested.

"Well, I just feel so washed out right now, so relaxed, so used up in a good way. I guess I felt like God was using me. It just seemed like the Spirit seized me and carried me forward. And then there was Kirsten! Oh, praise God, this was a great night!" She raised her eyes up toward God.

She went on to recount what Kirsten had said, and the others talked about the conversations in which they had taken part. It was a type of fellowship unique to Christian workers sharing a successful night of spiritual battle. Their sense of gratitude, their love for God and for each other was more tangible than at any other time. Before they parted, they had a short time of prayer together. At the door Jack had a special twinkle in his eyes. "What?" she asked.

"I'll have to talk to you about it later," he said looking down, embarrassed. "It's too late tonight."

She let him go with a peck and a quick hug.

52

Sherry was surprised during the next two days by the emotional price she paid for her successful teaching. She found herself apathetic, dull, and listless. It was all she could do to make it to work on Tuesday night and keep up with her classes. Negative thoughts about her life plagued her at times. At other times a deep-seated sense of satisfaction welled up in her heart. Time after time, she sought God for comfort, feeling a quiet, serene closeness that was better than ever. Her melancholy feeling was strangely enjoyable. She felt she could recline into God's arms, having spent herself for Him.

There was a new sense of destiny as she recalled the sensation of God's Spirit ripping through her during her talk. This experience of the power of God was something new, something marvelous—almost frightening. What did it mean? Would it happen again? People from the group were calling her repeatedly over the following days, saying they couldn't stop thinking about what she had said. Sherry just prayed that she would view the whole experience God's way, avoiding egotistical thoughts without putting herself down.

Spring comes late in Michigan, and this year it was later than usual. Although the buds were struggling to open during most of the month of April, the weather was so cold and rainy they seemed to be stuck. Sherry was frustrated by the slow movement as she walked to classes across the greens on campus. It was several weeks before the first string of warm days arrived. The long and cold winters made the arrival of the fragrant, soft spring more rewarding.

It was Wednesday morning, and Sherry wasn't sure what to wear. Women on campus were coming out in their spring clothes, which were often quite titillating. She had some clothes that were pretty hot, even by the world's standards, but she wasn't sure whether there would be a problem wearing them as a Christian. She hesitated in front of her closet for a minute, feeling some sense of resistance. Then she shook her head and grabbed the slinky white cutaway shorts-suit she wanted to wear, figuring she was just being paranoid. After all, this suit was good for sunning, which she wanted to do that afternoon while she studied by the lake.

While she was in classes that day, she kept thinking of Jack and the meeting at the union that night. Large crowds were still showing up—though not as large as before—and people in the group no longer knew what to expect from one week to the next.

Their home groups were proliferating also. The group at Jack's house had divided, planting a new group at Lisa's house. That group planted another only three weeks later. Ken and Lisa were planning to take half of the group that met in Sherry's apartment out to one of the lounges in the largest dormitory on campus and there form another home group. They were calling their group M.S.U. Home Fellowships now, and there was a growing sense that their approach might be the wave of the future for Christians on campus. Already they had four thriving home groups, with two more groups planned, but in virtually every one, there were also problems threatening the group's spiritual health. At least two key group leaders were experiencing heavy depression, and threatening to quit. Another leader had lost control with his girlfriend much worse than Sherry and Jack had. In yet another group there was some serious in-fighting. Sherry felt like they were onto something God could really use, but she also wondered whether their whole idea might come crashing down at any time.

As she lay in the warm afternoon sun trying to read her copy of the *Communist Manifesto* for modern Russian history, she heard Jack's voice: "Mmmmm, this is pretty hard to look at."

Rolling over and shading her eyes, she looked up and saw him standing over her.

"Oh, Jack, have a seat! What do you mean 'hard to look at'?"

"I mean, you look mighty fine!" He sat down and talked for a while, but he was acting ill at ease and nervous. He wasn't looking at her much—just stealing quick glances over at her. She thought he was acting as if she had forgotten to put any clothes on. Looking down at her revealing suit, she suddenly became very self-conscious. She drew her legs up and put her arms around them, laying her head sideways on her knees.

Jack was being a poor conversationalist. "Is anything wrong, Jack?" she finally asked.

"Uh, no. Why?" His shrugging nonchalance was unconvincing.

Sherry realized he was teaching that night, and she knew he was often emotionally messed up before he had to speak at the Wednesday meetings. She asked him what he was going to teach, and they talked on that for some time. Jack sometimes acted shy around her even after months of dating. At first, she felt like he might be losing interest. But by now she knew he was sometimes self-absorbed and somewhat insecure around her. Today he had one of the worst cases of jitters she had ever seen. They talked about things awhile, but it just wasn't working.

"Jack, you're acting distant and weird. Now what's wrong, honey?" she said as she reached out to put a reassuring hand on his back. He almost jumped when she touched him.

He looked at her in the eyes but no words came out.

"Come on, you can tell me about it," she urged.

Jack looked down, pondering something he didn't appear able or willing to explain.

Sherry decided to take a guess. "You're looking at me funny. Do you have a problem with the way I'm dressed today?"

"Uh, no! I don't see where you're getting that," he frowned.

"It seemed like you are embarrassed, like you are looking at me like I was nude or something."

Jack blushed deeply and smiled, again looking down and this time shaking his head. A moment later he looked up. "I'm sorry. I didn't mean to make you feel funny. I love the way you're dressed."

"Really? I thought you might find it too skimpy." She had a growing certainty she was on-target.

"Well, I guess I've never seen you . . . you know . . . I guess I've never seen so much of you before. You're really beautiful—and not just physically, of course." Now he was struggling. "But, I guess I would have to admit you're so good-looking, I uh . . . I guess it's a little . . . intimidating sometimes."

"I wondered whether I should wear something more this morning. I don't know what's expected with Christians, you know."

"Oh, I'd like to see you take it all off! I mean, well . . . I probably shouldn't say that, but I guess I wouldn't want you to think I don't like you . . . you know . . . the way you are."

Jack felt like a clumsy oaf in this conversation. He knew he wasn't communicating, and his face was burning with embarrassment as he confronted his own sense of weakness in certain intimate situations. He wasn't able to tell her he was really troubled because she was driving him crazy with desire. He didn't want to tell her he was craving her.

There was an awkward silence as she struggled to understand him and he tried to figure out what he should say. She finally tried to help again. "I guess I don't understand exactly what you're saying, Jack."

He looked at her with a pained expression that seemed to wish she would communicate for both of them. "Look, I'm feeling some things . . . and I can't seem to express them right now. Would it be all right if I thought about it awhile and we talk again, like tonight?"

She was worried now. "I hope it's nothing serious. I hope I haven't done anything."

"No, it's nothing serious, and it's nothing negative, either. I just have problems sharing my feelings sometimes, okay?" he said with some testiness.

"Well, yeah, that's okay," she said in a tone that made Jack kick himself even more. Now he had hurt her feelings.

"It's nothing negative! I feel real good about us. Okay?"

She forced a dutiful smile. "Yeah, sure. You shouldn't worry about me right now anyway. You have to teach in a few hours. Will you be at the prayer dinner?"

"Absolutely. I feel a real need for prayer tonight." He got up to his knees and gave her a quick kiss. Again, he seemed quite timid and distracted. "Bye, now," he said as he got up and strode off, waving over his shoulder.

Sherry was worried. The talk had been uncharacteristic, and she knew in her heart there was something wrong with Jack. He had something he hadn't been able to tell her, she was sure of that. Another woman? No way. Still, it wasn't like him to be moody or finicky. Despite the lack of proof, she continued to feel it had something to do with the way she looked. She wished she hadn't been wearing her sunning outfit. She decided to try not to think about it until she saw him that night, but it didn't work.

As she came out of German class late that afternoon, Jean met her on the steps of Cargil Hall. "Did you hear the news?" she asked.

"What?"

"Leslie has moved in with that guy from her skating class—the one she brought up to Monday night a couple of weeks ago."

Sherry felt like Jean had just punched her in the nose. "Moved in?! They're going to live together?"

"Yep. I don't think we'll be seeing her anymore around fellowship." Jean looked disgusted and angry. "I knew that guy was bad news."

Sherry felt her spirit sag down in defeat. She let out a big sigh and slumped onto a bench next to the steps. Leslie had been one of the first girls from the dorm to respond to Sherry's witnessing. Lately, Sherry could tell there was something wrong, but this was a complete shock. It felt like she had just been told a family member had died. She and Jean commiserated over it for a while, wondering what was happening. "Sometimes I feel like God might have taken away our protection," Sherry admitted. "How can the Devil just waltz in and carry off our sisters like this?"

It was the first time Sherry had felt the pain of seeing someone she had led to Christ defect, but certainly not the last. As she and Jean tried to wrestle with their feelings of despair and abandonment, neither of them realized this was the first of many such incidents they would have to fight through in the years to come.

Sherry began to tear up as they sat silently on the stone bench by the steps. Like a huge curling wave, heartache crashed down on her spirit. She threw her hair back as she looked up at Jean, now with a tear running down her cheek, and shook her head. "I just feel like the wheels are coming off, Jean. It seems like ever since I've become a Christian . . . well, at least ever since Christmas, it's just been one thing after another. Especially lately, it seems like every day my world is crumbling more. That nasty, wicked phone call I got from Jim Clemmons' mother has left me scared ever since."

"Oh, I heard all about it from Lisa. That sounded terrible!"

"And then there are these pastors after us . . . Jack said another guy left and went to that exit counseling group . . . I don't know. At one time, I was so sure God had called us to something special here. Now it just seems like nothing's working out. So many of our leaders are having troubles. . . ."

"Well, I don't look at it that pessimistically, but we sure have been taking a pounding lately."

"Something was wrong with Jack today. I know there's a problem there."

"What do you mean?"

"I don't know. . . . I guess I shouldn't jump to conclusions. He was just acting so weird . . . I think these negatives are building up. I feel like I'm being battered from every direction."

Jean reminded her that a lot of positive things were happening also. But as she walked to her apartment, Sherry was incredibly burdened and depressed.

Back in her apartment, about 4:00 in the afternoon, her anxiety crystallized into a conscious thought: *What if Jack leaves me someday?*

Sherry wasn't accustomed to men leaving her, and generally didn't fear such things. But this was different. She trembled inwardly at the thought of what it would be like to try to carry on with her life without this man she had grown to love so much. A deep sense of insecurity seized her. Even though she repeatedly assured herself there was no sign of any problems in their relationship—that there was nothing to fear—her anxiety continued to press down on her like a heavy weight.

Through her jumbled feelings she finally sensed God challenging her. Would she be willing to trust Him, with or without Jack? As she stared into the mirror in her bathroom, she realized she couldn't honestly answer the question. *Why would God want me to lose Jack? What's wrong with our love?* But as soon as she asked the question, she knew the answer. If she couldn't lay their relationship on the altar and inwardly commit to following God with or without Jack, it meant the relationship was an idol in her life.

She turned to God in prayer. "Lord, *please* don't ask me to decide this. Please don't ask me to offer to lose him. I've gone through enough lately!"

But she sensed God was refusing her request. She knew she *must* decide, she must offer him to God, not just temporarily, but permanently. Sherry had rarely had such a tangible feeling that God was speaking to her. It was as if He was standing behind her shoulder, looking in the mirror with her. "Will you surrender Jack to Me unconditionally?" seemed to be the gist of what He wanted to know.

She was miserable. By now, Sherry was certain enough of the reality of God to know the stakes—she knew if she offered to give up this relationship, God might call her on the decision. She realized she had to be willing to give the relationship up, not in theory, but in fact. She was caught in the middle. She knew she loved Jack, and she knew she had come to love God, also. Why must she choose between them? But she instantly knew why. There could only be one Lord in her life. *God wants to know what the integration point of my life is: Him or Jack. If I say Jesus is the center and Lord of my life, I have to be prepared to walk away from this relationship.*

For the next two hours, Sherry suffered as God continued to press her on the issue. The Holy Spirit confronted her squarely with her lack of fidelity and loyalty to Christ like never before. Everything within her cried out to cling to this love no matter what. But at the same time, she knew she had decided to follow Jesus, and she couldn't follow Him if she was going to question His instructions for her. She couldn't stand up and teach that He is Lord if she was going to insist on the right to supervise His direction for her life.

She sat in her chair fingering the plant-watering can in her lap as she stared out the window in sadness. It was time to go to the prayer dinner, but the issue still wasn't resolved. She decided not to go. It would have been too awkward to be at the dinner trying to pray with such inner conflict going on. It was the first time she had ever missed one of these prayer dinners, but she felt she had to deal with this question.

During the next hour, as she tried to plead her case to God, she found herself wondering about what it would be like to go back and live as a nonChristian. There would certainly be fewer attacks in her life, she didn't doubt that. But even as she toyed with the idea, she knew she couldn't do it. There was no way she could ever return to her former life. *It would be too trivial and stupid after what I've seen with You, Lord. How could I ever again think it's important to live for goals that are only temporary?* No. She had seen too much for that.

Then she considered whether there might be a compromise position between where she had been and this radical position God seemed to be calling for. It was hard to imagine. *Either I'll follow Christ, or I'll go back to leading my own life. I'm not going to be fake or mediocre. After all, if Jesus is God, how could I refuse to follow Him?*

It all made sense, but somehow that didn't seem to help. Her longing for Jack was stronger than ever as she entertained the idea of being without him. She could see his handsome face and his understanding eyes. She could feel his sensitive hands as they held her close to his heart. Tears of frustration welled up in Sherry's eyes as she struggled with the harsh alternative before her.

She took a shower. Afterward, standing in front of the mirror, she felt like she was standing naked before God. What if God wanted her to be a missionary for Him all by herself? She pondered this question long and hard as she dressed for the evening. She felt she was willing to be a missionary if that was what God wanted. But the idea of being one alone, without Jack, was a terrifying thought.

She dared not say yes to God unless she meant it. Her belief in Christ was too strong to consider trying to tell Him yes without meaning it. She knew God would find her out if she tried that.

At 7:30 p.m. she sat in her chair again and hung her head. *What do You want from me?* she pleaded. But she already knew. Suddenly she looked up as revelation dawned in her heart. *That's it! There's no alternative! What is there to think about, anyway? If You don't want me to be with Jack, it's because You have something better for me!* That was hard to imagine, but she realized in a moment God was either good and all-knowing, in which case He should be followed, or He was bad or limited, in which case there was nothing to follow.

She turned to God in her heart. With a level of awe equal to what she had felt so long ago when she faced Him for the first time, she offered Jesus the keys to her life. *From this day forward, Lord, I'm Yours without conditions or reservations. Use me any way You want to, Lord. I know this life will be over before I know it, and I'll be with You forever. Let that forever begin today. Please don't make me give up Jack. I love him so much! But if I have to . . . I'm sure I want to do it Your way.*

She paused and reflected. Then she added a qualification to what she had been saying. *I'm really not sure how faithful I'll be to this decision. I guess You're gonna have to help me. . . . All I can offer You is my willingness to do whatever You want. I'm not holding back anything.*

As she sat back and wiped a tear from one eye, she communed with God for a few minutes, a deep feeling of peace flooding her heart. She felt God's Spirit was ministering to her, reminding her of her security in Him.

She looked at her watch and got up to go to the meeting at the union, now already in progress.

53

Sherry alternated jogging and walking most of the way to the union. She didn't want to sweat too much, and her feet were sore from the shoes she wore. Still, she pushed hard, distressed that she was missing her favorite meeting. She knew Jack would be worried about her not showing up at dinner, and she worried that his anxiety might affect his teaching. Silently she prayed for him and for the group as she hustled across campus.

She burst into the hallway at the union at about 7:45 and ran down to the corner where the lounge was. There was Jack, intently arguing some point to a crowd of hundreds. The attendance had been down a little for the past month, but there were still several hundred students there every week. So far, the threat to attend Warren's group had been successful. They had not returned. She guessed the crowd was a bit over three hundred this week.

She stood at the rear in such a way that Jack would see her. She wanted him to know she was there and nothing was wrong with her. He didn't show any reaction, but she was sure his eyes met hers at one point.

As she leaned against one of the pillars in the large room and listened to Jack's melodious voice, she stared at him, wondering. Was this the man of her future? Would God test her by taking him away? Suddenly, she became aware of a noisy ruckus down one of the halls. Growing in intensity, it was the sound of many voices shouting as they approached. Sherry's brow furrowed in alarm as she realized some noisy group was about to burst into Jack's teaching. There was nothing she could do to prevent it, but she headed in the direction of the noisy mob anyway.

Looking around the corner, she was startled to see a large group of demonstrators carrying signs and yelling. They stormed right up to the lounge. Jack had already stopped speaking, and everyone's head was turned toward the noise.

There were angry faces calling out "STOP THE INQUISITORS!" "NO MORE GAY-BASHING!" and "DOWN WITH THE FUNDAMENTALISTS!" With horror, Sherry realized the demonstration was aimed at their Bible study. Looking at the signs, Sherry saw "Sexual Freedom, Not Judgment" and "End Prejudice!" along with gay-pride signs declaring that God loves homosexuals. It was obvious this was the militant Gay Defense League, or GDL. They poured into the rear of the room and continued their catcalls and chants.

Jack tried to manage the situation. "Can't we have some dialogue?" he called over the amplifier. "Are we just going to sit here and call each other names? What about some understanding?"

With horror, Sherry saw one of the protesters step forward from the center of the crowd of close to a hundred demonstrators. Wearing a clerical collar and black jacket, it was unmistakably Reverend Billings!

Jack picked him out immediately and called on him. "Dr. Billings! Won't you talk with us?"

The calling and chanting quieted down as Billings stepped forward. "This event is the expression of indignation at religious intolerance practiced by your group, Jack. I'm here in sympathy with people who feel you pose a threat to their freedoms and well-being. You teach their way of life is a sin. You dishonor them and disown them from your vision of society."

"You're wrong, Lowell!" Jack shot back plaintively. "I'm against compulsion in society! I believe in a pluralistic society!" he pleaded as catcalls and sneers sounded from the disbelieving protesters. "It's true! I'm against connecting church and state!"

"It isn't up to you!" Billings shouted back. "As long as you're teaching your narrow view of ethics and religion, you're contributing to a return to the Middle Ages. Your followers will take your judgmental teachings the next logical step and lash out in persecution, as they have so often in the past!"

Now a negative booing groan went up from the Christians, and this was met by angry affirmations by the Gay Defense League and their supporters. The noise grew quickly as the two groups fired taunts and accusations at each other. Sherry noticed several campus police appearing at the edges of the crowd as a number of Bible study people began standing up from their couches and turning to face the protesters.

At length, Jack was able to make himself heard again with the help of the amplifier. "Lowell! Can't we arrange a meeting between the leadership of your group and our leadership to discuss your grievances?"

Again the crowd quieted and allowed Billings to answer. "Jack, we've already scheduled a meeting for tomorrow. We're meeting with the university facilities management to protest the use of state funds for the establishment of fundamentalist religion. We're calling on them to expel you from the student union!"

This provoked a loud and angry cry of dismay from the Bible study group. The GDL members responded with shouting and finger pointing. She could hear Billings yelling that they intended to exercise their right to be in that room as a public place, and they were not leaving. Taunts and chanting continued.

Sherry looked at Jack, and he looked at her with a despairing shrug. It was clear the meeting was a complete ruin. Jack stared at the spectacle before him for some time and then took his microphone and called out to the group. This time the GDL would not quiet down for him. He had to shout over their voices, saying since these protesters were not willing to engage in constructive dialogue, the meeting was over. Then, after a pause, he also said he would close in prayer. The protesters called out even louder when they heard him say that. He nevertheless turned to God and continued to speak. "Lord, we see these people are angry at us for some reason."

Several called out "Yeah!" and "You better believe it, Bible-banger!"

"We pray we'll find a way to show them the love of Christ."

At this, some hissed and shrieked in rage. Sherry saw one loud guy near her with bulging veins on his reddened neck and face scream, "Take your love and shove it up yours!" She started walking around behind the group toward the stairwell they had come up. With her face burning in anger, she was determined to confront Billings this time.

Jack quickly closed the prayer as the protesters heckled him. He called on people to come out for fellowship, "you know where," referring to The Fireside.

As the Christians began to gather their things, some angry shouting occurred as some of the people from the Bible study told the GDL members what they thought of their intrusion. Some pushing broke out at one point, and people from both sides moved quickly to restrain the violence. The police looked nervous, and Sherry could see them on their hand-held radios calling for help. But at the point when it became clear the Christians were really filing out and the meeting was over, the GDL suddenly began to call each other to leave. As they headed for the exit, Sherry stood waiting for Billings, blocking his way out.

"So, out for a little time of unity in the community of faith this evening, are we?" she challenged.

Billings came right up to her. "I warned you about the antisocial, exclusivist tendencies these groups have," he said in a patronizing voice.

"Yeah, I guess I see some narrow judgmentalism here tonight," she acknowledged. "Maybe even a little hate! But I don't think it comes from the so-called fundamentalists."

"Look, we're just reacting in defense here. Jack is using a state-funded facility to attack others."

"Well, I'm sure glad you're not attacking anyone."

"Not as I see it," he shrugged. "It's not attacking someone when you defend yourself."

"You're a complete liar and a fake," she charged, narrowing her eyes and shaking her head in disgust.

"I see you've learned your lessons on judging others well," he smiled, and the GDL members behind him chuckled.

"You're the biggest judge on campus! Twice you've attacked this group entirely unprovoked—in the press, and here tonight. You're the most violent aggressor I've met in five years on this campus. But the disgusting thing is you launch all your attacks under the pompous guise of unity and nonjudgmentalism," she vented her fury.

"I'm sorry I don't meet up to your standards," he said with a plaintive look on his face.

"You're not violating my standards, you're violating your *own* standards. That's why I can't respect your stand. You're a hypocrite, a liar!"

"Well, I guess everyone who isn't in your narrow Bible group is a hypocrite. I just hope you don't burn us at the stake!" The other protesters laughed and cheered at this comment, and Billings turned to grin and nod at them.

They quieted down, apparently interested to see what Sherry would say. "I think, based on tonight, if there's enough hate here to burn someone, it would be you lighting the pyre."

"Oh, like all the other gays who have burned religionists at the stake?" He drew another round of laughter from his supporters.

"No, like all the men in priest outfits who have burned dissenters at the stake." She turned to leave, and as she walked by, some of the protesters made lewd gestures and called out names.

Finally, they left en mass, headed for some unknown destination, satisfied their protest had been effective.

It *had* been effective. As Sherry, Jack, Lisa, Ken, and a small group of Christians stood putting their things away afterward, they wondered whether they would ever be able to have another meeting in the union.

"How could this happen? Didn't you guys pray before the meeting? I thought we could bind Satan in prayer." Sherry began firing off questions as they came to her mind.

"We definitely prayed against Satan before the meeting," Lisa reassured her. "I don't know why it didn't work."

"Aaaagh, I just can't stand this!" Sherry held the top of her head with both hands. "It just seems like the Enemy's romping all over us on every front! Jack, you must be miserable! What do you think about it?"

He sat down heavily on a stool. "Yeah, this was a pretty amazing pounding we just took. I don't know."

"Why do you think Satan ignored our command we gave in prayer, Jack?" This time it was Lisa.

He looked down with a frown, thinking, as he rubbed his chin. "Well, I guess there's no prayer we can offer that will put an end to spiritual warfare. I guess what we really prayed was that his attacks would be ineffective, and, when you think about it, it isn't clear yet that he has been effective."

"Yeah, there you go!" Sherry's eyes lit up, as she pointed at him. "He may have scored a hit tonight, but that doesn't mean he's won!" Sherry could feel her blood rise as she went over from a perspective of defeat to the realization they needed to fight to win. In spite of the despair she had felt that day, she knew in that moment she was determined to go down fighting.

Lisa was glad for the ray of hope. "Yeah, we can't despair here," she said quietly, to herself as much as to anyone else.

"I agree," Amy spoke up. "Let's get over to the restaurant and talk to people. We need to help people work through this thing."

"Good idea," agreed Jack. "Let's get packed up and get over there."

"Why don't you take off now, Jack," offered Mark Grover, the guy who owned most of the sound equipment. "We can pick up here, and you need to be doing the talking over there."

"Okay. You guys can pray for us, too. Let's not let down. Lisa, Amy, Ken, and Sherry, I think you guys should come with me, too. Is that all right with you, Mark?"

"Yeah, sure. Go!"

The five leaders snapped into action and took off at a brisk pace toward the street and the two-block walk.

On the way, Jack was already coaching the others on what to do when they got there. "Look, there'll be close to a couple of hundred people in there. Start with workers and leaders. Let's be sure we're all on the same page here. We need to point out the basic facts we've already discussed, we need to get believers praying God will turn this into a victory. We also need to get people talking about how the whole thing affected them. I'm sure a lot of people feel really defeated right now. . . ." And so he continued to exercise his gift of leadership, casting a vision for what they could accomplish when they got there. Each step of the way, Sherry felt her determination and certainty about what to do growing.

As soon as they hit the door, Sherry glanced over at Jack and smiled as if to say she would see him later. They all split up and immediately became involved in animated conversations with various groupings of people who were at the meeting. Sherry felt excited and eager as she dove into spiritual warfare and Christian leadership. She was witnessing a tangible change of demeanor on the faces of people she talked to as she pointed out the main spiritual truths of the situation.

"Maybe you ought to help us get this perspective out to the others here and urge people to pray?" she suggested to one brother who had just expressed some relief at what she had shared with him. They agreed he would take one table and she would take the one next to it.

"Boy, we've never seen anything like that meeting tonight, have we?" she asked as she walked up to a table of six.

They shook their heads in dismayed agreement. "Sherry," asked one of the newer girls, "has anyone figured out what a priest was doing with the Gay Defense League?"

"He's not a priest, he's a Protestant minister," Sherry answered. "I know that creep. His name's Billings, and he runs that Unity place up on Decker."

"Oh! He's the guy who slammed us in the paper!" exclaimed one of the girls.

"That's him. He's a real two-face. He doesn't believe the Bible; he thinks it's all 'metaphors' or the 'spiritual interpretations of the ancients.'"

"That's really sick!" the girl wrinkled her nose.

"Listen, you guys need to consider this thing in the light of spiritual warfare. . ." and Sherry went on and explained things from a biblical perspective.

For over an hour the workers and leaders in the group scurried about in the restaurant, gathering their flock and steeling everyone's nerves for what looked like a serious battle. Some of them actually prayed in the restaurant. Others went to Lisa's house for a late-night prayer meeting. It was almost 12:00 by the time Jack came over next to Sherry as she said goodbye to a group from their own study in her apartment. They all called out their goodbyes and waved as they left. Sherry and Jack were left standing alone.

54

Jack turned and smiled at her with eyes full of love. All the uneasiness from that afternoon was gone. "We need to talk," he said.

"Yeah, I have something I want to tell you about."

"Let's get a table out of the way somewhere and have a glass of wine."

"Okay," she said as they strode arm in arm back to one of the many nooks in the very large restaurant. They each ordered a glass of white wine and turned to enjoy some time alone with each other.

Jack sighed audibly before breaking the brief silence. "Can you believe the day we've just been through?"

"It seems like it's been a week since I woke up this morning. I'm totally wiped out!"

"Maybe we should talk later."

"Are you kidding? I feel like I really need to talk awhile to get my head together!" she pleaded.

Jack smiled, "Well, I feel like I'd like to tell you a little about how I've been feeling. . . ."

"Wait. Would you mind if I shared first why I wasn't at the prayer dinner?" Sherry interjected.

"Okay. You go first." He seemed relieved.

She went on to give him a blow-by-blow account of her experience that afternoon. Jack listened carefully as she went deeper and deeper into the struggle she had experienced in her apartment. Several times, she paused, searching for words, and he patiently waited in silence as she worked out the whole story. He was fascinated, listening to a struggle that was so obviously authentic, not to mention that it centered on him.

Finally, she recounted the point of crisis, the point where she offered from the heart to give him up if God wanted her to. "I'm not saying He really wants me to, but I do worry that He might decide to test my resolve on this," she finished.

"If God did test you on this commitment, would you obey Him and break up with me?" he asked.

"Well, I don't want to sound too self-confident, but . . . at least the way

I see it now . . . if I could be sure it was His will . . . I think I'd try to break it off. Yes. What about you?"

"Uh, yeah, well . . . if He didn't want it, I'm sure it would be for a good reason. I've actually faced this question before, you know."

She raised a questioning eyebrow.

"Don't forget, early on, I actually had to do what you're talking about, in a way. This is what I was going through that night at your place when I told you I couldn't be involved with you. Of course, we weren't nearly as close then, but my feelings for you were already deep. I just didn't see how I could possibly cling onto something . . . someone, even you, if He didn't want me to. It would make a sham of everything I am."

She smiled. "I'm so glad to hear you say that. I'll tell you what, Jack. At one time, I would've felt rejection from that statement. But after tonight, I see I can trust you more because you say that. I now realize I'm going to be happier if I'm someone's girlfriend rather than his god. You know what I mean?"

He smiled in a deeply appreciative way. "I know exactly what you mean, and I'm so excited about your experience. It fits in strangely with what I've been going through."

"Okay, it's your turn."

"Well, this latest part started when I saw you this afternoon. I told you I'd never seen so much of you. . . ."

"Yeah." She smiled and looked down briefly with a little feeling of embarrassment.

"What was really happening there . . . I saw you in that sexy outfit, and . . . I just about lost it. I mean, it was intense desire for you that was making me act strange today."

"Oh, brother." She rolled her eyes. "I didn't realize that at all. I thought maybe it was almost the opposite." Now she felt put on the spot, but flattered at the same time.

"To be perfectly frank, when I saw your body in the sun, I just wanted you right there!"

She grinned and blushed as she looked down. "*Jack.*"

"Yeah. Sorry, but that's the truth. I was really losing it. That's why I was so uncomfortable."

"I get that sometimes for you, too, you know. This whole chastity thing's really new for me."

"Well, I feel like it's getting worse for me. I think our relationship's been developing really well, and the more I understand you . . . the more attractive you become. The more I see you deepening in the things of

God, the more I see your heart for ministry, the more desirable you are. I really feel like it's getting to the point where I don't know if I can keep my hands off you."

Again she had to grin and look away from him, shaking her head in embarrassment. "You're talking more like me now, and less like Jack Collins."

"Sherry . . ." he fell silent for a long moment during which her eyes came to meet his. The way he had said her name kept her from filling the void. He stared deeply into her eyes. "Will you marry me?" he pleaded.

She gasped and put her hand over her mouth in shock. Staring straight into those penetrating blue eyes, her tears began to well up as the realization sank in. This was it! Her life was on the line. Without much hesitation, she answered by shaking her head yes several times. Her hands reached out and met his in a desperate, loving clasp.

They stared into each other's eyes once again in the grip of a magical spell. At this moment, they looked at each other, not as boyfriend and girl-friend, but as life-partners.

"You really want to be with me forever?" she marveled.

"That's exactly what I want," he smiled, squeezing her hands.

There was another silence as they held on to each other and enjoyed their feelings. Sherry broke the silence. "How does this fit in with what I thought God was doing with me this afternoon?"

"Oh, I think it fits in beautifully! He was taking you to the laundry; you know, really working with your attitude, your values, *before* tonight, because He knew what He was putting on my heart from the other end."

"You really feel God has put this on your heart, Jack?"

"Oh, yeah! See, any man feels there are dangers in marriage, we're taught to value our freedom, all that stuff. But as my desire for you has grown, the fears I feel about marriage have stood in the way. Today, God finally convinced me I should 'be anxious for nothing' and just go ahead and lay my life on the line for you."

"I'm so excited! I want to be your wife!" She drew his hand up and kissed it, holding it to her lips as she leaned her head on his. There was another short silence. Sherry realized they were opting for a sexual rela-tionship. A moment later she looked up and blurted out the question that had been on her mind. "Jack, are you a virgin?"

"Yes, I am," he answered softly.

Sherry felt a pang of fear and sorrow sweep through her like a sword. How could she go into the bedroom with this man?

He saw her flinch and look away when he said he was a virgin. He reassured her, "Sherry, I really think any problems in that area can be worked out. Lee says when a virgin marries a nonvirgin, the problems are more in the mind of the nonvirgin. You know, you might feel more self-conscious than I will. Like, I'm there thinking, *This is the greatest thing ever!* and you might be thinking about your past or something."

She thought about that for a moment. "I feel like I can deal with that better than wondering what you're thinking of me."

"Believe me. When I have you in my arms I'll be thinking only of one thing—how beautiful you are."

She knew he was being nice, but her worries remained. Before long they got up and strolled out into the street. Jack walked her home, and they held each other in the fragrant spring night outside her apartment for a long time. Excitedly, they savored each other as much as they dared. "I wish we were already married and I could take you inside tonight!" he murmured.

"You're a hot man, Jack. It's going to be hard to wait. How long do you think we should wait, anyway?"

"Not very long, in my opinion. I've had too many friends who lost it during engagement. I think we should get you graduated next month, and that's it."

"You mean a June wedding?"

"That's what I'd like."

"Wow! I guess that sounds good to me, too. Let's do it! My mom's just going to die!"

"We'd better go and see your parents pretty soon. It won't be easy to see mine in Guatemala, but I bet they'll come home for the wedding.

"Here, I hope you can get into this." He pulled out a ring box and gave it to her. It was a small diamond ring.

"Oh, Jack! How could you afford this?" she gasped. "It's so pretty!"

"I had a few bucks back home in an account from years ago. It's pretty small, but I'm hoping you and I feel the same way about that."

"Absolutely. I wouldn't want to teach against materialism with a huge rock on my hand. This is perfect, Jack." She put it on and kissed him again. She held on to Jack's shoulders and buried her face in his chest. "Ooohhh, June might even be too far away!" she lamented.

"I'd better get out of here," Jack said, with a real note of alarm in his voice. He took her by the shoulders and moved her back. "I'll call you about the student union thing."

"Do I get to tell everyone?" she asked.

"I don't see why not." He gave her a hug and turned to go. "I'll call you." He ran toward home.

55

The next morning Sherry's phone rang. It was Jack. "I was just sitting here imagining me making us eggs in your apartment and then us sitting down for breakfast together at that little table by the window."

"Oh, yeah, that sounds fun!" she smiled. "I can't wait! I'd make us some coffee, and we could sip it together!"

After sharing dreams for a while, they turned to the crisis they faced over using the student union. Jack felt sure the union would honor the contract they had signed for the spring and summer quarters. But he had his doubts about fall quarter. He said he was planning to go over to the Office of Student Affairs, which controlled the space in the union, and try to head off Billings and his buddies.

Sherry had a class that day in the same building that housed Dr. Forsythe's office. She suggested she should talk to him about the situation, since he was a faculty member. They agreed to get in touch at dinner and see how things went.

She gave Forsythe a call before she left her apartment and arranged to stop by after class for a few minutes. Forsythe had been attending their home Bible study regularly since the first time, and had even brought his wife the last two weeks. Sherry could tell he loved the group, and his wife, Anne, seemed excited, too. Sherry was pretty sure he would come to their defense with the university.

As she talked to him later that day, it was clear he was deeply disturbed by her story of the protest. They spent some time talking about the alternatives. Forsythe warned her they might do better to find a place off campus. "After all, Sherry, it is a public place, and at the very least, they'd have the right to come back as often as they liked to protest."

"Yeah, that's a good point . . . wow, I hadn't considered that. I guess even if they continue to allow us to meet there it's no guarantee we won't be disrupted." She frowned at Forsythe's unusual blue cut-glass paperweight. "Boy, I don't know what we're going to do. It would take time to find a place, and we could be bounced out of the union immediately, or disrupted to the point we couldn't go on!"

After a moment of silence Forsythe offered, "Well, why don't you let me look into that? I know Jody Kear, who's pretty far up in the department that oversees campus facilities, and I think I could have some influence there."

"Oh, that would be so great! We'd appreciate the help," she beamed. "I really believe God's doing some amazing things through that study series. I've talked to so many who feel their lives have been changed there."

"Yeah, I feel like I've become a real supporter of what you guys are doing. I even feel like my own view of religion is changing from being around you kids."

"Are you trying to tell me you've received Christ?" she popped the question directly.

"Uh . . . well, I guess I've been praying some lately. Does that count?" He looked at her questioningly.

"You didn't used to pray?"

"Not really, I mean, I guess there have been a couple of times when things went bad, but no, I don't normally feel comfortable praying as such. I've gone back and forth about the question of whether God's a person or a principle. . . ." He ran his finger along the jagged edge of the blue paperweight. "I guess I've always sort of meditated on God . . . well, for the past few years I've leaned toward believing in the God of the Bible."

"This prayer thing sounds like your understanding is, that God is more personal."

"Yes, I'd say it's more personal. That's exactly what I'd say."

"Oh, Dr. Forsythe, I'm so happy to hear this!" she exclaimed, smiling.

He looked embarrassed, almost like a little boy. "Well, if we're going to be involved in the same fellowship group, you and Jack are going to have to start calling me Ray. I don't want to be 'Dr. Forsythe' for the rest of my life."

Sherry was glad he was feeling his way into a closer relationship with her and the others in the group. She could feel his desire to be a part, not just an observer. "Why don't you just go ahead and tell Christ that you're willing to come under His leadership, and His death, and the whole thing?" she challenged.

He paused for a minute before looking straight at her. "I guess, to be honest, I feel like I've done that."

Sherry sat spellbound as the reality of his roundabout profession of faith sank in. A huge smile spread across her face. "Boy, I think I'm going to die if another good thing happens! I'm just being blessed to death!" She laid her hand on her chest as though feeling her heart.

"This thing at the union didn't sound exactly like a blessing," Ray said with one eyebrow raised.

"Oh, no. But there are other things going on. Jack asked me to marry him!"

Now it was Ray's turn to be shocked. He drew his head back as though she had struck him in the face. "Are you kidding? I knew it!" He raised his finger and pointed at her. "I knew you two were made for each other! Congratulations!" She showed him the ring, and they talked for a few minutes about marriage.

At one point Forsythe seemed thoughtful. "You know, on this meeting place thing. . . ." He trailed off in thought.

"Yes, what?" she pressed.

He snapped out of his thoughts. "I was just thinking about some things. I need to think about this some more. Let's see what I can do." He sat in silence again with a thoughtful frown on his face.

Sherry thought he was acting strange as he seemed so absorbed about their space problems. He seemed to have more on his mind than his upcoming discussion with the administrator. She decided to ask him about his wife. "I've been really pleased to see Anna there the last couple of weeks."

"Yes, well, I have to tell you, she really likes your group, too. I thought she'd never question her loyalty to that boring church we're in. But lately, she's finding a lot of fault with it—especially the way they don't teach the Bible."

Sherry pressed further. "Really? They just sort of lecture on good and bad?"

"Yeah! You sound like you've been there. Anyway, she raised that complaint with the pastor, and he really put her down. Now I think she's pretty disgusted with their whole outfit."

"I'll never understand why these clergymen don't like the Bible," Sherry shook her head. "There must be something really sick there."

"I can understand." He nodded with pursed lips. "A lot of us have never been exposed to the kind of living understanding of the Bible you kids seem to have. Most scholars just view it as an ancient book deserving some respect because of its importance in Western culture."

"Yeah, I viewed it that way, but then I wasn't a Christian preacher either."

"I'll have to agree, that part's pretty strange."

Before long Forsythe said he had a lecture to get to, and Sherry got up to leave. "This has been the most exciting talk, Ray! I hope you can work out the thing with the union, but I hope you don't feel like you're being pressured or something."

"Don't worry," he said as he opened the door for her. "I'll let you know how things go with Kear. Would you like me to call you?"

"Oh, would you? That would give me so much peace of mind!"

"Sure. Let me get your number here." He jotted the number down on a Day-Timer he pulled from his vest pocket.

56

That evening, just before leaving to meet Jack for dinner, the phone rang in Sherry's apartment. It was Ray Forsythe. "Sherry, I wonder if you and Jack could meet me this evening if you're free?"

"Sure, I'm meeting him for dinner at Taco Bell in half an hour, and then I don't think we have anything planned."

"That's great. I'm not going to tell you anything right now. How about if we meet at the corner of Clark and State Streets in two hours? Is that too soon?"

"No, that's fine," she giggled. "But what is this? Why do you want to meet there? That's nowhere near the union."

"I have something to show you. You'll see. Why don't you bring some of the kids from the study group?"

"Well, yeah . . . I could ask the others to come . . . show us what? What is this? Come on!"

"No, you'll see. Bye now."

She tried to keep him on the line, but he hung up. She got ready and headed to Taco Bell, shaking her head. Things were happening at a blinding rate of speed. What would happen next?

She was already sitting at one of the stone tables out front when Jack walked up. It was no longer her boyfriend but her *fiancé* who squeezed in beside her at the table. They talked about how their friends had reacted to the news of their engagement that afternoon. So far, everyone seemed happy and positive about their plans, even though a couple of people were surprised they were moving so fast.

She was dying to hear how things had gone with the people at the union. Jack explained he had arrived at the office while Billings and the leader of the GDL, Matt Conover, were still there waiting to get in. "When Phil Frank, the manager of the union came out, I pointed out that neither of those two guys were students or university employees. I said they should have no say about activities on campus, and Phil agreed. He reaffirmed the union's commitment to our group until the end of the quarter.

"So Conover and Billings left, and they vowed to return with a student spokesperson. Then Phil warned me that the GDL would probably succeed in driving our fellowships out of the union. He said, 'I can keep you in there since the quarter's almost over and probably even through the summer. But you'd better find another place to meet.'

"I said, 'I can't believe you're letting the GDL tell you who can use the union, Phil. This is going to lead to a situation where any group can drive another out of university facilities.'"

"What did he say to that?" Sherry was expectant.

"Well, he sort of agreed, but there was something he wasn't saying, you know?"

"Yeah. . . ."

"And so then he admitted there were 'other factors.' He didn't want to say what, but I pressed him, and you won't believe it."

"Come on! What was it?"

"'Well,' he says, 'there have been some calls and letters to the university from prominent alumni, some big supporters.' And I'm like, 'Who? Other gays?' and he says, 'No. One of the most persistent has been a woman. She belongs to the chamber of commerce or city council.'" Jack just stared with a sardonic grin as the realization broke on Sherry's face.

"Oh, no. Not Mrs. Clemmons."

"Yep, Ruth Clemmons. He said she wrote him and sent copies to the university president and board members. He said the word has come down that he's supposed to 'investigate' the claims that they're supporting a cult in the student union."

As Jack recounted the story, Sherry's face paled with horror. She rubbed her arms, which were bristling with goose bumps. "I really can't believe this."

Jack went on, "They're going to throw us out. That's all there is to it. We have three weeks to get ourselves together. We talked about renting space, but that would be $480 a week! My main concern is, if we don't meet over the summer, I'm afraid most of the members would forget about us and the whole group will come unraveled. . . ."

Jack was still talking as they looked up and saw two couples approaching their table. It was Lee and Tory Carulo and Dan and Eileen Simmons from New Life Church. Dan was an elder at the church, and regularly prayed with Jack at their men's prayer meeting. Eileen had been meeting with Tory, Sherry, and Lisa, so they all knew each other. "Yeah, I told you we'd find them here," Lee smiled as they walked up and stood by the table.

"How'd you find us?" Jack looked befuddled.

"The guys at your house told me where you were, and your beautiful fiancée, too." He looked at Sherry who was beaming happily. "Are you sure you know what you're doing, young lady?"

"Well, it's too late to worry about that now," she smiled.

"I don't know, you can still get out of it." They were both chuckling now.

Jack put his hand to his forehead. "Oh, man, I can't believe you heard about it already!"

"Yeah, no thanks to you," said Lee.

"Hey, I was going to call you tonight!"

"I know, don't worry about it. I'm just giving you a hard time. We heard about it, and we thought we'd come down to campus and ride your case a little bit."

Tory and Eileen admired the engagement ring on Sherry's finger and bubbled with congratulations as they sat on the stone bench on the other side of the table.

After everyone was introduced and settled into their seats, Lee turned to Jack at one point and spoke in a more serious voice. "Jack, we heard about the attack by that militant group last night."

"Oh, you wouldn't believe it, Lee." Jack looked over at Sherry, who helped him as they poured out the story. They described the whole episode to Lee and Dan, who shook their heads slowly in dismay at the description.

"As it was in the days of Sodom . . ." Lee reflected quietly.

Then Jack filled them in on his successful meeting at the student union that day. "That's what we were talking about when you walked up," he finished.

"Well, I was going to see if you needed to use our church or something, but it sounds like you're going to be all right at the union for a while," said Lee.

"Yeah, but maybe in the summer . . ."

Sherry interrupted. "What we didn't get to yet, was my talk with Dr. Forsythe." They turned their attention to her as she related her conversation about Christ with Ray Forsythe. Jack was thumping the table and cheering out loud as she described his statements about prayer and receiving Christ. Lee and Dan joined him, caught up in the excitement.

"We've prayed for this man in our prayer group for months!" Dan beamed victoriously.

"I've been wondering if more was going on in Ray's heart than he was letting on," Jack exulted. "He's been asking all these questions during talks we've had lately. This is just too sweet for me to comprehend!"

"But that's not all," Sherry went on. "You won't believe what else he did."

"What now?" Jack looked like he couldn't imagine.

"Well, he was really being weird. He said he would talk to this guy who deals with campus buildings, you know? And then I gave him my number, and he was going to call me and let me know what happened."

"Yes," Jack said impatiently as she paused.

"So, he called me up just before I left to come here, but he was really weird."

"Yeah . . .what do you mean?"

"Instead of telling me about his talk with this guy, he said he wanted us to meet him tonight, and he's going to show us something."

"Tonight? When?"

She looked at her watch. "In about forty minutes."

"Meet him where? Show us what?" Jack pressed, still confused.

"At the corner of Clark and State Streets. And I don't know what!"

"He just said to meet him there and he'd show us something?"

"I told you he was acting weird."

"Oh, man. That really *is* weird! He's just going to meet us on a street corner and show us something?"

"Yeah, and he said to bring some of the people from the Bible study!"

For several minutes they tried to imagine what Forsythe might have in mind. Jack pointed out Forsythe didn't live anywhere near that corner. They finally gave up and went to call Lisa and Ken, asking them to invite any who were around at their houses who wanted to see what Forsythe had. Then they took off with Lee, Tory, Dan, and Eileen to walk the several blocks up to the rendezvous. The two older couples had made it clear they weren't about to miss whatever was going on.

By 7:30, the four older believers and six student members and leaders were standing at the corner talking about what they were doing there. It seemed hard to imagine that a professor had put them up to this. Sherry desperately hoped Forsythe wasn't going to turn up as some kind of nut after all.

A minute later, they saw him in the distance, walking up along with his wife, Anna. "Wow, this is really strange," Jack marveled from a distance. "What's she doing here? And look at that grin on her face."

"What are either one of them doing here? That's what I want to know," Sherry said in hushed tones.

Jack stepped out to shake Ray Forsythe's hand. "Well, you have our attention, Ray," he smiled. "And it's a surprise to see you here as well, Anna." Then he made sure everyone was introduced, especially the Carulos, and the Simmons. He turned back to Anna. "So, do you know what this is all about?"

"Yes, we've been talking about it for a while now," she seemed to beam with excitement. "It's something we want to do for the cause."

"Talking about what?" Jack sounded exasperated.

"About what we've come down here to show you," Ray said.

"Well, what is it?" Jack pressed. The others put up a chorus of agreement behind him.

"Yeah, what's going on?" "What's the deal?"

"Now, you're all just going to have to come along and see." Forsythe seemed to be enjoying himself immensely, judging from the huge smile glued on his face. He gestured for them to follow as he began walking down State Street with Anna.

Sherry, Jack, and the others looked at each other with confusion and amazement as they fell in and began following the middle-aged couple. Sherry saw Lee shaking his head in disbelief. Within half a block, they stopped, and everyone caught up.

"Well, what do you think?" Ray asked, turning to face the others.

"Think of what?" Jack queried.

"Your new facility," Ray answered, raising his hand to the left.

Ten heads rotated in the direction he was pointing as their eyes came to rest on the object they had been brought to see—the recently abandoned Fiesta Roller Skating Rink.

A soft "oooooh" sound emanated from the group as they caught their breath and tried to comprehend what he was saying. Jack looked back at Ray. "What?"

"Yeah, Anna and I have been the proud owners of this building since January. We're proposing that you use it for your meetings."

Jack looked like he was about to collapse. He turned back and stared at the building again, breathing deeply. "When will I learn to really trust You, Lord?" He looked at Ray again. "Why would you own this?"

"We inherited some money when my Mom died a few years ago. We were working with this guy on renovating it into a restaurant-club sort of thing."

"Well I don't see how we could consider interfering with your investment plans." Jack shook his head skeptically.

"Oh, don't worry. I'm not planning on giving up on my idea. We just think we can go ahead with the renovation and have you kids use it at the same time. Come on, let's look at it." He held his arm out toward the building, which had a chain hanging across the entrance. "It's walking distance from anywhere on campus, and it's pretty big."

"Wow, it's even closer to the dorms than the union is!" Sherry exclaimed as she moved toward the chain. "This would be the perfect place, Jack!"

They all stepped over the chain and spread out over the large vacant parking lot, tufts of grass growing everywhere through cracks in the asphalt. They headed toward the steel building with the stone facade, pointing at things and chattering as they went. Jack could hear excited comments being exchanged between the others. "What about occupancy permits and stuff?" he asked Ray.

"Well, we have city approval of our plans, and a building permit. But my buddy, who was going to actually do the renovation work, wasn't sure he wanted to get into the deal right now. I just dumped him from the deal this afternoon and I'm going to find someone else."

Sherry jumped in. "Jack used to work in construction, and he's looking for work this summer!"

"Yes, I know," was all Forsythe said as he looked at Jack.

"You don't mean you'd hire me to do the job?" Jack was having real trouble absorbing everything.

"Of course that's what I mean. This would pay a lot better than your job at the computer center, and I need someone who can manage here. In exchange, I'll let you hold your meetings here once we're open."

Jack ran his fingers through his hair. "Oh, I see. So you'd go ahead and remodel, and it's a profit-making venture, but we can use it maybe one night a week."

"Right."

"Well, I'm sure we could give your restaurant a lot of business."

"Yeah, that should sweeten the deal a little, but I'm not concerned about that."

The students, the Forsythes, the Carulos and the Simmons proceeded to walk excitedly from one area of the site to another during the next half hour as the evening light began to fade, pointing out features with future possibilities. There was a small trashy ravine in back that looked like it would clean up nicely. Lee and Dan joined in like the rest, feeling like students again themselves.

"I could see a little terrace out here for getting together afterward," Lee exclaimed, with his hands spread out toward the ground. "We ought to get the guys to come out here and build a terrace for these students," he urged. "Provided Ray approves, I guess."

"Oh, that sounds great to me!" Forsythe answered as he reached in his pocket and brought out a key ring. "I have a key here. There's no power inside, but I have a flashlight. Let's see if we can get this thing to work."

They got the door open and headed into the rather dark and dank building. Skylights provided a bit of light in the large lobby. They pressed through to the spacious rink, which had its own skylights. They could make out bleacher-style seating along one side. "We're planning to put in a large row of windows along that wall, which will overlook that ravine," Ray explained.

"This is just too perfect to be true!" breathed Ken in a low voice. He and Lisa stood with Jack and Sherry in the middle of the rink.

"Well, live performance was part of our plans, so it should work out well for giving talks and stuff like that," Forsythe observed.

"This place would hold hundreds! Maybe thousands!" Jack marveled. They wandered around trying to see more, but the light was fading and they decided they should get out before someone got hurt.

Sitting on the two benches facing each other by the entrance, they buzzed with excitement, imagining all the things they could do with such a facility. Concerts, social outreach meetings, large studies . . . it was like a dream come true.

They all sat and speculated with a mounting sense of excitement about what God would do though M.S.U. Home Fellowships. In the spiritual battle waged over the past year, they could all see stroke and counterstroke as the Evil One had used every imaginable tactic to raise barriers to their ministry. This seemed to be the perfect answer to every danger. Now they would be able to control who came to their meetings. Yet there was room for immense growth.

No one was more convinced than Sherry that Satan and his forces were behind the orchestrated attack they had experienced. It all spread out before her like a quilt. "The way I see it is, at the same time God was making choices and calling people like me to serve Him in this ministry, the Enemy was trying to energize all kinds of human agents to rise up in opposition. And, you know, none of them has been very successful until the GDL got us thrown out of the union. And now it turns out Jim Clemmons' *mother* helped get us thrown out!" She turned to the middle-aged couples and said, "It's a long story. Believe me, it's sick." She went on, "It's such a perfect area to strike, because we were able to overcome things like problems with our reputation and our division and stuff. But one area where we're really weak is that we have no money. I was worried that our whole momentum here was being threatened."

Several others agreed out loud. "Man, no kidding!" and "Yeah, that's right!"

"But God must have seen all of this ahead of time, and He's been working. . . ." She paused and looked over at the Forsythes. "To think Ray and Anna Forsythe would get behind us, and that they would just *happen* to have bought a skating rink that's closer to the dorms than the union!"

"Praise God!" Lisa cried out from her heart. The others joined in adding spontaneous praise and thanksgiving.

"I hate to bring in a negative note," cautioned Forsythe. "But we're a long way from being able to use this thing. We need an occupancy permit. Fortunately, the building is already rated for assembly, which is just what we need. But the city will have to approve plans, and it'll take time and a lot of money, probably at least $20,000, to get this place open, and our own plans called for closer to $80,000."

There was an audible moan as people reacted to this news. Forsythe went on.

"The reason we haven't already renovated it is we've been waiting to get a loan for the place and we're not getting any bites. And when I booted my ex-partner I lost a small share of the capital. Now I don't have enough on my own. I don't know what the answer is." He hung his head slightly. "I wasn't even sure I should get you guys all excited, but I just think we have to view this as a long-range thing."

Their emotions were immediately dampened as they had to adjust their expectations. "Well, we don't want you to feel hurried because of us," Jack offered. "But, if this isn't out of line, how long do you think these things will take?"

"Well, I'm going to have to apply to a couple of new banks. I may have to save up more cash to sweeten the loan. It could easily be another half year before I get a loan, and . . . the way things are with credit . . . there's no guarantee I'll get one even then. Then it'll take another three to six months to do the work. Maybe more."

The silence that followed this statement spoke eloquently of the concern and confusion the little band of Christians felt at his words. The location seemed to meet the need of the moment so perfectly, but their need was only weeks away, not months or a year.

Silently, they wondered what it might mean, and whether there was another way around the barrier. After a few moments, Lee Carulo looked up. "I think we might be able to supply that need."

Eleven sets of eyes snapped up to stare in disbelief.

"We have some money in our building fund at the church. I bet our people would love to be a part of what God's doing here."

"I agree," Dan joined in resolutely, his finger pointed at Lee for some reason. "We're doing pretty well, but we don't have the kind of action you guys are getting. This is a movement of God, and our people have already invested a lot of prayer—I think they'd want to see their wealth used in this situation."

"I don't understand," Ray said. "You mean your church would put up cash to help me renovate my restaurant?"

Lee answered. "We'll make a donation to M.S.U. Home Fellowships, which they can use to pay you in advance for a lease here. With that as collateral, you should be able to get your loan. In fact, if we made it $20,000 just to get the place open for the kids, you might be able to go ahead with work right away."

"We'd have to submit a new plan to the city but . . . yeah," Forsythe breathed. "That would work! Are you serious? Your church would do this?"

"Well, we'd have to check with the other elders, but . . . what do you think, Tory?"

"I think it's a marvelous idea, and I can't imagine the church saying no," she said with certainty in her voice. Eileen was nodding vigorously in agreement.

"Oh, I don't know whether we could allow you to take your money and use it for us," Sherry suggested.

"It's not our money," Tory argued. "That's what it's there for. We collected our money so we could use it for Christian ministry . . . for the glory of God. I think this effort is glorifying God tremendously. Lee and the rest of us have wished we could be more involved down here on campus. This is money that's been given to God."

There was a significant moment of silence as the others seemed to wait for someone to react. Jack finally spoke up. "I can see where you guys are coming from, and I agree. I hope when I'm older I'll have the level of spirituality you guys have. I hope I . . . we . . . get to the point someday where our group is so mature we're prepared to take our own funds and give it to another ministry because God's behind it. I really thank you guys . . . not just for the gift, but for showing us an example here we'll never forget."

"I'm stunned." It was Ray Forsythe. "Your church must be different than most."

"Oh, it really is, Ray," Jack looked around toward him. "You and Anna ought to go there and listen to Lee preach. You'd meet some serious believers your own age there, too . . . of course we'd want you to keep coming to our meetings, too. We love having you guys there." The other students again chimed in with agreement. Jack went on, "But now that we mention your spiritual life, it sounds like you opened up with Sherry today a little more than you have with me."

"Yes, but you never asked, and she did." Forsythe grinned. Then, facing the whole group, "I guess I should tell you kids . . . as my friends . . . that, uh . . . I've had a change in my life. . . . I guess I've done what you guys call 'receiving Christ.' Anna has, too."

A minor pandemonium broke out as the ten others all cried out in joy and encouragement at once. Now they were actually swimming in a sense of excitement and Christian unity so vivid and tangible that a brief, rich silence of spiritual communion ensued. Nothing but silly smiles and shaking heads could express the sheer joy shared among the group.

Lee suggested they pray right there that God would grant them the opportunity to have their own place to meet and to carry out their mission without hindrance. For the next twenty minutes, they fellowshiped together in prayer and worship.

Afterward, Lee pointed out that the campus group ought to start passing the hat at meetings and get an account at the bank so they could move toward paying their own bills in the future. "It's time to begin teaching your group about stewardship in earnest," he admonished. "We won't be doing you any favors if we always come in and pay your bills for you."

"Maybe it would be good for the group to pay the church back for this?" Ken suggested.

"No," Lee shook his head. "I don't think we would want to loan it. We want the chance to be involved directly in this ministry ourselves, and this is a solid way we can. I think you guys should take a series of collections, though, and donate the money to Ray in addition to what we give."

They all murmured agreement to that suggestion.

Several announced they had to go, and gradually the others wandered off to go home. Finally, the Carulos, the Simmons, and the Forsythes left, agreeing to stop at a coffee shop together on the way home. Sherry was so glad to see Ray and Anna Forsythe with people their own age who were deep, committed believers.

Finally, Jack and Sherry were left sitting alone on a bench as darkness descended on the warm, humid spring evening. They looked out over the grounds of the rink, and drew in the scent of late spring life, wondering if this area represented a big part of their future together. Jack looked over to watch Sherry's sharp eyes as they scanned the scene before them. Suddenly he saw her break into smile.

"What?" he challenged.

She shook her head, still smiling. "Oh, that's just too weird!"

"What? Come on."

"you see that yellow lit sign on the other side of the river? You can just barely see it through the trees."

Jack craned his head to see what she was talking about. "Yeah, I see it."

"That's the sign for the *Acropolis* restaurant."

"Right . . ."

"Well, that's where this whole thing began." She turned to look at him, radiant in her beauty. "That's where I was sitting the night I first realized I had to have a change in my life—I was there with Clemmons the night he attacked me the first time."

"Oh." Jack wasn't sure how to respond.

"And now, it's like I've come full circle, but I'm on the other side of the river. Doesn't that sound corny?"

"No, I don't think it's corny! I think it's kind of cool." He put his arm around her shoulders and gathered her in. "You're a completely different person than you were then," he smiled.

"You're not kidding."

As they again stared at the grounds of the rink, they speculated about what God was going to do with them now that He was bringing them together into one life—forever. They could see endless possibilities, but there was also much they could not see.

They didn't know how big the spiritual fire storm lying ahead would be. They had no idea, as they sat pondering, how difficult it was going to be to fight the powers of hell for each square inch of spiritual territory they would take for God. They had no idea how many lives God would change through their ministry—it could be thousands. Without intending to, they were already laying the foundation for serious future problems in their own group. Like most young couples, they didn't realize what marriage was or how difficult the adjustment would be. They didn't know how having children would affect their lives and their ministry in the years to come. But they did know they were in a wonderful position—in love, both with each other and with God, and on track with His purpose for their lives. It was with excitement, not fear, that they faced the future.

NOTES

1. Edward Norbeck, *Religion in Primitive Society* (New York: Harper & Row, 1961), page 71.
2. Norbeck, page 72.
3. Douglas Davies, "Myths and Symbols," *Eerdmans Handbook to World Religions* (Grand Rapids, MI: Wm. Eerdmans Publishing Company, 1982, page 36.
4. Norbeck, page 73.
5. Anthony F. C. Wallis, "Rituals: Sacred and Profane—An Anthropological Approach," in *Ways of Being Religious: Readings For a New Approach to Religion*, Jay T. Allen, Charles L. Lloyd, Jr., Frederick J. Streng (Englewood Cliffs, NJ: Prentice-Hall, Inc., 1973), page 158.
6. Wallis, page 158.
7. Wallis, page 159.
8. Wallis affirms that "the ritual process, as described above, is a universal human phenomenon" and "one—but only one—way of institutionalizing the ritual process is to interpret and apply it within the context of a belief in supernatural beings." Thus, the notion of religious ritualism is not dependent on belief in personal deities. Even things like patriotic meetings could fit this description. Wallis, page 160.
9. Mircea Eliade, *Patterns in Comparative Religion* (Cleveland, OH: The World Publishing Co., 1958), page 370.
10. I have substituted the term "sacred event" for Eliade's more complicated term "heirophany," which means a manifestation of the sacred, throughout the paper. Mircea Eliade, *Patterns in Comparative Religion*, pages 371 ff.
11. Eliade, page 368.
12. Turner agrees that designating sacred space gives man control of sacred experience, and adds that the same is true of sacred times. Harold Turner, "Holy Places, Sacred Calendars", in *Eerdman's Handbook to World Religions* (Grand Rapids, MI: Eerdmans, 1982), page 20.

13. Eliade, page 370.
14. Geoffrey Parrinder, *Worship in the World's Religions* (New York: Association Press, 1961), page 27. Wrongly, see Sir James George Frazer, *The Golden Bough* (New York: Macmillan Company, 1940), page 55, who thinks magic precedes religion in an evolutionary process. Actually, there is *never* an absence of religion in "primitive" societies, nor is there an absence of magic in the so-called "civilized races of the world," as I hope this paper shows.
15. Eliade, page 369.
16. In Catholicism the relic is placed within the altar of the church, thus "sanctifying" the church.
17. Norbeck, page 56.
18. Norbeck, page 82.
19. This is the interpretation favored by Wallis for many objectified aspects of religion. For instance, "The simple ritual act of crossing oneself, in Catholic custom, by touching the fingers to the forehead and chest in four, must be understood as a statement of intent to secure divine power as a protection against danger, spiritual or physical. The 'sign of the cross,' the extremities of which are indicated by the points touched, invokes the whole story of Christ and its complex meanings; the accompanying litany—'In the name of the Father, Son, and Holy Ghost, Amen' . . . constitutes both a prayer and a primitive magical conception of power inherent in naming. Thus, this simple act may be a statement . . . of beliefs based both on ancient Christian mythology and even more ancient conceptions of magic." Wallis, page 156.
20. It could be argued that the anointing with oil mentioned in James 5:14 and the laying on of hands practiced in Acts were elements of objectification also (Acts 13:3; 1 Timothy 4:14, 5:22; 2 Timothy 1:6). However, I think these were cultural features that were not directly related to the worship of God—that is, they deal with ways believers relate to each other rather than to God. Namely, the one laying on hands or anointing with oil *identifies* him or herself with the recipient.
21. Norbeck, page 74.
22. See 1 Thessalonians 5:27, Philippians 1:1, and parallels.

Note to the Reader
from Dennis McCallum

Somehow the detailed teaching outlines from Jack's series on the Gospel of John fell into my hands. I took those outlines and presented them to another group almost exactly as Jack gave them originally. The similarity is uncanny! Sherry's notes also mysteriously made their way to my desk and I repeated her teaching. For those who would like to listen to Jack's and Sherry's teaching (at least as close as we can get), I have collected eleven lectures from the Gospel of John and Sherry's teaching on Colossians 2 into a cassette tape album. If you'd like a copy, just send $45 plus $3 for shipping to MEDIA CONCEPTS, 611 E. Weber Road, Columbus, Ohio 43211. Also available for $2.50 plus $.50 for shipping is Jack's paper on Stephen's speech in Acts 7. If you decide to order, allow four weeks for delivery.

I hope you enjoyed the book.